RETURN OF THE PALADIN

BOOK IV OF
THE BLACKWOOD SAGA

Layton Green

To Wick Sewell, old friend and partner in imagination

Published by Cloaked Traveler Press.
Cover design by Sammy Yuen
Interior by QA Productions

Books by Layton Green

THE DOMINIC GREY SERIES
The Summoner
The Egyptian
The Diabolist
The Shadow Cartel
The Resurrector
The Reaper's Game (Novella)

THE BLACKWOOD SAGA
Book I: *The Brothers Three*
Book II: *The Spirit Mage*
Book III: *The Last Cleric*
Book IV: *Return of the Paladin*
Book V: *Wizard War* (Forthcoming)

OTHER WORKS
Written in Blood
A Shattered Lens
The Letterbox
The Metaxy Project
Hemingway's Ghost (Novella)

THE TALE SO FAR . . .

The Brothers Three

The Blackwood brothers have very different outlooks on life: Will is a dreamer and fantasy addict stuck in a dead-end job; middle brother Caleb is a charming, happy-go-lucky bartender; and the eldest, Val, is a driven corporate attorney. One night in their hometown of New Orleans, after receiving a strange inheritance from their father—a pair of bracers, a staff, and a sword with a silver hilt—the Blackwood brothers are attacked by a necromancer named Zedock who raises a manticore from a bag of bones and stops bullets with a glance. Fearing for their lives, the brothers accept a key from a mysterious old man named Salomon and are transported to an alternate Earth ruled by wizards, where magic is real and monsters prowl the land. To survive in this deadly new world, the brothers hire a band of mercenaries to recover a trio of magical items from an abandoned sorcerer's keep. Led by an alluring but deadly adventuress named Mala, the brothers manage to recover the items, take a portal back to New Orleans, and confront Zedock in a cemetery. Will and Caleb follow the necromancer through a portal and manage to defeat him, but end up trapped on Urfe.

The Spirit Mage

Desperate to help his brothers, Val enlists the Myrddinus Society to help him return to Urfe. After landing in the dangerous underbelly of New Victoria, he concludes the only way to find Will and Caleb is to enroll in the Abbey—the school for wizards—and somehow gain access to a gateway called the Pool of Souls.

As Val struggles to survive, his brothers undergo an even deadlier trial. Reeling from the loss of Mala, who is adrift in the mysterious Place Between Worlds, Will and Caleb and Yasmina are captured by slavers and taken to the mines beneath Fellengard Mountain.

Trapped in a land of dreams and nightmares, afraid of losing their home world forever, the brothers manage to survive but are forced apart yet again. Val is thrown into an unbreakable prison for trying to use the Pool of Souls, while Will and Caleb escape the Darklands only to find themselves under siege by wizards in a city called Freetown, home of the Revolution.

The Last Cleric

The Blackwood brothers have become entangled in events that threaten to upend the Realm. Sentenced to die in wizard prison, Val wins his freedom by undertaking a quest to an alternate dimension for the Congregation—but taints his soul in the process.

Reunited with an old lover, Caleb braves the dangers of the Barrier Coast to warn his ancestors of the coming invasion. He survives the journey, but at a cost so high—the death of his wife and adopted child—it will change him forever.

And in a distant unexplored jungle, Will finds his warrior spirit as he and Mala lead a party of adventurers in search of the Coffer of Devla, a fabled artifact thought to reside in the lost pyramid of a sorcerer king. Used to annihilate the enemies of its possessor, the Coffer might be the only hope for the struggling Revolution. While the expedition is a success, prophecy holds that the Coffer can only be used by a cleric of Devla—and yet it mysteriously opens for Caleb during an attack by the Congregation.

Dramatis Personae

EARTH

Will Blackwood: The youngest brother; apprentice builder; wielder of the legendary sword Zariduke

Caleb Blackwood: The middle brother; bartender; thought by the followers of Devla to be the Templar, a warrior who prophecy has foretold will lead their people to freedom

Val Blackwood: The oldest brother; attorney; spirit mage and member of the Congregation

Yasmina: Zoology PhD Student; budding wilder of the Realm

The Brewer: Former rock star from New Jersey; bard

Lance: Former police officer and Marine; Will's best friend in New Orleans

URFE

Lord Alistair: Chief Thaumaturge of the Congregation; arch spirit mage

Mala: Adventuress; master thief and swordswoman; daughter of Clan Kalev

Allira: Healer from a land beyond the oceans

Marguerite: Member of New Victoria Rogue's Guild; Caleb's deceased wife

Luca: Roma child adopted by Caleb and Marguerite; deceased

Dalen: Young illusionist from Macedonia

Mateo: Roma warrior and cousin to the Blackwood brothers

Tamás: Leader of the Revolution

Adaira: Cuerpomancer and daughter of Lord Alistair

Dida: Bibliomancer from the Kingdom of Great Zimbabwe

Synne: Majitsu loyal to Val Blackwood

Kjeld Anarsson: Tenth Don of the Order of Majitsu

Yasir Ookar: First General of the Protectorate Army

Alaina Whitehall: Governess of the Protectorate

Rucker: Adventurer

Professor Groft: Dean of Spiritmancy at the Abbey

The Prophet: Leader of the followers of Devla

Salomon Elder: Spirit mage searching for his lost son

Core Disciplines of the Congregation

Pyromancy (fire)

Aquamancy (water)

Aeromancy (air)

Geomancy (earth and stone)

Sylvamancy (the natural world)

Cuerpomancy (the human body)

Alchemancy (transformation)

Spiritmancy (spirit and astral travel)

Other Disciplines

Electromancy (lightning and related phenomena)

Necromancy (scrying and the dead)

Menagery (adaptation, breeding, and fusing of species)

Illusomancy (illusion and light)

Artisamancy (magical artistry)

Entomancy (insects)

Cyanomancy (sound)

Relicmancy (creation of magical items)

Bibliomancy (runes, wards, and lore)

Phrenomancy (exploring the inner mind)

PROLOGUE

On a lonely country road outside New Orleans, at the entrance to a sanatorium nestled among a grove of live oaks, the old man with silver eyes appeared out of nowhere.

Humming a folk melody from his youth, a time forgotten by all but the most knowledgeable of bards, he strolled right through the security gate and onto the manicured grounds. The morning sun warmed his chest and fingers, breathed life on weary bones. When one of the staff glanced in his direction, sensing a presence but seeing no one, the employee's eyes lingered and then slid away with an uneasy feeling. Some of the patients, whose minds were tuned to a different station, had better luck. They noticed a displacement of the air or even, in one or two extreme cases, saw the old man outright.

One of these outliers, a slender woman in her mid-fifties with gray hair that retained a smattering of sunflower strands, her fine-boned features reminding the old man of her middle son Caleb, bore an inquisitive expression as she watched him approach. She smiled as he handed her a bouquet of gardenias, her favorite flower.

"Thank you," she said, inhaling the aroma and then peering over his shoulder. "Is Dane with you today?"

Salomon gave a sad smile. "I'm afraid not."

"That's okay," she said lightly. "I'm sure he'll come by later."

"Maybe he will."

"Did he ask you to bring me these? It's our anniversary, you know."

"I do," Salomon said gravely.

"He was here last night and asked about the boys. Do you know where they've gotten off to? Maybe the beach?"

He patted her on the shoulder. "I'm sure they'll come around."

With the wistful sigh of a mother who wishes her children were still nestled at her bosom, she said, "I'm just glad they've stayed close over the years. Family has to stick together, you know."

Salomon's eyes slipped downward, a sadness whisking through him at the thought of his own child, lost in the vastness of the multiverse so very long ago. "I know," he whispered.

He chatted with the woman, whose name was Elaina Blackwood, for most of the afternoon. At her husband's funeral, Salomon had wondered at the strange absence of a spirit signature. The body was Dane's, there was no doubt about that, yet Salomon had expected more evidence of a battle between wizards, or a flight to another plane of existence. He suspected Lord Alistair had slain the elder Blackwood, but Salomon had never known for sure. Because the Blackwood brothers were very special—anomalies—he had often come to Earth while they matured.

And he had watched.

During this time, Salomon brought Elaina flowers every year on her wedding anniversary. Many centuries ago, he himself had made the sword that had caused all of this poor woman's troubles. Flowers was the least he could do. He had also harbored the selfish desire of hoping Elaina could shed light on Dane's final hour. When her condition failed to improve, he gave up on that, and he knew his magic couldn't help her, either. Unraveling the mysteries of the human brain was beyond the powers of a spirit mage.

Beyond even him.

"Excuse me, sir," she called out, as he headed for the gate.

Salomon turned.

"Why is your head glowing?" she asked.

He stared at her, a wave of gooseflesh prickling his arms. In his dream the night before, one of the strangest he had ever had, Elaina had asked the exact same question.

She giggled. "It glows, like Dane's. Only brighter." She raised the flowers above her head and twirled as if she were a young woman, then crossed her arms and shivered. "I like your visits much better than that other man. He pretends he's friendly but he's not."

Salmon watched her closely. "What other man?"

"His name is Alistair. He says he knew my husband when they were younger." She frowned. "*I've* never heard Dane mention him. I asked him about it just last night, but he said not to talk about him."

"You asked who?"

"Dane, of course."

On every single visit Salomon had made to the sanatorium, Elaina had claimed that Dane visited her. He gave it no credence, chalked it up to the imbalance in her mind.

"How long has Alistair been coming?" he asked.

"Oh, just the once. Sometime recent, I can't keep track of the days anymore. He wanted to hear all about the children." She giggled again. "His head glows, too."

"Mrs. Blackwood!"

She turned as one of the male orderlies strode towards her across the lawn. "It's time for lunch. Where did you get those flowers?"

A patch of sunlight illuminated her face. She shielded the sun with one hand and pointed right at Salomon with the other. "He gave them to me."

The orderly took her gently by the arm. "Did one of your sons stop by? Or do you have another secret admirer?"

"I just told you," she said, as the old man with silver eyes waved goodbye. "That man right there brought them."

The orderly patted her arm and guided her towards the cafeteria.

Salomon released a heavy sigh as he walked down Magazine Street. As always, the arch mage felt a melancholy descend after leaving Elaina. Before the injury, she must have been an extraordinary woman.

He always suspected her husband's death was not the sole cause of her mental state. His guess was Lord Alistair or one of his emissaries had entered her mind after Dane had passed, searching for knowledge of the sword, and left a broken vessel behind.

The recent visit from Lord Alistair, or someone claiming to be him, did not bode well. At the very least, it meant the Chief Thaumaturge of the Congregation knew of the Blackwood children, and likely Val's true identity.

So be it. Salomon had long ago decided not to intervene. If the smallest chance existed he could still find his own son, then extraordinary measures had to be taken. Unpleasant choices made. The outer limits of technology, the source of magic and human consciousness, the origin and meaning of the universe . . . so many secrets remained out of reach, even from the arch mage. Every time he found a new world or dimension, delved deeper into spirit or unlocked a treasure chest of knowledge, he only seemed to encounter more questions.

Questions that dwarfed the ones that came before.

As much as it pained him, he had to let the events surrounding the Blackwood brothers follow their natural course. The three siblings were unique among human beings, as far as he knew. Children of two different worlds, born to parents with vastly different—incompatible—spirit signatures. He sensed there were powers involved in the brothers' struggle beyond any he had ever known, perhaps even a prime force of the multiverse. If he watched closely enough, perhaps one or more of these entities would appear in some way or reveal a deeper truth, and bring him closer to finding his son.

As he neared Will and Caleb's old neighborhood, deciding to re-examine the residual currents around their apartment, someone called out to him.

"Hey you! Old man!"

Startled, Salomon turned to find a familiar, square-jawed face limping towards him down Magazine Street. A former police officer named Lance, the young man still kept his head shaved in military style, but his once-muscular body had gone to seed, swollen with fat. An accidental companion of the Blackwood brothers on their first visit to Urfe, Lance had been badly wounded in the battle with Zedock, enough to ruin his career.

Salomon felt a chill when he saw him, a tingling that left him feeling as shocked and uncertain as a boy wizard discovering the power of magic for the first time.

The dream. First Elaina, and now Lance. Calling out to me on this very street.

"Wait up!" Lance said. "I know you! You were there, in the cemetery!"

Salomon stood in the middle of the street, unsure if he should talk to Lance or disappear. What did this mean? How did the dream affect his own promise not to intervene? From where had the dream come?

"We have to talk," Lance said, breathing hard.

The arch mage ignored him and shuffled down a side street, deciding to test the power of the dream.

Lance finally caught up to him and grabbed his arm. He had a crazed look in his eyes, and spittle flew from his mouth. "I know it's you. You have to tell me, old man. You have to tell me if they're still alive."

The exact same words I heard last night.

Stunned by this manifestation of his nocturnal vision, a connection to the netherworld of the deep subconscious that not even the phrenomancers understood, Salomon tried to pull his arm away.

Lance gripped him harder. "Where are Will and his brothers? You're from there, aren't you? The other world? You sent us there and you know things. *Where are they?*"

Feeling unsteady, Salomon gave a furtive glance around the street and found a grove of banana trees that would shield them from view. He knew powerful forces were at work, and he had to accept that he, too, had a role to play.

Salomon beckoned with a curled finger. "Come with me."

-1-

"Did you clean your shield, Will the Builder?"

Sitting cross-legged on the beach behind Freetown, right at the edge of the surf, the sound of Mala's voice caused Will Blackwood to turn his head. Her lilting accent was less mocking than usual, and as she sat next to him, the breeze scattering her hair while the dusk light seemed to float within her violet eyes, she laid a sympathetic hand on his arm.

He looked down at the battered, teardrop-shaped buckler he had taken from the tomb of the sorcerer king. The heraldic design on front, a set of runes almost faded to obscurity when he had found the shield, was now clearly outlined in a platinum hue which matched the wooden buckler's metal edging.

"It's strange," he said, in a toneless voice. Two days had passed since the attack by the Congregation and the theft of the Coffer of Devla. Though he wondered what had caused the runes to illuminate—perhaps residual magic from the Coffer—he was too grief-stricken over the death of Marguerite and Luca, and worried about his brother, to care about anything else.

"She was my friend, too," Mala said, staring at the waves thumping ashore in a steady rhythm. In place of her old amulet, she wore a stylized rose pendant hanging from a silver chain. "A fine companion."

"The finest," he agreed. An image kept crowding his mind, that of the Congregation electromancer sending a lightning bolt arcing into Marguerite from a dozen feet away, her smoking body falling next to the boy's.

Caleb had still not left his room or allowed anyone inside. Not even Will.

He balled his fists. "We can't let them get away with that."

She gave him a sharp look. "It's the Congregation. They get away with whatever they choose."

When he pulled his arm away, annoyed, she said in a gentler voice, "Have you spoken to your brother?"

"He won't let me in. I've never seen him like this."

"He's never lost a wife and child before."

"Tell me something I don't know." His blond hair had grown half as long as Mala's, spilling past his shoulders, and he ran a hand through it before cupping the back of his head and squeezing his eyes shut.

Marguerite and Luca murdered. Val still imprisoned by the Congregation, as far as anyone knew. The Coffer of Devla stolen right out from under them, dealing the Revolution yet another devastating blow.

After a time, Mala said, "Everyone's looking for you."

"Who's everyone?"

"Tamás. The council."

"Why?"

"To discuss whatever business it is that important councils discuss."

He opened his eyes. "Is that why you came to find me? Because the council sent you?"

"I came because I knew where to look."

"How? I haven't seen you all day."

"Are you not a dreamer, Will Blackwood? A lover of the promise of foreign shores, of uncertain currents and the wild, untamable things in life?"

Her mocking grin had returned in full. Despite the edge to her words, he knew she hadn't been forced to come. They could have sent someone else to find him. In her own way, Mala was letting him know she cared.

He just didn't know how much.

"Shall I tell them you're unavailable?" she said. "You don't have to take part, you know. You brought the Coffer home. You don't owe them a thing."

"I never did, and the Coffer's gone." He pushed to his feet. "But I'll come."

With a resigned shake of her head, Mala sighed and rose with him.

The night air brought a chill to the Barrier Coast. After throwing on a light cloak, Will swung by his brother's room and knocked on the door, over and over, until Caleb shouted at him to go away.

"It's me," Will said.

No response.

He stood quietly by the door, troubled. Always cool and collected, Caleb had not been this upset since their father had died. And despite the crushing nature of that blow—the shock and despair all the brothers had experienced—Will knew it paled in comparison to the deaths of Caleb's new wife and adopted child. Their dad hadn't been slaughtered by a Congregation electromancer right in front of their eyes.

Unsure what to do, Will backed away from Caleb's door and left the inn, brushing past two men standing at attention on either side of the entrance. Clad in hooded gray caftans, a triangle of blue dots on their foreheads marked them as devoted disciples of the Prophet. Because Caleb had opened the Coffer, the Devla worshippers believed him to be the legendary Templar foretold by prophecy, and insisted on posting an honor guard outside his door—despite the fact that Caleb despised the Coffer and refused to talk to his own brother, let alone a kooky cult that didn't even know he was from another world.

Yet the Devla had a few thousand followers camping in the forest just outside the city, waiting for Caleb to make an appearance.

To do what? Will wondered. The prophecy, which derived from the Romani Canticles, spoke of someone who would lead their people out of bondage and crack the spine of the world. Not only had his brother been an atheist for as long as Will could remember, but Caleb was also an avowed pacifist. He winced at cracking an egg.

Aching with his brother's pain, Will walked slowly across the courtyard to the Red Wagon Tavern, saddened by the solitude of the streets. The boisterous soul of Freetown had been cowed by the wizards. Oh, how he hated bullies and tyrants.

Something creaking in the wind caught his attention. He looked up and saw the two majitsu he and Mala had killed hanging from a makeshift gallows near the beer fountain. Only ashes remained of the electromancer, incinerated by his own spell when the power of the Coffer had flowed through Caleb and redirected his attack.

How much power did the Coffer possess? How many wizards could it combat?

They might never know.

He entered the back room of the inn and found every seat at the long oaken table filled with members of the Roma High Council, as well as elders who had trickled in from the clans strung along the Barrier Coast. Mala was also present, as was Will's cousin Mateo. Due to their valor on the expedition to the tomb of the sorcerer king, the surviving members of the journey, including Will, had been given seats at the table.

There was another new addition, sitting at the end near the door: a lean man with wheat-colored hair and intense eyes, wearing a belted tunic woven from coarse animal hair. The Prophet. The eyes of the council members seemed both repelled and attracted by his presence, as if buoyed by his faith but wary of being judged.

Once, Will had approached the Prophet about Caleb, asking how his brother could possibly be the Templar. "The Creator works in mysterious ways," was the infuriating reply.

Both Tamás and Mateo greeted Will with a warm arm clasp. Standing alone by the fire, Mala watched the proceedings with a cool stare, her eyes unreadable. Along with the usual assortment of jewelry and pouches and weapons, she carried the scourge she had recovered in the pyramid, a weapon she called Magelasher. A cat 'o nine tails not particularly fearsome in appearance, yet the azantite tips had pierced the magical defenses of a majitsu.

A feat Will had not thought possible—except of course with the blade of Zariduke, his own sword.

"Are we all gathered, then?" Tamás asked, trying to speak over the pockets of conversation filling the room. No one else seemed to be paying attention.

A moment later, without warning, Tamás slammed his palms on the table, shocking everyone into silence. Having gained the room's attention, the leader of the Revolution began to slowly walk around the table, his eyes burning with passion.

"Enough," Tamás said, with barely controlled fury. "Enough senseless murders of our people, enough pogroms in the plains, enough fens and prisons, enough degrading oaths that aim to destroy our heritage. *Enough*. I don't know what you expected from this meeting, my brothers and sisters. Perhaps another reasoned consideration of our plight." He shook his head as his gaze swept the room. "I did not come to debate whether or not we should strike back at the wizards." He stopped at the head of the table, raised a clenched fist, and pressed it to his heart. "I came to declare war."

After a moment of stunned silence, there were murmurs of assent from Jacoby Revansill, Merin Dragici, Tinea Alafair, and the other assembled elders. Will felt chills running down his arms, both from the power of Tamás's words and the terrifying thought of attacking the Congregation.

Will exchanged a troubled glance with Mateo.

"Foolish," Mala muttered, loud enough for everyone to hear. "You're all foolish."

Tamás turned on her, his handsome face contorted into a snarl. Despite his much larger stature, Mala didn't flinch when he stalked towards her.

Will's hand slid to the hilt of his sword, worried Tamás might strike her. "You've never been one of us," Tamás said, his face inches from hers. "And I'm not interested in your opinion."

"We should not shy away from dissenting voices," the Prophet murmured in the background, causing Tamás to stiffen.

Mala's lips curled as she faced Tamás. "If my opinion is not wanted, then why invite me to the meeting?"

"In case you have any wisdom on the course of action I'm about to propose," Tamás said.

"If it involves an attack on the Congregation, then I do not."

The revolutionary flung a hand towards her. "What would you have us do, Mala of Clan Kalev? You have the means to roam the world as you please, without restraint or obligation. Your way of life is not in danger. We, on the other hand—your people, I remind you—are facing genocide."

"What would I have you do? *Flee.* Go somewhere. Anywhere. We're gypsies. That's what we do. We leave our homelands and wander the earth, cursed to roam like dogs, begging for scraps."

He raised his arms. "Flee to where, pray tell? The ancient country is too far. We have no way to undertake the journey, and even if we did, the Congregation wizards—or the sovereign countries that await on the other side—would simply sink our ships. The Mayan Kingdom has rebuffed our requests for resettlement. The Northern Forests are too far, and ruled by trolls and giants. The Barrier Coast is our homeland now. Our last place of refuge." He shook his head and backed away. "The decision of the council has been made. If Devla has ordained the destruction of our people, then so be it. Better to die in battle, fighting for our honor and our lives, than to wait like sows for the slaughter. We go to war, and we go now. While we still can."

"How?" Will asked. "How do you fight the Congregation?"

"Alone, we don't. That I grant you." He glanced at the Prophet, sitting expressionless at the end of the table. "Our only hope lies in the power of Devla."

Merin stood and raised a fist. "The Coffer has been opened! A true cleric has returned to the Realm, the Templar come to fulfill the prophecy! Devla has not abandoned us!"

As a chorus of excited, agreeing shouts rose from the council members, Mala tipped her head down and shook it. Will slumped in his chair, aghast that these people believed his brother was the Templar foretold by the prophets of Devla.

"You scoff?" Tamás said to Mala, incredulous. "Even after what you witnessed? An agent of the Congregation—an elder electromancer, no less—consumed in an instant by the power of the Coffer?"

"Impressive, I grant you," she said. "But that was one mage, far from his stronghold. The Congregation commands thousands, who will act in concert to destroy us. Not to mention their majitsu, and the Protectorate army, and their allies, and their magical weapons and defenses. It's madness. Suicide. Nor do you have proof that Devla acted through the Coffer."

"If not Devla, then who? Faith is not something you can prove, Mala. That is the nature of it."

"This, then, is your plan? To march into battle trusting in a god who, even if he exists, abandoned our people thousands of years ago?"

"Who are we to judge the ways of the Creator?" Tamás said.

"Wise words," the Prophet said softly, causing all heads to turn his way. "The Templar has arrived, and the will of the Creator shall prevail."

Mala waved a hand in disgust. Will agreed with the sentiment, but he understood the council's hopes. He, too, had seen a lightning bolt reflect off his brother and disintegrate an elder mage. Whatever its nature, the Coffer had power.

Major League power.

"What's your plan?" he asked. "For war?"

Tamás glanced around the table as if gathering strength from the presence of the others. "We'll hide those who cannot fight in the forests, and we'll build an army of those who can. A select band will travel the Ninth in preparation, gathering our forces and recruiting allies."

"In preparation for what, exactly?"

Tamás leveled his gaze at Will. "For the return of the Coffer, and our march on New Victoria."

Will swallowed.

"With the Coffer and Zariduke, we have weapons to combat the wizards." Tamás held Will's gaze—the wielder of the sword—to let the implication of his words settle in. "Is it enough to topple the Congregation? Doubtful. But we do not have to destroy every last oath-taking wizard in the Realm. I suspect there are many who stand with Lord Alistair out of fear. We simply have to last long enough to sway the opinion of the public, or the majority of the Congregation, to our cause. Let them know we can oppose the wizards, and will not be massacred by death squads. We will fight until they agree to let us, and every non-Oath taker, live in peace in the Ninth."

"They'll never agree," Mala said. "The Realm covets the resources of the Ninth, and acceding to your demands would show weakness to their enemies. Not to mention the memory of the Pagan Wars."

"I think you're wrong," Tamás said grimly. "But if you're not, then so be it."

"Aren't we overlooking one extremely important detail?" Will asked. "The theft of the Coffer?"

Tinea Alafair, the eldest council member present, a stooped figurehead of scars and bones and wrinkled skin, addressed Mala. "Thanks to your swift assessment of the manner of thievery—a gateway bauble rather than a mage portal—our wizards were able to trace the residual magic in the tellurian lines. We don't know who utilized the gateway, but we've uncovered where the Coffer was taken."

Will leaned forward. "And?"

The proud old woman grimaced. "To a city built by a race long since vanished from Urfe. A city that has survived centuries of war and pestilence and plague, and bears little resemblance to the legends of old. At least so I'm told. Neither I, nor anyone else at this table save perhaps Mala, has laid eyes on it. It's rumored to be a lawless place, home to thieves and assassins and worse. Some believe it to be the most dangerous city on Urfe."

"Does it have a name?" Will asked, thinking *the most dangerous city on Urfe* might get annoying to repeat in conversation.

"It goes by many names, though it's true one is Praha," Mala said, earning a nod of approval from Tinea. "Yes, I've been there, and yes, it's exceedingly dangerous."

Will made a choking sound, drawing stares from the elders. Due to a life-long fascination with places on Earth that resembled fantasy cities, he knew Praha was the local spelling on Earth of Prague, capital of the Czech Republic. "Sorry," he muttered. "Not what I was expecting."

"You know of it?" Tinea asked.

"Just by reputation."

"This reinforces my theory," Mala said, "that the Alazashin are involved. My guess is one of their order traveled to Praha to purchase a gateway bauble in order to conceal their origin."

"What do you mean?" Will asked. "Why conceal it?"

"To keep their identity secret, of course. Meaning I do not think the thief was an agent of the Congregation."

"Because the Congregation wouldn't *need* to use subterfuge," Will guessed.

"Precisely. Why send an electromancer to presage the thief? Why use a gateway bauble instead of their own magic?"

"All good points," Tamás murmured.

Mala crossed her arms. "I do not think the Alazashin would risk the wrath of the Congregation. But they *would* steal something for the highest bidder."

"Another bidder?" Tamás asked in amazement. "Who? And why?"

She shrugged. "I can only speculate. We all witnessed the power of the Coffer: what collector would not desire such an item? Urfe is an immense world, with many powerful interests. We tend to focus on our own. Perhaps a foreign monarchy desired the artifact, or a rebel faction from abroad, or simply a wealthy hoarder of magical items seeking to increase his collection."

"The only thing that matters is retrieving the Coffer," Kyros Toth said. "And now we know where to start. The only remaining question is who will lead this most important of quests."

Tamás walked over to lay a hand on Will's shoulder, startling him. "Though it pains my heart, I am needed here, to prepare for war. There is surely the power of a wizard behind the theft of the Coffer. We have asked much of you already, my friend and brother, but I fear that without the strength of Zariduke and your steady hand to guide it, the quest for the Coffer is doomed from the start. Should you choose to aid us once again, placing us forever in your debt, we will supply you with the finest assistance at our disposal. I will enlist the strongest mage we can spare."

"Like you enlisted Selina?" Mala asked.

Mateo jumped to his feet, gripping the necklace of his fallen love. "She loved her homeland, and betrayed us only because Lord Alistair threatened her daughter. Never dishonor her name!"

"Selina was a brave woman who gave her life for us," Will said, taking his cousin by the arm to calm him. "But Mala's right. Lord Alistair could have leverage over anyone."

"Not anyone," Jacoby Revansill said. "Not all of us would choose a single life, even our own child, over the fate of our people."

"Easy to say when it's not your child," Will said. "How long is the journey to Praha?"

Tamás looked away. "Too long for our people to survive the death squads, once the Congregation receives word of the demise of their electromancer. If they have not already."

Will was perplexed. "Then how do you plan to find the Coffer?"

"The storehouse of our people, though limited, is not barren. We have a portal of our own, of geomancer origin, an item that will transport four people along tellurian lines to a destination of their choice."

"Why didn't we use that to find the Coffer?"

"The portal only works once, and the Mayan Kingdom is within easy reach of the Yith Riders. Praha is two continents away, across a vast and dangerous ocean." He exchanged a glance with Tinea and Jacoby. "We thought to use the gateway to strike a blow at the heart of the Congregation. But if we don't retrieve the Coffer, all is lost."

"You said only four people can go?"

"That is all the item will bear."

With all eyes on him, Will slowly stood. On the beach, he had already been thinking about the Revolution and what they would ask of him. Even if Caleb was not the Templar, Will could not deny the Coffer might be their only hope.

"I have to talk to my brother first. I won't abandon him in this state."

Tamás gripped Will's shoulder as the council looked on with expectant faces. "Fair enough."

2

Val went back to the beginning.

To the Minotaur's Den in New Victoria, the same pub in which he had laughed long ago with his brothers and Lance, before a group of mercenaries had rolled them and stolen their inheritance, before Mala and Allira had agreed to take them to Leonidus's castle to find a trio of magic items to kill Zedock.

Helpless as babes, Val and his brothers had scurried behind the deadly adventuress and her companions, setting in motion the incredible string of events that had led back to the table at the Minotaur's Den at which he now sat, completing the circle.

Fate was a funny thing.

Especially when it spanned worlds.

The night before, Lord Alistair had asked him to recover the Coffer of Devla on behalf of the Congregation. If successful, Val would join the Realm's powerful society of wizards not just as a full-fledged spirit mage, but as Lord Alistair's apprentice. To Val's great shock, the Chief Thaumaturge had even given his implied consent for Val to marry his daughter Adaira.

It seemed appropriate to surround himself with memories as he considered the full implications of his decision. So much to process. So many angles and emotions. He did not find it distasteful—not at all—to agree to everything the Chief Thaumaturge was offering. He could not deny that he was falling in love with Adaira, though he had hardly considered marriage. He enjoyed being a wizard and the power it conferred.

And becoming the apprentice of the most powerful spirit mage in the Realm? Possibly the heir apparent? The offer made being a partner in a New York City law firm pale in comparison.

Val was not even sure, after the terrible things he had done on Urfe, that he belonged back home. Helping his brothers was still his first priority—it always would be—but rejecting Lord Alistair's offer would not further that cause. Val needed training, knowledge, and resources to find Will and Caleb, and the best place for that was in the Wizard District. He could deal with everything else, the choice between worlds, when the time came.

Mug of ale in hand, he stared into the fire whose smoking remains, buried deep within the cavernous stone hearth, gave off more atmosphere than heat.

"That's a lot of table for a lone bloke, eh? How about ye move aside?"

The voice, coarse and challenging, had come from Val's right. He swiveled to see a group of six ruffians, laden with weapons and armor, crowding his table.

Moving with casual poise, Val rested his hand near the crescent moon of azantite topping his staff. "I'm fine right here."

The men took in his high-collared white shirt, the traveling cloak of fine wool the Queen had gifted him, his staff, and the glint in his green eyes as he leveled his gaze at them. The leader stumbled over an apology as the other men lowered their eyes and hurried to the next table over.

A few things had changed, Val thought, since his first visit.

As he continued pondering his decision, enjoying a meal of fire-crisped elk and wild boar called the Li'l Wolf's Platter, he couldn't help overhearing the subject of the men's conversation. It seemed a member of the Wizard's Council, an electromancer named Garbind Ellhorn, had been recently murdered, pierced through the heart with a sword. An unheard of event in the Realm.

Val knew full well, even before he heard the lead mercenary say it, what sort of blade had the power to pierce the defenses of an elder mage. As far as he knew, there existed only one.

Zariduke.

Forcing himself to remain calm, he rose to approach the men's table. "Do you mind if I join you?"

The mercenary who had accosted him earlier, an enormous man with tattooed hands and a braided red goatee hanging down his chest, spluttered into his mug. "No, sir. Pleased if you do. Make yourself at home." He threw the scrawny man next to him out of the seat by the scruff of his neck, then waved Val over.

After taking a seat, Val placed the bottom of his staff on the floor and held it upright beside him, in case the mercenaries forgot their manners. He swept his gaze across the group. "I just arrived in town, and will be appearing at the Sanctum in the morning." The mention of the headquarters of the Congregation caused a collective shiver to sweep through the group. "I'm curious about the rumors on the street about the death of Garbind."

One of the men spat on the stained wooden floor. "Got to be the gypsies, sir. The Black Sash."

"Aye," another agreed.

Val leaned forward. "But how? Even with a sword as powerful as Spiritscourge, how did the Black Sash penetrate Garbind's stronghold?"

He had used the common vernacular for Will's sword, due to the rough nature of the men. They looked nervous at the question, wondering why a Congregation mage was asking for their opinion on the matter, perhaps seeking to entrap them. "Don't seem likely, does it?" another man said. "I 'eard they had help on the inside."

"What do you mean?" Val asked. "One of the servants?"

The red-bearded leader shook his head, keeping his eyes low. "Another mage, sir. Least that's the rumor. One at the very top."

"Who?"

The man swallowed. "Dean Groft himself."

Val was stunned by the answer. *Dean Groft*? He had to find Adaira immediately and find out what they had missed during their journey. "What's the basis for that?" he challenged.

"Dunno, sir, I just 'eard the dean's working with the Black Sash. Everyone 'eard. Tis common knowledge, though, that 'e disappeared a few days back."

"Is this true?" Val asked, sweeping his gaze across the table. "You've all heard the same?"

They all agreed.

"Do you mean that Groft killed Garbind himself," Val ruminated, thinking it through, "or just aided and abetted?"

The men looked confused.

He leaned forward, intense. "Have you heard about anyone else involved, besides Dean Groft? Someone who might have used the sword?"

Someone like my brother?

No one had heard of a description floating around. He didn't hear anything else useful and returned to his table. Truth be told, if Dean Groft had gypsy sympathies, Val wouldn't be shocked. The dean had seemed like a man with secrets. While he didn't come across as a traitor or a murderer, one never knew how far a man's beliefs could take him.

Could it be true? Had someone wielding Zariduke managed to kill an elder mage? If so, how had his brother's sword arrived in New Victoria? Were Will and Caleb close by?

He tried to tell himself that Will would never have anything to do with such a thing. Yet he knew the youngest Blackwood all too well. Born with a hero's complex, Will had always been quick to take the side of the underdog, and if someone had convinced him to take up the fight against the wizards, or if he thought he might be helping his older brother . . .

Val pushed his plate away, his appetite ruined. If Will was involved, the Congregation would find him and crucify him. Val had no doubt about this. He no longer believed the Congregation was a force of evil, and in fact he thought it preferable to the murderous anarchy of common rule he had read about in the history books and seen firsthand in the alternate universe to which the Star Crown had sent him.

Still, the wizards would act to protect themselves. Zariduke was a threat that had to be eliminated.

He took a deep breath. This changed things. If there was any truth to the rumor, then Val had to find Will before the Congregation did.

The next morning, Val met one of Lord Alistair's personal majitsu at the entrance to the hulking, midnight blue pyramid known as the Sanctum: the headquarters of the Congregation. Two colossi flanked the columned entrance, thirty-foot tall guardians made of living stone who never seemed to move. As always, they gave him the shivers.

Val followed the silver-robed majitsu in flight high above the manicured gardens and pathways of mosaic tile separating the wizard compounds, weaving through the forest of colored spires that was even higher and more awe-inducing than the skyline of Manhattan. Only a rare few of the war-rior-mages possessed enough magic to sustain flight, and Val could feel eyes from the towers of rival strongholds tracking their progress. He had the feeling Lord Alistair had orchestrated such a public performance in order to demon-strate his intention to usher Val into the inner circle. Soaring into the Chief Thaumaturge's tower with a personal bodyguard would make an instant im-pression.

Which made Val's decision that much harder. He had no idea how Lord Alistair would react to Val's rejection of his offer, and now it would embarrass him even further. He might send Val back to prison.

Yet he didn't think Lord Alistair would go that far. As the Chief Thauma-turge's stronghold came into view, Val ran through his strategy in his mind. He planned to seek a grace period in order to tend to his ailing mother. Everyone believed he hailed from the far north, which should buy him some time to find Will and Caleb.

If things went well, Val hoped to find his brothers and convince them to lay low until he could recover the Coffer, return to Lord Alistair's good graces, and find a way to get them home. Whether or not he went with them, well, he could worry about that later.

The wind rushed through his hair as he flew, but the real chill came from the knowledge that he was playing a very dangerous game, with one of the most dangerous men on Urfe.

The majitsu angled towards Alistair's graceful central tower, topped by a bluish-white needle that soared high above the sprawl of topiary and polychro-matic fountains. Gothic bridges and archways linked a nest of beehive-shaped towers to the central one, a sprawling citadel of dun-colored stone flowing in fantastical patterns, dreamed up by a team of the Realm's most talented artis-amancers.

He followed the majitsu through an open window near the top of the tow-er. Lord Alistair must have deactivated the wards for Val's entry. Once inside, the majitsu returned to the sky, leaving him standing inside an observatory that took his breath away. Detailed celestial maps and astrological charts cov-ered the walls, made of vibrant magical dyes which made the artwork look three-dimensional, as if Val could slip through the walls and enter a new dimension or realm.

And maybe he could.

A midnight-blue glass ceiling evoked the splendor and mystery of the heavens. Artistic renditions of other planes of existence—at least Val assumed they were artistic—wrapped the support columns and flowed onto the silver tiles covering the floor. Sumptuous bronze telescopes and other stargazing devices dotted the room. A trio of azantite cases with glass doors showcased a stunning collection of artifacts.

His skin tingling from the power and knowledge on display, Val almost jumped when he noticed Lord Alistair observing him from beside a wizard chute in the corner.

"Welcome, Valjean."

He tipped his head with just the right amount of deference. "Lord Alistair."

"I trust you've had a chance to consider my proposal?"

Val looked him in the eye for a long moment. "I want you to know how flattered I am by your offer. It's one I would be foolish not to accept. And I do plan to accept it. But first, there is something I have to do—"

Lord Alistair raised a hand, cutting him off. Val tensed.

Can he read my mind? Does he know the lie I have prepared?

The Chief Thaumaturge clasped his hands behind his back as he bent to inspect a line of obsidian helms hanging above an ivory pew. It was an odd collection, and Val wondered at their purpose.

"Before you say something that might be difficult to retract," Lord Alistair said, "I have a question."

Val lowered his eyes. "Of course."

"Why did you not bring your staff today?"

The floor seemed to shift beneath Val's feet.

"The one bearing the crescent moon of azantite," Lord Alistair continued, still running his hands over the strange helms. "The staff of a spirit mage."

Val stood very still, wondering if these were his last moments as a free man. His true identity was a secret he had gone to great lengths to protect. Could Lord Alistair know the staff once belonged to Val's father?

Trying not to panic, he debated summoning spirit fire, but discarded the idea at once. Lord Alistair would incinerate him in an instant.

"Queen Victoria inquired about it upon your return. She thought it looked familiar and wondered where such a young mage had come upon it." He turned to face Val. "I have not been fully truthful with you. When I learned of the staff, which I recognized at once, I finally realized why you had always looked so familiar. I can't believe I didn't see it from the start. You're Dane Blackwood's son."

It was posed as a statement, not a question. Val didn't bother denying it. Instead he listened in stunned silence, scanning the room for an escape route he knew didn't exist.

Lord Alistair approached to lay a hand on his shoulder. "I understand why you kept the knowledge from us. You grew up on a different world and were unsure whom to trust. I have to say, what you've accomplished in the time you've been here is nothing short of remarkable. Your father told you nothing, did he? Else your choices make no sense."

"No," Val said truthfully. "He did not."

He felt Lord Alistair's eyes boring into his, probing for the truth. Val forced himself not to flinch as he met the gaze of the elder mage.

How much does he know? What game is he playing?

Lord Alistair's smile was wistful, faraway. "Your father and I were once very close. He was an amazing man. I never knew why he didn't come back from his mission to find the sword—until I discovered the lies of Dean Groft."

"The Dean—I don't understand."

Alistair looked at him sadly. "You've heard the recent news? Of the death of Garbind Ellhorn?"

"I heard talk of it last night."

"I'm afraid the rumors are true. Dean Groft conspired with the revolutionaries to murder one of our own. Unbeknownst to any of us, all those years he's been after the sword himself, in service to the Revolution. It was Groft who killed your father and sent Zedock after the sword."

Val took a step back, reeling. He did not exactly trust Lord Alistair, but from Val's years of interviewing clients and witnesses with his law practice, he had become an extremely good judge of liars. As far as he could tell, Lord

Alistair appeared to be telling the truth. Val would try to verify the story, but why would Alistair lie? He had nothing to fear from Val. And apparently the whole town knew about Dean Groft's connection to the Revolution.

Ever since Val had learned his father was a spirit mage, he had doubted the accidental nature of his death. He was barely able to croak out his words. "Dean Groft killed my father?"

"I doubt any other mage could have accomplished the feat. But the *Revolution* killed your father, Valjean. The *ideas* it represents. Do you see how dangerous it is?"

Val felt a cold weight settling into the bottom of his gut. "If Groft killed him, why didn't he take the sword the first time?"

And how did he get it this time? Did he kill Will, too?

"That I have yet to learn," Alistair said. "My guess is your father arranged a spell to hide the sword and scramble the spirit pathways to your world. It must have taken all those years for Groft to find it again."

Val felt wobbly on his feet, nauseated and confused by what he was hearing.

"Such a tragedy," Alistair said. "All that promise lost. Not to mention the unnecessary trials of you and your brothers. You must have been through so much."

"My brothers?" Val said, his voice returning in a whisper.

"Our spies tell us the Black Sash is in possession of a journal of your father's, likely stolen by Dean Groft or one of his agents."

"Zedock," Val said grimly.

"This journal discusses the inheritance Dane left for his three sons, which confirmed my suspicions. They're not like you though, are they? Not possessed of magic. Not meant for this world."

Val took a step forward. "Will and Caleb are alive? You know this for sure?"

"At last report, yes."

"I see."

"Unlike them, you inherited your father's power. You belong here, Val, in this world." His eyes flicked to a picture of Adaira on the wall near the wizard chute. "With us."

"How much does she know about this?"

"I've told her nothing. I leave that to you, at your discretion." Lord Alistair clasped his hands behind his back and began to pace. "Do you know your brothers have joined the Revolution, no doubt poisoned by lies?"

"I didn't."

"They're alone on the Barrier Coast, embroiled in a mutiny that will only get them killed. We all know the history of the Age of Sorrow, but you've seen what happens with your own eyes when the superstitions of the common born are allowed to fester, haven't you?"

Val tightened as he thought of the villagers hustling Adaira through the village, seeking to sacrifice her in a misguided attempt to appease the demons outside their walls. This after Adaira had saved the life of a village child. "I have."

"You understand, then, why we take a firm hand in these matters?"

"Yes," he said, almost inaudibly, thinking only of his brothers.

Lord Alistair steepled his pointer fingers. "My proposal to you still stands."

Val blinked when he realized what he was offering, stunned yet again.

"You must be wondering why I did not tell you all of this before last night," Lord Alistair said.

Val thought about it. "You wanted to know if I had any connection to the Revolution."

"As always, your instincts are unfailing. I've had you followed from the moment you returned from Londyn. I'm curious; did Groft ever approach you about joining him?"

"Never."

"There's one thing of which I'm uncertain—how did you arrive in this world?"

The thought of his father's role in all of this, the lengths he went to in order to protect his sons, caused a lump to rise in Val's throat. He thought about Lord Alistair's question and decided to withhold Salomon's name, not knowing what response it would elicit. "A portal our father left us. A friend of his, our godfather, helped us escape when Zedock came for us. He left us the sword and the staff but didn't have time to tell us much else. Or maybe he didn't know. Our father left us a journal, but Zedock stole it."

"You never had a chance to read it?"

"No."

Lord Alistair's face tightened in sympathy. "What an unfortunate turn of events. I can't imagine the shock you must have experienced upon your arrival on Urfe."

"No. You really can't."

Alistair began to pace again. "I said my proposal still stands, and I'll go a step further. I understand family, and what your brothers mean to you. Find the Coffer, and I'll return them to your home world unharmed."

Val was stunned once again. "You can do that?"

A thin smile appeared on the Chief Thaumaturge's lips. "Once we find them, of course. I've no interest in punishing them. This is not their world. They do not understand their choices."

Val sagged in relief. "I just want them home safe."

Alistair laid a hand on his arm. "I had a brother once. He died when I was young, and I was devastated." He released Val's arm and wagged a finger. "As long as we find your brothers before a battle erupts that they cannot win, they should be safe. Now," he said, crossing his arms and raising his eyebrows, "what was it you were about to tell me?"

Val's smile was swift and wolfish. "I seem to have forgotten."

3

After the council meeting, Mateo and Tamás tried to get Will to join them for a late dinner at the tavern. Dalen offered as well, once Will returned to the inn where they were sleeping.

He refused them all. Not even Mala could have kept him from his vigil on the stairwell outside Caleb's room that night. At some point, his brother had to leave for food or to relieve himself, and Will planned to corner him. As the grandfather clock down the hall ticked away, he slumped on the second-floor landing of the inn's battered staircase, stained with time and spilled ale, the floorboards stripped of shine by the tread of adventurers past.

Midnight came and went. Late-night guests had to maneuver around him as they returned to their rooms. Their annoyed stares turned incredulous, and then reverential, when they recognized him. Months before, Will would have questioned whether the residents of Urfe were even real people, or just figments of his imagination.

But now, in this world where dreams came true and nightmares stalked the land, where he was an adventurer with a magic sword instead of an assistant builder struggling to pay the rent, he had never felt so alive.

He missed home desperately, as all childhood homes are missed, but he had come to love the world from which his father hailed.

He loved it, but he also respected it.

Feared it.

He stared down at the scars on his hands and forearms, badges of honor from the construction sites he used to work. Less than a year before, he had thought of the jobsite as a theater of war, the one place in all the world where he was bold and respected.

The foolishness of that sentiment caused him to cackle out loud at his naiveté.

Now he worried about staying alive, on a daily basis.

There was another concern. These people—*his* people—thought of him as a hero. That was a title he had always dreamed of holding, but which he had never understood. No one had told him about the weight of expectation it carried, the desperate fear of failure. If Will botched this insane quest the Council was proposing, he didn't just fail himself, he failed an entire people. So was he up to the task?

Hell no, he thought. *What kind of egotist actually thinks he's prepared to be a hero?*

Caleb's door banged against the wall as it flung open, causing Will to leap to his feet. His brother's red-rimmed eyes flew wildly about the hallway, as if he had just awakened from a dream. Rushing past Will as if he hadn't seen him, Caleb bounded down the stairway carrying a backpack and wearing the black traveling cloak with silver stitching he had pulled out of the Coffer.

"Caleb!"

His brother turned at the bottom of the stairs, blinking as if he had just noticed Will. "What are you doing here?"

"What am I *doing*? Holding an all-night vigil in a desperate attempt to see my brother for the first time in days. What are *you* doing? It's three in the morning." He glimpsed the edge of Caleb's black leather vambraces poking out from the sleeves of his cloak, and he noticed a new addition to his wardrobe: a leather thong necklace with Marguerite's wedding ring attached. "Are you going somewhere?"

To his surprise, Caleb gave a single, grim nod.

"Um, where?"

"I had a dream," he said.

"What are you talking about?"

"There's someplace I have to go. Something I have to find."

"Because of a dream? What is it?"

"I'm sorry, Will. You'll just try to interfere."

As Caleb started down the stairs, Will hurried after him, catching up with him outside the inn. The two Devla sentries looked stunned by Caleb's sudden appearance. They bowed deeply before trying to engage him, but he pushed them away and kept walking. After a moment of confusion, they ran off down a side street.

The courtyard was dark and quiet, the glow lanterns extinguished by decree of the council in order to make the city less visible from above, in case of another attack. Will hurried forward, grabbed his brother by the shoulder, and spun him around. "This is crazy, Caleb. You can't just leave."

"You're getting ready to, aren't you?"

Earlier, while he was waiting outside Caleb's door, Will had told him about the council meeting. He thought he was talking to a door, but he supposed his brother had been listening after all. "That's different. I've told you everything I know. You can come with me to Prague."

"I have a different path now," he said, looking right through Will. "For the first time in my life, I have purpose."

"Which is?" Will asked, expecting him to say he was going to drink the Barrier Coast dry, or honor Marguerite's memory by burying her ring someplace special in the Blackwood Forest.

Instead his brother drew up straight, the cowl of his cloak shadowing the handsome lines of his face, his six-foot-two frame looming over Will. "To kill Lord Alistair."

Will's first instinct was to laugh at his brother's joke. But then he saw the deadly glint in Caleb's eye, the clench of his jaw, and his fists balled against his sides.

Will rocked back on his heels. "What are you talking about?" he whispered.

"Just what I said."

"That's impossible."

"Maybe. I don't care. Don't you understand that I don't care about *anything* anymore?" He took a step closer, his stare so intense it felt as if he were soldering two pieces of metal. "Except for revenge, my brother. I care about revenge."

When Will stepped closer to grip his arm, Caleb shook him off with a growl. "I don't want your sympathy."

"This isn't you. You can't... you're a pacifist, Caleb. Not a fighter or revenge seeker."

"I made an exception once, for Zedock. I'm going to make another one."

Will stared into his brother's eyes for a long moment, hoping to see a frantic but dying resolve, or even a touch of madness. Instead he saw calculated fury, burning with the passion of a zealot. "You're serious."

"More than I've ever been."

"Then I'm coming with you."

"*No*. You weren't in the dream, and I'm not risking your involvement. Both because I don't want you in danger and because it might upset the balance."

"Upset the balance?" Will pressed his fingertips against his temples. "This dream, did it involve you fighting Lord Alistair?"

"Among other things."

"Did it say, um, who won?"

He could tell by his brother's eyes that the outcome wasn't desirable.

"It's a chance," Caleb said. "Nothing more."

Will gripped his brother by the shoulders. "This is madness, Caleb. At least wait until the morning. Dreams can be so vivid at the time. We'll have coffee and talk it out. I'll take as long as you need. *Please*."

Caleb turned and strode away. Unable to let him go, Will hurried across the courtyard, pleading with him to wait. Caleb turned, grabbed him by the collar, and shoved him away. "You're not coming," he said, with a snarl. "I mean it. Don't try to follow me, either."

Stunned, Will stood in the street with his hands hanging helpless at his sides. As much as he and Caleb had teased each other over the years, they had never laid a hand on one another in anger. "I can't just let you go."

"You want to help me, Will?" Caleb called out as he walked. "Give me a chance to survive? Then go get the Coffer. Bring it back to me, and help me use it against Alistair."

Will hurried to catch up to him again. "You're talking like it's yours."

"You saw what happened."

"Yeah, I did. Can we talk about that?"

"There's nothing much to say. I didn't even touch it. My hand got close and the lid lifted by itself. I don't know what happened, or how, or why. Just that it did."

"What was inside the Coffer?"

Before he strode off again, Caleb shrugged and said, "Nothing except this cloak. But for some weird reason I can't explain, I feel like the Coffer is a part of me."

Will had never felt so helpless in his life. His brother had always been as wise as an oracle when dishing wisdom at the bar, yet hapless with his own life decisions. Principled in all the wrong situations.

But going after Lord Alistair? A virtual god among men?

What had Caleb seen in that dream?

When he reached the next intersection, Caleb stopped to pound on the door of another inn. Will watched as the Brewer, a former musician from New Jersey also trapped in this world, a minstrel with the power to affect people with his music, stepped outside with sleep-filled eyes and conferred with Caleb. The two had met in the Blackwood Forest when they were imprisoned inside a fairy ring, and had grown close. Will stepped nearer and heard Caleb telling the Brewer to pack a bag and meet him at the stable.

"He's going, too?" Will asked, after the Brewer disappeared inside and Caleb started walking again.

"Yes."

Will threw his hands up. "Why him and not me?"

"Because he was in the dream. And because I don't know how to cook."

The Brewer emerged, throwing a helpless look Will's way before leaving with Caleb. Will tried one more time to follow, and his brother rebuffed him again. Not knowing what else to do, Will stood in shock as he watched them walk away, glad at least his brother wouldn't be alone.

Just before they turned down a wide boulevard, Will saw the Prophet emerge from an alley and hurry to meet Caleb, his palms held up in supplication. He was alone and wearing his traveling cloak, his intentions clear. Caleb dismissed him with a flick of his wrist.

After watching Caleb leave, the Prophet turned his gaze on Will for a brief moment, then melted back into the shadows.

At noon the next day, Will strode into the Red Wagon Tavern to join the council meeting. The room was full again, though Mala was nowhere to be seen.

"Have you considered our proposal?" Tamás asked, thrusting his palms on the oak table.

"I have."

"And?"

Still devastated by Caleb's departure, terribly frustrated he was unable to help either of his brothers, Will took a deep breath and stood at the head of the table to address the assembled elders and council members. His only consolation was that he felt the spirit of his father in the room with him. Will was sure that he, too, had been a revolutionary, and would have approved of his decision. Not only that, but getting the Coffer back might be the only way to help his brothers. If nothing happened to upset the balance of power, Will knew Val would rot in wizard prison and Lord Alistair would slaughter Caleb like a lamb, even if his brother did manage to get within a thousand miles of the Chief Thaumaturge.

"I'll go to Praha," Will said, eying the assembled crowd. A cheer broke out, and he walked over to stand near Mateo. "Will you go with me, cousin?"

Mateo jumped to his feet and embraced him in a fierce hug. "I was going to insist."

"An excellent choice," Tamás said. "I figured as much. I've asked three mages as well, and each agreed that—"

"I'm taking a wizard," Will interrupted, "but not one of yours."

There was silence in the room.

"After what happened with Selina, I have to have people I can trust. With my life."

Mateo shuffled his feet as the elders murmured amongst themselves and exchanged nervous glances.

"Who, then?" Tamás asked.

As if on cue, the door to the back room opened, and Dalen walked inside with a sheepish expression. "Lucka, I hope I'm not late," the young illusionist said, looking nervous at the grim faces around the table. He turned to face Will. "You told me to wait a few minutes and then, aike, I wasn't sure if I should knock and then I thought—"

"It's fine," Will said, quieting him with a finger as he cast his gaze around the room. "I've decided to take Dalen as my mage."

Tamás looked ill at the proclamation. Merin Dragici, a wealthy trader, stood and pointed a gnarled finger at the young illusionist. "He's not Roma, or even a full mage. We cannot leave the fate of our people to an unproven boy."

"He's as old as I am," Will said, "and in case you've forgotten, he was an integral part of our escape from the Darklands. Dalen is growing in power, he trains harder than anyone I've ever met, he's clever, and most importantly—" Will leveled his gaze at Merin and then Tamás, "I'm not going without him."

Shouts filled the room, followed by a heated discussion, but Will wouldn't budge from his position. Dalen's face grew redder and redder, until Tamás cut everyone off. "Enough! I've traveled with Dalen myself, and can attest to his bravery. If Will desires him as a companion, then while I may not agree, I will accept his demand."

Merin continued to disagree, but Will wouldn't relent. Unwilling to lose the support of the wielder of Zariduke, the council was forced to approve the choice.

"And the fourth companion?" Tinea Alafair asked Will. "Who will it be?"

"When do you want me to leave?"

"This evening, if possible," Tamás said. "I'm afraid there's no time to spare."

Will nodded and started for the door. He had expected that answer. "I'll return before nightfall with my fourth companion," he said, with a confidence he did not feel. "Prepare the gateway bauble."

"No," Mala repeated. She was curled into a worn armchair in her room at the inn, wearing leather pants and a scarlet blouse with a matching headscarf. "I will not accompany you on your foolish journey."

Will sank into a twin armchair, bitterly disappointed. He had found her packing for her own journey, the purpose of which she would not reveal. Something she needed to do alone, she said. Unfinished business from her past.

Why wouldn't anyone he loved tell him where they were going?

"We'll fail without you," Will said.

"This is your expedition to lead," she said. "Its failure or success depends on you and not me."

"I agree. And as the leader, I want the fiercest warrior and most knowledgeable traveler I know by my side. Someone who has been to Praha before."

"Capable I may be, but I'm no wizard."

"You killed a majitsu."

Her eyes moved to the corner, where the azantite-tipped cat o' nine tails rested against the wall. A surprising range of emotions flickered in her eyes. He saw fury, satisfaction, and longing wrapped inside a distant sadness, as if she were thinking of something lost long ago. Most of all, though, he saw fear—and that both surprised and unnerved him.

"Magelasher is a powerful weapon," she said softly. "An artifact from a long ago age meant to combat majitsu. Not wizards, Will. *Majitsu*. Warriors with a touch of magic. Though a powerful item, Magelasher is a pale shadow of Zariduke."

"You knew it was in the pyramid somewhere, didn't you?" Will asked in sudden understanding. "You wanted it from the start. That's why you were so interested in the journey."

Her eyes lingered on the scourge. "You should accept their offer of an experienced mage. Praha is full of strange magic and powerful creatures. An extremely perilous place."

"I can't be betrayed again. It almost doomed us last time. I trust Dalen, and he's much stronger now."

She gave a harsh laugh, ever the pragmatist, and Will looked away. He knew that his friend, while more capable than when they had met, would still rank among the weakest of mages. In the Realm, illusionists were considered second rate wizards, more fit for a sideshow carnival than for serious magic.

Mala had visited Praha once before. Over the next hour, she told Will everything she knew about the city. "Don't do this, Will. Gallantry is a fool's path. As foolish as a revolt against the Congregation. Show me a room full of people who believe a story about a hero who lived to old age, and I'll show you a room full of fools."

"Wow," he said, rising off the chair, "I would almost think you cared."

Her cynical smile appeared like the crack of a whip. "As I said, don't be a fool."

He stepped right next to her and cupped the nape of her neck. The supple smoothness of her skin sent a shiver coursing through him. He still remembered their kiss before the surprise attack on Freetown, the taste of plum and spice, danger dancing in mystery. "Would you respect me if I stayed?"

"I'd rather share ale with the living than respect the dead."

"Is that all you want from me?" he said as he moved even closer, until their lips were almost touching. "To share a good ale?"

As the moment stretched, he felt the warmth of her breath on his face, smelled the floral musk of her perfume. He moved to kiss her, but she put a finger to his lips.

"I won't kiss the hero before his ill-fated journey," she said, though her fingers caressed the edges of his mouth, "like the village lass who lives inside her skirts and waits patiently for his return."

"And if I stayed?"

A flicker in her eyes caused him to think she was about to change her mind. Yet instead of leaning into him, she held his gaze and took a step back. A distance that, to Will, seemed as if a mountain had just landed between them. "You won't."

Her answer caused him to flinch. As much as he wanted to, he couldn't deny the truth in her words. He loved her, but he could never live with himself if he chose desire over what he thought was right. He knew Mala was not the same kind of person and, while it did not make him love her any less, it was a barrier between them he didn't know how to cross.

She crossed her arms against her chest, as if drawing herself tight. Protecting. He knew she could read his thoughts in his eyes. "Go," she said, her voice barely above a whisper. "Perform your duty."

Unable to bear the distance between them, he took her by the arms and moved to kiss her, but she turned her head and slipped out of his grasp.

He stood in the center of his room, feeling hurt and foolish.

"It's time for you to leave," she said coldly. "You have a quest to attend to."

The guarded look had returned to her eyes, the one that had been there for as long as he had known her—except for the last several minutes.

"Tell me where you're going," he said.

"I cannot."

"How will I find you again?"

"You probably won't."

Feeling as if the ground was slipping out from beneath him, he stepped forward and placed his hands on her shoulders. She tensed as if ready for a fight, but didn't pull away.

He looked her in the eye. "I love you, Mala. I have for some time."

She started, as if that was not at all what she had expected to hear. A flicker of confusion entered her eyes, and he relished the emotion, the spark of uncertainty.

"I just wanted you to know," he said. "Take care of yourself. I hope we meet again."

Without waiting for a response, he grabbed his sword and closed the door behind him.

Reeling, feverish with disappointment, Will trudged through town towards the Red Wagon Tavern. The sun had almost descended. He had no fourth companion and no idea whom to choose. He supposed he could limit it to three people, but as dangerous as this journey promised to be, that seemed foolish.

Yet whom could he trust? He wished Marek were still there, but the big warrior had returned to his family while Will was away in the Mayan Kingdom.

As he passed the beer fountain, he heard a familiar voice calling his name. Not the voice of someone he knew from Urfe, but from back home.

Could it be, he thought? Or am I hearing things?

He turned and saw a tall, beautiful woman, her hair and skin the color of a light roast coffee bean, riding through the square on a handsome chestnut stallion.

A shrill cry split the air. Will looked up and saw a massive bird land atop a nearby rooftop, settle its mottled wings, and watch over Yasmina's approach as if protecting the young wilder. The wounded harpy eagle Yasmina had rescued in the Yucatan forest, now healthy and strong.

His old friend's countenance had changed from the last time he had seen her. They had not been apart that long, but she looked wiser and more competent, as if her wilder powers had grown during her absence. An aura of power enveloped her, not just in the traditional sense, but the sort of personal power that comes when someone figures out exactly who she is.

Yasmina still carried the owl staff Elegon had bequeathed her, as well as the pewter-colored traveling cloak she had worn on the journey to the tomb of the sorcerer king. She dismounted and embraced Will with a warm smile, which relieved him. He was afraid she had turned into some sort of wisdom-spouting recluse who spoke in riddles and had changed her name to something unpronounceable.

"Yasmina?"

"Yes?"

"Just checking. What are you doing here? Where did you go?"

"North," she said. "Beyond the Protectorate."

"How did you get there and back so fast?"

She gave a mysterious smile and didn't answer. He reassessed his earlier conclusion.

"It's good to see you, Will." A conflicted look shadowed her face. "I'd love to catch up soon, but is Caleb here?"

"He left."

Her face tensed. "Left? Where did he go?"

After a shake of his head, he told her everything that had happened since she had left their party atop the pyramid, including the recovery of the Coffer and Caleb's marriage to Marguerite. Yasmina stood very still as he told her about the murder of Marguerite and Luca, and the circumstances of Caleb's departure.

She whispered, "It's as I feared."

"How could you fear something when you haven't even been here?"

"I . . . knew something had happened to him."

"How?"

"I can't explain. I just did, and I knew I needed to help."

"Was it a wilder thing?"

"Maybe. And maybe . . ."

"You two have a connection," Will finished for her. "Magnified by the weirdness of this world, or your wilder powers. Or both."

Her eyes gave a mute assent.

With a sigh, Will eyed the shadows collecting on the streets, the purple hue bruising the sky. He had to get to the Red Wagon Tavern.

"Will?"

"Yeah?"

"Do you really think recovering the Coffer might help your brothers?"

"I don't know, Yaz. I don't know how much trouble Val is in, and I don't know if anything can bring Caleb to his senses. But I feel in my gut this is the right thing to do, both to help my brothers and these people."

Yasmina's hand moved to the top of her staff, and she looked past Will to somewhere distant. "Do you think it was an accident I arrived here at this very moment?"

"I have no idea. Do you?"

"I don't believe in fate in the traditional sense. But I do believe that sometimes, things happen that are beyond our ability to understand. Is there any way you might consider taking another companion on your journey?"

He hadn't told her about the gateway bauble and the limit on the number of people.

But now he didn't need to.

Sky merged with earth, a cloak of darkness settling on the land as Tamás led Will, Mateo, Dalen, and Yasmina on a well-trod horse trail out of Freetown, up into the high green hills overlooking the ocean. The council had decided to keep the method of the journey a secret, in case more spies were about. If anyone saw them leaving town, Tamás could claim he had seen Will and his companions off on horseback, on an expedition to find the Coffer in the Dragon's Teeth.

Each member of the party carried a backpack full of rations and miscellaneous items. With no idea how long they would be gone, the packs were stuffed as full as each member could handle. They also had a single bottle of healing salve, one of the few left in Freetown after the wizards' attack.

In addition, Will carried Zariduke, his new buckler shield, the supple leather armor he had worn on the Yucatan journey, and his magical armband that

translated foreign tongues and had eluded all attempts at removal. The armband made him nervous, but there was nothing he could do about it. Would
it not fall off until his death, as with the ogre-mage? Was it a sentient thing?

Mateo rode beside him, his flexible urumi sword worn as a belt, the two of
them ensconced in a comfortable silence. In place of his left hand, his cousin
bore a magical chain mail glove he had found in the tomb of the sorcerer king.
An archer as well as a swordsman, Mateo claimed the five-fingered glove did
not afford him the nimble dexterity needed for a bow, though it possessed
other advantages. Mateo could now break the bones of a man's hand with his
grip, or smash through a brick wall with his fist.

Dalen rode just ahead, chattering to himself, excited and apprehensive.
Will still didn't know the young mage's true background, or what had led to
his capture by the tuskers. He sensed it was a sore topic, perhaps because his
family had abandoned him.

At the front of the group, Yasmina rode beside Tamás, conversing softly.
Ever since he had met her, Tamás had harbored an attraction for the striking
wilder. They seemed to be getting along, though Will could not tell whether
Yasmina had started to return his feelings, or was just being nice.

Before they set out, Will had asked her about the harpy eagle. Yasmina said
she had sent her off on an errand, but had refused to elaborate. He wondered
if it had anything to do with Caleb.

The long-haired, handsome leader of the Revolution led them to a majestic
redwood grove high above Freetown. In the distance, stars glittered above the
velvet canvas of the ocean. As Will dismounted, he noticed a handful of elders
assembled beside an enormous tree with a hollowed-out space in the trunk. He
tried to shake off his nerves and the memory of his last encounter with Mala,
wondering if they would ever meet again.

As they dismounted at the base of the redwood, Will noticed Jacoby Revansill, Merin Dragici, Tinea Alafair, Kyros Toth, and a gray-haired sylvamancer
named Grelick, Tinea's brother, who had recently arrived from his homestead
near the eastern edge of the Dragon's Teeth. Grelick had visited Praha once
before and would handle the shaping of the gateway bauble.

The Prophet was also present, standing by himself at the edge of the wood,
observing the proceedings with a serene air. Will had the sudden urge to grab

him by the collar and shake him. *Stay away from my brother, you zealot. He's not who you think he is.*

When Tinea saw Will, she gasped and clapped a hand to her mouth, pointing at his shield. "Where did you get that?"

He looked down at the battered, teardrop-shaped buckler. "I found it in the treasure room of the sorcerer king. Why?"

Though unimpressive to look at, its weight had felt right in his hand, lightweight and maneuverable.

"When I saw it on your return, it didn't look like this. The runes . . .so vivid . . ." She trailed off and stared at the shield in wonder.

He hadn't thought it was a big deal. "The Coffer did that when Caleb opened it. I assumed the residual magic affected it in some way."

"The Coffer?" Tinea gave a strangled cry, though the other elders looked as confused as Will. "Does no one recognize the pattern on this shield? What he is holding?"

Kyros Toth snapped his fingers. "By the queen . . . *could it be?*"

Tinea approached Will and laid her withered hands on the buckler with reverent care. "Perhaps I'm the only one here ancient enough to remember the old books. This is a *paladin's* shield. Not just any paladin, either." She turned her piercing gaze on Will and pointed at a rune that resembled a squiggly line wrapped around a sword, piercing a seven-pointed star. "This is the personal insignia of Fieran Blackwood. Captain of the paladins under Priestess Nirela, devoted servant of Devla and a true cleric of our people."

Tamás gaped at the buckler. "A paladin's shield has not been seen in ages. And now one is revealed by the Coffer? Fieran Blackwood's, no less?"

"Does this mean Will's a paladin?" Dalen blurted out.

"Only a true cleric of Devla can anoint a paladin," Tamás said, gripping Will by the shoulder. "But this is surely a great honor. Yet another sign from Devla that our path is true!"

Mateo was looking on with wide eyes as the elders gathered around Will, inspecting the buckler with awe. All the attention embarrassed him. "Does it do anything?" he asked gruffly. "Any powers I should know about?"

Tinea said, "It's said that under the aegis of a high cleric, the shields are enhanced in some way. What those abilities might be, I'm uncertain. The lore has long been lost."

Will let his gaze rest on the rune-covered buckler. He had always been drawn to the concept of the paladin, a warrior with an allegiance to a greater cause, something more than just a sword-for-hire. Despite the unknown nature of the runes, the shield seemed a symbol of everything that had happened since he and his brothers had arrived on Urfe: his journey to become a warrior, becoming entangled in the Revolution, and now the weight of undertaking a journey that might be the last hope of his people.

"We should go," Tamás said.

Will took a deep breath as Grelick, the sylvamancer, took a glass bauble the size of a grapefruit out of a cloth sack. He bent and carefully placed the bauble inside the hollow of the tree.

"It helps to keep the bauble in a confined space," Tamás said quietly to Will. "To ensure it stays contained."

"Uh, what happens if it's not contained? Like if one of our arms is sticking out?"

Tamás's face turned troubled. "Do not allow that to happen. It is why only four people can be taken."

The hole in the trunk was so large Will didn't even have to duck as Grelick ushered the four companions inside and asked them to link hands around the bauble. Once they were positioned, the old sylvamancer smashed the artifact with his foot and backed out of the tree. Strangely, the sound of his footsteps was muffled as a dense mist rose out of the shards and swirled around the companions. Everyone pressed close together, ensuring they were inside the mist. Grelick was staring intensely at the fog, which had no smell or taste and began to move rapidly, as if the wizard was sifting through it.

Will looked down and noticed his hands had started to merge into the ephemeral gray substance. He gritted his teeth and forced himself not to panic. Tamás and the other elders observed the process with tense expressions from outside the tree, their hopes resting on the fate of the four companions.

Grelick moved his hands in the air like a conductor. The fog started to congeal as the bodies of Will and his friends grew more and more transparent, and then an image emerged in the soupy haze, surrounding them as if they were in a Cyclorama theater with a three hundred and sixty degree view: a cobblestone street set beneath a slender, crumbling archway spanning the air between two black obelisks. As the vision solidified, the trunk of the redwood tree and the faces of the elders grew ever more distant.

Eventually the fog dissipated and, with a start, Will realized he and his companions were corporeal once again. They were standing on that very cobblestone street, staring up at the archway and the obelisks, drinking in the same dystopian cityscape of soot-blackened buildings, cracked bridges and arches, and nests of maze-like alleys they had glimpsed through the escape portal taken by the Coffer thief.

"Praha," Dalen whispered.

-4-

Ringed by columns of red-gold marble, the Hall of Wizards was a rectangular, hundred-foot tall building that stretched the length of a football field. Inside the open-air structure, a frescoed ceiling depicted conquests from the Pagan Wars and the Age of Expansion, looming high above the statues of deceased wizards filling the hall.

Those statues looked so real, Val had learned, because artisamancers trained in geomancy had fused the corpses of deceased mages with solid chunks of granite, immortalizing them in a process he did not fully understand. Each figure held or wore the wizard stone they had carried in life, scepters and wands and crowns and bracelets, adding splashes of color and majesty to the somber display.

Val strode to the rear of the Hall, awed by its grandeur, then stood in front of a plaque with a list of names bearing a birthdate followed by a dash. The roster of wizards whose fate remained unknown, including the second name on the last row: Dane Blackwood.

Except his father's fate, if Lord Alistair was to be believed, might no longer be a mystery.

Had Dane Blackwood died on Earth, killed by an agent of the Revolution? Murdered by Dean Groft?

Maybe that was why the Dean had treated him kindly. Out of guilt for his deeds. He might even have liked Val's father and slain him to get the sword, due to zealous belief in the cause.

Head bowed and eyes closed, Val took a knee, honoring his father's memory. He gripped the azantite-topped staff he no longer had to keep secret, a birthright for all the Realm to see, then whispered a vow of revenge as he choked back his emotions with a snarl.

He did not have time for weakness. Not with so much at stake.

As he always did, Val focused on the big picture, which to him was quite clear.

First, recover the Coffer and use his leverage with Lord Alistair to find his brothers. With any luck, they were safe on the Barrier Coast, in the bosom of the Revolution.

After he sent his brothers home, he would find a way to get to the bottom of his father's death.

Save his family. Avenge his father.

The rest was details.

Using the staff to push to his feet, Val touched his fingertips to his father's plaque and murmured goodbye. He needed to get going. The shadows had lengthened outside the hall and, oddly, Lord Alistair had requested that Val meet him at the Sanctum at midnight to discuss how to recover the Coffer.

Before that, Val had a dinner date with two very special people.

"The Duck and Fig, is it?" Gus spat out a gob of tobacco as the two horses pulling his black carriage clacked down Magazine Street. The dappled steeds splashed into puddles of muddy water that had gathered on the cobblestones during the afternoon deluge. "Fanciest new restaurant on Canal, they say."

Though Val could have flown or even walked to the restaurant, it was customary in New Victoria for wizards to travel by carriage outside the Wizard District, unless taking flight over long distances. The murder of Garbind had everyone spooked, causing even the elder mages to travel with caution. If Dean Groft truly had Zariduke in his possession, then it was doubtful anyone, even Lord Alistair, could stand against him.

Most of all, Val enjoyed his driver's company and found him a valuable source of information. Gus had his ear to the ground, and he and Val had developed a close bond.

"I've heard good things," Val replied.

Though used to dining in New York City's finest restaurants, the cuisine of New Victoria impressed him. The ingredients were always fresh from the soil, and some of the dishes were so original and delectable that Val suspected the hand of magic.

But at the moment, the gastronomy of Urfe was a distraction.

Gus took notice. "Something on your mind?"

Val leaned back and turned his head to the side, absorbing the city. "Lots, Gus."

"I've heard some rumors about ye. What ye did for the Queen. They say Lord Alistair is right appreciative."

"Word travels fast."

"Always does, laddie, always does." Gus looked back and grinned through tobacco-stained teeth. "Especially in low places."

"What else have you heard?"

"Nothing new about yer brothers. I've been asking hard, too. It's impossible to be sure, but no one's seen a pair like the two of 'em around, especially with the sword."

"I'm sure they'd keep the sword hidden."

"Aye. But eyes in the gutter have a way of noticing hidden things."

"What about Mala or Allira?"

Gus slapped at a mosquito on his neck. "The gypsy hasn't been seen in New Victoria since she left town with ye and yers. They say the dark one, though, has joined the Prophet."

Val's eyebrows rose at the mention of the leader of the gray-clad followers of Devla. The wizards wanted the Prophet's head on a platter, and for good reason. He symbolized a return to ignorance and persecution of the wizard-born. "Why?"

"Dunno, lad. I s'pose she found religion, though 'tis a right dangerous thing to find around here." He spat again and looked as if he wanted to say something else, then cut himself off.

"You can speak freely," Val said quietly. "It's me."

The increased Protectorate patrols, inquisitions, and other harsh measures against those who had not taken the Oaths had incensed some of the population. Val understood his friend's wariness, but he also understood the Congregation's response to the threat of the Revolution, especially after the murder of Garbind.

"It's just that yer moving up in the wizard world, and I know ye've heard me speak ill of them in the past. I want ye to know my loyalty is with ye, lad, whether ye be a commoner or a tax collector or the Chief Thaumaturge him-self."

Val leaned forward to lay a hand on his driver's broad shoulder. "I know, Gus. And I want you to know you never have to watch what you say around me, even if it's negative."

Though Gus looked relieved, Val could tell he wasn't entirely convinced. But that was okay. Val did not want blind devotion. Full disclosure was a fool's game, and Gus was no fool. Val would prefer his driver to keep his harshest criticisms to himself and preserve their relationship.

They navigated the cobblestone streets of the Central Business District and its dizzying array of shops, taverns, and markets. Val felt a pang of sadness as he recalled the wonder in Will's eyes when they first beheld the Adventurer's Em-porium, the Museum of Curios and Oddities, and the New Victoria Magick Shop.

After skirting the Government Sector and the Guild Quarter, they passed through one of Val's favorite neighborhoods, a bohemian district full of street-side cafes tucked under a sheltering canopy of live oaks. Finally they reached Canal Street and its legendary row of high-end restaurants. The arrival of dusk had sparked the glow orbs arcing over the street, casting a silver glow on the finely brocaded carriages and velvet-draped entrances. At the end of the street, a golden bridge spanned the river, and Val heard the sounds of revelry from the parks and cafes stretching along the banks.

The beauty of the wizard capital took his breath away. New Victoria, he realized, had almost come to feel like home.

As they drew closer to the bridge, some of Val's goodwill faded when he saw a pair of ten-foot iron cages flanking the entrance, each holding a prisoner in-side. The captives' wrists were bound to iron rings at the tops of the cages, their soiled black sashes still around their waists. Val thought they were dead until one of them twitched. A pair of silver-robed majitsu stood guard with folded arms by the entrance to the bridge.

"Gibbeted without food or water," Gus said, "as a lesson to the rest of 'em. Tis harsh, but can't say I lose any sleep over *their* ilk. Right vicious ones they are."

Val firmed his jaw before looking away. War was a harsh business, and he had seen first hand the brutal tactics of the black sash gypsies. One of them had gutted Mari like a fish, and he would never forget it.

An arched entranceway and a glowing emerald sign heralded the entrance to the Duck and Fig. As they approached, he heard Dida calling his name from a flagstone patio built around an enormous jacaranda. After Val asked Gus to wait nearby, a hostess opened a gate built into the low stone wall separating the patio from the street. Val walked through and embraced the bibliomancer, who almost tripped over a chair as he rose to greet him.

"My friend!" Dida cried. The light from clover glow orbs set on stands around the patio gleamed off his eraser-shaped bald head. "It is so good to see you."

"And you," Val said warmly, taking care not to hug his friend too hard. Dida had been gravely injured in the fight with Asmodeus, and Val had last seen him in the care of the cuerpomancer in the Queen's infirmary in Londyn. Though Dida looked thinner as he limped back to the table, his mahogany skin bore only faint traces of the dagger-like barbs that had pinned him to the demon lord's torture wheel.

In contrast to the earnest greeting of the bibliomancer, Adaira eyed Val from across the table with a coy twist to her lips, her pale blond hair caught above her head in a turquoise circlet that matched her eyes, drawing the stares of every man in sight.

"Valjean," she said, extending her hand in mock formality.

He took a knee to kiss her hand. "Milady. Mine eyes have never witnessed such a bounteous vista as thee," he said, imitating the archaic speech of Queen Victoria and her court.

Adaira laughed and traced a hand across his cheek. Val took a seat between them, ordering a glass of granth as they exchanged pleasantries. He decided to wait until he and Adaira were alone to discuss the truth about his past and her father's offer.

"What do you plan to do now?" he asked Dida. "Finish out the year at the Abbey?"

Dida pulled out a scroll from his orange chidakor, a strange hybrid between a silk robe and a business suit favored by the mages of Great Zimbabwe. "After our return, I was granted an honorary diploma."

"Dida, that's excellent news!" Adaira said.

"The accolade itself is unimportant," he said modestly. "In truth, I valued the exchange of knowledge and the camaraderie." He broke into a slow grin. "But the diploma is why I have applied for and been granted another year of post-doctoral study at the Abbey. The Archivist General has granted me full access to the library and rare manuscript rooms!"

"Another year in New Victoria?" Val said, clapping him on the back as Adaira rose to hug their friend. "Even better news."

"And you?" Dida asked. "Will you return to your studies?"

"Val completed the Planewalk," Adaira said, fingering the black pearl choker resting on her sleeveless dress of matching color. "Technically, he's now a spirit mage and member of the Congregation."

Val could tell from her eyes that Adaira knew more than she was letting on. He began to question how much her father had told her.

Dida clapped a hand over his chest. "By the moon, I hadn't considered that! Is it true, then? Will you be the first spirit mage in generations to accelerate your studies?"

"I don't know," Val mumbled, as a man in a chef's apron approached. It was customary in the finer restaurants on Canal Street for the head chef himself to take the orders of respected guests. Val was grateful for the interruption, though he started when he noticed that the chef was Mattie, the owner of the country inn to which Mala had taken them on the journey to Leonidus's Castle.

Hard times must have forced the chef to return to the capital. Val saw a flash of recognition in his eyes, but after seeing the look of warning Val gave him, he took their order without comment.

Val was relieved. A question from Mattie about Val's brothers would have forced an uncomfortable conversation with Dida and Adaira. He hoped he could confide in them soon, but now was not the time.

Dida lowered his eyes. "What terrible news about Dean Groft. Quite hard to fathom, I must say."

"He seemed like such a kind man," Adaira said. "Val, you've met him. What did you think?"

"The same," he said, balling his fist at his side. "We never really know anyone, though, do we?"

"I don't know," Adaira said, looking right at him. "Do we?"

How much does she know?

"Being kind yet secretly devoted to an unpleasant cause are not mutually exclusive," Dida said.

Val slammed a fist on the table. "Killing someone in cold blood is hardly a kind act."

Dida looked startled. "You're quite right. Forgive me. All I meant was—"

Val put a hand out, surprised at his own outburst. It was unlike him to lose control. "I'm sorry. You're right, sometimes people do things for a cause, a deeply held belief, that they otherwise wouldn't do."

"And sometimes," Adaira said softly, looking right at him, "they do them when there is no other choice."

She knew Val was still troubled by two things that had happened in the strange nether world from which they had just returned. In a fit of bloodlust when the villagers had tried to sacrifice Adaira, Val had accidentally killed a young girl with Spirit Fire. He thought an adult was trying to grab him, and would never forgive himself for the girl's death.

The second incident was the cold-blooded murder of Tobar Baltoris. Though a catatonic who probably would never recover his mind, Val had nevertheless put his own life and those of his friends above Tobar's, and killed him with magic.

If needed, he would do it again, too.

Though he wasn't sure what kind of a person that made him.

"There's always a choice," Val said roughly.

Adaira found his hand under the table and squeezed it.

"And you, my dear?" Dida asked Adaira. "What are your plans?"

"I'm returning to the Abbey to finish my studies. I feel it's important for the daughter of the Chief Thaumaturge to follow the same path as everyone else. My dream is to restore cuerpomancy to the discipline of public stewardship it was meant to be. I don't want an air of nepotism to cloud my mission."

Val took a sip of granth. "It's a worthy cause."

The meal arrived, and the bounty from Mattie's kitchen was just as amazing as Val remembered. Yet he couldn't relax enough to enjoy the balmy night air, the dome of stars above, or the laughter of his companions. Whenever his eyes roamed to his left, the tortured bodies of the black-sash gypsies were visible at the end of the street, a visceral reminder of the Revolution raging over parts of the Realm. While Dida and Adaira and the other well-heeled diners on Canal Street might not be affected, at least not that night, his brothers were embroiled in the conflict, lost far from home. If Val didn't intervene, they were in danger of becoming casualties of war.

During a restroom break, he cornered Mattie near the kitchen and asked if he had heard from Mala or Allira. With a subservient politeness that made Val uncomfortable, as if Mattie were afraid of him, the corpulent chef denied having any knowledge of the two women since that night at the inn. Val believed him, though he also came away thinking that if Mattie knew where either woman was, the chef wouldn't have told him.

The night lingered. By the end of the meal, Val longed to accompany Adaira back to her lodging and take her in his arms. Instead he embraced Dida with a forearm clasp and kissed Adaira on the forehead, then walked away and instructed Gus to take him straight to the Sanctum.

He had a meeting with Lord Alistair to attend.

As the carriage delved into the heart of the Wizard District, the tip of a midnight-blue pyramid came into view, followed by the pair of colossi with giant swords crossed over their chests, guarding the columned entrance. Multidimensional wards protected the entrance to the Sanctum, and Val knew that each member of the Congregation bore a magical imprimatur somewhere on their bodies, the same multi-hued octopus carved into the rear of the building. The symbol of the Congregation.

As Val stepped down from the carriage, since he had not yet received the mark, he gripped the colored disc Lord Alistair had given him to bypass the wards. Gus clicked his tongue to spur the horses, tipped his top hat, and headed off. When Val flew over the bridgeless moat and between the two colossi, one of the giants blinked, a torpid movement that almost caused Val to crash into the wall. The enormous beings existed in a different temporal state from humanity, though Val had no doubt they could spring to life when needed. With a shudder, he flew through the opaque doorway, the disc in his hand pulsing as he crossed the wards. He did not want to know would happen to an interloper who entered the headquarters of the Congregation unprotected.

Since he had never been inside the Sanctum, he took a moment to gawk at his surroundings. Topped by a twenty-foot ceiling made of black marble, the ground level was a cavernous lounge area furnished with an array of stunning wizard art. Taxidermy of exotic beasts that felt real to the touch. Bronze planters containing bouquets from a boggling array of climate zones, no doubt maintained by a floramancer. Urns of living fire. Beautiful slivers of disembodied waterfalls that plunged through the floor. Freestanding sculptures combining shapes, colors, and metals at the limits of the imagination. Some even seemed to span dimensions, drawing Val's gaze into a vortex of impossible shapes and hues that reminded him of his gazing journey with Alrick the phrenomancer.

Plush divans, groups of high-backed chairs, and the occasional gemstone table dotted the room, encouraging private conversation. Alcoves recessed into the smooth amber walls sheltered displays of weapons, ceramics, and cultural artifacts from around the globe.

Instead of stairs and hallways, a nest of wizard chutes bored into the ceiling and the floor, including a central chute with a wider circumference than the rest. Azantite-framed signs beside the wizard chutes provided direction. *Administration. Gathering Room. Banquet Hall. War Room.*

Despite the late hour, a number of mages sat alone or in groups. A stern-faced majitsu Val had seen before, another of Lord Alistair's personal attendants, approached Val and guided him into a chute in the floor that read *Diplomacy.*

Ruby glow orbs lit the way down a fifty-foot obsidian tunnel that had to be reinforced with magic, since the water table in New Victoria was so low. The wizard chute branched in three directions. The majitsu chose a horizontal passage on the right. After another branch and another right turn, the majitsu stopped but told Val to keep going. His disc glowed again as he passed another ward and entered a large stone room that again caused him to stare in fascination.

Rows of arched doorways with mirror-like faces were interspersed every five feet along the walls. He peered closer and realized they were not reflective surfaces, but silvery and opaque, almost molten. Names were carved into the granite floor at the base of each portal. Tikal. Tower of Londyn. Charlemagne City. Carthage.

"Welcome, Valjean," Lord Alistair said.

He turned to find the Chief Thaumaturge standing in front of a portal on the far right of the room, joined by a handful of familiar faces, and one unfamiliar one. Braden Shankstone, Kalyn Tern, and Professor Azara he had met before. The hulking, red-bearded man in the black majitsu robe was new to him.

Val tipped his head in greeting. "Thank you."

As his eyes met Braden's, Val caught a flicker of jealousy before the cuerpomancer smiled back at him.

Lord Alistair's right hand man is worried he's being supplanted.

And maybe he is.

Kalyn afforded him her typical icy greeting, though he detected a note of grudging respect in her voice. Professor Azara was cool and unreadable as always, and Lord Alistair introduced the enormous bearded man as Kjeld Anarsson, First Don of the Order of Majitsu. Val had heard of the fierce leader of the warrior-mage sect. Reputed to have enough magical ability to become a full wizard, Kjeld preferred to specialize in physical combat instead. One of the most feared men in the Realm, his capacity for cruelty was as legendary as his battle tactics. Val wondered at his presence.

"You must be quite confused," Lord Alistair said, and Val had a brief stab of fear that they had all gathered to kill him. "I said we would meet to discuss the return of the Coffer, and that is true. But that meeting will not take place here, or even in the Realm. I'm sure you've gathered that this room houses diplomatic portals to various kingdoms and organizations around the world." Dressed in a formal heraldic coat, wearing his silver azantite bracelet and bevy of rings, Lord Alistair beckoned to Val. "Step forward, please."

Still unsure whether to trust the situation but knowing indecision would be a sign of weakness, Val moved to stand beside the Chief Thaumaturge.

"Though anyone can use the portal," Lord Alistair continued, "only a spirit mage can successfully protect against an attack while inside. You're not trained for this, of course, but I hope that one day you will be."

Val could feel the envy radiating from Braden.

"This is an unusual situation, as I am going myself, and our contact has no knowledge of our arrival. Too long have they dabbled in our affairs without fear of repercussion. First the acolyte murders, and now this. An impression needs to be made, a message sent."

Val finally read the name engraved at the foot of the portal next to Lord Alistair. Neither a country nor a kingdom like the others, but instead the home of a legendary group of assassins, the name caused a shudder of fear to roll through him.

"It is time," Lord Alistair said, "to call upon the Grandfather of Alazashin Mountain."

5

"Want to tell me where we're going?" the Brewer asked, as he and Caleb rode south along the Barrier Coast.

"Nope," Caleb replied without emotion, focusing on the steady rocking of his mare.

Though his back ached and his thighs kept cramping, the physical pain helped numb the dull roar that filled Caleb's mind, unrelenting since he had buried Marguerite and Luca's charred remains.

"Seeing as we've been gone almost a day and you haven't so much as said hello, told me our destination, or mentioned anything at all about why you dragged me out of bed, I think I'm entitled to a little repartee." The Brewer rubbed the back of his neck. "I'm also starving, the horses need rest, and my back feels like a team of delvers are pounding it into mush."

They were riding through a valley full of wildflowers and knee-high grass. A canopy of twisting oaks defined the forest on their left, a rhythmic series of waves pounded the shoreline.

"Why did you come with me?" Caleb asked.

The Brewer was quiet for a moment. "Because I had a dream, too."

"You and me, the journey, a tower on the coast?"

He gave a single, grim nod.

"Was that it?" Caleb asked.

"What do you mean?"

"Was there more to the dream? Did you see a battlefield with New Victoria in the background?"

The older man looked confused. "No. Just the tower."

Caleb did not have to search his memory to recall the dream. The entire jumbled sequence was still vivid in his mind, a living thing that had not dissipated with the morning light.

A freestanding cylindrical tower, slender and crumbling.

Ancient as the pyramids.

White as sun-bleached bone.

Caleb inside the tower, climbing a spiral staircase that never seemed to end, strange beasts carved into the walls in bas-relief, a feeling that time had no meaning, the floor disintegrating, and a mace with a diamond-shaped head floating in the darkness.

And then the part that had shaken him to his core and caused him to jump out of bed soaked in sweat.

A battlefield on the outskirts of New Victoria, a slaughterhouse of bodies and fallen trees, the city on fire in the background. Caleb strode at the head of one army, wearing his black cloak and holding the diamond-headed mace he had seen atop the tower, the Coffer of Devla carried by porters on a carved wooden stand beside him. High above the other army, Lord Alistair hovered with an imperious gaze, black lightning sizzling up and down his arms.

Despite the smoking buildings, Caleb's army was not faring well. Scores of wizards lined the rails of airships drifting behind the Chief Thaumaturge. On the ground, the Protectorate Army was a swarm of iron locusts standing between the battlefield and the city. The armies clashed and the dream muddled the images, as dreams do. Then it skipped forward, and somehow Caleb was clashing with his nemesis alone in the middle of the sky. The Coffer opened, the sky pulsed, and bodies fell like hail. A furtive shape closed the Coffer, and the Congregation mages rained fire and destruction on the forces gathered beneath them. As the wizards slaughtered Caleb's army, he surged towards Lord Alistair with the diamond mace in hand, revenge and bloodlust thrumming in his bones. Lord Alistair smiled and held out a palm. Black lightning issued forth, the dark energy swarmed over Caleb—

And the dream ended.

Recalling it had caused Caleb to break out into a cold sweat and start breathing heavily atop the horse. Could the mace he glimpsed in the tower pierce magical defenses, like Will's sword could do? Had he made a mistake in the dream by leaving the Coffer unattended?

What did it all mean? Was any of it real?

He also had the sense he could still affect the outcome of the dream—except there was no chance of victory without the Coffer at his side and the mace in his hands.

He had to have them.

If Will failed to recover the Coffer, then Caleb would go after that, too. But for now, for whatever reason, the dream had shown him the path to the mace.

I need to stop calling it a dream, Caleb thought with a grimace. Dreams were not real enough to compel him to act so rashly, not even in his present state. What he had seen the night before was as real as the flesh on his bones and the grief in his heart.

What he had seen was a *vision*.

He eyed the beauty of the descending sun, a tangerine plunging into an inkwell. In his vision, waves had crashed against a rocky shore beneath a tower that rose high above the Barrier Coast. He wasn't sure how he knew it was the Barrier Coast, except he and the Brewer had ridden south out of Freetown, just as they were now.

Later that night, when they finally stopped at the base of a sand dune covered in scrub grass, Caleb helped the Brewer with the horses and then collapsed on his back. Before they left Freetown, the wise older man had the presence of mind to pack two sleeping rolls and a few days' rations. With the movements of an automaton, Caleb accepted a water skin and a stick of dried beef.

The Brewer was sitting cross-legged, his linen sleeping roll spread atop the sand. Caleb laced his hands behind his head and stared at the stars, remembering how much Marguerite had loved to sleep beneath them, and how Luca had snuggled between them. The electromancer's lightning bolt might as well have cut through Caleb as well, because he felt hollowed out inside, seared and cauterized.

"I miss them, too," the Brewer said quietly. When he still didn't get a response, he said, "What do you think the dream means? Since it's the only thing you'll talk about."

"I have no idea. I just know I have to go."

"Have you ever seen it before? The Tower of Elarion?"

Caleb sat up as if given a shot of adrenaline. "You know what it's *called*?"

"What do you mean?" the Brewer said. "I'm following you, aren't I?"

"In the dream, we were traveling south. I'm just going along with it."

The Brewer stared at him, then rasped a chuckle. "I assumed you'd heard the legend and knew where you were going."

"What legend?"

"That the tower is haunted. They say it's been here, watching over the Barrier Coast, for as long as anyone can remember. Not even the nomad tribes from the southern desert know its origin. According to their lore, a cleric-mage named Elarion once lived inside, before the Roma arrived. Most think Elarion himself is a myth, though *someone* built the tower."

"A cleric-mage?"

The Brewer nodded. "That's probably a legend, too. The Roma aren't short on faith or stories."

"What's the history of the tower? Is the mace supposed to be inside?"

"Mace? What mace?"

"You didn't see it? A diamond-shaped head with a black wooden handle?"

"No."

"It's why I'm making this journey. In my vision, I found it in a room atop the tower."

The Brewer looked as if he had tasted something unpleasant. "The top?"

"Yeah. Why?"

He rested his elbows on his knees. "The tower is supposed to be haunted, but no one really knows for sure, because everyone's afraid to go inside. Even wizards. The last one who did never returned."

A flicker of fear penetrated Caleb's despair. "A wizard didn't return?"

"I was sort of hoping you wouldn't have to go inside."

"If you didn't know I was after the mace, then why are you here?"

"Who else is going to sing about the exploits of He Who Opened the Coffer?

There aren't that many true bards around, you know. I'm kind of rare in these parts. Maybe even unique."

Annoyed by the attempt to lighten the conversation, Caleb's voice turned sharp. "What did you see in your dream?"

The Brewer took a long drink of water. "It took me a while to orient myself. You know how dreams are. When I finally realized I was staring up at the Tower of Elarion, I turned and saw you lying on the ground, outside the door.

I started playing my lute and . . ." he waved a hand and yawned. "That's about the size of it. Listen, I'm turning in."

"What else?"

"What do you mean?"

Caleb rose and stood over the older man. "What happened to me in the dream?" His roiling emotions turned his voice into a growl. "I need to know."

The Brewer's eyes, sad and knowing, lifted to meet Caleb's. "Some things in life are better left unspoken."

"Bruce."

"It was just a dream."

"*Tell me.*"

The Brewer's gaze slipped into the darkness that surrounded them. "I was playing my lute because I was trying to revive you. I don't have healing powers or anything, but I can take people out of a trance sometimes, just like I can put them into one."

"So was I in a trance?"

"I'm not sure." He let out a slow breath. "In the dream, I couldn't tell if you were alive or dead."

6

As soon as Will and the others materialized in Praha, Will spun, sensing eyes on his back. A one-armed beggar lying on a piece of frayed sackcloth was watching the four of them with rheumy eyes. After ensuring the vagrant meant no harm, Will scanned the rest of the street, its ancient cobblestones worn down to smooth nubs. He realized the view through the portal had been limited, and they had landed in a courtyard ringed by stone buildings stained almost black, as if from a fire or from centuries of grime. Upon closer inspection, he noticed the cobblestones were silver-plated artisanal tile that had long since lost its gleam. The tiles were exquisitely patterned, and the workmanship must have cost a fortune.

Just behind them, the crumbling archway they had seen provided egress from the courtyard. A hint of gray dawn light illuminated the tapered points of the obelisks on either side of the archway, two black thorns jutting skyward. The ruined city took naturally to the morning gloom, though Will could tell it had once been very beautiful. He recalled the history Mala had told him, though she admitted no one knew how much of the story was myth.

Many eons ago, ancient records told of a city called Enokkadi, built by a race of tall and splendid immortal beings called the Nephili, long since vanished from Urfe. The name caused Will's eyebrows to rise from the similarity to the word Nephilim, a legendary race of giants mentioned in the Bible. If he recalled correctly, the Nephilim were said to be descendants of fallen angels who had coupled with humans.

Whether the Nephili were native to Urfe, created by menagerists, or had arrived from some other world or dimension, not even the legends opined. But the Nephili capital of Enokkadi was said to be the most exquisite city on Urfe, filled with wonders beyond imagining and magical technologies that had never been equaled. The Nephili themselves possessed powerful innate magic, though not the ability to work spells like human mages. A proud and beautiful race, the Nephili passed ruthless laws allowing only their best and brightest to reproduce, which led to inbreeding among their elite and a gene of madness that took root in their society. Somehow, the magic that lived within them and which they had corralled to build their city became corrupted, unleashing a plague of unknown origin that annihilated their race (not so immortal, Will thought) and festered in their walls and homes. It had turned their city into a twisted, nightmarish version of itself that remained uninhabitable for a thousand years, until the infection burned itself out.

Or so the story went.

Whatever the true origin, no government desired to rule the accursed place. Long ago, one of the kings of Bohemia had renamed the city Praha and tried to reclaim it, though no upstanding citizen would live inside its walls, and soldiers sent to explore its depths kept disappearing. The king gave up and declared the region an independent city-state, and Praha remained an autonomous entity to this day, ruled by no one except the thieves, beggars, hardened adventurers, and other dangerous sorts who called the city home.

A door slammed in the distance. The odor of musty clothes and rotten vegetables spoiled the air. Will shivered beneath his leather jerkin, since the temperature was much chillier than on the Barrier Coast. Mateo's loose patchwork cottons seemed to provide more warmth, and Yazmina looked snug in her pewter cloak. In order not to attract attention as a mage, Dalen had opted for gray cotton breeches and a brown tunic.

Like Will, the others were gazing at their new surroundings with a mixture of wariness and controlled amazement.

"Praha exists," Dalen breathed. "I thought it was a story of my Da." His expression dimmed as he turned in a slow circle, staring open-mouthed at the city. "Lucka, how it reeks of weird magic. I'm no augur and even I can feel it."

On the other side of the archway, the street curved into the distance, walled in by a corridor of blackened buildings that rose to uneven heights far overhead. As Will stepped beneath the arch, the others pressed close behind, and they found themselves in an intersection which the obelisks had shielded from view. The street on either side looked similar to the narrow one twisting ahead.

"Mala said we need to find the docks," Mateo said, "but which way are they?"

"She was there when the Coffer thief disappeared," Will replied, "but she didn't recognize the particular street. We'll have to find a map or a better vantage point."

Zariduke was strapped to Will's back, and he drew it out. He didn't like the feel of these silent streets, the menace and forbidden history hanging in the air like a cloud of pollution. Tall buildings abounded in the skyline, towers and minarets and larger structures of exquisite design, often connected by walkways and bridges and arches high above the streets. The architecture rivaled or even surpassed that of the Wizard District, though Will feared what lurked in the blackened recesses of Praha's buildings. Nor would he risk having Dalen fly above the sight line unprotected, where an arrow from a watchful brigand could bring him down.

Mala had suggested they seek out an old contact of hers named Skara Brae who called Praha home. If anyone could help them discover who had hired the Coffer thief, Mala had said, it was Skara. The adventurer lived inside a nilometer, a type of old well used to measure water levels, near the city's docks. Will had no idea how someone lived inside a well, but Mala said if they found the docks, they couldn't miss it.

He hoped she was right, but that didn't help with their current predicament. As they trudged into the heart of the city, seeking an open establishment to inquire about the docks, the streets became grittier and more mazelike. At times, a panhandler would appear in a doorway, though Will wondered who they were targeting. Twice a pair of passerby scurried past the party with cloaks drawn tight, hoods shielding their faces. It was only a matter of time before the party encountered a more dangerous group. Due to the narrow, curving, labyrinthine nature of the streets, and the immensity of the city, even Will quickly lost his bearings.

What I wouldn't give for a pencil and some graph paper.

The party stopped for a drink of water as they considered their options. Mala had said certain areas of the city were populated, including taverns and inns, though the options were sparse and seedy. They must have landed in a mostly abandoned neighborhood. "Yaz, any way you could help? Summon a giant bird or something?"

Yasmina gave the leaden sky an uneasy glance. "The bird life here is wary, unfamiliar with wilders. I'm afraid I would need time to earn their trust."

Mateo scratched at his fluffy beard. Similar in age to Will, he had brown hair that fell past his shoulders, a lean but muscular build, and khaki-colored eyes. "We might need to risk a climb into one of these towers. The sun will set early here, and I don't fancy sleeping in the open."

"Aike," Dalen muttered. "I feel as if thieves are already scouting us."

"Agreed," Will said in a tight voice.

Mateo pointed out an arcing walkway to their left, at least two hundred feet overhead. The aerial bridge connected a cylindrical tower to a squat building capped by a field of twisting spires. "If we can reach it, that walkway affords a good view."

There were no objections, and after a few minutes of winding their way through the streets, they found the base of the slender tower. Will pulled on an iron ring set into a doorway covered with faded carvings in bas-relief. The bulky stone door swung open with a creak. Stale air leeched out of the tower. After Dalen summoned a ball of light to illuminate the interior, Will stepped warily inside, sword at the ready.

From up close, the cylindrical tower was wider than he had thought, at least a hundred feet across. A spiral staircase with no railing or support system filled the center of the room, disappearing into the darkness overhead. More decorative carvings enhanced the walls, though the staircase and the rest of the interior was almost as ruined and blackened as the outside. Will had the feeling that furniture had once filled the bottom of the tower. Had someone once lived inside? Was the structure magisterial, defensive, ornamental?

"Let's try it," he said, testing the marble stairs with his boot. They felt solid. The stairs rose two and a half feet from one to the next, as if built for occupants much taller than the average human.

Owl staff at the ready, Yasmina stayed close behind Will, followed by Dalen and then Mateo, who was gripping his urumi blade. Their footsteps echoed in the open interior.

Except for a bat swooping through the gloom, nothing else stirred. As they climbed, Dalen's light rose with them, illuminating walls covered in the same bas-relief carvings. Will goggled at the time and artistry they must have taken to design. Every now and then an oval window frame, its glass long since shattered, offered a glimpse of the city.

"I can see the entrance to the aerial walkway," Yasmina said, twenty feet before the rest of them noticed the high arched opening. Her owl staff enhanced her powers of sensory observation in a way Will knew she did not fully understand.

As they approached the opening, they saw the aerial bridge arcing in a gentle convex, spanning the fifty-foot gap between the tower and the spires of the squat building. They could now see that the spires were covered in circular baubles that resembled, except for their grimy appearance, gumdrops atop a gingerbread house.

Was it an aesthetic addition? Or an infestation?

Remarkably, as the party edged onto the walkway, Will realized it was made of natural black stone streaked with color, perhaps opal. A fifty-foot long gemstone arch with no seams and no visible support, somehow attached at that height.

A cold wind buffeted them as they walked far enough out to get the full view. Will did not suffer from vertigo, but he saw Mateo's face whiten as the city sprawled around them, immense and threatening. From above, the layout of the ground level looked even more confusing, a nest of high-walled alleyways and dead-end courtyards and twisting, serpentine streets. Yet what rocked Will on his heels was the bird's eye view of the construction. The skyline abounded with bridges, archways, and other connectors that defied gravity. Many of them changed direction or arced in midair, a spider web of architecture that looked designed by a graphic artist on acid. It wasn't just bricks and mortar, he knew, that kept the mesmerizing structures from falling.

Except for a few low hills, the enormous city sprawled flat to the horizon. In the distance, behind the tower they had just climbed, an ash-colored river cut through the middle of the buildings. Yasmina pointed out a thicket of masts clustered around a portion of the riverside marked by canals and low structures. "Those must be the docks!"

Though excited by the discovery, they realized the river was too far away, and the city too confusing, for blind wandering. What they did see, not far from their position, was a section that looked more populated, with smoke pouring out of chimneys and people scurrying around on the streets.

Will and Yasmina had walked three-fourths of the way across the arched walkway to get the best view. Just before they turned back, a pack of lizard men brandishing shields and broadswords rushed through the empty doorway leading into the maw of the spired building. They wore thick breeches and soiled breast tunics that displayed their scaly, muscular arms.

Startled by the sudden attack, Will stuffed the panic down and grabbed Yasmina, prepared to race back across the ten-foot wide archway, when he noticed one of the lizard men nocking an arrow. The bowstring twanged, and Will whipped his buckler shield in front of his body just before the missile thunked into the wood.

With a grunt and a flick of his tongue, the nearest lizard man attacked with his sword as a dozen more surged forward. Mateo's battle cry from behind gave Will courage, and he parried the leader's sword thrust. When their weapons clanged, Will used the momentum of his swing to spin and drop, slicing deep into his opponent's thigh. The lizard man fell back as green blood spurted from the wound.

Three more took his place. Will and Yasmina scrambled backward, to the apex of the arch, nostrils flared with adrenaline. His friends caught up to him, though the precipitous walkway provided a terrible battleground. If they turned to run for the stairs, they would expose themselves to the archer. There was just enough room on the elevated walkway for the lizard men, who seemed much more comfortable in the constricted space, to surround them.

Will felt fear surging through him. They were outnumbered, and a single misstep would send them plunging to their deaths. As the archer lizard nocked another arrow, a bright orange light flashed in his eyes, causing him to slap at the flame and drop the bow. The light sparked brighter and spread along his body, driving the lizard man back. He stumbled at the edge, lost his footing, and pitched off the walkway, screaming as he plummeted to the ground.

"Guard my flank!" Will roared, knowing Dalen had bought them a moment to act. Still, the arch was too treacherous to risk a pitched battle. They needed to escape. "Fall back!"

Using her walking stick as a quarterstaff, Yasmina jabbed with the owl tip to keep the lizard men at bay. Mateo cracked his flexible urumi sword at the feet of the attackers on the other side, and they hesitated, confused by the weapon. Will fended off two more, working furiously to keep them from slipping past him.

One of the lizard men picked up the bow and quiver and took aim, hiding behind a companion so Dalen couldn't blind him. Instead the clever illusionist caused the bow to turn into a writhing cobra, which snapped at the lizard man's face. He yelled and threw the weapon to the ground. The bow returned to normal as it bounced off the archway.

Will kicked another of the lizard men in the solar plexus, stealing his breath, then sliced through the leather breastplate of another. After glancing to either side and noticing a lull in the attack, he shouted, "Go! Now!"

Yasmina and Mateo turned to rush through the narrow archway, pulling Dalen along with them. Will followed behind, backing away as Zariduke danced. The entire group of lizard men surged forward, trying to swarm him, but Will scrambled backward quickly enough to reach the opening.

Then he made his stand.

With a howl, he gutted the first lizard man who approached, and clanged blades with the next. Only one body at a time could fit through the tall, narrow entrance. Dalen threw light into the second attacker's face, Will cut him down, and the third took a step back as he glanced at the bodies of his slain companions. Realizing Dalen was a mage of some sort, and that Will was more than a match for any single one of them, the remaining attackers hissed and snarled before slinking back into the darkness of the larger building, leaving their fallen companions on the archway.

They descended the long spiral staircase and hurried into the street, worried the lizard men would regroup or gather more allies. Will kept looking over his shoulder as the party fled towards the busier section of the city they had spied from above. For all he knew, the lizard men might be the least dangerous brigands in the city.

They needed safe shelter.

A map.

A solid meal would be nice, too.

They passed what he mistook for a pair of elongated pillars standing side by side, before he looked up and saw how they conjoined high above the ground. He craned his neck even further, having to walk backwards to realize the pillars were the legs of an enormous statue, an angular being at least five hundred feet tall.

He walked closer again and noticed, barely visible in the blackened state of the granite, carvings covering the surface of the statue that depicted smaller and more lifelike versions of the same type of humanoid. Tall and lithe and beautiful, clothed in elaborate outfits with high collars and flared shoulders, the androgynous beings had long pointed ears that curved gently backwards, causing Will to start.

Were they elves?

On some of the figures, slender wings could be seen poking out of their backs from various angles. Elves did not normally have wings, he thought—though neither were elves typically associated with the offspring of fallen angels, which legend claimed had built the city.

As Will stared dumbstruck at the building, drinking in the fallen splendor and mystery, Mateo put a hand on his arm. "We shouldn't linger."

"I know," Will said, continuing down the street. He noticed Yasmina pulling her gaze away from the building.

"Lucka, has anyone seen anything like that before?" Dalen asked. "Were those Nephili?"

No one had an answer.

After crossing a bridge spanning an empty manmade canal, rats scrabbling on the muddy bottom, the party saw more signs of life. Humanoids of varying sorts passed by, crows picked at trash, and the smell of ale and baked goods emanated from doorways. The architecture was less grand, now marked by three and four-story buildings with tall arched doorways, often with a commercial establishment at the bottom. Blacksmiths, curio shops, alehouses, bestiaries, lodging houses, black lacquered doorways with ominous shrieks coming from inside, an old temple covered in scrollwork and repurposed into a brothel. It was odd, given the danger and mystique that enveloped it, to think of Praha as a functioning city.

Or semi-functioning. As they passed through the district, sporadic fights broke out on the street around them, and grimy drunks stumbled out of the taverns to urinate. Hard-eyed thieves seemed to eye the party from every corner, angled doorway, and hidden alley.

"This is the Wild West of Middle Earth," he muttered to Dalen.

"What?"

"Nothing."

His companions' ignorance of fantasy trivia made Will long for a night out with Lance, peeling crawfish and swapping stories. He wondered where his old friend was at that very moment, and prayed he had survived the encounter with Zedock. With a start, he wondered if Lance, too, might have landed in wizard prison along with Val. Though it was Val's voice he had heard in the tavern in Freetown, he had not seen either of them since the night in the cemetery in New Orleans.

Most of the buildings in this section were made of pockmarked marble, blackened and crumbling like the rest of the city. Mateo stopped in front of a chalkboard sign with a drawing of a satyr. The half-man, half-goat creature was quaffing a beer as he dragged a bloody unicorn through the woods. *Goat and Stag*, read the sign.

"Anyone fancy a rest?" Mateo asked. "This seems as good as any."

Will had never been so ready, but Yasmina glared at the sign in distaste. "Not here."

Respecting her wilder sensitivities, Will trudged to the next tavern, whose sign bore an image of a pale, long-fingered hand holding a mug of ale. *The Cryptic Cellar*, it read.

"This will do," she said, planting her staff on the ground.

They entered through a wooden door and immediately had to descend a claustrophobic staircase made of forest-green marble. The steps were scuffed but solid, and had retained some of their original color. At the bottom, they found themselves in a torchlit grotto strewn with rotting furniture. Will's eyes widened when he saw the crypts dotting the gloom, scattered among the furniture and placed in alcoves set into the walls. The elongated coffins were twice as long as normal caskets, and many of them were overturned or lying on their sides.

The walls shone with a dull white gleam. Will peered closer and noticed the strange radiance emanating from thousands and thousands of human bones inset into the wall, top to bottom, backlit from an unseen source.

Maybe they were short on building materials.

Much of the furniture was occupied, and he realized the patrons all wore cloaks, shawls, or concealing clothing of some sort. The face of the first one who turned their way seemed made of smoke, with eyes that glowed like coals.

Conversations paused, and a door creaked in the darkness to Will's left. Something skittered in the shadows of the alcove. The mugs of the patrons looked filled with a thick red liquid, and before anyone could utter a word, Will rushed the party up the long staircase and out the door, hurrying down the street until they could no longer see the entrance to *The Cryptic Cellar.*

"Great choice, Yaz," he said, stopping to catch his breath. "What's next, *The Dragon's Breakfast Buffet? Cannibal's Delight?*"

She swallowed. "Bad call. I'm sorry."

"Aike," Dalen said, with a shiver. "I'll be having nightmares about that for weeks. What about this one?"

He pointed out a sign that read *Tiny's Inn and Tavern.* Outside the doorway, two bearded ruffians were clinking glasses and roaring with laughter.

Mateo eyed the sky, which had already begun to darken. "We need to get off the streets. I vote yea."

Everyone agreed, and Will led the way inside, more cautious this time. He was relieved to find that, while the place was filled with the sort of hard-edged mercenaries he had expected to find in Praha, they were human. No one paid them much attention. Yasmina's willowy figure drew some stares, but her cool gaze in return caused the leers to evaporate or seek out more pliable targets.

Will tensed when he saw a group of albino dwarves—delvers, on Urfe—at a table in the corner. Yasmina squeezed his hand, a gesture of shared distaste for their former captors, as well as an admonition to keep his cool. Women sprinkled the crowd, and Will realized he had not seen a single child in the city.

That's probably a good thing.

Despite the grim environs and the omnipresent danger, or perhaps because of it, Will felt a titillating excitement at their quest. Wandering into the unknown in pursuit of an ancient artifact, battling monsters along the way, the specter of myths and ancient riddles. It was the same sort of excitement he used to feel at cracking a new D&D module or buying the latest role-playing video game—a pale imitation, he now realized. On Urfe, that initial rush was but a taste of the terrifyingly real adventure that awaited. Some or all of his companions, including himself, might perish on the journey.

He had become a true adventurer at last, with all the thrills and rewards and bone chilling, life-or-death stakes it entailed.

Rough-hewn wooden tables filled the room in a haphazard pattern. The ceiling was at least twelve feet high. Judging by the dusty bookshelves and elegantly carved sconces set high on the walls, it had once been a library of some sort.

The floor was sticky with spilled ale, the air smelled of leather and body odor. Patrons were hovered over mugs of ale and platters of meat and dumplings, and Will realized he was starving.

As he scanned the room for a seat, a drunken brawler got in his face. Will pushed him away, then stared him down while putting a muscled forearm on the hilt of Zariduke. Mateo bristled beside him until the drunk backed down, and no one else accosted them. Finally Will spotted an empty line of seats at the end of the bar.

A huge barkeep approached them when they sat. He was a head taller than Marek, with reddish skin and one-inch horns poking out from the top of his bald head.

"What are ye, a gazer?" he said to Will.

"Um, not that I know of."

"Then what're ye staring at? Haven't ye ever seen a half-darvish before?" He grinned and rubbed at a wet spot on the bar with his towel.

"No, actually."

"That's okay. Me either."

"Sorry," Will mumbled, wondering if the bartender was speaking the truth about his heritage. During their escape from the Darklands, Will and the others had freed a young darvish woman named Lisha, kept chained to a rock by delvers. The cruel humanoids had forced her to survive on raw fish and heat the basin of water surrounding the rock for their barracks.

"Four mugs of house ale?" the bartender said.

"Sure," Will said.

"Good thing, because there isn't any other." His laughter as he walked away seemed to vibrate the stone floor.

Tiny, Will presumed.

Dalen tried to disappear inside his cloak, not wanting to stand out. Mateo placed their packs along a wall where they could see them, and Yasmina surprised Will by taking a long drink of ale. He had thought her wilder diet might consist of roots, berries, and herbal tea.

The ale was only passable, the platter of meat greasy and tough. Still, it was a warm meal, and they didn't have to dip into their supplies.

As they ate, Will overheard wild tales of adventures from the crowd. Halfway through their meal, a leather-clad female warrior stood on a table and offered a share of the loot to four adventurers who would join her on a quest to recover treasure in a dungeon beneath the slave pits of Karlovy, an abandoned island fortress just downriver from the city. She unraveled an old map to prove her claim, and at least ten people raised their mugs and stepped forward. Will observed the negotiations in fascination, watching as the woman interviewed the volunteers to judge their experience and try to select the best mix of talents for the campaign.

After a while, he decided Tiny himself was probably the best source of information, but the hulking bartender rebuffed Will's efforts to engage him in conversation.

"Hey, Tiny?" Will said.

"Ready for another?"

"I need to ask you something."

After grunting in annoyance, the burly giant finished with another patron and sidled over. "Another round?"

"Are you really half-darvish?"

Tiny gave a wicked grin and offered his hand. Will accepted the gesture, and the bigger man engulfed his hand in a fierce grip. As Will wondered what was going on, he felt a prickle of heat spread outward from Tiny's palm, growing in intensity until he felt a searing pain. He tried to jerk away but the barkeep gripped him tight. When Will reached for his sword with his other hand, Tiny finally let him go, guffawing. "Believe me now?"

Will jerked his hand back as the other patrons snickered. Not wanting to show weakness, he resisted the urge to dunk his hand in his beer. Mateo rose in his chair, furious at the slight, but Will eased him down.

"Bah," Tiny said. He opened his palm to reveal a telltale red glow, though it was much duller than Lisha's would have been. "That's about the size of it. I don't know if the real darvish can do more than warm up a good handshake. My ma went camping in the Carpathians when she was a young lass, and had a fling with one o' the bastards. Must have been a handsome rogue, to sire a face like this!" He rubbed his chin and roared with laughter, though Will could see the bitterness behind his eyes.

"Your ma doesn't know anything about them?" Will asked.

"Twas a story of true love, as they say. One whole night of it."

"Ever wondered what the darvish are really like? Where they live, what sort of powers they have?" Will leaned forward. "Ever wondered about your father?"

"Course I have. But since no man alive, or at least no man I've ever met, has seen a darvish, then I don't s'pose I'll be gettin' any answers to those questions, will I? But thanks for probing that wound, *friend*."

Tiny smacked a towel on the bar and turned to walk away. Will grabbed his arm. "I've seen one."

The big man tried to jerk away, but Will's forearms, naturally strong and hardened by years of construction work and his recent adventures, kept the grip.

"Eh?" Tiny said in anger, looking down at Will's hand as a number of other patrons slid their stools back, ready to jump to the barkeep's defense.

"I haven't just met a darvish," Will said. "I've seen their *city*."

He released Tiny's arm as the bartender stood with a dazed look. Then Tiny slapped the bar and howled with laughter. "Ye hear that, laddies? This one here says he's been to the land of the darvish. Which is real interesting, since my ma said they have streets of lava and no human can survive the heat."

"I didn't say I'd walked the streets," Will said. "I said I had seen it, from high above, inside a cave deep in the Darklands. And I'm no liar." With Yasmina vouching for the tale as well—her word as a wilder seemed to carry great weight—he gave a brief recounting of how the darvish girl had helped them escape Fellengard and led them into the Great Chasm, right up to the precipice overlooking the last darvish city on Urfe.

The bartender's face grew paler and paler. "It's just like my ma said," he whispered. "What my pa told her. The colored walls and geysers and canals—" He grabbed Will by the shirt. "It's true? You've really seen it?"

"I have."

"Then tell me everything you saw, everything about them."

Will swiped the bartender's hand away before it burned him again, and raised his empty mug. "I'd be happy to discuss an exchange of information."

After Tiny rushed to the cellar to procure bottles of his best ale and aged cuts of elk, he ordered one of his employees to take over the bar, then cleared out a party of delvers from a table in the corner so he could dine with Will and the others. Yasmina and Will tensed at the interaction with the delvers, sworn enemies of the darvish, but Tiny explained that everyone who came to the ruined city left their patriotism behind and switched their allegiance to the gods of loot, vice, and buried treasure. In its own way, the city was one of the more accepting places on Urfe—if one could manage to stay alive.

Judging by the way the delvers were staring at Tiny, Will wondered if the hard-eyed albinos shared his egalitarian outlook. The bartender might want to lock his doors a bit tighter that night.

As Tiny recounted some of his life history, Will grew saddened by the tale. The bartender's mother had died young, stricken by a coughing disease that sounded like tuberculosis. After she passed, Tiny became an expert spelunker and explored Urfe's cave systems in search of his father. Though he had many extraordinary adventures, he finally gave up and settled in Praha. The cool climate suited him, his odd appearance didn't raise as many eyebrows, and if people did want to mock him, he said with a grin, he was free to bash in their skulls.

He told Will where to buy a map, and said they were currently in the most settled part of the city. Much of Praha had not been mapped or explored for centuries. A constant stream of expeditions left from Tiny's inn to explore the dungeon of some dead mage or find the hidden loot of an outlaw who had come to Praha to escape the authorities. Ages ago, the city was the unofficial capital of the menagerists, after the discipline fell into disfavor. The bounties placed on the heads of the renegade mages had attracted bounty hunters to Praha, which had driven those who dared practice the forbidden art of fusing species even deeper underground.

"Lucka, where are all the mages?" Dalen asked. "Why don't they rule in Praha like everywhere else?"

"Oh, they're around. Usually outcasts or deviants of some sort. No self-respecting wizard wants to sully their reputation by living here, and even if they did, it's dangerous for them. The thieves and assassins don't want them spoiling the fun by imposing the rule of law or hoarding all the treasure, so they tend to pick off wizards when they can." Though Dalen tried not to react to the statement, Will saw his hand tighten against his mug.

"Not only that," the barkeep continued, "I've been told by more than a few mages who passed through that sometimes their magic doesn't work the same here."

Will and Dalen exchanged a nervous glance. *Good thing the illusions worked atop the arch, or we might all be dead.*

"Do you believe the rumors?" Yasmina asked. "About the Nephili and the magical disease that ravaged the city?"

Tiny leaned back in his chair and finished half a mug in one quaff. "Live here long enough, and there's no rumor about it. You see it in the architecture, you feel it in the air. Something happened here. Something powerful and alien. And then there's the Old City," he said mysteriously.

Mateo looked up from his meal. Unlike Will and Dalen, who had barely touched their food as they listened, Will's cousin had not let his curiosity affect his appetite. Yasmina ate quietly as the bartender talked, absorbing the conversation with calm, watchful eyes.

Tiny noticed their blank looks. "The Old City is a walled section to the north, on a bluff above the river. You have to walk through the Agora to get there, which no sane person would do, then scale the Wailing Wall atop the bluff and deal with the Skinwalkers." He pulled a hunk of meat off a bone with his teeth.

"What about a powerful mage? Could one get through?" Will asked. "If he wanted?"

"Maybe they have, lad." He licked a spot of grease off his fingers. "And maybe they haven't."

"What's in there?" Dalen asked, leaning forward. "Inside the Old City?"

"No one I know has ever been. Or maybe I should say no one has ever returned. Every now and then an expedition will set out to explore it, because the talk of danger inside its walls are outweighed only by the rumors of the treasure. They say it was once the palace of the Nephili. They also say," the bartender said after a long swallow, "that one of their kind still lives there."

Will couldn't keep the stunned look off his face, and Tiny gave an uneasy laugh. "Not many believe that rumor. Alive for thousands of years, right here in the city? Bah."

In his fascination in learning about the city, Will had almost forgotten to ask about their own quest. "We're looking for someone named Skara Brae. Do you know anything about him?"

Tiny wiped his mouth with the back of his hand. "Never heard of him."

Will sat back, disappointed. Had they wasted the entire conversation?

"But I've heard of *her*. Skara's a lassie, you fool. Though no lassie I'd ever like to cross."

Why hadn't Mala told him Skara was a woman? Then again, why had he presumed she was a man? "Who is she? Where can we find her? We're told she lives in the Nilometer."

"Does she? I wouldn't know. The Nilometer's on the maps, though. You won't have any trouble locating it, though the docks be one of the more dangerous parts of the city. Watch your backs, and don't ever go there at night. Oh, and if you do happen to find yourself within a hundred yards of Skara Brae Tenjilk, you better make sure she knows you're coming."

7

The morning after Will and the others stepped through the portal to Praha, Mala left Freetown in the company of a gypsy caravan bound for the plains west of the Great River. By the second night of the journey, deep into the Valley of Cyrmarcyth, she knew someone—or possibly something—was following the caravan.

Someone who had left fresh boot prints, glimpsed through a spyglass at daybreak, on the muddy bank of a stream the caravan was paralleling.

Someone who traveled after the sun went down, and avoided notice during the day.

Someone who had approached the camp the night before, evidenced by the panicked whinnying of the horses, and who was deterred by a nightflare and the rattle of clanging swords.

Mala's gaze swept the terrain, the sprawling grasslands visible for miles in either direction, searching for incongruities. A raven cawed as it launched off a tree and flapped towards the white-capped mountains rising like bleached arrowheads on the eastern horizon. Iron-grey mullets made playful leaps out of the rushing stream, and a pair of squirrels scrambled across the broad limbs of a cottonwood.

Danior Whitehill, a tall, lean man with scarred forearms and a pronounced widow's peak, climbed up beside her in the cramped viewing box that topped the observation wagon. After Mala, he was the caravan's best fighter—though a vast gulf separated the two.

"Who do you think is out there?" he asked.

She lowered the spyglass, a three-foot long tube mounted on a swivel. Though a day's ride inland from the coastal road, the Valley of Cyrmarcyth was not a particularly dangerous stretch. It was too exposed for most bandits or a Protectorate death squad, either of which they would have seen coming from miles away.

Nor were the plains known to be home to creatures dangerous enough to attack an armed gypsy caravan, even one as small as the six-wagon party in which she traveled. Thus she had elected to tag along with a group for this leg of the journey. Alone, she exposed herself to more risk, especially at night. She would not want a night shamble or a burrow wyrm to catch her sleeping.

Still, it was the Ninth Protectorate. Something dangerous could have wandered down from the Dragon's Teeth, or a renegade menagerist might have unleashed a new creation on the Barrier Coast. The footprints had been human, but that didn't rule out shapeshifters or a handful of other possibilities.

"I'm unsure," she answered. "I hope it's nothing more than a curious village lad."

"I haven't seen any villages in some time."

"Perhaps the lad is en route to a destination, staying close to the caravan for safety. Traveling at night to avoid questions."

Danior grunted and waved a hand at the brown, windswept scrubland marking the southern reaches of the plains. "You said the footsteps were fresh. So where did they come from? Where did they go?"

"If I knew the answer, I wouldn't still be looking."

Danior was a hard man, unperturbed by her sarcasm. "Maybe someone is concealed in one of the cottonwoods."

"The closest footsteps to the trees are clustered near that rock pool, almost a hundred feet away." Mala returned to watching the terrain, her hand slipping instinctively to the smooth silk of her weighted sash.

"And? What course of action do you propose?" Danior was the only member of the caravan who did not seem uncomfortable in her presence.

That's fine. Let the others be wary. These are not the sorts of times in which one's guard should be relaxed.

"We should travel through the night and keep a constant watch," she said, "resting only as the horses need. If we've entered someone's territory in error, perhaps a peaceful exit will suffice."

"And if it doesn't?"

She turned to face him. "Need you ask that question, Danior? What else, at the moment, would you suggest?"

With a curt nod, he descended the ladder and left her with her thoughts. As she continued her watch, sipping on a steaming mug of coffee to relieve the chill of the morning, the rest of the caravan staggered to life and spurred the horses southeast, towards the Shoehorn Pass at the southern edge of the Dragon's Teeth. From there, it was a day's ride to the Koraxi desert, an old Romani name for dry and blasted land. Their ultimate destination was the vast grasslands west of the Great River, where Mala planned to purchase a horse from the plainsmen and continue on her own to New Victoria.

The thought of her ultimate destination caused her hands to feel clammy, despite the warmth of her mug. Most people thought that courage went hand in hand with fighting prowess, but in Mala's experience, most people were fools.

Over the course of her life, she had learned to control her fears and make swift and rational decisions in the face of great danger, but she did not consider herself a courageous person. That particular trait was the domain of simpletons and dreamers and heroes. Though all the heroes she had known had finished their lives gutted by a spear, a sword, or an arrow.

Most who sought to be heroes did so for the wrong reasons. Tamás, though valiant, longed for glory and had a petty streak. The previous leader of the Revolution had died screaming at the hand of a pyromancer, his flesh melted from his bones by a Fire Sphere, too foolish to realize his rescue mission in an abandoned building in the Gypsy Quarter was a trap.

Gunnar, may he rest in peace, never had the ambition to be a hero, and she had loved him for that. He had saved her life more than once and was a hero in his own way. No other man with whom she had dallied had possessed half of Gunnar's strength of character.

Except for Will Blackwood, that was. The blond-haired young warrior who, until recently, she had thought of as little more than a village dreamer with a nice sword. Yet he had gained prowess as quickly as any warrior she had ever known, and had proved himself time and again.

Did he have a pure enough heart, a clear enough head, and a strong enough arm to be a hero one day?

She rolled her eyes at the thought.

Will Blackwood. A hero in training he was, indeed.

Another pretty face with a death wish.

She had known that he loved her before he said the words. She wished she could say the same. She preferred taller men with darker hair, men with a rougher edge who did not talk so much and who had fewer designs on saving the world. She could admit that her flavor of lover would probably never win her heart, not truly, but she had no desire to relinquish the key to that particular lock.

Mala did not need home or hearth. She needed adventure, excitement, and someone as wayward and ignoble as she felt herself to be.

She could admit that when Will had kissed her at the inn, his calloused hands cupping her face and his long blond hair brushing her shoulder, she had felt a thrill of attraction for the first time. She told herself it was the heat of the moment, the sweet seduction of parting ways.

Or had the balance between them shifted? The thought annoyed her, for while she thought he possessed true courage—and admired him for it—she thought him foolish for the very same reason.

So, no, it was not bravery that drove Mala towards the wizard capital of the Realm to confront the man who haunted her darkest nightmares. Nor was it a promise to herself, because Mala thought promises were also the domain of fools. A promise was ignorant of the future and impervious to changing circumstance.

She had never told anyone, not even Allira, the story of how she became an orphan. Not because of lingering trauma, though shock and fear had governed the early years of Mala's life. And once she discovered the identity of her parents' murderer, she knew enough of the world to know the knowledge was best kept to herself, lest the man hunt her down and finish the job. She had kept her secret all these years, a burden like a two-ton anvil on her back.

Even now, the memories caused her to wince inside, though she fought against the pain with a vengeance.

Pain was weakness, and in her world, weakness meant death.

Most people thought that Lord Alistair's massacres in recent years against gypsies—she refused to use the term Roma, because *gypsy* was what her people had become—were a new development. The prevailing wisdom was that one did not hear about the persecution of the gypsies in old Albion because there were almost no gypsies left.

Mala knew otherwise.

The wizards, she knew, would never forgive her people for their refusal to give up their pagan beliefs, and for their role in the revolutions and uprisings over the centuries. As long as her people continued their foolish belief in Devla and asserted their right to worship as they pleased, the ruling thaumacracy would always consider them a threat. The proud Roma clans, widespread across the continents since the Age of Fire, had been reduced to beggars and slaves and itinerant wanderers, shepherded like three-legged livestock into the last outpost of the Barrier Coast, their only plan for survival a desperate hope that Devla would send someone to save them.

Oh, how she hated the prophets who came and went like pollen on the wind, spreading lies and desperate hope. The latest debacle was almost beyond imagining: the current Prophet had proclaimed that Caleb Blackwood, Will's brother, was the Templar. Did the man even know that Caleb was from another world? A pacifist and a layabout? Even if the Prophet did, he wouldn't care. Caleb had opened the Coffer and was a tool for the man's gain.

Despite the muttered whispers of *gadje* she caught when no one thought she could hear, Mala loved her people. She truly did. But she thought they were all fools who would end their lives rotting away in the fens or burned alive by wizard fire.

The return of Zariduke and the appearance of the Coffer—whatever its true nature—were remarkable events. Yet they were pebbles in the river of history, a mote in the Congregation's eye. Mala did not believe in salvation from the gods, especially not one particular god who was supposed to look after his people.

Any chance of that had died with her parents.

The attack had come when she was ten years old, traveling with her clan in the countryside outside Londyn. In broad daylight the raiders had arrived, unconcerned with reprisal, a band of mercenaries and strange men and women in black robes led by a beast of a man, coarse and vile, red of hair and beard and with eyes that burned hotter than a blacksmith's hearth. Her father called him the Despiser. Like the other black-robed killers leading the attack, a silver belt cinched his black robe at the waist, and he did things no normal human could do. Things like stopping swords with his palm, thrusting his fist straight through a man's heart, and even taking flight during battle, as only a wizard was supposed to do.

She didn't know what to call them at the time, as these were the first majitsu Mala had ever encountered.

The other four warrior-mages were powerful, easily strong enough to overcome the gypsy fighters, but the Despiser was another thing entirely. A force of nature who seemed to be twice, three times the strength of the others. Not only that, but he enjoyed his work. A cruel smile lit his features as he made his way through the ranks of Mala's people, breaking bones and smashing skulls, flipping over wagons with his bare hands. Her father and mother were the last two standing, the leaders and most skilled sword hands of the Kalev clan. Mala watched, covered in filth from the latrine hole her father had dug underneath the supply wagon, as the Despiser snapped her mother's spine. He took his time killing her father, twisting his arms and legs into unnatural angles before Mala turned away, losing the contents of her stomach.

She shuddered at the memory, so alive after all these years. She had loved her parents more than life itself. Dreamers they were, fighters and poets and lovers and seekers. They had come to Albion from the Old World to help the remaining gypsies escape the death squads.

Yes, dreamers they were—and it had gotten them killed.

Mala never forgot the lesson.

Orphaned on the streets of Londyn, she turned to thievery to survive. She excelled so much that her handler sold her for good coin, at the tender age of eleven, to a guild master seeking youth for a traveling carnival that stole twice as much as it charged for entry. The carnival toured the continent, from the gateway city of Myzantium in the east, full of learned mages and soaring minarets, to the great city of Scythia in the frozen north. Along the way, she became an expert acrobat, horsewoman, archer, actress, and sleight of hand artist. Due to her athletic ability and a natural feel for the blade, as well as a rage at the world burning inside her, the guild master created an act just for her, in which

Mala fought grown men with her hands or wooden blades. She rarely lost, and became the carnival's highest earner.

She loathed her status as a virtual slave, and her plans to escape were accelerated when the guild master tried to force himself on her. Pretending to give in, Mala let him undress her to her boots and climb on top of her, then sprung a hidden knife out of her heel and stabbed him in the back. She silenced his scream with a slice across the jugular.

Mala fled into the night. Soon after, realizing how dangerous it was to travel alone as a teenage girl, she used her savings to board a ship bound for New Victoria, a place of fabled wealth and promise.

A new world, a new beginning.

Like all dreams that are realized, the reality was a far cry from what the stories and her imagination had led her to believe. New Victoria was indeed a wondrous place, but it was no less dangerous than most of the other places she had traveled, especially for a gypsy. The racism was palpable. Still, she wanted a home base to explore the promise and mystery of the lands beyond the Western Ocean, and joined the New Victoria Thieves Guild.

Trained at the feet of the best rogues and cutpurses in the land, a favorite of the masters from the start, Mala's skills increased tenfold. Her wanderlust blossomed, and she struck out on her own, this time with a reputation that preceded her, an adventuress who would undertake difficult tasks in faraway places, often of a dubious nature. As soon as she acquired enough funds, she decided to specialize in the retrieval of magical items. This took her around the world, acquiring items for a client list that included wealthy collectors, generals, wizards, criminals, and even a few museums.

Her specialization served another purpose. Mala had never forgotten the man who had put her on the streets in the first place, the one whose red beard had split with a wide grin as he tortured and killed her parents. By this time, Mala knew his identity. He was a towering majitsu, Kjeld Anarsson, who had risen through the ranks of his order to become First Don, the supreme majitsu in all the Realm. He sat on the War Council and had the ear of Lord Alistair himself.

Even without the protections of his position, such a man could never be bested by Mala alone. Knowing that cold hard fact, she had searched and searched for the weapon, scroll, or potion that would allow her a chance to prevail against this monster of a human being. Despite her achievements, Mala had seen firsthand what a majitsu could do, and her knees turned watery at the thought of confronting him.

Yes, the great Mala herself, adventuress supreme and explorer without equal, was nothing but a little girl cowering in a hole, arms hugging her knees, when faced with the prospect of avenging her own parents.

As the wagon rumbled past a swath of wildflowers, her fingers again found purchase on the contours of her sash. Reinforced with strong and pliable wire, weighted at both ends with tiny balls of iron, the sapphire band could entangle the limbs of a foe or crush a man's face from afar. Yet she knew the sash—and all her weapons—would fall short against Kjeld. In all her travels, she had never found an item she thought would give her a chance of victory.

Until Magelasher.

Long ago, she heard rumor that an Alazashin expedition had carried the fabled weapon into the tomb of the sorcerer king. A cat o' nine tails with eight magically hardened azantite tips, a mockery of an octopus in defiance of the Congregation, Magelasher had been designed by a gypsy mage to attack majitsu from all sides and overcome their defenses.

Even when she had embarked on the expedition with Will and the others, she had not fully thought about the consequence of her success.

What it would mean to hold Magelasher in her hands and feel its power and make a conscious decision to pursue Kjeld.

She was truly terrified of this man. The weapon would give her a sliver of a chance, nothing more. Yet her fear drove her. She would let no man have such power over her. Live or die, she would face him at last and gain her freedom.

The feeling of incompleteness that had never gone away—*this* was what drove Mala. The knowledge that this man, this murderer of her family and thief of her childhood, still owned a part of her.

Another day in the valley came and went. Meals prepared, wagons circled, stories swapped. As the sun descended and the dances around the campfire began, time-honored twirls of patchwork skirts and booted gypsy heels beneath the moonlight, Mala observed the festivities alone, from atop the observation wagon. She liked to dance, and perhaps she would join them the next night, if she felt secure. She even allowed herself a few thimbles of grog, enough to relax the mind but preserve her reflexes.

As the festivities wound down, she slumped lower in her chair, ceasing all movement so she could hear the sounds the wind carried. Nothing stirred except for a lonely cricket and the gurgle of a nearby stream, and no movement disturbed the night until she saw the red eyes of a hyena wolf creep out of the darkness and slink towards the caravan.

She sat up at once. Uncommon but not unheard of in those parts, a hyena wolf was a dangerous adversary, especially if traveling in a pack.

It squatted on its front paws, supporting the weight of its huge neck and shoulders, the ridge of its coarse gray mane raised like arrow fletching along its back. The creature raised its head to peer at Mala and then loped back the way it had come.

What strange behavior! It caused Mala to think the creature was either unwell or under the aegis of a mage. A hyena wolf that did not howl or travel with its pack? Drawing so close to a group of armed humans?

Bizarre.

Yet it was not until she recalled a sighting earlier in the day, a lone raven alighting from a tree, that she realized who was following them, and what they were truly facing.

No, she corrected silently. Their pursuer was not following the entire caravan; he was following *her*. It was not Kjeld, but someone almost as dangerous.

The sudden knowledge of her adversary, swift and sure, brought a stab of fear like an ice pick to the back of the neck. So much so that Mala sounded a horn and released a nightflare, spraying red and gold light into the darkness.

As the caravan's archers and a bevy of swordsmen gathered outside the wagons, she called Danior to her side. She knew of only one dhampyr who assumed the form of a hyena wolf.

The grizzled warrior rushed up the ladder of the observation wagon and joined her as she peered into the belly of the night. "What happened? Why the outcry?"

Mala debated how much to tell him, deciding for the safety of the caravan that he should know the truth. Or at least some of the truth.

"I noticed a lone hyena wolf observing the caravan. Slinking towards one of the wagons."

"Here? Perhaps it smelled one of the chickens. Though why didn't the horses catch the scent? A steady wind has blown all night."

"Because this was no normal hyena wolf. Do you remember the raven we saw earlier? By the stream?"

Danior squinted as he thought. "Yes, I believe so."

"I believe a were-creature is following us."

"What sort of creature assumes the shape of both raven and wolf—"

Danior cut himself off, a look of fear spasming his hardened features. "Surely you don't imply a dhampyr?"

"Aye," Mala said. "Though each dhampyr can only shift to one form, the appearance nearby of other avatars of their kind, ravens and bats, often signal their presence."

"Dhampyrs exist?" he said rhetorically, as if dazed. "Here, on the plains of the Barrier Coast?"

Mala turned back to the spyglass. A dhampyr was the Romani name for a half-human, half-vampire hybrid who could walk in sunlight and assume the full powers of a vampire at night. An extraordinarily rare and potent foe who possessed the strengths of both races. Belonging fully to neither the world of the living or the undead, dhampyr were often embittered by their isolation.

She did not believe this was a random sighting, though her suspicions as to the identity of this particular dhampyr was a tale she was unwilling to tell.

"What do we do?" Danior continued. "Have you faced such a creature before?"

"Aye."

His eyes widened, awaiting an explanation that never came.

"Ready the horses and put every sword on guard," she said. "Give everyone a torch as well. Non-magical weapons will do little damage, but a dhampyr fears fire. We will travel through the night and pray it does not attack."

"And if it does?"

"Then some of us will die. It would be bold, however, for one dhampyr to attack a caravan en masse, when we are on guard."

"You refer to him as a male. Do you know this pursuer?"

"For whatever reason, most dhampyr are male," she said, avoiding the question. "And all are sterile."

Danior gave a sober nod of acceptance. "When the morning dawns? What do we do?"

"Is there a town within reach?"

"Talintock is a walled village half a day's journey. 'Tis on the way, but deeper into the valley."

"That should suffice." Mala returned to scanning the ground around the caravan with the spyglass, dismissing Danior with a wave. "Go. Spread the warning. We will reconsider our options, Queen willing, within the walls of Talintock."

8

As he awaited instruction from Lord Alistair, Val faced the arched doorway of mercurial silver, a portal that existed in a state of matter he did not understand.

Magic, he thought. *That's the state of matter it's in.*

He could feel the eyes of the others on his back, especially Braden Shankstone.

"When we step into the doorway," Lord Alistair said, "we're entering a fixed portal inside the realm of spirit. We will be neither here nor there, yet can be seen and heard in both places. As I said, you're accompanying me merely to observe."

"Understood," Val replied. "When we open the portal, it flows both ways, doesn't it? That's why the others are here. In case someone comes through."

Lord Alistair nodded in satisfaction. "Yes, but also to observe. In addition, I wanted you to experience the magic of the portal when we enter. It was built by spirit mages and designed for our use."

Again, Val could feel the jealousy radiating out from the non-spirit mages in the room.

"Come behind me, please." The Chief Thaumaturge stepped right into the portal and disappeared. Val followed suit, realizing the silver doorway was not substantial at all, since he passed through without any physical resistance. Or perhaps it had been ensorcelled to dispel sensation.

For the briefest of instants, Val passed into a shadow land of dull gray hues, like a ghost passing through an odorless steel vault, and then he materialized beside Lord Alistair in front of an iron throne occupied by a man clad in loose black silks. The man was so old the skin of his brown face and hands resembled pieces of chewed leather, spider-webbed with wrinkles and stained by liver spots. A beard of coarse white hair, scraggly with age, came to a sharp point beneath his chin. In an alcove behind the throne, there was a replica of the silver doorway through which they had just passed, a companion portal. Val could tell the magic was linked in some way.

Feeling eyes on his back, he turned to find a pair of leather-clad assassins standing right behind him, swords poised in midair as if awaiting a command to strike. It took all of his self-control not to flinch. Behind the two Alazashin, in an egg-shaped cavern the size of a small auditorium, lurked dozens more cutthroats, both human and non-human, male and female, bristling with weapons and quiet menace, gathered into groups or slinking into position along the walls. Archers in the wings had arrows trained on Val and Lord Alistair. The silhouettes of more bodies lurked in the shadowy passages leading out of the cavern.

Expecting a grand hall full of riches, as the wealth of the Alazashin was legendary, Val was surprised to find a fortress of rock and iron. He gaped at the plates of azantite worked into the natural rock floor and walls for reinforcement, the largest quantity of the priceless substance he had ever seen in one place. Iron pillars buttressed the ceiling, flames leapt out of tall braziers lining the walls, and a grid-marked steel grate formed the floor. He peered through the latticed iron and saw nothing but blackness, wondering what lay below.

The old man's eyes gave a flicker of surprise at the sudden appearance of Val and Lord Alistair, then tightened in anger. From the left side of the throne hung a gauntlet of azantite and a curved dagger with a black tip. The Grandfather of Alazashin Mountain slipped on the gauntlet as he addressed Lord Alistair. His thickly accented voice was hard and brittle, like the unsheathing of a blade. "What is the meaning of this? Unscheduled visits are strictly prohibited by the accords."

Val looked closer and realized the entire throne was made of interlocking daggers of azantite and iron. Protection against attacks both magical and physical.

The Alazashin, it appeared, was not an order softened by the fruits of its success.

"The Congregation," Lord Alistair replied, "does not take well to the assassination of our students."

"I am sure you do not," the old man said coldly. "Yet that is the way it is, how it has always been. You have used our services yourself, and know we take no political position. We are tools for hire, nothing more and nothing less. To act otherwise would be to break our code. Our reputation is everything to our clients. The wellspring of our power. And if we are killed in the line of duty, then so be it. No repercussions are sought."

Val kept waiting for the Grandfather to lower his hand and call off the legion of assassins standing behind them. It made Val afraid to move, though when he tried to clasp his hands behind him and felt nothing but air, he realized their physical presence was merely an illusion. In fact, tuning his senses to the world of spirit, he realized he could feel the silver doorway in his mind, invisible and waiting.

Lord Alistair spoke with quiet menace. "Political assassinations are one thing, untrained students another. Did you know that my own daughter was a member of the targeted class?"

The old man's expression softened a fraction. "I am sorry to hear that."

He might be sorry, but he didn't say it was a mistake. The tension between the two powerful men was like syrup in the air.

"I'm afraid that an apology," the Chief Thaumaturge said, "is not sufficient."

In the ensuing silence, Val saw movement at the edges of his vision, and heard shuffling in the darkness beneath them. While Adaira claimed the Alazashin did not allow mages among their ranks, they had amassed some of the most powerful artifacts on Urfe, and surely had ways to combat spells. He resisted the urge to whip around or raise a Wizard Shield, trusting in Lord Alistair's control of the situation.

"Do you threaten us," the old man asked, his gauntleted hand twitching, "in our own home?"

"It has been far too long since our two nations have negotiated an accord," Lord Alistair said, ignoring the question.

"The Alazashin negotiate price," the old man rasped, "and nothing more. To change our accord with one party would weaken our reputation in the eyes of all."

Lord Alistair gave a cold smile. "You're correct, and I misspoke. I am not here to negotiate. I am here to make a demand."

More silence from the old man, his face a stoic mask. Val knew he was in the presence of two masters of the political game.

"Speak," the Grandfather said finally, "and we shall see where we stand."

"I wish to know," Lord Alistair said, clasping his hands in front of him, causing Val to realize he could control the illusion, "where the Coffer of Devla now rests."

"No one knows the location of this artifact. It has been lost for millennia."

Lord Alistair stared into the old man's eyes as if trying to pry loose his secrets. "It is lost no longer, as you well know. It was recovered from the tomb of the Sorcerer King Yiknoom Uk'ab K'ahk, then stolen by someone I believe to be your agent."

"Even if this were true, you know I will never break our silence. Not for any price."

Lord Alistair seemed to grow taller, his brow darkening. "I am not offering you payment."

"No?"

"I am offering you your life."

Rough laughter tumbled out of the old man's mouth, shaking his time-ravaged frame like a child's ragged doll. "You dare? We who have agents in every city on Urfe, who can strike in any location at any moment? You *dare*? We both know your manifestation is dependent on the portals and that you cannot harm—"

A patch of darkness coalesced in Lord Alistair's hands, flickering with the raw energy of Spirit Fire. When he turned, reaching out with both hands, black lightning lanced from his fingertips into two of the iron pillars. Instead of dissolving, they exploded into a million pieces, piercing the assassins in the path of the deadly shards.

Azantite-tipped arrows flew across the cavern. Val cringed as the arrows ripped straight through his and Lord Alistair's illusory images and struck the walls or those assassins unlucky enough to be caught in the crossfire. The Alazashin nearest Val snarled and tried to knife him in the back. Val forced himself to stay calm as the knife slashed through his insubstantial form.

Chaos reigned until Lord Alistair magically projected his voice above the din and caused everyone to cease moving. "Spirit mages built this portal, you fools, we who search the heavens and bring the world of the unseen to life. Behold, King of the Alazashin," he said, sweeping his hand across the rubble-strewn room filled with corpses, "a sliver of my power. I should kill you for the murder of our acolytes, but instead, I will let you barter for your life. I ask a final time: where is the Coffer?"

The old man stood, quivering with fury. A slew of his subjects lay dead or dying in the throne room, filling the cavern with their moans. "I know not how this is possible, but no matter. You believe a threat on my life is enough to break our code? We are legion, spiritmancer. I am one man, old and weary, but thousands await my command, and the chance to take my place. Destroy me if you will, destroy this entire mountain, and we will rebuild and hunt your kind to the ends of the earth, to the very end of time."

"Such melodrama," Lord Alistair mocked. "Please, accept my invitation to visit New Victoria at any time. I think your thieves and murderers would enjoy the outcome of that encounter even less than the travesty they have witnessed here today." He raised a hand, palm up. "Again, I am not here to destroy you. But I *will* have my answer."

The old man made a slight movement, a twist of his wrist, and a cone of brown light shot out from a ring that had appeared on his finger during the melee. The light enveloped the silver portal behind the Throne of Daggers and melted it into a puddle of dirty liquid that dripped through the grate.

"You think we are defenseless against wizards?" the old man inquired softly. He laid his arm across his lap, displaying the azantite bracelet. "Consider the accord terminated."

"Agreed. Though if you believe the destruction of the portal will stop me from leaving or returning as I wish," Lord Alistair's lips curled, "you understand even less than I thought. From this moment forward, be warned the Alazashin are not welcome in the Realm, upon penalty of death. I have no wish to engage in an unnecessary war, so I will ask one last time. *Where is the Coffer?*"

The old man tightened as if ready to engage Lord Alistair in a fight, and Val wondered at the power of his ring, the azantite gauntlet, and whatever other magical items he possessed. Still, he would not bet against Lord Alistair, especially when not even present in corporeal form and seemingly impervious to harm. *How had he used Spirit Fire?*

"If a client had engaged us to steal the Coffer," the old man rasped, sinking back onto the throne, "we would let you and your whelp test the full might of Alazashin Mountain, and see how long your power would last." After letting his statement sink in, he said, "As it stands, I can tell you that no one under my authority took possession. I do not know who took the Coffer or where it is. That is the truth, sworn upon my oath as Alazashin, and my final word on the matter."

Val cringed, waiting for an explosion from Lord Alistair, but instead the Chief Thaumaturge bore a satisfied, if disappointed, expression. "So be it. I will not insult your honor by inquiring further. Though if our students are ever again troubled by one of your kind, I will return myself, in a much fouler mood."

The old man's eyes sparked with a lifetime of power and secret knowledge. "And next time, I will ensure you have a proper greeting."

Lord Alistair didn't bother responding. Instead he stepped backward, nodding at Val to do the same. The mountain disappeared as they returned through the portal.

Once Val emerged in the room beneath the Sanctum, he blinked, trying to orient himself. He didn't know whether they had traveled in their mind or through spirit or both, but one thing was sure: his definition of reality was changing by the day.

"You heard?" Lord Alistair asked, striding for the door. Everyone else fell into step behind him, the hulking form of Kjeld bringing up the rear, looking over his shoulder at the Alazashin portal as if ensuring the enemy was not going to pour through.

"All of it," Kalyn Tern responded. "I thought your hand well played."

Lord Alistair preened at the compliment.

"A masterful stroke indeed," Braden Shankstone said, "though it still begs the question of who stole the Coffer."

"The Alazashin are hardly the only thieves of note on Urfe. The outcome is disappointing, but we shall widen the search."

"You believe him?" Val asked, daring to comment. Though he knew his place at the moment was to watch and listen, he also knew one did not get ahead in life by sitting in the corner. "A professional assassin?"

"There are two things sacred to the Alazashin, and two alone," Kalyn said, surprising him by not pouring venom into her words. "The confidentiality of their missions, and their oath to the Alazashin."

Lord Alistair knew he wouldn't get a name out of the old man. The trip hadn't been made to gather information, though the knowledge was a bonus.

The trip was a lesson: assault a Congregation wizard, even one in training, at your peril.

Professor Azara was the only person who did not look pleased by the outcome. "Are you sure it was wise," she said in her haughty and hyper-cultured voice, "to anger the Grandfather so? Your actions might destroy relations with the Alazashin for decades."

"The Realm has tolerated these assassins inside our borders for too long, unafraid to poke the hornet's nest. I, too, wish for peace and prosperity in a kind and gentle world. But reality dictates otherwise."

"A statement had to be made," Braden said.

"The nature of man ensures that an empire which rests on its laurels," Lord Alistair continued, "no matter how beautiful its streets or well-structured its policies, is an empire doomed to fall. To stay static is to wither and die. For this reason, at the next meeting of the Conclave, I will declare a new age upon the Realm, one led by the unequalled might and enlightenment of the Congregation of New Victoria. An age in which we will spread our prosperity and values to the rest of the world."

Lord Alistair's chin lifted high as his voice rang throughout the corridor. "An age, my friends, of expansion."

As they exited the Sanctum, Lord Alistair asked Val to accompany him to his study, earning yet another resentful glance from Braden. When they had returned to the Chief Thaumaturge's highest tower, glasses of granth in hand, the city a child's bauble beneath them, Lord Alistair folded his hands in his lap. "You're wondering why I have supplanted Braden so quickly. One might even say cruelly."

Val had been thinking about just that; he and Lord Alistair had the same instincts. In truth, Val assumed there was a good reason for his callous handling of Braden. The Chief Thaumaturge was too smart for petty politics.

After a careful sip of granth, Lord Alistair said, "Leadership is not fatherhood, or even friendship. There is no place for sentimentality. I will talk to Braden, but he is learning a valuable lesson. That a ruler must exercise, above all, expediency. Power. Wisdom and empathy and charity are also important traits—unless one desires to rule a hell dimension—but the Realm has too easily forgotten its past, become too inured to the illusion of peace. Braden has never known the horrors of war or the threat of an invasion. Before we expand our borders, we must use the annoyance of the Revolution to strengthen the will of our populace. Remind them of what they have to lose."

"Garbind's murder helped that cause," Val said. "If the Revolution can reach an elder mage, they can get to anyone."

"Yes. Indeed. I'm glad you understand. Kjeld understands, too. He has traveled Urfe under the aegis of the Queen, with experience in innumerable conflicts. And Kalyn and Professor Azara are a century older than Braden. They remember war, though Professor Azara has philosophical differences that will . . . be addressed." He stroked his chin with a finger bearing a ring of intertwined onyx and white gold. "Braden's life has been one of privilege. Before he can progress, he must feel the sting of disappointment. He needs to understand that you will one day be a stronger mage than he, and that no one's position by my side is assured."

Lord Alistair's pointed stare told Val that he was also included in that statement. Val leaned back in his seat, expression unchanging. He understood the nature of the game, and it was nothing new. Not to this or any other world.

Power.

It was always about power.

Lord Alistair opened a palm. "Understood?"

"Perfectly," Val replied, wondering if the entire speech about Braden hadn't been meant for him.

Lord Alistair reached for his granth. "It's time to move forward with the search for the Coffer."

"What do you have in mind?"

"To be honest, I'm surprised the Alazashin were not involved. I did not expect them to divulge their client, but there are other ways to glean information. I'll send political emissaries to other kingdoms. I still believe a thief was hired for the job, and that is where you should focus. There will have been talk. Rumors. Perhaps bids for service in certain channels. To catch a thief, we must talk to another of their ilk. To the King of Thieves."

Val recalled a memory of a canvas yurt in the Goblin Market reeking of perfumed oil and incense, of a feeble glow orb illuminating a man in the shadows with patterned leathery skin and a slender tail coiled behind him. "Sinias Slegin," Val guessed, remembering the name of the serpentus, or snake-man, who many said was the most powerful figure in the New Victoria underworld.

"Not Sinias, though you raise a good point. Let's consult him. His guidance might be beneficial with the one I seek. Are you familiar with Undertown?"

Val had heard rumor of a section of New Victoria that lay below ground level, a ruined labyrinth of sewers, forgotten watery channels, and buildings that had long ago sunk into the swamp, reclaimed by nature and creatures unknown. "I know of it."

"A mermerus called Zagath lives in Undertown. Aboveground, he is called the King of Thieves. Due to the nature of Undertown, he is able to exert his influence in every part of the city where the sewers and swamp channels touch the surface. If the rumors are true—the Congregation does not consort with such types, as long as they stay underfoot—he has amassed an immense fortune and his standing in the underworld exceeds even that of Sinias."

"A mermerus?"

"Forgive me. Sometimes I forget your origins. A mermerus is a merman, one who is half human and half kethropi. An advantage, of course, to surviving in those watery depths."

"Should I consult an aquamancer?"

"Mermen cannot live underwater, and Undertown is not wholly submerged.

I could send an elder aquamancer with you, but then the quest and the result-ing political capital would not belong to you, would they?"

Lord Alistair was always scheming, Val realized. Always playing the game.

He realized something else, as well: that for all of Lord Alistair's talk of a successor, Val was still an expendable asset, full of promise but unproven, in a way that an elder aquamancer was not.

"Agreed," he said. "And understood."

"Excellent." Lord Alistair clapped his hands and rose. "I suggest leaving in the morning."

After the Congregation mages left Alazashin Mountain, the Grandfather called for servants to remove the remains of the shattered pillars, ordered the dead collected, sent the injured to the infirmary, and authorized the use of healing salves.

Once a measure of order had been restored, he called for his closest ad-visers. Not for many moons had anyone dared attack the Alazashin in their home, and the mages he had hired to inspect the spirit portals had assured him the illusory appearances they facilitated could do no harm.

Were the mages lying? Or had Lord Alistair somehow transcended the magic of the portals?

It had also shocked the Grandfather that Lord Alistair had broken an ac-cord that had stood for centuries, and the old man wondered whether the more reasonable voices of the Congregation had been silenced in recent years.

They say there is no honor among thieves, but the old man knew that am-bitious rulers were the most accomplished thieves of all. They stole kingdoms, precious resources, the hearts and minds of generations.

As the present members of the *Zashiri*, twelve of the world's deadliest as-sassins who would give their life at the Grandfather's command, knelt in front of the Throne of Daggers, he felt the long and bloody history of the mountain, the storied legacy of his order, thrumming in his bones. The Alazashin had influenced world events for two millennia, deposing kings and emperors with the prick of a poisoned blade long before the Congregation had held its first Conclave.

He pushed to his feet at the foot of the throne, quivering with barely re-
strained fury, the hundred and fifty years of his battle-hardened flesh held together by elixirs and force of will. "We know we have not the strength to oppose the Congregation in battle. Yet open conflict has never been our weapon.
Our payment for this incursion, this desecration of our home, will be taken
from the intruders a piece of flesh at a time, cut by cut, sliver by sliver. Over the
years, the decades, or even the centuries, as need be." The Grandfather paused
to catch his breath, inhaling the smell of old stone steeped in sandalsmoke that
wafted through the cavern from the braziers. "Has there been word?"

A tall woman with charcoal skin and the unblinking eyes of a predator held
up a bauble swirling with blue fog. "Not from Ferala, Grandfather. But Nagiro
draws closer." The woman spat. "He has the heretic in his sight."

The Grandfather had a thousand and more assassins at his command, but
the best of the best were the twelve *Zashiri*. The two missing members, twins
who had climbed Alazashin Mountain in their adolescence, legends in their
own time, had been sent out on missions.

Long ago, a tracking crystal had been implanted in the hilt of Magelasher,
a priceless weapon crafted for another Grandfather by one of Urfe's greatest
relicmancers. When Magelasher reappeared in the Kingdom of the Mayans,
the magic of the tracking device no longer interrupted by the powerful cloaking ward surrounding the sorcerer king's pyramid, the Grandfather had sent
Nagiro, the younger of the twins, in pursuit. The cat o' nine tails had traveled
to Freetown, and a spy reported that Mala of the Kalev clan held possession.
This pleased the Grandfather greatly, since he had once sworn an oath not to
pursue her—the only living person who had been offered a place in the *Zashiri*
and refused. The Grandfather had to live with the consequences of the bargain
he had struck. For a time, it had almost cost him his grip on power.

Yet he had made no promise not to pursue the weapon. Mala would fight
Nagiro when he came to take it, and the gypsy adventuress would die. The
thought caused the old man a moment of grief, for he had once loved her. Yet
mostly he was glad.

The older of the twins, Ferala, had a more difficult task. No tracking device
existed on the Coffer of Devla. Stolen by an unknown entity, the future of the
mysterious artifact remained in limbo.

Perhaps the Alazashin could not field an army with the might to confront Lord Alistair. But the Grandfather could find and steal that which the arrogant mage desired most, and either keep it for the Alazashin's own defenses, or sell it to the enemies of the Chief Thaumaturge. No one understood the power of leverage better than the Alazashin.

Lord Alistair desired the Coffer?

Then let the race begin.

9

At first, Caleb thought the two brown shapes moving swiftly down the steep hillside were some type of animal, perhaps an antelope or a mountain goat. It seemed like strange behavior, but what did he know about wildlife? The Brewer was riding a few yards ahead, his gaze focused on the waves crashing against the rocky shore on their right.

"Bruce," Caleb said, startling the older man. The sun had begun to set on the first day of their journey, and Caleb had not uttered a word all day.

"Yeah, pal?"

Caleb pointed towards the line of golden-brown peaks to the east, the foothills of the snowcapped Dragon's Teeth. "What do you think those things moving towards us are?"

The Brewer studied the hillside for a moment, frowned, and took out his spyglass. After taking a moment to focus, he scanned the hills and sucked in a breath. "Those are mountain trolls. They have excellent vision, and I think they've already seen us."

"Mountain trolls? What do we do?"

"We ride, kid. As fast and as far as we can."

The Brewer flicked his reins and urged his dappled white mare into a gallop. Caleb had no choice but to follow, adrenaline gushing into his veins, cool air searing his face as his cloak flapped around him. Gripping the saddle with one hand, he turned and saw the shapes growing closer, materializing into a pair of long, angular humanoids atop muscular steeds. The distance rendered their size hard to judge.

Caleb shouted as they rode. "Can we outrun them?"

"They're on ridgebacks. Larger and faster than normal horses. They won't last as long as ours, but they don't have to."

"So what's your plan?" Caleb said as he caught up to the Brewer, both men's knees clamped against the sides of their mounts.

"Plan?" When he glanced over, Caleb saw a look of wild surging in his friend's eyes. "Ride until they catch us, and pray for a miracle along the way."

Watching the mountain trolls gain on them was one of the most terrifying experiences of Caleb's life. Every time he looked back, it seemed the creatures had closed another hundred yards, until they drew close enough for him to get a good look at them. What he saw caused his stomach to lurch in fear, and he gripped Marguerite's wedding ring that hung on a leather thong about his neck.

Taller and much leaner than their hill troll cousins that Caleb had encountered before, the two mountain trolls wore tattered loincloths with bear pelts draped across skeletal shoulders. Guards of spiked bone protected their shins and forearms. Hairless, their exposed gray skin had the rough texture of bark stretched over sheaths of sinewy muscle. When they rose in the saddles of their enormous steeds, hefting roughhewn spears as they approached, Caleb knew that if he had not been so devastated by the deaths of Marguerite and Luca, he might have fainted from fright. "Can you sing?" he shouted.

"Sure," the Brewer said. He held his broadsword in one hand, the reins in another. "But it won't stop those two. Why don't you try praying?"

"What?"

"You opened the Coffer, right? Ask for some lightning."

Caleb looked over and saw that the Brewer was serious. Despite the thunder of hoof beats pounding twenty yards behind them, Caleb laughed, loud and harsh. "I tried that when Marguerite died. Nobody brought her back."

"Maybe try asking for something more modest? Like snapping those whale-bone spears in half?"

"God is a fairy tale," Caleb said with a snarl, reining in his horse and wheeling around to confront their pursuers.

"And mountain trolls aren't?" the Brewer muttered.

One of the trolls flew past Caleb, bearing down on the older man. The other monster stopped near Caleb and stood to his full height in the stirrups, at least eight feet tall. With catlike agility, one of its spindly arms thrust his spear straight at Caleb's chest.

But Caleb was quicker. A flick of his left wrist brought his vambrace into play, turning aside the troll's spear. His ensorcelled bracers only shattered metal, but they were an effective shield against other materials. The troll thrust again and again, thwarted each time by the vambraces. Caleb was an ace tennis player in his youth, and possessed excellent reflexes. He had no way to hurt the troll, but he began to cackle, maddened by fear and adrenaline.

Bruce cried out behind him. Caleb couldn't turn to see what had happened. The troll attacking him snarled with frustration, but then its eyes took on a triumphant gleam. It stabbed downward, too low for Caleb to block.

Right into the chest of his mare.

The animal cried out and stumbled. Caleb rolled off before she went down, but the mountain troll had already vaulted off his steed, scarily fast, and grabbed Caleb by the throat with a knobby hand. Caleb roared, trying to free himself, but the monster lifted him straight into the air and started squeezing his neck. Caleb flailed in midair, trying to pry its fingers off him, but the mountain troll's grip seemed made of iron.

Caleb fought for a moment more, and then he saw black.

When Caleb woke, the back of his throat felt like someone had rubbed sandpaper against it all night. He opened his eyes at the same time he smelled the stink of the mountain trolls: decaying bodies in a nursing home, wrapped in moldy coats of fur. Mingling with their stench was the smell of greasy animal fat cooking over a fire.

Caleb was lying on his side at the back of a shallow cave, bound hand and foot with heavy rope that cut into his skin. Beside him, the Brewer lay unmoving with a dark, matted stain on his head. After watching him for a moment, Caleb saw the rise and fall of his chest.

Twenty feet away, at the mouth of the cave, the trolls gnawed on a pile of stringy roots as they conversed near the fire. Four squirrels roasted on sharpened stakes were arranged in a tee-pee above the flame pit.

Fireflies danced in the woods outside, a parody of freedom. Caleb still vividly remembered the night the tuskers had captured him and Will and Yasmina. The terror had gripped him for weeks, paralyzing him. He felt a surge of familiar panic well up deep inside, but this time something else lived beside it, something dark and fierce. A new and unfamiliar presence coiled in his essence, something with its mouth open in a soundless scream, burning for blood and justice.

For his entire life, Caleb had abhorred the thought of harming another living creature. When he had stabbed Zedock to save Will and Yasmina, he sensed the barrier start to waver, though he had tried not to think too hard about that. Living on Urfe had slowly carried him down the path of violence, like a cult member starting to believe, and Marguerite's death had tipped him over the edge. All he wanted to do was free himself, kill these two filthy monsters licking their chops by the fire, and watch Lord Alistair draw his final arrogant breath.

Caleb's passions had always ruled him, and he supposed they still did.

Because now he had a passion for revenge.

The trolls were laughing cruelly as they took long drinks from a cloth-wrapped gourd. He wriggled to free himself, careful not to alert the creatures, but nothing he did seemed to work the ropes loose. Inch by inch, he wormed his body into a position where he could see the Brewer's face. As soon as the older man's eyes fluttered open, he drew his attention with a hiss.

"Bruce," he whispered. "Keep quiet but look around."

The older man blinked and stifled a groan. His eyes flew to the front of the cave, quickly grasping the situation. "Yeah?" he whispered back.

"Can you get us out of here?"

"I'm fine," he muttered. "Thanks for asking."

"We don't have time for that. I don't want to be dessert."

"I'm not too keen on it, either."

"I was captured once," Caleb said. "I'm not going through it again. I'll kill myself if I have to. Knock my head against a rock."

"Geez, kid, calm down. From what I know of mountain troll lore, we have at least a day before they carry us home and eat us." The Brewer struggled with his bonds, and the combination of sweat and blood running down his forehead caused him to squeeze his eyes shut from the sting. "We're not getting out of this rope."

"I know. Can you sing us out of here?"

The Brewer was quiet for a moment. "I can try something, but it's risky. If it backfires, they might kill us on the spot."

"What is it?"

"I can't sing us out of here, but I can tell a story."

"A story? What do you mean?"

The Brewer gritted his teeth in pain. "Just listen. No matter what, don't interrupt. Got that?"

Caleb wanted to inquire further, but a glint in the Brewer's eye made him decide to trust him. He didn't see another option, so he nodded in acknowledgment.

"If it doesn't work, and they guess what I'm doing . . . well, it's been real, kid."

Caleb let his gaze bore into the older man's eyes, trying to pour all of his innate movie star charm into his next words. He had never really used his charisma before in that way. "Stop thinking about failure. Whatever it is you're doing, make it work."

The Brewer swallowed, gave the smallest of nods, and let his eyes go distant. Just as Caleb wondered if he had lost his nerve, the older man called out to the trolls. "We're a little hungry over here."

The creatures whipped their long necks around, stretched and leathery faces gleaming by the light of the fire. Most frightening of all was the cunning intelligence shining in their feral gray eyes.

The troll on the left was missing the top half of one ear. He looked at the other and said, in a voice like chewing nails, "I think it speaks to us."

The other troll turned to speak to the Brewer. "What say you, little man?"

"I said we're hungry."

The sound of their laughter, jagged and intelligent, made Caleb's skin crawl.

"So are we, yes? Such is why we took you."

"You don't want us too thin before you throw us in the pot, do you?"

The troll walked over to him and stroked his chin with a long, crooked finger tipped with nails sharpened into claws. "Not to worry, morsel. A short journey up the mountain will not strip the flesh from your bones."

The Brewer's voice turned pleading. "A final meal before we die is our custom. Please, consider this last our request."

After another harsh laugh, the troll drew a line of blood on the Brewer's cheek with its sharpened nail.

"How about I make you a deal," the Brewer continued. "I'll tell you a story, the best story you've ever heard. If you think it's worthy of a meal, even just a few bites from your squirrel, that's all I'll ask in return. And if not, well, what have you lost?"

"You seek to bargain in your position? A bold little man you are!"

The other troll stuck a long, hardened arm into the fire and stoked the flames with its fingers. It blew the ashes off its hand and raised its gourd. "Tell us your story, grub. The night is young." It bared his yellow teeth with a slow and sinister smile. "If it's not the best story we've ever heard, the very best indeed, then we eat one of you while the moon still glows."

The Brewer hung his head and started to protest. "How about we-"

"Silence!" the troll by the fire thundered. Caleb lay very still on the ground, not daring to lift his eyes.

"You wanted a bargain, yes?" The troll rose to walk over to them. Caleb could see the gnarled bunions on his feet and a thick scar that ran the length of his left calf. "Now you have one. Speak. Entertain. We shall see if your words gain you another sunrise."

After the troll backed away, Caleb risked lifting his head and saw that it had rejoined its companion by the fire. They turned the squirrels and drank lustily from the gourds as the Brewer began to speak of a prince in a faraway kingdom, a land of science and enlightenment with machines that produced everything imaginable. Giant mechanical birds carried hundreds of passengers through the sky, food was made in factories, and homes were heated and cooled by metal boxes that harnessed the power of lightning. This particular kingdom, the Brewer said as the trolls grappled with the concept of science, was a mountainous country like the homeland of the trolls, one known for its crystalline lakes and bountiful game. Its people wanted for nothing. Yet for all of its advantages, the young prince of this kingdom was very wicked. So wicked that even the mountain troll chieftains who dwelled deep in the hollows of the Dragon's Teeth would look in awe upon his cruel nature. So wicked that the prince, who would one day go to war and use his machines to slaughter millions of people in unimaginably horrific ways, would one day be known as the most wicked person who ever lived, his very name synonymous with evil. Perhaps expecting something different, the trolls looked pleased at the turn the story had taken, and asked for it to continue.

The Brewer droned on and on, continuing to speak in detail of this strange and fascinating land, of its descent into war and chaos, of how the young prince stuffed his citizens into ovens and tortured them to death in prison camps. The trolls grew more and more riveted, forgetting about their dinner and listening to the story with rapturous eyes. The Brewer spoke so long that his voice grew hoarse, and one of the trolls, moving as if in a trance, brought him a gourd to drink. The story continued until the moon rose to its peak and fell again, and the stars began to merge with the sky. As the charred corpses of the squirrels fell in ashy chunks to the floor of the cave, the trolls grew heavy-lidded and fought to stay awake, not wanting to miss a single word. Still the Brewer carried on with his tale of secret meetings between nations and ever more death and destruction, ending with a weapon that could incinerate an entire city in the blink of an eye. Caleb grew as weary as the trolls, and he fell asleep to the sound of the Brewer's hypnotic voice, whispering his tale of horror into the night, too hoarse to speak any louder.

Caleb felt a hand shaking him roughly by the shoulder. At first he thought it was a dream, and then he heard the whisper of his friend in his ear, still scratchy from the long story.

"Wake up, kid!"

Caleb blinked and found himself staring into the morning gloom of a steeply wooded slope. "Where are we?"

The Brewer was gripping the reins of their remaining horse, glancing over his shoulder with a worried expression. "I carried you a hundred yards from the cave. Hurry, now!"

"A hundred yards—what about the trolls?"

"They're still sleeping, and I set the ridgebacks free. The nasty beasts tried to bite me. I wouldn't be surprised if they came back to warn them."

After climbing onto the back of the horse, Caleb held on for dear life as they pressed down the hillside, trusting the horse's instincts to guide them safely to the bottom.

"Thanks," Caleb said.

"Don't mention it."

"How does it work? That was like . . . magic."

"Dunno, kid. I guess I've got the gift of gab. I know that back home, studies were done about how music rewires the brain. Quantum physics and all, I got bored with the details. And story is story, right? Whether spoken or sung. Back home, a powerful storyteller can impart empathy and change your worldview, make a real difference in your life. Over here, well, let's just say the effect is a little more direct."

They rode the horse as hard as they could with two people, desperate to create distance. When Caleb asked whether the Brewer thought the trolls would pursue them, he shrugged and said it could depend on how far they were from home, what their orders might be, and how bad they wanted to catch them. None of that made Caleb feel comfortable. They rode through the night along the shore, stopping only to rest the mare.

Early the next morning, they reached a prosperous fishing village and bought another horse, a powerful young stallion the color and temperament of a leaden sky, gray and foreboding. It fit Caleb's mental state. The spirited horse had a white streak along its back, and he named her Margo.

A sign beside the door of the village tavern advertised mouthwatering local prawns. Caleb insisted on pressing forward. They warned the villagers about the trolls, refilled their water, and bought lobster bread rolls for the day's ride, then continued south along the coast.

Not until two more days of hard riding passed with no sign of the trolls did they start to relax. No other bandits or large predators approached them. They camped each night without a fire, and the constant presence of the ocean lent a false sense of security. Like a child pulling the covers over his head at night, Caleb could hide inside the rhythmic pounding of those vast blue waves until the danger and memories faded.

As the dusk chill set in on the fifth night out of Freetown, purple light creasing the sky like crushed velvet, the Brewer stopped at the edge of a cliff overlooking a five-fingered promontory jutting into the ocean.

Caleb pulled alongside him, joining him in silent contemplation. In the palm of the promontory, just off the rocky shoreline, sat a cylindrical white tower a hundred or so feet tall. It had long since lost its gleam, and a columned façade twisted around the tower in a spiral pattern that must have been an optical illusion, because as Caleb gazed upon it, he couldn't seem to figure out where it began or ended.

"There she is," the Brewer said quietly.

Caleb didn't need to ask whether this was the legendary Tower of Elarion. Whatever the name of this strange anomaly in the forgotten reaches of the Barrier Coast, sitting proud and alone on the shore, a lighthouse without a light, he already knew this was his destination.

He knew it because, right down to the moody sky and heaps of kelp strewn along the beach, the crash of the waves and the cry of the seagulls flitting above the rocks, this was the exact same tower he had seen in his vision.

-10-

Tiny rented out rooms above his tavern. Three were unoccupied, so he put Will and the others up for the night. Judging by the layout of the rooms and the authentic feel of the construction, all of which looked carved from soot-stained quartz, Will guessed the second floor of the inn had been repurposed from an original dwelling.

The house of a Nephili family, perhaps?

Somehow the thought seemed mundane, as if the builders of the ancient city could only have lived in palaces or soaring obelisks.

Yasmina took a room to herself, and Will wondered what was going through her mind. She had transitioned so quickly from grad student to enigmatic wilder, from studying at the library to wielding the power and responsibility of a steward of the Realm. The emotional impact must be tough—which he knew all too well.

The friendly conversation with Tiny had caused Will to lower his guard, but as he stared out the window at the shroud of darkness settling over the city, soaking into the tips of the spires and spreading down the tops of the ruined arches like an oil stain, as he listened to the streets come alive with raucous laughter and the occasional scream of terror, he drew his sword and decided to post a guard in the hallway. He took first watch, twitching at every scrape of furniture or creak of a door, hoping the pitter-patter of tiny feet in the walls belonged to rodents and not malicious imps waiting for Will and the others to fall asleep.

Sometime after midnight, he woke Mateo to take his place. Bleary-eyed, his cousin squeezed his arm, sat cross-legged in the hallway, and laid his urumi sword across his lap. As skittish as Will was about their first night in Praha, he had barely slept in days.

Dreaming came easy.

*   *   *

The night passed without incident. After preparing a breakfast of eggs, sausage, and spicy duck hash, Tiny wished them luck and pointed them to a general store where they could buy a map.

Except for the shopkeepers sweeping the streets in front of their establishments, the city was calm. Scores of drunks slept in doorways, and a man dragging a burlap sack collected broken bottles with a set of iron pincers.

In the general store, Mateo bought a map for a silver florin, which Will had learned was equal to one tenth of a gold piece. An exorbitant price for a worn piece of parchment, but given the dearth of shops in Praha, they were lucky to have found one at all. He also picked up some blank parchment and a silver pencil with extra lead, almost laughing out loud at the thought of mapping an actual adventure. It brought him back to winter nights by the fire as a kid, sprawled out on the floor with his friends, crafting nefarious dungeons on graph paper to explore.

As soon as they left the store, everyone crowded around as Will unfurled the map on the ledge of an ornate fountain that had long stopped flowing. Though disappointed by the lack of detail, he stared in fascination at the rough outline of the city. Running north to south, the river dissected Praha like the faded scar in the middle of Mala's forehead. The shopkeeper had pointed out the section in which they stood, an area called Burgher's Blight on the eastern side of the river. At the northern edge of the map, the river made almost a closed loop, a reverse C. The mysterious Old City lay inside that loop, bounded by a high wall. A black citadel loomed right in the middle of the Old City, and a sprawling area called the Agora, marked by a jumble of broken columns, butted up against the curve in the river.

Miles and miles of wasteland surrounded Burgher's Blight, interrupted by the occasional temple, graveyard, tower, or other landmark. Isolated districts dotted the city on both sides of the river, all with colorful names: Aganon's Demise, Ye Olde Ruined Bower, Pilferer's Pantry, Corner of Broken Souls. Will pulled his eyes away from the tantalizing mysteries of the map, dungeons and crypts and shadowy areas marked by question marks or danger signs. He concentrated on the docks, located several miles downriver from the Old City.

"Lucka," Dalen muttered, "it's a long way from here."

Will studied the legend of the map and made some scale calculations. "It's only about three miles as the crow flies. Though since few streets are marked, we'll have to find our way through, and who knows how long that will take."

"Or what else we'll stumble upon," Mateo said darkly.

Yasmina planted her staff. "Can we not hire a guide to the Nilometer? Perhaps Tiny can help?"

"Not a bad idea," Will said.

They returned to the tavern and told Tiny what they needed, causing him to grimace and shake his leonine head. "Plenty of willing guides be cozying up to my bar, though only a handful know the city well enough to help. The problem is knowing who to trust—and trust, me new friends, is as rare in this city as a barrel full of azantite. Give me a few days, though, and I'll try to sort you out."

Will exchanged a glance with the others. Time was one commodity they did not have. "What if you had to choose today? Right now?"

"Then I suppose that'd be Trigell Kolivar. He just returned from the Flats and is eager for coin. I'd say with him," Tiny lifted a palm and shrugged, "you've got a fifty-fifty chance of being led into a trap."

Will rolled his eyes. He was getting the hint. They were simply too new in Praha to trust a mercenary guide they didn't know. It made him question asking Skara for help, but Mala had vouched for her, and they could cross that bridge when they came to it.

"We'll go ourselves," Will said. "How dangerous is the journey to the docks?"

Tiny prepped the garnish tray as he talked. "About as safe as any in Praha, I suppose. Which isn't saying much. You've got a map, you say?"

"We do."

"Let's see it."

Will unrolled the map on the bar, and Tiny bent over it. With a stubby finger, he traced a rough path from Burgher's Demise to the docks, pointing out landmarks and showing them the areas to avoid. "I hope you've got a good memory, because the city's a maze."

"We'll get by," Will said. *Better to be stuck in a maze than rolled by our own guide.*

Tiny stuck a plate of beer pretzels on the bar for the group to munch on. "A couple of things, then. Never go inside any building you're unfamiliar with. Which, I suppose, is all of them. Avoid contact with strangers, especially outside the settled portions. Watch out for sewer entrances and traps laid by thieves. And most of all, under any circumstance, don't find yourselves out after dark."

As they entered the marrow of the city, weapons drawn and nerves on a razor's edge, Will found himself questioning his ability to lead, and wished Mala was there to guide them. That train of thought led to an ache deep inside. The doubt, the uncertainty, the thrill, the passion. God, how alive he felt with her. How *right*. He knew she wasn't perfect, but her imperfections only made her more desirable in his eyes. More human. He felt as if he knew the Mala that no one else did, knew her better than she knew herself. The spark of goodness behind the armor.

Leave it behind, Will. Distractions will only get you killed.

With a deep breath, he pushed forward, keenly aware of the position of the sun. Three miles across the city. How hard could that be?

Once they left Burgher's Blight, the city resembled the section in which they had first arrived. Rubble and debris and the occasional pile of bones littered streets that curved through contiguous buildings of granite and marble rising high overhead like the walls of a canyon, colossal basilicas and sweeping cracked arches and towers that kissed the heavens. As before, walkways and aerial bridges of all sorts spanned the tops of the monolithic buildings, a plague-blackened vision of gloom under a sky perpetually thick with clouds.

After reaching the first landmark Tiny had given them, a trio of spires in the center of a courtyard jutting upward like a colossal fork, Will stopped to take out his pencil and parchment. "I'm already confused."

"What kind of city planner made a mess like this?" Yasmina said.

"My guess?" Will said, looking skyward in awe. "One who planned it from the top down. I think they made the buildings and the walkways in the sky, and then the streets on the ground came later, as the need arose."

Everyone's gaze roamed skyward, thinking about the implications of his words.

What kind of beings had once called this city home?

Will made a smudge near the right-center edge of the paper to denote their starting point. According to Tiny, the docks lay due west from their position. At least the map should give them a general sense of direction.

Their first encounter came when they ducked into a jagged hole someone had made in the rear wall of a courtyard. When the street dead-ended in the direction they wished to go, they decided to risk the shortcut. As soon as Will clambered through, something snatched him off the ground, causing him to drop the handle of his shield. He recoiled in the grip of a hairy, eight-foot tall humanoid with a bulbous nose, flabby but enormously strong arms, and knuckles that dragged the ground. Its head was elongated like a crocodile's, teeth bristling from a slavering jaw, and its bulging belly looked as if it still contained its last meal. The creature squeezed Will in its one-armed grip and bounded away before the others could get through the hole.

"Help!" he managed to roar as he fought to free his sword arm, gagging at the stench of the thing. He could see maggots writhing in the coarse, matted hair.

The monster bounded towards another hole torn out of a ziggurat the size of a city block. The thing's lair might encompass the entire building, Will realized in terror. He couldn't let it carry him inside.

"Will!" Mateo shouted. Dalen cast a spell, a rapid-fire blast of colored light that exploded like fireworks, right in the monster's face. Neither slowed the creature, though Dalen's light show did cause Will to lose his vision for a few moments. *Thanks, buddy.*

When his eyesight cleared, Will saw the monster grasping onto an iron beam to pull itself through the hole in the ziggurat. Inside, he saw a darkened interior littered with bones and discarded weapons. Gurgling and the scrabble of tiny claws arose in the darkness, and he looked at the creature and its distended belly with new eyes. Is this thing *pregnant*?

The thought that he might be the next meal for a bunch of slavering, tiny hairy monsters gave him a burst of adrenaline. He threw his legs up and wrapped them around the iron pole, crossing his ankles and clamping on for dear life. When the monster tried to yank him off, he felt as if his arms would come out of their sockets. The others shouted his name as they sprinted down the street after him.

The scrabbling in the darkness drew closer. Will grew more and more desperate. When the monster reached up with its free arm to pry him lose, Will reared back as hard as he could with his head, catching it under its jaw. It shrieked and let go. Will dropped off the pole, reaching for his sword as he crash-landed on his back. The fall had knocked the wind from him, and he gasped as he struggled to his feet, dizzy from the head butt. The creature swung a long arm and raked its claws across Will's chest, shredding the front of his leather armor. He freed his sword at the same time five smaller versions of the beast emerged from the interior of the ziggurat, salivating with hunger. They were the size of small monkeys.

The larger monster was right in front of him. Will whipped his sword down, trying to slice through its chest, but the creature's left arm came up shockingly fast and gripped him by the wrist. He booted it in the stomach and jerked on his sword to free it. The creature rushed forward, clawed arms extended, as Will feinted and took a step backwards, towards the hole. He wanted to dive out to the street but knew that if he turned his back, the monster would tear him apart.

The fastest of the children was steps away, and it launched itself at Will. Despite the threat to his life, he couldn't bring himself to kill it, so he used the flat of his sword to smack it away. Worried the distraction had given the mother an opening, Will spun to find that a much larger monster had appeared out of nowhere, a serpentine body with red scales and a gaping maw so wide it caused Will's knees to quiver as he backed away.

A dragon? Where had that come from?

Eldritch wings furled at its side, its sinewy form stretching into the darkness, the legendary beast turned its baleful gaze on the creature that had grabbed Will, causing it to scamper away in fear.

Before Will had a chance to ponder why the dragon hadn't moved or why the hairy creatures seemed so surprised to find another occupant in their lair, a pair of strong hands pulled him through the hole and into the light of day.

"An illusion," Mateo whispered, as he handed Will his shield. "*Run.*"

Will didn't need any urging. Beside them, Dalen was staring intently into the hole, hands waving and mouth whispering. At Yasmina's urging, Dalen turned and followed the others as they sprinted back into the courtyard. Moments later, they heard a roar of irritation, followed by desperate scrabbling on stone. The party ran for their lives, heedless of where they were going, dashing down the clearest streets they could find.

Heaving with exertion, Will put a stop to the retreat with a raised hand. Once he caught his breath, he clasped Dalen on the shoulder. "You saved my life."

"How did you do that?" Yasmina marveled.

Though Dalen's eyes shone with pride, his expression was grim. "Queen fortune and the cover of darkness, that's how. That illusion is far from ready. Aike, we're lucky those things were dumb enough not to question how a red dragon appeared suddenly in their lair."

Will gave a rueful grin. "Color me stupid as well, Dalen. Trust me, when a monster like that appears out of nowhere, your first thought is not *now where is that pesky illusomancer*? Are you sure you didn't accidentally summon a real one?"

"It did look authentic. Maybe the weird magic here enhanced the illusion. Lucka, I don't know. I'm just glad it worked."

Everyone heaped on more praise, which caused the little mage to blush. After the party took a drink of water, Will searched his map for the route they had followed before the attack. He thought they had fled parallel to the street leading to the ziggurat, but he couldn't seem to find the way back.

He frowned down at the graph paper. "I suppose I'll have to start again."

Mateo glanced at the sky. "'Tis midday already. With this cloud cover, I fear an early sunset."

Sobered by the thought of being stuck in no-man's land after dark, they hurried forward, working their way westward as best as they could. The curving streets were maddening, zigzagging across the city with no apparent reason and dead-ending at courtyards or into the sides of buildings. Though Will's map saved them from running in circles, progress was slow, and the faint halo of sun behind the clouds seemed to sink faster than they could gain ground. As they passed a deserted block of buildings, Will thought he heard a slithering sound, and stopped to pinpoint it.

After cocking her head to listen, Yasmina pointed at a rectangle of open space beneath the lip of marble curb that lined the road. They had seen these openings before, on almost every road, and speculated they served as entrances to the city's sewer system.

They backed away, nervously eying the opening. Yet as they continued walking, they heard the sound again and again, on multiple streets, as if something below had somehow caught their scent.

During the journey, they encountered a handful of beggars, as well as a band of adventurers who seemed more nervous of Will's party than they were of them. Every now and then a thief would appear, skulking in a doorway or disappearing from view inside a building. Once, at an intersection of wide roads, a party of heavily armed adventurers passed by with booted feet stomping, both groups warily eying the other. Will breathed a sigh of relief when they disappeared from sight.

Dusk cloaked the buildings as they broke free of the maze and finally saw the sprawl of the docks in the distance, fronting a river that cut a wide brown swath through the city. Relief poured through him as they stopped to absorb the sight.

Why is it brown? Will wondered. *Did the plague affect the water as well?*

The only bits of evidence of the original city were giant slabs of marble, spaced a hundred yards apart, jutting into the sluggish water. Will could almost envision the exotic vessels that used to sail from the docks of Praha and travel to the ends of the earth. The spices they would bring back, the creatures and adventurers ferried to and fro, the wizards from far off lands.

The present reality was far more banal. A nest of makeshift wooden planks connected the marble slabs, reminding Will of the Fens. Shacks and houseboats lined the shoreline, and he didn't see a single vessel on the open water. He wondered if something about the plague limited river access, if something lurked in the water, or if no ships dared to pass through.

Though elated to see the docks, he grew apprehensive as he stared at the teeming chaos of activity, human and non-human, swarming the riverside. Everyone was armed and edgy. Fights broke out as they watched. He realized they might be worse off trying to find a place to spend the night in the docks than holing up in one of the abandoned buildings, and he relayed his thoughts to the group.

Yasmina drew her cloak tight and had no opinion on the matter, other than the need to hurry and find shelter. "My wilder senses are not attuned to this place," she said, gazing nervously at the bruised sky. "And I'm not sure I want them to be."

Dalen sat on the curb to take a breather. He opened his water skin and gave the docks a sideways glance. "I think I'd feel better away from people. You heard what the thieves think of wizards here."

Without warning, Mateo slapped his blade on the ground beside Dalen, jolting Will to his feet. His cousin's face had turned white, and Will followed his gaze to a piece of mottled green tentacle, at least a foot thick, writhing on the street at Dalen's feet. There was a sewer opening beside it, and Will caught a flash of movement, something long and thick and slimy receding into the darkness.

Dalen jumped off the curb. "Queen's Garters!" he said, kicking at the detached tentacle before stumbling away from the opening. "What was that?"

"Something that wanted to invite you below for dinner," Mateo said grimly, cocking his wrist for another swing.

"That thing just made the lodging decision for us," Will said as he backed towards the docks. "Forget staying in an abandoned building tonight."

No one disagreed, and Will led the way into the center of the grimy riverside district, Zariduke in hand, breathing in the stench of stale beer and rotting fish. His eyes roved from face to shadowy face. "I vote we find the Nilometer tonight," he said, not liking what he saw one bit. "Right now."

"Maybe Skara will know a safe place to spend the night," Yasmina added.

"Aye," Mateo agreed, weaving his urumi sword rhythmically beside him as he walked, as a warning to thugs and muggers. "'Tis our best course of action."

Three narrow streets lined with unsavory establishments, running parallel to the river, comprised the backbone of the district. Taverns and brothels made up the bulk of the storefronts, though Will saw pawn shops, an armory, and various other shops.

Thinking there might be safety in numbers, they returned to walk along the river. A hundred feet in, a drunken lizard man lurched out of the crowd and grabbed Yasmina by the arm. She twirled away and cracked him on the wrist with her staff. With a bellow, he charged right back at her. She lowered and swept his legs, then pointed the bronze owl head at his chest.

The lizard man started to rise, then looked in her eyes and thought better of it. Those who noticed gave the party a wider berth.

Growing increasingly nervous about the darkening sky, wondering who they should dare approach to ask about the Nilometer, Will was stunned when they found an ancient sign post, an arcing silver pole with letters carved in elegant vertical script, pointing the way to a handful of sights—including the Nilometer.

"That helps," he said.

As the crowds thinned they found themselves in an area of the city filled with plazas and green spaces long since gone to seed. A dark mass of unkempt vegetation had overtaken what must have once been beautiful parkland. As they took in their surroundings, a series of shrieks and growls emanated from the foliage, causing the party to clump together. Weapons in hand, they followed the signs deeper into the labyrinth, increasingly unnerved by their isolation, the city a receding memory. Just as they debated turning back, a pathway of broken mosaic tile led them right to the edge of a huge chasm a stone's throw from the banks of the river.

After a nod from Will, Dalen congealed the twilight to illuminate the hundred-foot-wide perimeter of the Nilometer. When the party peered cautiously over the edge, they saw an enormous well with smooth sides extending deeper than Dalen's light could penetrate. A staircase spiraled downward along the perimeter of the ivory-colored walls, and the structure seemed to have escaped the ravishing effect of the plague.

Will dropped a stone into the giant well. Long moments later, a faint splash echoed back. "My guess is a few hundred feet," he said. "At least."

"Lucka, did Mala say *where* in the Nilometer Skara would be?"

"I wished I'd asked more questions," Will muttered.

I was too busy thinking about how her lips tasted.

Yasmina glanced down the well, then peered into the dense vegetation surrounding them. "I don't like the feel of this place. There are things inside those woods we don't want to encounter. Things waiting for the cover of darkness."

"No offense," Will said, "but I don't need a wilder to figure that out."

"Should we retreat to the city while there's still light?" Mateo asked. "Return in the morning?"

Will's grip tightened around the hilt of Zariduke. "Every day counts, and I'm not sure spending the night in the docks is an improvement over the current situation." He peered inside the Nilometer and saw, along the staircase, a number of alcoves dotting the interior of the cylindrical structure. "I think we take our chances here. Maybe Skara lives in one of those alcoves."

Dalen looked very small within his cloak. "Maybe something else does, too."

"Even if we don't find her," Mateo reasoned, "it could be an advantageous place to spend the night."

"Agreed," Will said, "assuming there isn't another occupant." He turned to Yasmina. "What do you think? Can you see the bottom? Sense anything dangerous down there?"

The wilder peered into the depths of the well. "I can't see the bottom, but yes, something lurking in the water. I can't tell what, though I think it's very large."

"Is the weird magic of Praha messing with your abilities?" Will asked.

"Perhaps," she said, with an enigmatic smile. "I'm not a seer or a wizardess, Will. Just someone attuned to the land. And this particular land is as foreign to me as it is to you."

The wild shrieks and bellows from the undergrowth around them grew louder and more intense. Urgent.

Ready for a meal.

"We should decide, cousin. Night closes in."

Will's eyes flicked from the darkened woods to the Nilometer, immense and silent. "I vote to descend. If we don't find Skara, we pick an alcove and hole up until first light."

"Aye aye," Mateo said.

Yasmina gave a single nod, and Dalen agreed as well. Will led the descent, creeping down the staircase with his shield raised and Zariduke gripped tight. Yasmina followed a step behind, and Dalen illuminated their passage with a halo of insipid gray moonlight. Mateo brought up the rear, letting the tip of his blade trail on the steps, ready to whip into action.

The interior smelled of dampness and old stone. Ten feet down, Dalen shone his light into the entrance to the first alcove, revealing an ivory corridor extending into the darkness. Elaborate etchings covered the walls, too dim to be made out. Will noticed a pair of metal hooks set into the wall of the Nilometer just above the alcove.

"Skara!" he called out, deciding to take a risk. "Skara Brae!"

No response.

"Should we explore the corridor?" Mateo asked.

"Let's go further down," Will said. "Get the lay of the land first. I don't like surprises."

Step by step, they continued spiraling down the perimeter of the well, casting light into each and every alcove. While some dead-ended, most heralded the entrance to a passage delving deeper into the interior. *Where did they lead? How big was the complex?*

A hundred feet down, Yasmina announced she could see the bottom. "We're about halfway."

"What's down there?" Will asked.

"Just water, as far as I can tell."

"Lucka," Dalen muttered, "we know it's not just water."

Why so deep? It can't be the river.

Still, no longer feeling as if the Nilometer was a bottomless pit, he picked up the pace, slowing whenever they passed an alcove. Once the rest of the party had laid their eyes on the dark surface of the water, far below ground level, they stopped to consider their options. As they were discussing which alcove to hole up in, Dalen yelped and slapped at his back.

Mateo called out Will's name in a sharp voice. He turned to find his white-faced cousin plucking a dart out of Dalen's back. As the illusionist stumbled to a knee, Will felt rough fibers tightening around his middle, pinning his arms. Struggling to get free, he looked up and noticed Yasmina and Mateo also caught by lassos. He looked even higher and saw at least a dozen people sliding silently down the perimeter of the Nilometer along lines of rope clamped between their knees, clutching weapons in their hands.

11

Using their entire stash of nightflares, probing ground and sky for a sign of the dhampyr, the Roma caravan made it safely through the night. While the appearance of such a legendary creature was cause for grave concern, Mala's people did have experience dealing with their kind, and as she had told Danior, a single dhampyr pitted against an entire caravan did not overly worry her.

But if her suspicions proved correct, this was no ordinary dhampyr.

Mala shuddered at what might have happened had she not spotted the hyena wolf. They might all have been dead by morning, killed one by one under cover of night.

As they pressed on towards Talintock, wary of stopping outside a smaller and less-protected settlement, Mala's thoughts turned to another time and place, a journey with a very different purpose.

A few years after she had left the comfort of the New Victoria Thieves' Guild to travel Urfe and ply her new profession, she made a rash decision to attempt to join the Alazashin, a secret society of thieves and assassins rumored to be the best at their craft in the world. No one was born into the Alazashin. Every member had to earn his or her way in, and the ritual was the same for everyone.

Appear at the foot of Alazashin Mountain at dusk. Wait three days, then ascend.

Face the trials alone. Attempt to reach the top. Pass a final test.

Then, and only then, would the legendary order offer a seat at the table.

To this day, Mala was not quite sure why she had made the journey. Part of her wanted to train with the best, to *be* the best. Part of her was attracted to the mystery of the order and yearned to discover its secrets. Those parts, in fact, she did not regret. But part of her had been young and reckless, and brushed aside the reality of the Alazashin: a mercenary criminal organization

that worked for the highest bidder and had no qualms about murdering innocent human beings.

Mala went to the mountain. She had stayed for three days, sleeping on cold
stones, consuming water and dried rations. The mountain simmered in silence
above her. On the third day, as the shadow of night consumed the towering
peak like a snake swallowing its prey, she set out upon the crooked footpath
that led up the mountain, sword and sash in hand, confident and eager.

Ten hours and many trials later, tests of skill and intelligence and endurance
that left her barely alive, she reached the summit, a windswept aerie of searing cold and isolation. Though the moon was full, a layer of mist blurred the
boulder-strewn landscape and restricted her vision. She breathed in the heavy
damp of incipient snow, and her feet crunched on shattered rock from some
long ago explosion. Dangerous crevasses lay hidden beneath the mist.

When she saw the nature of the final test, a man who could change from
wolf to human in an instant, a dhampyr, she stumbled to a knee and placed a
hand on the ground. Blood poured from the wounds she had suffered during
the other tests, and fear of the creature standing before her stripped her of her
will to stand.

"Greetings, seeker," the dhampyr said, with a cruel smile.

Mala said nothing, trying furiously to think of a strategy. Even at full
strength and with her best weapons, she might not prevail against a dhampyr,
especially under cover of night. And a vampire half-breed who was one of the
Alazashin, trained by the best assassins in the world?

Madness. Suicide.

Yet she used her sword to push to her feet, palming a handful of fire beads.
If she must die on this forsaken peak, she would not go out like a lamb. "Come,
then," she said, twirling her blade and eying the nearest crevasse. Perhaps she
could use her acrobatic skills to trick the creature into plummeting to its death.

He stepped aside to reveal a staircase cut into the rock, leading down into
the mountain. "Your apprenticeship awaits," he said. "You need only pass
through me to accept it."

With a howl, Mala rushed forward, tossing her fire beads and then whipping off her sash. The dhampyr avoided the fire beads with a chuckle, flowing

under them like quicksilver, his form blurry as if in the midst of a transformation. He disappeared into the mist, and Mala's will to battle curdled into fear.

"What magic is this?" she whispered to herself.

Having used up her store of items on the ascent, she darted for the staircase,
hoping to catch the dhampyr off-guard and circumvent the test. The creature
re-emerged right in front of her, knocking her down with a backhand to the
face. "If only it were so easy," he mocked. She recognized his accent as from the
ancient city of Myzantium.

They fought for an entire hour, until Mala could no longer hold her sword.
Her numbed fingers dropped the blade and the dhampyr kicked her to the
ground. She had not even landed a blow. The dhampyr was extremely fast and
seemed to merge into the mist at will. Every time she got close, he disappeared,
only to reappear behind her without a sound. He had toyed with her as a jungle cat might play with a wounded rabbit.

"If I gave you a choice," he said, standing over her, "to die or become like me,
a cursed eternal thing, which would you choose?"

"You mock me at death's doorstep? Everyone knows the dhampyr cannot
sire others of their kind."

"Do you think, little lass, that I am the only creature of the night who belongs to the Alazashin?"

Little lass? Mala whipped her sash around his ankle and jerked, pulling him
off his feet. Fast as a snake, she whipped out a dagger and lunged for his heart.
He caught the blow an inch from his chest, gripping her wrist in his hand.
"You must know that a stab to the heart will not kill me."

"You must know," Mala snarled, "that I'd rather die than join your infernal
kin."

The dhampyr gave a soft, low laugh as he plucked the dagger from her
hands. "Another choice, then. Would you rather die tonight, at my feet, or
swear lifelong allegiance to the Grandfather of Alazashin Mountain, on pain
of torture and death should you choose to leave?"

Mala started. "What?"

"The test, dear mouse, was not besting me in battle. That is not the prov-
ince of your kind. You proved your skill and stealth by reaching the summit.
You proved your fortitude and will by battling me unto the threshold of your

demise." He produced a silver ring bearing an image of a pair of crossed daggers beneath a crown. "Now you must prove your fealty by swearing an oath."

Left with little choice, Mala had kissed the ring and sworn, before she entered the mountain, to carry out the will of the Grandfather and have no other family besides the Alazashin, for as long she lived.

I didn't ask for this, she remembered thinking. I wanted adventure and training, not blind allegiance to a deadly cult.

Yet she knew she had been naïve, and reckless, and blind. What had she thought was going to happen?

As the dhampyr watched, Mala took the oath, knowing he would kill her if she refused. Once inside, the Alazashin gave her a healing salve and brought her before the Grandfather, who seemed bemused but impressed by her youth and small stature. She underwent more training and passed more tests and uncovered many, but certainly not all, of the secrets of Alazashin Mountain. Along the way, she learned the dhampyr she had fought was named Nagiro, and that he and his twin sister, Ferala, were part of the *Zashiri*, the twelve assassins of the Inner Circle. Not only that, but Nagiro and Ferala were considered the class of the twelve, due to their vampiric lineage and the weapons they wielded. Ferala carried a knife imbued with a magical poison that never dried up and whose touch meant death. Nagiro wore a garment called the Mirrorcloak that allowed him to flow into the mist and approach almost any enemy unseen.

It was not just a dhampyr that Mala had fought. It was a dhampyr who also happened to be one of the world's best assassins, armed with a cloak of immense power.

No warrior had bested one of the dhampyr twins in single combat, she had learned.

Ever.

In time, Mala began to undertake missions of her own, rising through the ranks of the Alazashin. She became a favorite of the Grandfather and was able, for the most part, to select her own assignments. This allowed her to undertake jobs that involved stealth and theft, and avoid assassinations of which she did not approve.

Yet her ascension worked against her. The Grandfather thought so much of her talents that he offered her a place in the *Zashiri*.

No, he did not offer: he ordered.

The price of admission? An assassination of the Grandfather's choosing, carried out to perfection. Perhaps knowing of her qualms, the task he chose for Mala was the murder of a fourteen-year-old Mayan princess, at the request of a rival kingdom. The Grandfather gave Mala one month to complete the task.

That night, Mala returned from the Throne of Daggers and sat lotus style at the foot of her cot, deep inside the mountain. She was no assassin and never had been. She had yet to kill someone who did not deserve to die, in her mind at least, and she knew that if she crossed that line, then she herself would not deserve to live.

How had she let this happen?

Instead of planning the assassination, Mala spent her time planning her escape. In the end, she came to the conclusion that while she might leave the mountain, she would never escape the Alazashin. There was nowhere on Urfe she could hide. The Grandfather would send his assassins after her until one of them found her in a remote village, or on a heath-covered moor, or in a cavern at the bottom of the Darklands. Someone would find her and kill her.

So she made a choice. A terrible one.

Or at least convinced the Grandfather that she had.

One of her previous clients had hired her to retrieve a magical shield from a wyvern's lair in the Ural Mountains. Along with the other loot, Mala had found a curious philter in a small, stoppered jade bottle. She had it analyzed by a potion master and was told it was a reverse love potion. A Tincture of Desire, the potion master called it. An insidious magic used to both ruin and ignite relationships, the tincture worked by imparting the memory of a night of unbridled passion to two people who shared the same drink, spiked with the elixir. Anyone unaware of the potion would never know the difference.

As did most men she had met, Mala knew the old man desired to possess her. Seducing him was not hard. It was considered a rite of passage for female members of the Zashiri and, if rumors were to be believed, some of the males. Yet Mala had always resisted, and she knew it had inflamed his passions. The next night, before she left on her mission, she entered the Grandfather's chambers and told him she was ready to succumb. The old man smiled and ordered his guards to leave. Mala debated killing him but chose not to. She would never have escaped the mountain alive, and even at his advanced age, she feared his knife hand and his legendary stock of magical items.

With a deep breath, Mala emptied the tincture into a glass of shared granth when the Grandfather turned his back. They both drank deeply. The room swam, and she fell asleep on his bed. When she woke, the Grandfather gazed at her with eyes of satisfied indulgence. Though she knew the truth in her mind, she would have sworn with all her being that she had spent the night in his arms.

She resisted his advances that morning, claiming she did not want to spoil him further until she was a member of the *Zashiri*. Now, she said, it was time to complete her mission. He agreed, and claimed she had inflamed his desire to an unbearable level. He claimed, in fact, that he loved her.

Six weeks later, when Mala returned from hiding and the Mayan princess yet lived, the Grandfather summoned her into his chambers, as she knew he would.

"What is the meaning of this?" he demanded. "I cannot save anyone, not even you, from the fate of neglecting a mission."

"What about your unborn son?" she lied. "Can you save him?"

The Grandfather took a step back, his face crumbling as if she had just speared him through the heart. It was common knowledge he had no heirs worthy of undertaking the trials, and was desirous of a strong son. In fact, he looked so stricken she feared he might have a stroke and ruin her plan.

"I'm leaving the Alazashin," she continued, pulling a dagger from her sleeve and pressing it to her own belly. "I will hide our child until his eighteenth birthday. Only then will I tell him of his lineage. If you do not release me from service—and I know that you have this power—then I will kill your child myself, right now. Before your very eyes."

"How do you know the child is a male?"

"How do you know it's not?"

He clutched his head. "You would do this? To your own child?"

Mala pressed the knife tighter, looked into his eyes, and made him a believer. As the old man reeled, she forced him to perform the rite that would release her from her death oath to the Alazashin. As far as she knew, the rite had never been used in the order's long history.

There was a first time for everything.

After the rite was complete, Mala forced him to reveal his decision in front of the *Zashiri*, though she allowed him to keep the reason for her release unknown. She could tell it gravely wounded his pride, though his eyes kept slipping to her stomach, longing for a child that did not exist. A proper heir, born from a member of the Zashiri.

It was a cruel trick, but the Grandfather was a cruel man.

She had left the mountain that very day. The Grandfather kept his word, and she knew he would never reveal the truth for fear of losing face. For her part, she had gained a wealth of knowledge of the dark arts, a greater appreciation for her own life, and a vivid and rather revolting memory of a night of passion that had never actually occurred.

The towns between the Barrier Coast and the Dragon's Teeth were friendly to the Roma. At Talintock, the caravan was able to stable its horses and take shelter in a pair of inns near the center of town.

Of course, the local people had no clue that a dhampyr stalked the caravan.

After lunch, Mala approached Danior in the common room of the inn. "I'm leaving," she said.

Altruism alone did not spur her decision. The caravan would never be able to outdistance the dhampyr, and he would pick them off one by one, at his leisure.

Danior's face darkened. "You would leave us to face the dhampyr? I suppose the rumors about you are true."

When she was younger, the comment might have wounded her. "Stay the night," she said, with quiet authority. "In the morning, continue your journey as before. The dhampyr will follow me."

"Why? And why would you do this?"

She crossed her arms, her jewelry gently chiming. "Because it knows me."

Danior's eyes widened. Though she refused to elaborate, she gave him a physical description of Nagiro, so they could spot him during the day. "Do as

I say and barricade your rooms tonight. Post a guard as you travel for the next week, just in case. Remember to keep fire on hand at all times."

After gathering her belongings, she paid good coin for the caravan's fastest horse and snuck out of town through an emergency escape tunnel that burrowed beneath the ten-foot wall. The town alderman was all too happy to help.

Under a sinking tangerine sun, Mala took flight on the plains, praying she had bought herself enough time. She had left a note on her bed, taunting the dhampyr, hoping it would divert his attention from the caravan.

Yet if he decided to drink from a few gypsies before he tracked her, that blood would be on her hands.

So be it. It was a harsh world with harsh choices.

At least that was what she told herself.

Spurring the horse into a gallop, dark hair flying in the wind, she considered the dhampyr's presence on the Barrier Coast.

Why had he come? What did he want?

She thought she might know.

The Grandfather would never break his oath that afforded Mala his protection until the fictional child's eighteenth birthday. Of that she was sure. Once that day came, not too many years in the future—that was something she would address if the Grandfather lived that long.

Why, then, the presence of his best assassin?

Magelasher. It was the only conclusion she could draw. Her suspicion was that the weapon contained a tracking device. Perhaps the cloaking power of the sorcerer king had interrupted the signal. The retrieval of the weapon must have alerted the order somehow.

The thought stopped her cold. She reined in her horse and gave it water while she inspected the cat o' nine tails. A typical weapon of this sort possessed a two-foot long handle an inch in diameter. Nine strands of tightly-braided cotton or leather cord typically extended from the hilt, whip-like thongs whose lashes caused intense pain.

Magelasher was similar in size and appearance, but had a black-and-red bloodstone hilt that gave it extra heft. Instead of cotton or leather, ultra-thin black wires of unknown material formed the thongs, tipped by azantite barbs with enough magically-enhanced power to pierce the shield of a majitsu.

She ran her hands over the weapon. Her eyes narrowed as they moved to the worn leather wrapping the bottom half of the hilt. After checking her spyglass to ensure the dhampyr was not in sight, she unraveled the leather, cutting into the adhesive with her dagger. It took some time, but she managed to remove it all, exposing more of the bloodstone.

As well as a tiny crystal embedded into the underside of the hilt.

Mala used her dagger to pry it out, recognizing a common device of the Alazashin. Tracking crystals were pieces of a larger crystal, ensorcelled by a geomancer to connect the pieces of the stones over long distances.

Mala started to grind the crystal to dust with the hilt of her sword, then gave a thin smile and carried it to a nearby stream. She set the crystal adrift on a small wooden barge and wished it a very long journey.

Breathing a little easier, she drank from the stream and spurred her horse forward. The dhampyr did not know her destination. If she were lucky, he would lose the trail. She checked the spyglass until night fell with no sign of her pursuer, ate a handful of dried beef and coffee beans, and kept moving.

The dhampyr did not know her ultimate destination and, without the aid of the tracking device, might lose interest in the chase. She rode swiftly southeast, still heading for the pass. Once she cleared the southern edge of the Dragon's Teeth, she had a long ride through the desert, many days of scrounging for water and cactus fruit, before she reached the treacherous, wide-open vistas of the plains.

Her reprieve didn't even last until the afternoon. During the horse's midday rest, an hour before the Shoehorn pass, Mala raised the spyglass and glimpsed the dhampyr riding a horse in the distance. He was close enough that she could recognize the untamed dark hair and cold, Oriental, flat-faced features of Nagiro.

By the Queen! How had he found her so quickly?

At this rate, she wouldn't last the night. Once darkness fell, the dhampyr would change form and quickly outpace her. He would have to rest during the day, but she would never make it to the next dawn.

After a moment of panic, she reached into her Pouch of Possession and withdrew a map of the Ninth Protectorate. The atlas contained a number of villages, trading outposts, and other locations of interest she had discovered on her travels. Yet what could help against a dhampyr?

As her hopes began to dim, she focused on a place she had visited only once, but which had seared into her memory. A place of great power, known as the Crater of the Snow Moon. It was a land of stark and exquisite beauty, sacred to the nearby tribes for millennia untold. No one lived permanently in the valley except for a shaman rumored to understand how to harness the power intrinsic to the red and cracked earth. Though Mala had met him once, she did not know if he could help—or if he would. But it might be her only chance.

She thought the valley could be reached by nightfall. If darkness came too soon or the horse gave out or the shaman refused to help, then the dhampyr would find her, and she would likely die.

Mala lowered the spyglass and affixed Magelasher to her belt. With a snarl of anger at feeling so helpless, she flattened on her horse and rode for her life.

12

Adaira leaned forward to clasp her hands atop the blue quartz table. "Let me go with you."

Behind her, a line of arcing glow orbs illuminated the bend in the Great River. Lush vegetation surrounded the table for two in the city's most renowned pleasure garden.

Val enfolded her hands in his own. "I'm not the one who made the decision."

"My father doesn't control me."

He adjusted the cuff of his high-collared white shirt. "No, but why anger him? He believes I should do this myself. I agree. We've talked about this, Adaira."

"I just . . ." She caressed the inside of his palm with her finger, frustration swimming in her turquoise eyes.

"Don't want to miss out on an adventure?"

She removed her hands and cupped a tabletop glow bauble. It changed color to match her eyes when she touched it. "I can accept that for now. I need to finish my studies."

"Then what?"

She pressed her lips together and, after a moment, said, "No one knows much about Undertown. It's never been mapped or studied. Why doesn't my father just send for Zagath?"

"I'm not aware of a line of diplomatic communication with the sewer."

"My father has ways," she muttered.

"I gather the journey itself is part of the plan to let me prove my worth to the Congregation."

"As if you haven't already," she said sharply. "We almost gave our lives in pursuit of Tobar."

"Which secured my release from wizard prison, and kept you out of it. Heavy lays the crown, Adaira."

His comment caused her to stare off into a hedge of vivid tropical flowers, artfully entwined with streaks of Spanish moss. A pattern too dazzlingly intricate to be anything other than the work of a floramancer.

The intoxicating scent of the blooms, combined with her perfume, made him light-headed. He reached for her hands again. "I'll have a guide," he said gently. "Someone who's dealt with Zagath before."

"I thought it was a solo adventure."

"Your father wants me to be the only wizard. He never said I couldn't use help."

"Who are you taking?"

"Sinias Slegin. Though he doesn't know it yet."

"Lovely," she muttered. "Another thief."

He didn't quite understand her concern. Though dangerous, a guided trip to Undertown should not elicit this kind of response.

As if responding to his unspoken question, she fingered her black choker and glanced around the pleasure garden, probing for unseen eyes. "I don't trust him," she said finally.

"What do you mean?" Val asked, knowing she meant her father and not Sinias. He had to tread carefully here. Both in case someone was watching, and because familial relationships were delicate things.

"It's not that I think he means you harm. On the contrary, I think he genuinely respects you, and wants you by his side. But he always has an agenda and is not exactly known for . . . let me just say I believe he'd put the interests of the Realm above yours."

"Welcome to politics," Val said wryly, though he squeezed her hands, moved by her concern. As she bit her lip, he admired the pale curve of her neck, revealed by a diamond circlet that swept back her hair. The worst part of his upcoming journey was leaving Adaira behind. He told her as much, and she reached up to cup his face.

"Val, I'm a little afraid of admitting this, but I think I'm falling in love with you."

Her words stirred something inside him that he was unused to feeling. Something much deeper than simple attraction. As their gazes met in the soft light of the glow bauble, he felt intoxicated by the milky smoothness of her skin and the hidden depths in her turquoise eyes, and in that moment, he realized things had changed.

Changed very much indeed.

He traced her lips with a finger. "You're not falling alone."

The next morning, Val strode through the front entrance of the Goblin Market, head high and eyes sweeping the crowd. On this occasion, he did not desire to blend, so as to avoid the grasping hands of pickpockets.

He wanted people to clear the way.

And part for him they did. From the moment he passed through the creaking wooden gate marking the entrance of the city's largest bazaar, a dizzying collection of stalls and smells, grimy tents and babbling vendors, the bystanders in his path hurried to give way to the wizard with the azantite-tipped staff striding purposefully into their midst.

I'm a spirit mage now. An emissary from the Chief Thaumaturge of the Congregation, on a mission for the Realm.

Following in my father's footsteps.

Despite his confidence, the swarms of buyers and the patchwork of canvas roofs hovering over the labyrinth of narrow lanes, combined with the thick clouds of incense from the braziers, felt smothering. Val was not naïve enough to believe that all of the cutpurses were dissuaded by his appearance. With a grimace, he pushed away a growing sense of claustrophobia, trying not to breathe in the nauseating aroma of animal dung and roasting meat and exotic oils that swirled in the air like a noxious cloud. Gripping his staff, he burrowed into the heart of the market, moving largely on memory. Yet he quickly grew lost, and sensed the position of the lanes had shifted since his last visit. Perhaps they changed on a daily basis. He hated to appear vulnerable but was forced to ask directions from some of the vendors, an unsavory collection of lizard men and ferret-faced humans and short, wart-covered tuskers.

Relief flooded through him when he finally left the chaos of the market behind and stepped into a familiar beige yurt. Yet the calm interior felt more sinister than welcoming, as if the rest of the market dared not intrude.

A pungent and unsettling aroma, tropical flowers soaking in grease, caused his stomach to lurch. It took his eyes a moment to adjust to the insipid yellow light leeching out of a glow orb suspended from the apex of the yurt.

"I know you, yesss?"

A lithe figure in a silky black robe was watching Val from the rear of the enclosure, legs crossed beneath him. Though Val knew what to expect, the sight of the flat nose and manicured pincers, the patterned scales and slender tail coiled behind the serpentus, still unnerved him.

"I was here once before," Val said. "With a few friends of mine. We purchased a Shadow Veil from you."

The slit-orbed, jaundiced eyes of Sinias Slegin narrowed even further, followed by a flash of recognition and then distaste. He made a sound somewhere between a hiss and a purr. "Ah, yesss. I remember. You came with the daughter of Alissstair."

"That's right."

"What isss it that you now ssseek?"

The flap to the yurt must have magical properties, Val thought, because not the faintest sound from outside could be heard.

"Guidance."

"Ah." The forked tongue of the serpentus flickered. "The most precious commodity of all."

"Not that type of guidance," Val said. "Actual guidance."

"I do not appreciate sssubterfuge."

Val spread his hands. "None was intended. Are you aware of a mermerus in Undertown called Zagath?"

"Of courssse."

"Do you know how to reach him?"

"There isss only one way."

"Which is?"

"A persssonal audience in Undertown."

Val nodded. He had figured as much. On any world, kings of the criminal underworld tended not to venture far from their lairs.

"You wisssh a guide procured?"

"No. I wish *you* to guide me."

The serpentus gave a prolonged hiss before he spoke. "I choossse when I leave my home, human. Not you. And I certainly do not ssserve as a tour guide, not even for apprentice wizardsss."

Val gave a thin smile, then reached for his magic and caused a spark of Spirit Fire to play across his fingertips. "An apprentice no longer, Sinias. I'm a full mage now. A spirit mage."

The serpentus gave a supple roll of his neck that Val couldn't interpret. "Isss it, then? Very well. I do not often receive requesssts from membersss of the Congregation. Yet it doesss not change my reply."

"I'm not requesting a favor. I'll pay well, and in advance."

"For an entire day of my ssservice? With sssuch danger?" His tongue flicked. "Expensssive."

"I can offer you one hundred gold pieces."

"Enough for a different guide, perhapsss."

Val frowned. "Two hundred, then."

"One hundred *platinum*, wizard."

Val laughed and shook his head. "Robbery, Sinias. And you know it."

"Perhapsss a handful of other guidesss could lead you through Undertown, but no other can asssure an audience with Zagath. We have done busssinesss, he and I."

Val considered the offer. Each platinum piece equaled five gold coins, and his treasure chest was running dangerously low. A very hefty sum—far too hefty for the service on offer. Still, Val did not calculate on present value alone. If he completed his mission and one day joined Lord Alistair, rising to the very top of the wizard food chain, then a hundred platinum pieces would be a pittance.

"Three hundred gold, a meeting with Zagath, and guidance there and back," he said. "Final offer."

The tongue of the serpentus flicked greedily. After a seated bow of acceptance, he turned to the side, exposing a burn scar warping the scales on the left side of his face. He called out in a string of hisses with varying pitch. A female voice responded in the same language from behind a curtain in a corner of the yurt.

After their conversation, the serpentus said to Val, "A pleasssure doing busssinesss. When do you wish to leave?"

"As soon as possible."

Sinias conversed with his unseen assistant again. "We will leave tomorrow at dawn. From here."

"Dawn?"

"I have businesss to conduct, yesss? The daylight hoursss are more expendable."

"Fair enough. There's just one more thing."

"Yesss?"

"I came alone today, but I'm acting under the aegis of Lord Alistair. Not only that, but my visit to Zagath is of utmost importance to the Congregation. Should anything . . . untoward . . . happen to me in Undertown, or our bargain dishonored, it will not go unnoticed."

Sinias's shrewd eyes narrowed almost to a close.

"I just like to cover my bases," Val said.

"I am unfamiliar with this colloquialisssm."

Val chuckled to himself. "I believe you can guess the meaning."

Sinias pointed a black-lacquered pincer at him. "Undersssstand I cannot ensssure a sssafe journey through Undertown. But I can asssure you my bargain includesss my faithful ssstewardsssship."

The corners of Val's lips upturned. "I suspected it might."

The next morning, when Val stepped outside Salomon's Crib with his staff in hand, ready to journey to Undertown, his mouth fell open when he found Synne sitting cross-legged on his doorstep. Dressed in the thin black robe and silver belt of the majitsu, she carried nothing other than the small backpack she had worn on the journey to find Tobar. She had also adopted a silver patch over her left eye, to cover up the missing orb the demon lord Asmodeus had plucked from its socket.

While Val had gotten used to having the young warrior-mage by his side, and missed her steady presence, the queen had rewarded her role in the mission by reinstating Synne into the Academy of Majitsu.

"It's great to see you," he said, as she rose to greet him with a forearm clasp. "You could have knocked, you know. I've been awake for hours."

She gave a small smile and didn't respond.

"Are you going to kill me with suspense?" he asked. "Shouldn't you be off learning how to punch through walls and fight whole regiments of Black Sash gypsies?"

"I've been given a leave of absence," she said, in a neutral voice. "By the Congregation."

"A leave of absence? For what?"

"To accompany you to Undertown, and wherever else the search for the Coffer might take you."

The news both surprised and pleased him. Having Synne by his side would be a huge advantage. Still, as Adaira had intimated, it made him wonder if Lord Alistair didn't think the journey was more dangerous than he had let on.

Moreover, while she looked pleased to see him, Synne did not seem excited by the arrangement. "Is there something I'm missing?" he asked.

"Missing?"

"Will this set you back at the Academy?"

"On the contrary. I was promised that if we recover the Coffer, I would be exempt from further studies and afforded the rank of full majitsu."

Seeing the set of her jaw made him withhold his praise. "You don't like that for some reason, do you?"

"I'd prefer not to discuss it."

"We're friends, Synne."

After a moment, she said, "There is tradition, and a certain honor, in the successful completion of my studies. It would be untoward to jump rank in that manner. There are also awards to be won at the Academy, commendations to be earned, that can never be regained."

He folded his arms and considered the problem. "Can you not re-enter the Academy after the Coffer is recovered?"

"Once assigned to a wizard," she said, "I am not free to make my own decisions."

"You've been officially assigned?" he said, both humbled and slightly amazed. "To me?"

She gave a single, firm nod.

"Are you happy about that? Is there another mage with whom you'd rather work?"

"No," she said fiercely. "It would be an honor to serve with you."

"It's an honor for me as well," he said, waving at Gus as the carriage approached from the other end of Magazine Street. "And I suppose that once we recover the Coffer, the first order I'll give you is to return to the Academy and graduate with as many medals as you can fit in your backpack."

With a broad grin she quickly smothered, the first true smile he thought he had ever seen from her, she sprang to her feet and gripped his forearm so tight in gratitude that he yelped.

"Full of surprises, ye are," Gus said to Val, after Synne climbed into the carriage behind him. The driver looked nervous at the presence of the shaven-headed warrior-mage.

Val introduced the two. "Synne and I have been through a lot together," he said to the bearded driver. "She's with me, now."

"Good enough for me," Gus said, touching his fingers to the tip of his black top hat.

"What do you know about Undertown?" he asked his driver as the horses clacked down Trafalgar, a wide cobblestone street lined with contiguous homes and shops.

"Not much, laddie. Never been there meself, though I know blokes who have." He gave a low chuckle. "Plenty o' people where I'm from end up in the gutter, but no one talks about what lies below it."

"Is it dangerous?"

Gus turned to display a tobacco-stained grin. "For the pair of ye? I'd worry more about the health of whatever's down there. Still, they say there's Undertown and then there's *Undertown*. One's a well-trod grid of old sewers and underground byways, but the other's deeper even than that. Home to some things that, well, aren't fit for the light o' day. I don't know how much truth is in the rumors, but as always, laddie, never trust the situation, no matter how powerful ye've become. Ye just watch your back, now and forever, ye hear?"

"That's what I'm for," Synne said, with a cold smile intended to put Val at ease, but which instead gave him a shiver.

Dressed in a cowled gray cloak that shadowed his face and concealed his tail, Sinias Slegin met Val and Synne at the entrance to his yurt. The serpentus carried a wooden staff with a hooked blade on one end and a spiked iron bauble on the other.

From where does his race hail? What are their customs?

With a sinuous wave of his hand, the snake man turned and led them through the Goblin Market. The other residents scurried out of the way as soon as they glimpsed the hooked staff and gray cloak. On the far side of the market, Sinias approached a corner of the wall that abutted the river, shielded by the backs of a line of canvas stalls. After glancing to each side, he depressed one of the blocks on the stone wall, made a motion like turning a wheel, and a door-size section of the wall hinged open, exposing an iron ladder set inside a narrow hole. A *plop* of water sounded from below, and the stench of sewer drifted to Val's nostrils.

The snake man rasped a chuckle. "The entrance of kings."

"Easy access from the Goblin Market to Undertown?"

"Yesss."

"Works for me," Val muttered, hoping the forest-green cloak and boots he had purchased at the magick shop, ensorcelled with a waterproof spell, would hold up. On Earth, the heart of New Orleans was a saucer-shaped depression surrounded by water, much of the land below sea level. Besides the levees, the city relied on an enormous underground sewer system to pump waste and rainwater into Lake Pontchartrain. He didn't even want to think about what sort of nasty conditions and vile creatures existed in his hometown's sewers.

And that was back home.

After shaking out a jade glow rod, the serpentus led the way into the claustrophobic shaft. He had a bowlegged, rolling gate that reminded Val of a sailor stepping off a ship after a long voyage.

The ladder deposited them in a tunnel with a low, rounded ceiling and smooth rock walls. Val's boots sank ankle-deep into a thick layer of muck and sewage. The stench was almost unbearable.

His flat nostrils wrinkling in revulsion, Sinias retrieved a stoppered glass vial from inside his robe. He opened the bottle and held it up to his nose, breathing deeply. "Better," he said, after a prolonged sigh.

The serpentus offered the vial to Val, and he gratefully accepted. It smelled like a stronger version of the perfumed oils in Sinias's yurt, and left him feeling light-headed. Not too much, he cautioned himself.

With a grimace, Synne refused the vial and cast a wary eye around the sewer tunnel. Val assumed a geomancer had played a part in forming the slate-gray walls, since no seams were visible in the twenty-foot cone of light emanating from the glow rod. Water dripped from condensation formed by the humid air, creating a steady rhythm as they followed behind Sinias.

"How far to our destination?" Synne asked.

"An hour walk if there isss no flooding."

"It hasn't rained for days," Val said. "But what do we do if the tunnel's flood-ed?"

"There are other waysss. Other passsagesss."

"More sewer tunnels?"

Sinias flicked his forked tongue. "No, mage. Deeper."

"Who made them?"

"They were here before the tunnelsss were built, before even the native tribesss. Older racesss or culturesss, perhapsss."

"Are they dangerous?"

"Of courssse. All of Undertown hasss peril. But the common routesss are a known commodity. They are not caussse for concern."

"What are the chances we're alone down here?" Val asked.

Sinias turned, his shrewd yellow eyes flickering inside the hood. "The upper level belongsss to Zagath."

"Meaning he's watching us already?"

The serpentus didn't answer.

*   *   *

At periodic access points, water and sewage would spill into the tunnel from smaller pipes above. When they reached their first intersection, the rush of running water could be heard down the intersecting tunnel. Probably a channel to the river. Straight ahead, the tunnel continued sloping downhill. Of principal interest was the jagged hole in the floor, and the bolt attached to a heavy metal chain that led into it.

Sinias stood beside the hole and lowered the glow stick to peer inside. Twenty feet down lay another tunnel. Unlike the polished sewer walls above, the constricted passage looked formed of crumbly rock and hardened sand. The first layer of bedrock, Val assumed.

"Why doesn't it flood down there?"

"Who sssaysss it doesss not?"

"Good point," Val muttered. He didn't like the thought of a whole other level or levels down there, hiding who knew what. He could tell by her frown that Synne didn't, either.

"Ssstrange," Sinias said.

"The hole?"

Another supple weaving of the snake man's head. "The sssilence. We should have ssseen othersss by now, passsing beneath the city. Travelersss. Begarsss. Thievesss."

Not having a choice, they continued walking until, just past another intersection, the disgusting sewage was piled even deeper. They pressed forward until it reached their knees, and Val exchanged a concerned look with Synne.

"I don't like it," she said. "I cannot move as well in this environment."

"Thisss isss the way. We mussst not deviate."

"Is there not another—"

A large plop interrupted her. Val jumped, startled by a small round ball the size of a grapefruit that had fallen into the water at their feet. At the same time Synne yelled "Stunsphere!" he looked up to see a ragtag band of men and women in patchwork cloaks and black sashes surging down the passage, wielding an assortment of weapons.

Ready to blow them back with a Wind Push or a Fireball, Val was not too worried until the ball at their feet exploded, causing a stinging paralysis to spread down his limbs and arrest his movements. The last thing he saw before he fell was a trio of black-sash gypsy sorceresses hovering above the muck, their eyes gleaming like feral witches, linked arm-in-arm as they drifted closer.

13

A hazy afternoon sky welcomed the crowd gathered in the tiled public square fronting the Fifth Protectorate Capitol Building. An imposing monolith of bronze and limestone, two sphinxes flanked the onyx marble steps that led to the entrance of the rectangular façade. The building housed both the High Courts and the Legislative Assembly, integral components of New Victoria's Government District.

Facing the crowd, Lord Alistair stood atop a dais of hardened spirit that hovered high above the steps. Though the pair of sphinxes at his side appeared to be made of stone and almost never moved, they were very much alive, relics of an age whose history was lost to the ravages of time. As with the pair of colossi guarding the Sanctum, no one knew the exact origin of the mysterious wardens. They required no sustenance, were charged with defending their respective structures, and responded only to commands read from a set of scrolls in the possession of the Keeper, an elder mage charged with overseeing the ancient guardians of the Wizard District.

On the steps below Lord Alistair was a roster of Important People: the entire Conclave; a smattering of other elder mages and politically important wizards from the Congregation; Kjeld Anarsson looming above a contingent of honor guard majitsu; Yasir Ookar and a handful of lesser generals from the Protectorate Army; Alaina Whitehall—Governess of the Protectorate—accompanied by a row of high-ranking officials from the Assembly; and a personal steward of Queen Victoria, sent to bear witness to the public marshaling of the Protectorate into a state of war, as well as the ascension of Lord Alistair to Chancellor of the Protectorate.

The title was meant to be a temporary one, giving the person designated by the War Council autocratic authority in time of war. Yet if that war never ceased, and if the War Council happened to be fully under the control of the

Chancellor, then Lord Alistair saw no reason why that particular state of affairs should not extend for a very long time.

Perhaps, he thought with a thin smile, it would extend indefinitely.

The presence of the Queen's chief steward—a minor functionary—was a sign of Londyn's disapproval. Yet Queen Victoria and her Mage Council had chosen not to intervene, as Lord Alistair had gambled. The old empire was an ocean away, and both sides knew that should the Protectorate choose to secede, its wizards and defenses and artifacts were at least the equal of Londyn. No, better to preserve the integrity of the Realm, keep the peace, and let the upstart Protectorate flex its adolescent muscle.

Speaking of youth, as the pomp and circumstance began, Lord Alistair cast his gaze on the youngest mage allowed a presence on the steps of the capitol building: Melina of the Randor Clan, a talented gypsy sorceress who had become one of Lord Alistair's favorite devotees—and one who had an important role to play in the day's proceedings. Melina was a strikingly beautiful young woman with full lips, lavender eyes, and long blond hair that was quite unusual for the Roma clans. The irony of her presence was quite delicious to Lord Alistair, as she was the daughter of Selina, the sylvamancer Alistair had blackmailed into becoming a spy for the Congregation.

Alaina Whitehall led the initial proceedings, her voice magically amplified as she read from the Protectorate Bylaws and announced the State of War. At her side was Yasir Ookar, his gloved hands clasped in front of him, reptilian eyes flat and steady. At the conclusion of the speech from the Governess, the crowd gave a thunderous ovation, causing Lord Alistair to preen with satisfaction. *Nothing unites a populace,* he thought, *like a declaration of war.*

Let the Age of Expansion begin.

After the applause died, Lord Alistair gave a rousing speech outlining his goals as Chancellor.

"I pledge to stamp out the vulgar Revolution that seeks to impede the progress of our great civilization. The gypsies would have us return to the darkness of the Age of Sorrow and destroy our way of life. Does anyone long for a future in which our cities' water is not clean, bandits control the byways, and we are ruled by ignorance and superstition? I promise you I will punish, to the fullest extent of the law, those who assassinate our civic leaders, waylay innocent travelers visiting friends and family, cause law-abiding citizens to live in fear. Nor will I stop with the Revolution. I also pledge to secure the Ninth, as well as our Southern and Northern borders. This will allow us to fully exploit our natural resources, bringing prosperity to all and quelling the ambitions of our warmongering neighbors."

As shouts of approval shook the plaza and fists pumped in the air, Alistair promised to take an even firmer stance on prosecuting Oath avoiders and re-distribute their land to proper citizens, including vast tracts of mineral-rich property in the Ninth. This caused the greatest uproar of all.

When he finished speaking, Kalyn Tern waited on the top row of steps to present the Chief Thaumaturge with a scepter traditionally given to rulers of the Realm during times of war. The head of the scepter, azantite and bronze interwoven in an intricate floral pattern, was symbolic of the union between mage and common-born. It was sent from Londyn as a gift from the Queen, yet Lord Alistair saw it as another slight: a reminder that he served the inter-ests of the common born as well as wizards.

The Queen would do well to remember how the common born once sought to eradicate the mage-born from the face of Urfe.

The applause increased as the Chief Thaumaturge dissolved the spirit dais and drifted down to meet Kalyn Tern, dressed in a regal silver gown set off in a lovely manner by the onyx steps. Many had urged Lord Alistair to consider marrying Kalyn, a powerful aeromancer who hailed from the most prominent family in the First Protectorate. He had to admit the political capital from such a union would be potent. Yet despite his ambition, he could never re-marry. Along with his daughter, Lord Alistair cherished the memory of his deceased wife above all things.

When Lord Alistair touched down on the step, authority and wisdom etched into the proud lines of his face, his arm outstretched to receive the scepter, a tight circle of fire erupted around him, shooting skyward at least fifty feet. Kalyn Tern, along with everyone else near the Chief Thaumaturge, gasped and drew back, staring in horror at the blazing inferno that had just enveloped their ruler. All of the mages could be seen waving their hands and whispering words of power, but the fire raged unabated, impervious to their efforts.

The roar of approval from the crowd turned to wails and shrieks of dismay.

An elder aquamancer raised her hands, blowing off a sewer grate as she summoned the nearest source of water. As the water gushed to the surface, someone pointed at the wall of fire, where a glowing outline of the Chief Thaumaturge had emerged in the center of the inferno, bluish-white in color. Lord Alistair was no longer holding the scepter. As he held his arms straight out, palms up, the glow around him spread to consume the wall of fire. Once the blaze had been subsumed by the bluish-white hue of his magic, he cleaved the wall in two, shrinking each half into a sphere which he held in the palm of each hand. Then he started to expand, growing in size until he reached twenty feet in height, looming above the crowd.

His voice boomed into the ear of every single person congregated in the public square. "Behold the treachery of the Oath Avoiders."

"He lives!" someone in the crowd shouted, followed by "Destroy the Revolution!"

"Kill the gypsies!"

"All hail Lord Alistair! Preserve the Realm!"

Lord Alistair still had his arms extended. "They would strike at the very heart of our republic! Yet another cowardly act of terror!"

The members of the partisan crowd—virulent Protectorate nationalists carefully selected by the Congregation—had whipped themselves into a frenzy, stomping their feet and shouting for the heads of those involved in the assassination attempt. In the back of the public square, a commotion was taking place. A circle had formed around two majitsu, each dragging a black-sash gypsy through the crowd. The eyes of the gypsies, a man and a woman, were looking wildly about as they tried in vain to free themselves.

With a snarl, Kjeld Anarsson rushed into the crowd, causing it to part like a hot knife through butter. He flew low above the ground to meet the two majitsu, exchanged words with them, and grasped the two prisoners by the necks, holding one in each of his enormous hands. The crowd cheered as he flew them above the crowd, returning to the steps of the capitol building.

When the woman captive saw Melina, she gave a strangled cry. "You *traitor*! You betrayed us!"

Melina's mouth twisted into a smirk. A few feet away, Kjeld shouted up at

Lord Alistair, who made sure the words of the Head Don were amplified to the assembled crowd.

"Milord, here are your attempted assassins. We caught them fleeing the scene after trying to witness the result of their murderous intentions."

"You're sure of this?" Lord Alistair asked. Earlier in the day, after learning of the planned assassination attempt and capturing those responsible, he and Kjeld had prepared a dialogue for the masses.

Melina pointed at them. "These are the two. I overheard their plans myself."

"Thank you, Melina. And you as well, Don Anarsson. What do you recommend?"

Before Kjeld could respond, someone in the crowd shouted, "Kill them both! Kill the gypsies!"

"Death to traitors!" another shouted, and the rest of the crowd picked up the chant.

"'Tis true, milord," Kjeld said, "that treason is a crime punishable by death."

"Indeed it is. Yet I alone cannot command such a fate. Since the Firesphere of the traitors has consumed the Scepter of Peace, in the spirit of cooperation, why not let the will of the people decide?" After a long and dramatic pause, he continued, "Who here would have these traitors stand trial for attempted murder?"

Except for the cries of the two black sash gypsies still struggling in Kjeld's iron grip, not a single voice could be heard in the ensuing silence.

"And those in favor of execution?"

The roar of approval seemed to shake the foundation of the stately Fifth Protectorate Capital Building.

"Then let it be so," Lord Alistair's giant form boomed above the crowd.

Under Protectorate law, a death sentence—even for black-sash revolutionaries caught in the act of attempting to assassinate the Chief Thaumaturge of the Congregation—was only available after trial in a court of law. The prisoners knew this, the assembled mages and political leaders knew this, the crowd knew this—and that was exactly the point.

In the new state of affairs, the new Chancellor was the arbiter of life and death.

After Lord Alistair's proclamation, Kjeld flung his two adult prisoners through the air as if they weighed as much as a bag of beans. Alistair turned his palms towards them, and the baubles of white-blue light he had captured shot towards the prisoners, hitting them in midair and expanding until they were large enough to encompass the prisoners, high enough for all to see.

"They wished for someone to burn," Lord Alistair said calmly, "and so it shall be."

As he swept a hand towards the prisoners, the bluish-white globes started to rotate and change color, adopting a pinkish hue that deepened to orange, and then bright red. The crowd cheered as the captives writhed in agony, screaming for release while the Firespheres roasted them alive.

-14-

The harsh reality of the situation flashed through Will's mind as the lasso tightened around his waist and arms.

Trapped on a precipitous staircase halfway down a gigantic nilometer in the middle of the most dangerous city of Urfe.

A group of armed attackers sliding down on ropes.

Dalen slumped on the ground, felled by whatever drug the dart had contained, a smart decision to take out their wizard at the start of battle.

Mateo and Yasmina were also ensnared around the waist, their arms pinned to their sides. As Yasmina bucked to free herself, Mateo grasped onto the rope with the fingers of his chain mail glove and ripped it away.

Though he couldn't lift his arms, Will was able to flex his wrists. As the first assailant drew near, hanging ten feet above his head, he gripped Zariduke and, with a twist of his powerful forearms, began to saw his bonds with the blade. Will's attacker, a middle-age woman dressed all in black leather, dropped the remaining distance and landed in front of him. She dangled a small cudgel in one hand and an odd weapon in the other, a cane with a blade sticking out of the end.

Will felt his bonds give just in time to block a swing of the cudgel with Zariduke. Three more strikes came in rapid succession, forcing him down the staircase and into a defensive posture. He parried furiously and, as soon as he saw an opening, thrust forward. Quick as a snake, moving in a strange fighting pattern he didn't recognize, the woman cracked him with the cudgel on his sword arm, causing him to drop his blade. He turned to find that three more attackers, dressed in a variety of clothing, had dropped down behind him. Mateo was also surrounded, Dalen lay unconscious on the ground, and Yasmina was still caught by a lasso, her wrist gripped tight by a man twice her size.

As Will scrambled to pick up Zariduke, the cudgel cracked on the ground beside him, cutting him off.

"Skara Brae!" he shouted. "We're looking for Skara Brae!"

The woman's blade stopped a millimeter from his eye. A tan headscarf swept her blond hair off her face, and he noticed a set of brass knuckles on her left hand, daggers in her boots, and a hatchet attached to a chain looped around her belt.

"Who," she said, pressing the bladed cane against the tip of his closed eyelid, "wants to know where to find her?"

Sweat trickled down Will's back as he spoke. "I'm Will Blackwood, leader of this expedition."

"And where are ye from?"

"Freetown. It's on the Barrier-"

"I know where it is," she snapped. "If it's Skara Brae yer after, then yer looking right at her. Who sent ye to kill me?"

"What? We're not here to kill you."

The blade pricked tighter against his eyeball. He tried to lean back but she pressed the cudgel into his back with her other hand, keeping him still. With a snarl, she said, "Speak yer piece and convince me otherwise. Ye have to the count of three before I take yer eye and drop ye into the kraken's mouth."

Having no desire to lose his eye or to find out whether the kraken was metaphorical or real, Will told her the truth. "I led a different expedition that found the Coffer of Devla in a pyramid in the Mayan Kingdom, in the tomb of the sorcerer king. We took it back to Freetown, but a thief stole it and carried it here. To Praha."

Her eyes bored deeper into his. "How do ye know that?"

"It was a gateway bauble. A mage traced it back. We thought you might know something about it. If you do, we'll pay good coin for the knowledge. Is my friend going to live?" he said, glancing at Dalen's prone form.

"Good coin, is it?" She started to laugh, causing a ripple of chuckles to spread through the crowd. She slid the cane into a long sheath on her back, gripped the front of his shirt, and brought their faces close. She was a few inches taller than he and smelled of olives and shoe leather. Though a handsome woman, scars crisscrossed her exposed skin, including an ugly welt on her left cheek that resembled a cigarette burn. "Saying I believe ye about the Coffer, which I don't, then the last time I hired out me services, half a decade ago, was for two thousand gold pieces."

The council had reached deep into the treasuries of Freetown and given Will two hundred gold pieces for the journey, in anticipation of just such a scenario. He swallowed. "We don't have that much."

"Then my people will escort ye to the surface, and if I catch ye near me Nilometer again without an invite, I'll kill ye meself."

"Wait!" Will said. He hadn't wanted to mention Mala's name, in case there was bad blood between the two. Mala had never told him how she knew Skara, and seeing how volatile the woman was, mentioning the wrong name might get him killed. But if he didn't figure something out, the quest would be over before it began.

"Mala sent us to you. Mala of Clan Kalev."

Skara's eyes narrowed, a mixture of wariness and grudging respect. "Mala, is it? Why would she send ye here?"

"She said you knew the city better than anyone. That you might be able to help."

"She got the first part right. As for the second, she knows as well as anyone there are two things alone I care about. One is finding new breeds to mount on me walls, and the other is, well, don't ye worry yer short little head about that."

Little? Dalen stirred beside him, until one of Skara's cohort shot another dart into his back. They weren't taking any chances with a mage.

"Unless ye can lead me to the lair of an intelligent beast I've never encountered, which would surprise the boots right off me, then we 'ave nothing to talk about." She smacked his thigh with the cudgel. "Ye have two minutes to reach the surface."

"What's the other thing you care about?" Will said. Some of her people had started climbing back up the ropes they had descended.

Skara ignored him and gripped one of the ropes.

"Hey!" he shouted in desperation, ignoring the looks of warning both Mateo and Yasmina were giving him. Still the black-clad woman didn't pause, and he roared her name again.

Finally Skara turned, a dagger in her hand and fire in her eyes. "Ye have a death wish, Will Blackwood? One minute and counting."

He planted his feet and thrust his jaw forward. "You said there were two things you care about. What's the second?"

Skara gave an ugly laugh and leapt onto the rope, almost as agile as Mala. "I need a way through a magic door that can't be opened, not even by wizards. So you see, ye've just wasted precious more seconds, and I'm beginning to doubt whether ye'll make it out of the Nilo alive. When I said two minutes, ye should know, it's not *us* ye need to worry about."

At that moment, something caused the water below to displace and lap against the sides of the Nilometer. Skara's crew jumped onto their ropes and scurried upwards, hand over hand.

"The kraken feeds at night," Skara finished, flashing an evil grin before she resumed her climb.

Mateo scooped up Dalen across his shoulders, as Yasmina grabbed her staff and urged Will up the stairs. He shook her off and called out to Skara again as he retrieved his sword. "I can help you!"

"Eh?"

"I can open that door."

The water below grew more and more agitated, swirling and lapping against the walls of the Nilometer. He had to make Skara believe him without tipping his hand completely, since he was at her mercy and didn't trust her not to kill him and take the sword.

"And how, pray tell, might ye accomplish such a feat?"

"You'll have to trust me. But I swear it on my life."

"Why would I trust ye? Especially when yer life is about to be forfeit."

"Because I'm standing here to gain your help when I could be running up those stairs." The others were tugging at him, but he looked up the rope, staring right at Skara. "And because whatever lies behind that door you want opened so badly, I promise you'll never get another chance like this."

The spark of interest in her eyes turned to curiosity, and then a quiet desperation harbored over long years. As the water exploded beneath them, revealing a huge, mottled gray body that turned Will's stomach to jelly, Skara slid down the rope and vaulted off, somersaulted in midair, and landed on her feet at Will's side.

"Quick!" she said. "After me!"

Skara dashed up the steps, hurrying past the first alcove that appeared and darting into the second. Will, Yasmina, and Mateo, still carrying Dalen on his shoulders, raced after her as something vast and scaly shot out of the water and surged upwards, almost filling the Nilometer with its bulk.

As Will entered the alcove, terrified they wouldn't make it in time, Skara stopped him with a hand on his chest. "If yer lying to me, I'll slit yer throat meself."

"I'm not."

With a grim nod, she removed her hand, threw something on the ground that exploded in a puff of dense smoke, then dashed into a curved, narrow stone tunnel looming beyond the alcove. It was too dark to see the end of it.

As Will and the others raced down the tunnel, a fat and slimy tentacle with suckered appendages shot through the cloud of smoke, probing, grasping, reaching. It fell just short, slapping wetly against the stone behind Yasmina and then retracting into the depths of the Nilometer.

Though Skara slowed to a walk, another tentacle smacked against the ground, causing Will to jump.

"It's just probing," Skara said. "It can't reach us here."

"That's the kraken?" Will asked.

"Aye."

"How do you know for sure it can't reach us?"

An amber glow from somewhere ahead lit the smooth stone passage as they walked. "Because I've measured the length of its tentacles, down to the millimeter, and marked them on the corridors. I also know the circumference of its maw, how many pounds of bite force it can produce, and a host of other statistics that will make ye lose sleep over how close ye just came to death."

"I don't need any help with that," Will muttered. "Is it really a kraken?"

"It is *a* kraken. One of many in its phyla. I claim discovery over this particular species myself," she said proudly, "which I've termed Skaraticus Lesopteridus. It surfaces at regular intervals in the Nilometer to feed on the waste flushed out by the sewer system. As well as anything else unfortunate to cross its path."

"Ick," Yasmina said.

When the tunnel spilled into a larger room, Will took a step inside and then stumbled back, thrusting his shield forward in defense. A spindly, ten-foot tall humanoid with the long ropy neck and sword-like beak of a heron stared back at him, poised to run him through. Lurching backwards caused him to collide with Mateo. As Will scrambled to right himself, he looked to his left and saw another monster, this one even taller than the first, with the body of a woman but the head of an owl. White wings curled into its back, and it clutched a sword with a bronze hilt.

He heard Skara laughing at the same time his eyes adjusted to the brighter light and he realized neither of the two monsters was alive. Though extremely realistic, and suspended from the wall by slender wires that made them appear to be looming threateningly above them, he noticed the waxen nature of their skin and the glassy rigidity of their stares.

A chorus of raucous laughter filled the room. After exchanging a sheepish glance with Mateo and Yasmina, Will crossed his arms as he took in the enormous, alabaster amphitheater in which they stood. Circular and at least fifty feet high, filled with a tiered seating arrangement reminiscent of the Roman Colosseum, the underground stadium must once have been able to host thousands of spectators. Twelve-foot high walls encircled the bottom level, and throughout the amphitheater hung a startling variety of monsters. All of them were different, each more terrifying than the last, and Will gaped at the exhibition. It was like looking at a life-size display of a Monster Manual.

"Ye like me taxidermy?" Skara asked as she gazed reverently around the room. Some of her followers had climbed down to stand guard around her, and some lounged in the seats above to play dice games.

Will turned in a slow circle, mesmerized. "It's unbelievable. You've . . . *killed* all of these?"

"Me or me disciples." She took off her headscarf and shook out her long blond hair. Both of her eyes were as white as eggshells, including the irises. "Though I've killed more than half meself."

"Why?" Will said.

The question seemed to amuse her. "Why does a painter paint? A minstrel sing? I like monsters, Will Blackwood. I like to find them and I like to kill them."

Yasmina's eyes flashed. "I see very few monsters here. Only creatures whose habitats were disturbed." She waved a hand around the room. "And these abominations . . . how would you feel if a family of trolls had taken someone you love and mounted them on a wall? You think you know these creatures, you study and hunt them, but you know *nothing* of them."

The sound of conversation and dice games ceased. Skara's hand moved to the hatchet at her side. In the corner of his eye, Will saw bowstrings stretched taut and pointed at the party. Skara took a step towards Yasmina, a dangerous glint in her eye.

Will stepped between them. "She's a wilder," he said. "She has . . . different priorities."

He glared at Yasmina, praying she had the good sense to leave it alone.

"A *wilder* should know better than to enter my own abode and insult me. Ye must be new to yer profession," she said to Yasmina, then pointed at the white-winged humanoid. "Or do ye not agree that the owlshrike has a heart of pure evil, and loves in particular to dine on the flesh of young children?"

Yasmina swallowed her first retort. "I'm not saying you shouldn't defend yourself at times."

"What would you say to the parents of those children? Would you describe your respect for the habitat of the owlshrike, and explain how you once stayed my hand?"

"That's just one example."

"How about the terrengar?" Skara said, turning to point at a six-legged reptile with huge incisors and curved tusks on either side of its snout. "A species also fond of human flesh. Or the Carpathian banderfiend, which skins and tortures its prey for weeks in its lair before the kill?"

Her jaw tight, Yasmina turned away and said nothing.

Mateo had eased Dalen to the ground. The illusionist stirred on occasion as if dreaming, but he was still out cold. "When will he recover?" Mateo asked.

"When I deem it so," Skara said coldly. "We do not look kindly on mages around here. Now," she said, turning to Will. "I'm waiting for ye to tell me how ye can diffuse magic?"

"Sure. But there's some information we need from you as well."

Skara chuckled. "Yer not in much of a position to bargain."

"I am if you want that door opened. We're not asking for much. We just want to know who stole the Coffer, and where he is now. The thief came from Praha, so we thought you might know something about it. That's all. A fair exchange, I think, for what you propose."

The adventuress tapped her thumb against the hilt of her hatchet, then fingered the chain to which it was connected. "I've no idea who stole the Coffer. There are legions of thieves in Praha." As Will's hopes fell, she continued, "But not many are able to afford a gateway bauble. Not only that, a gateway, as you know, leaves a magical residue." She gave a mysterious smile and said, "It appears our interests may be more aligned than we realized."

After her enigmatic proclamation, Skara waved for Will and the others to follow before disappearing down one of the corridors exiting the amphitheater. Mateo picked up Dalen again, and Skara's bodyguards led Will and the others through a twisting series of passages into a modest-size chamber with a hodge-podge of velvet furniture that looked stolen from a Victorian mansion. There was a stocked liquor cabinet, lit torches hanging from sconces just below the ceiling, and mortarless stone walls covered in maps, charts, and anatomical drawings of monsters. Will saw a list of exotic creatures on one wall and wondered if it was a wish list of targets, or some kind of danger metric.

The adventuress flopped onto a sofa as one of the bodyguards took a bottle of amber-colored liquid out of the cabinet. "Drink with me," she said, after pouring herself a glass.

Will looked at the others and shrugged. He accepted her offer and watched her pour a glass from the same bottle, in case it was poisoned. Though Will wasn't too worried about that. At that moment, deep inside the mazelike corridors of the Nilometer and surrounded by allies, Skara held all the cards.

The smooth but fiery drink tasted like a vanilla-coated bourbon, the best he had ever had. "It's delicious."

"Granth came from Praha," she said, "though the original recipe has been lost. Some of the finest granth in the world," she raised her glass, "was recovered from abandoned Nephili manors."

"So you believe in the legend?" Will asked.

The corners of Skara's lips upturned, and she peered into her glass as if enjoying a private joke. "It's impossible to trace magic from within Praha," she said after a moment. "The energies are too scrambled. Which is why, of course, your thief departed from here."

"Who might have sent him?" Mateo asked. "A wealthy guildmaster? A warlord?"

"There are no guilds within the city. And the residents are too factious to unite under any warlord." She smirked and swept a hand down her chest. "As far as I know, I command the largest number of loyal subjects in all of Praha." She buried her nose in her glass, inhaling deeply. "I've no idea who stole the Coffer, or how to go about finding them. But I know someone who might."

Will exchanged a glance with the others.

"I said it's impossible to track magic within Praha—and that is true. At least for a *human* mage. A being exists who might be able to unravel the skein of magic surrounding the use of a gateway bauble. The problem is, ye'll never receive an audience."

"Who?"

"A being who might be insane, or who might as easily decide to extinguish your life for having the impudence to gaze upon the visage of such an exalted creature. I speak, of course, of the former rulers of this city. Those who created this otherworldly architecture, invented these marvelous feats of engineering, and who might hail from some other world or dimension. I speak," she said softly, almost reverently, "of the Nephili."

Will swallowed as Skara's eyes sparked with an intense light. "I *want* one, Will Blackwood. I want one for my collection."

"You're mad," he whispered.

As the light in her eyes dimmed, she eased back in her sofa. "Mad I may be. But driven and capable I am, too. Imagine the treasures, the wonders we would find in the palace of the Nephili! No one has breached the walls above the Agora since the Plague." She rose and wagged a finger as she paced. "Yet

I, Will Blackwood, have spent my life studying the byways of Praha. I have all the maps and know all the legends. I've ferreted out the records of the ancients, and all those explorers who came before me. Yet even if we navigate the Agora and face the guardians of the Wailing Wall, the only way to lure such a being into our midst—if the legends are true—is to present it with a wafer."

The Nephili love vanilla wafers?

Will opted not to express that particular thought in front of Skara.

Skara returned to her seat, her long blond hair swishing against her leather shirt. "There is a door to a storehouse in a forgotten part of the city—forgotten to all but me. I've seen it with my own eyes, yet its magic is impenetrable to every device I've tried. This includes enlisting the aid of a powerful geomancer who lost his life trying to dismantle the door."

"The wafers are in this storehouse?"

"Yes."

"What are they?"

"They're called the Wafers of Sephyr. It's said they arrived with the Nephili when they came down from the heavens, and are the source of their eternal youth. It's said they desire them above all else."

Will steepled his fingers on his forehead. "So you want us to open this door and go with you to the Old City—which no one has entered since the plague—in the hope that one of these beings, who may or may not exist, can tell us who stole the Coffer?" His eyes flicked to Yasmina and Mateo. Both looked slightly ill.

"If the Nephili lives and knows the answer to your question, it will tell you. I'll stake my reputation on it. It will tell you in exchange for the wafer."

"I don't understand—why do you think one of the Nephili still exists? Wouldn't they be, like, thousands of years old? I know there's a rumor about it, but rumors exist about a lot of things that aren't real."

Though Urfe has proven a lot of those rumors true.

She spread her hands. "A fair question. There are signs. The presence of the Skinwalkers—the guardians on the Wailing Wall—are one. They're said to draw their life force from the Nephili, and I've heard them with my own ears. The density of magical energy that persists in the Old City is another. Perhaps it's residue from the plague, perhaps not. And what if they do not still exist?

We will still have gained access to untold treasures in the palace, and what have we lost? Maybe ye'll find something else to aid yer quest."

"How about our lives?"

She opened a palm. "Ye risked yer life to come to Praha and seek my counsel. Would ye stop now?"

He didn't need to look in his cousin's eyes to know the answer to that question. They all knew how much was at stake. If they failed to find the thief, they had no other way of finding the Coffer.

And Praha was their only lead.

Another thought came to mind. What if this Nephili being knew something about Val, and could be persuaded to help him? What if he could help the Revolution *and* send them all home?

"Why would the Nephili help?" Mateo cut in. "Why not just take the wafer and kill us?

"Because I can only imagine that any surviving Nephili are too old and plague-ravaged to leave. Else why stay in the Old City for so long?"

Will thought there was more to Skara's story than she was letting on. Even with her obsession for tracking monsters, she seemed too calculating to embark on a mission without knowing more about it.

He couldn't force her to reveal her hand. Not yet. And she was right: for the moment, their interests were aligned.

"One step at a time," he told Skara. "That's all we can promise."

The wintry eyes of the adventuress shone bright in the torchlight. "A most excellent choice."

15

The Tower of Elarion had no windows, and only one entrance: a wooden door at the base of the structure. No one, the Brewer had said, knew the true purpose of the freestanding tower. It could have been a lighthouse, except there was no light. Or maybe a campanile, except there was no bell. The best guess was that a wizard made the tower long ago, perhaps an adventurous mage who had flown across the oceans long before the Age of Sorrows, and established a home on the Barrier Coast.

With the Brewer snoring softly beside him, Caleb lay on his back and stared at the tower, backlit by a panoply of stars glowing like exploded quicksilver. In the morning, with his energy restored, he would walk through that simple wooden door from which it was said no one ever returned.

Who was this person inhabiting his body, he wondered, who would attempt something so foolish? Something that *wizards* had failed to do?

Did he have a hardened inner core that defined who he was, a Caleb in the back of the cave, or was his true self a mutable thing, changing with time and circumstance on a continual basis, second by second, pinwheeling in response to fortune and tragedy and all the little variables in between, as ephemeral as a summer breeze?

Because the Caleb that he and everyone else knew was someone very different from the man who was about to walk through that door, and most probably never come back out. That Caleb's credo was *chill and let life flow*. That Caleb would never have left Freetown in the first place. That Caleb's idea of an adventure was trying out a new bar in the Faubourg-Marigny. That Caleb had traveled to Costa Rica with his inheritance, yes, but only because he could make the money last longer in another country, live in flip-flops and board shorts, and smoke in peace on the beach.

True, that Caleb was the brother who cared about living life to the fullest, and was always trying new things. Will was a man of causes, Val a power broker and successful attorney. Caleb relished sampling different cuisines and craft beer and women from around the globe.

But those sensual experiences he had always craved most definitely did not include putting oneself in danger, ever, for any reason. That Caleb was a pacifist, a preserver of life and limb, a coward.

As well as an atheist.

"What is this," he whispered as he stared at the bone-white tower in the darkness, wrapped in a cloak he had pulled out of a Coffer with eerie parallels to the Ark of the Covenant, and which the Roma worshipped as a religious artifact of immense power.

He barked a laugh, which caused the Brewer to stir. *Why me, of all people? A nonbeliever and a case study in lack of ambition and wasted youth? Has there ever been a greater irony?*

The thing was, he really didn't care about any of that. The reasons behind these miracles did not interest him. What he cared about was the awesome power that had surged through his bones and leapt out of the Coffer to incinerate an elder mage. He cared about picking up that diamond-headed mace he had glimpsed in his vision and carrying it into battle.

He cared about anything, anything at all, that got him closer to ending the life of the man who had given the order to murder Caleb's wife and adopted child.

Content in his thoughts at last, he closed his eyes and fell into a deep, dreamless sleep.

The aroma of fresh coffee eased Caleb awake the next morning. He opened his eyes to sunlight spilling over the hills, then turned to see a watery horizon with a dreamy hue that reminded him of the orange sherbet push-ups he had loved as a boy.

He and the Brewer ate and drank in silence, sipping coffee as the chill of the night receded and the haze burned off the tops of the peaks. Sunlight glistened on the jellyfish and shells that had washed ashore. It was a beautiful day.

"We're really doing this?" the Brewer asked.

"*We're* not doing anything. It was just me in the dream. So I'm going in alone."

"Maybe together we can change what . . . what I saw." He opened his mouth and then slowly closed it, having seen Caleb's dark expression and the futility of further argument. "I'll forage while you're inside," he said quietly. "Try to replenish our supplies."

"Good idea." Caleb drained the last of his coffee and stared at the empty cup.

"Take my sword," the Brewer said, holding out the blade.

"Whatever's inside, I don't think that's going to help. How could anything be alive? Plus, I don't know how to use it. I'd probably just stab myself."

The older man let out a deep breath and clasped Caleb on the shoulder. "Then be careful, kid, as if I need to say it. And listen—I didn't make this trip for nothing, okay? Give me something to sing about. I need some new material."

"Rock and roll all night, man."

The Brewer grinned and thrust his left hand skyward, holding up his pinky, thumb and index finger, the only appropriate response to Caleb's words.

With a smile, Caleb started walking across the beach. The Tower of Elarion rose above him, tall and silent, the white stone pockmarked with age. Thoughts of his past flashed through his mind as he plodded through the sand. The taste of a cold beer with his friends after his shift ended, his parents surprising him with a birthday party at Chuck E Cheese, going to the first crawfish boil of the season with his brothers, young and carefree.

He also remembered a parade of gorgeous women that had never satisfied him, not even Yasmina, and the feeling of guilt from knowing he was using them in some way. He didn't deserve the peace and happiness he had felt when he bent down on one knee to propose to Marguerite on a rock in the middle of a forest stream as sunlight streamed through the trees. Yet that wasn't how life worked. The undeserving got what they wanted all the time—and the very best of us, like Marguerite and Luca, were often taken too early.

Before he knew it, his hand was on the iron pull ring set into the door.

It wasn't even locked.

*   *   *

Inside the tower, the first thing Caleb saw was a spiral staircase, the same dull white color as the stone on the outside, twisting into the darkness above. In fact, the staircase was the *only* thing he saw, so wide it took up almost the entire bottom level. The rest of the tower was empty as far as he could tell, and appeared pretty much exactly as he imagined a thousand-plus year old abandoned tower would appear: silent and creepy, full of cobwebs and dusty stone and gloomy upper reaches.

When he turned back to close the door, it had disappeared, leaving Caleb facing a blank stone wall.

Of course the door disappeared.

Despite the lack of an opening, a lambency of daylight remained, though he couldn't tell why. As his eyes adjusted to the dim light and he gazed upward, searching for answers, he realized the staircase was a tightening spiral that wound almost to a point at the top. It was weird, and he had no idea what that meant. Will would know. He always knew about those weighty sorts of things. Val would be pounding on the stone where the door used to be, trying to get out, while Will would be expounding about some geeky trivia concerning the mythological significance of a tapering spiral staircase and what sort of monster was about to come bounding down it.

The disappearing door and the thought of his brothers, that window into *old Caleb*, caused a little shiver of fear to sweep through him. He took a deep breath, looked down at the first step, and saw an inscription carved into the stone.

KNOW THYSELF

The cryptic words caused him to chuckle. *Know myself. That's always been the problem—I know exactly who I am.*

After staring down at the step for another moment, he tilted his head back and howled, in defiance of the perverse creator of the tower and the mystery of the two worlds and the cursed shadow land of human consciousness.

And then he started to climb.

On the third step, the tower disappeared.

A vision of heaven replaced it. Instead of a deserted stone building, Caleb found himself lounging on his back in a sea of cushions and plush Persian carpet, surrounded by dozens of the most beautiful women he had ever seen, women of all colors and cultures, half-naked, their delicate waists wrapped in colored silks. A white stone ceiling rose high overhead. Looking around, he couldn't even see the end of the room. He saw colonnades and shallow basins, tables laden with exotic foods, pleasure devices of all sorts, women and more women. The aroma of the place almost caused him to swoon, and he realized with a start that he recognized the scent. When Caleb was eleven years old, an eighth grader had sat next to him on the bus and kissed him. He had never forgotten the illicit taste of her lipstick, the warmth of her tongue, and the intoxicating smell of her, a rosewater and cinnamon blend that was probably a cheap perfume but which had metastasized in his memory as the most sensual of all fragrances.

All the women in the room smelled exactly like her.

The first one to approach, a dark-haired temptress with sky-blue eyes, slid into his arms and nuzzled his neck. With a shudder, Caleb eased her away and stood, blinking to see if the room would disappear, pinching his own skin and the cushions and one of the women, who giggled at his touch. He even picked up a fig, shrugged off the myths about eating food in strange locations, and bit into it.

Everything felt real.

He started wading through the harem, confronted at every turn by willing women. The food became more delicious with every step, all of his favorites. Some of the women were playing board games, or poker, or drinking whiskey and reading horror novels. There was even a tennis court and a section with a movie screen and video games. He had to blink a few times at that one.

In short, the room had everything on offer that Caleb Gideon Blackwood found desirable in life. And it didn't appear to be a trick.

He kept walking, just to see how far it would go, but it never seemed to end. Pleasure after pleasure after pleasure. Yet how was he supposed to leave?

Or was this it? Was the Tower of Elarion a gateway to heaven, Caleb's heaven, and the rest of his days would be whiled away in this pleasure palace? There were definitely worse fates. No wonder no one had ever left.

He engaged some of the women in conversation. They spoke English and were happy to talk. He thought they would be robots, but they were knowl-edgeable about both worlds, and could talk about almost anything, from base-ball and television shows to the price of milk in New Victoria. They talked about everything, that was, except where they actually were or the nature of the tower. When asked a direct question about these items, they would stroke his arm and coyly change the topic.

Sometime later—he had lost track of time and felt dizzy from the effort of resisting temptation—he froze when he saw a spiral staircase in the distance. *The* staircase. He started walking towards it, brushing away the women that approached, and then started running. The tower itself had not reappeared, but it was the same spiral staircase, no doubt about it, ascending through the ceiling of the harem.

Just before Caleb arrived, a woman stepped into his path who caused him to slow and then stop, catching his breath as he stared in disbelief at the slate-col-ored eyes and pixie-cropped auburn hair, the playful lips, the waifish face tilted up at him with a knowing expression.

It was not Marguerite—he knew that. But it was as close as a woman could possibly resemble her. She was even dressed in her favorite attire, leather breeches and a high-necked riding shirt.

"Stay with me, Caleb," she said, in that low and throaty voice that haunted his dreams.

The spiral staircase flickered. Caleb's eyes whisked over to it, and he noticed that it looked less substantial.

"We've got some catching up to do," she said. "And we 'ave all the time in the world 'ere."

So that *was how it is.*

This is the game.

At first he thought it would be easy to pull away and leave this doppelgang-er behind, this cosmic joke of a consolation prize. The staircase grew even less substantial, and he started to walk towards it, but she caught him by the arm and stroked the back of his hand in exactly the same way Marguerite would.

"I know I'm not her," she said. "I'm not trying to fool ye. But I can be exact-ly like her, for all eternity."

Caleb swallowed. She gently took his chin, turned him to face her, and kissed him. She tasted and smelled just like her. He sank into the kiss, unable to resist, almost weeping when their lips parted. She held him close and stroked his cheek, lost in his eyes.

In the corner of his vision, the staircase grew even less substantial.

He forced himself to stare at it, and then at the woman in front of him. Did he need revenge that much? So badly that he would forsake the opportunity of a lifetime?

"It's not a trick," she whispered. "Ye can stay here with me. Forever."

The longer he looked at this woman, the less he could tell the difference between her and Marguerite. Almost as if she was perfecting the memory from his own thoughts. "What's your name?" he asked.

"Ye know it already," she said. "Say it for me, love."

The staircase had almost disappeared. Somehow, he sensed it wasn't coming back. That this was his one chance at leaving this place and returning to Urfe.

"Say it," she said.

Despite his better judgment, he mouthed the name. *Her* name. She smiled in response.

"That's a good lad," she said. "It isn't just me, ye know." She swept a hand around the room. "This can all be yers. I'll be 'ere, too, whenever ye want, but ye know I'm not the jealous type."

Her words caused Caleb to blink as if coming out of a dream. Whether unintentional or the final test, it was the one false step she had made. Marguerite *was* the jealous type. Caleb didn't want a thousand other women, tens of thousands, and he didn't want this imitation, this *thing*, standing in front of him. She might have been genetically identical to Marguerite, crafted by some arch mage just to lure him here for some reason—but it wasn't her.

She pulled him in for another kiss. He took her face in his hands, closed his eyes and thought of the real Marguerite, and kissed her, long and passionately, one final time.

It was one of the hardest things he had ever done, but as tears blurred his eyes, he turned and sprinted for the staircase, leaping onto it just as it began to disappear.

The world swirled around him.

*   *   *

A long, disembodied moan was the first thing Caleb heard. It sounded like a prolonged groan from one of the horror movies he had loved so much back on Earth. A voice full of pathos, desperate and angry, hungry for warm-bodied souls.

After shuddering away the touch of the quasi-Marguerite, he blinked to re-orient himself and realized he was standing in a large, open-walled dungeon. Skeletons hung from manacles along the perimeter of the rough stone walls. The air felt damp, and puddles of water pooled in the corners.

He closed his eyes and willed away the image of Marguerite. *Simple. I just have to resist temptation to get through this. A few months ago, I never would have made it out of that harem. But whoever made this tower doesn't know me as well as they think they do. In the past, boredom was my greatest fear. But once I found Marguerite, all I wanted to do was grow old and gray with her—and only her.*

My greatest fear was losing her.

So what else do I have to fear?

When Caleb opened his eyes, he noticed two corridors leading out of the room, and a wooden door that looked exactly like the one at the base of the tower. He went over to it. Locked. He pulled on the iron pull ring as hard as he could, then kicked and shook the door. It wouldn't budge.

There was one difference with this door. It had a keyhole, while the real door to the tower did not.

This was the exit, he could feel it.

And the test was to find the key.

A long moan sounded down one of the corridors. Caleb turned one way and then the other, trying to discern the source.

Okay. So this scenario isn't as tempting.

He chose the passage on the right. Except for the intermittent light of a glow orb, set high on the wall in clawed sconces, the corridor was similar to the room in which he had landed. Damp stone walls splattered with spooky dark stains. A musty odor laced with the putrid stench of the dead.

The hallway spilled into an intersection with decaying corpses hanging on the walls. Caleb shuddered and continued forward as another prolonged groan came from one of the side corridors. This time he broke into a run.

The dungeon was a maze of moldy corridors, hanging skeletons, darkened pits he had to jump over, and torture devices. At last he found a set of spiral stairs, dull white like the tower, and he shivered with relief as he dashed up them. They led through a trapdoor and into a room that resembled the parlor of a Victorian aristocrat in an old horror movie. The lair of a vampire.

Except Caleb knew this room, and its previous owner was far more dangerous than a simple bloodsucking nosferatu. He recognized the stone floor and the spiral staircase, made of iron and much narrower than the one inside the tower, in the middle of the room. He noticed the same standing candelabra and medieval tapestries and black-upholstered furniture from his previous visit, the familiar vertical shaft leading to the higher levels.

A wizard's shaft.

Somehow, Caleb was inside Zedock's stronghold.

Things were different, though. Aged. The tapestries were more faded, the upholstery in tatters. Where the air had once smelled faintly of cloves, an odor Caleb would never forget, it now smelled of formaldehyde and decay, as if someone had tried to mask the stench of death.

Zedock's Obelisk, a hundred years in the future? What the hell?

As Caleb tried to decide what to do, he heard voices from the levels above. Two he recognized. One was the majitsu Will had killed, though it sounded softer, the voice of an older man.

The other voice was Zedock, and it had barely aged.

As he glimpsed the high-collared shirt of the necromancer floating down the wizard chute, Caleb scurried out of their line of sight. *Those men are dead. This can't be.*

He debated climbing back into the dungeon, then discarded the idea. The trapdoor was right below the staircase. They would see him for sure.

Left with little choice, he fled into the spooky swamp surrounding the obelisk, heaving a sigh of relief when he didn't find the other majitsu standing guard by the door. Caleb breathed in the cloying humid air and examined the outside of the stronghold. It looked much as it had before, a huge black obelisk surrounded by water the color of chocolate. Stands of bald cypress ringed the lake, ghostly tendrils of Spanish moss dipping into the water.

And, same as before, a pirogue was secured to a small dock at the end of a long wooden walkway leading away from the obelisk.

The same pirogue he and his brothers had used.

Except it was still here.

The dock was missing some boards, and looked much more weathered. Caleb rushed to the end of it, hoping to untie the boat in time to escape.

Halfway down the walkway, the door to the obelisk opened, forcing Caleb to slip quietly off the platform and into the algae and scum coating the top of the water. The swamp full of zombified humans and animals that Zedock kept for his experiments. A morass of horrors that haunted Caleb's dreams to this day.

He couldn't risk confronting Zedock, who would snuff Caleb's life as easily as pinching an ant. Even if this was a test, Caleb had the sense it was all very real, and his choices were life or death. Choking back his disgust, he held his breath and sank beneath the fetid water, hiding among the cypress knees that rose like the stumps of severed limbs from the bottom.

He saw them at once, the pale and bloated bodies floating by in various stages of decomposition, the grasping fingers hungry for life. The lidless eyes of a kethropi, the gills of its cheeks flapping in a useless rhythm. Though nothing attacked, they brushed against him, the spongy touch of their skin causing him to recoil.

Caleb gritted his teeth and swam towards the rear of the obelisk, hoping to put distance between him and Zedock. To take his mind off the loathsome swamp, he thought about what he had seen. Either this was some kind of trick, or he was in an alternate universe or dimension, one where Zedock was still alive. As the import of that thought hit him, he looked down and found himself staring right at Val.

Caleb thrashed in the water, unable to believe his eyes. Biting off the bile surging into his throat, he grasped the thing by the arm and pulled it towards him.

No recognition in the eyes.

But it was Val.

Caleb had been hoping the appearance of Zedock meant that he and his brothers had never been here, but now he had to face the awful truth of the alternative scenario.

They had been here—and failed in their attempt to kill him.

Which meant he and Will were dead, too.

Somehow, Caleb knew what he was supposed to do. Where the last test had been one of temptation, this was facing his worst fear, the most gruesome thing imaginable, and fighting through it.

Caleb had a good guess as to where the key was, and after surfacing for a quick unseen breath, he dove down to find it.

Resurfacing whenever he needed air, it took him long, torturous minutes of swimming through the muck and zombified bodies, his soul shrinking at his task, until he found what he was looking for just off the pier, right near the base of the obelisk.

He found himself: a twin Caleb, bloated and decomposing on the bottom of the lake. Lying right next to Will. With a shudder, Caleb swam closer and saw a leather cord hanging from his own neck, with the end of it in his mouth.

He gagged as he plunged his hand inside the putrefying mouth of the corpse, fished around as the teeth fell off, and lifted the key out. None of it made any sense. Why did he have the key? Who had put it there? Had he put it there himself, in this other world? If so, why?

Trying not to look into his or Will's eyes, Caleb rose to the surface and huddled in the trees behind the obelisk until nightfall, wet and miserable. The mosquitos eviscerated him, but he didn't dare cry out. When the moon rose, he crept back to the main door, eased it open, and peered inside.

No one.

Using the stealthy movements Marguerite had taught him, Caleb crept to the trap door and opened it. A voice shouted from above. The majitsu's voice. With a surge of adrenaline, Caleb threw himself through the opening and bounded down the staircase. Gasping, he sprinted back into the dungeon, hoping he remembered the way.

He heard the majitsu enter the corridor behind him, followed by Zedock calling out for Caleb to stop. He pressed forward, his skin on fire from mosquito bites, running harder than he ever had. He rounded a corner of the dungeon and saw the wooden door. His hand shook as he inserted the key, and someone grabbed his shoulder. Trying not to scream, he turned the key in the lock as he felt the strength of magic-hardened fingers digging into him, tearing him away from the door.

The key clicked once, and the dungeon disappeared.

16

Fleeing the dhampyr, Mala rode hard through the Shoehorn Pass, pushing her mount to the limits. The brown rocks and succulent-strewn landscape of the Karaxi Desert awaited on the other side, and further on into that forbidding wasteland, through a narrow crevasse in the sandstone, lay the anomaly that was the Crater of the Snow Moon.

The pass was aptly named, a tongue of sun-blasted scrubland that ran as flat as a shoehorn between two isolated, snow-capped ranges. At times, the sheer walls of the pass rose thousands of feet into the air, making Mala feel like a mouse trapped inside a gargantuan hallway, pursued by the demon behind her.

She wasn't worried about Nagiro catching her during the day, while on foot. He was no match for equine legs. What she feared was the descent of the sun and Nagiro's transformation, the howl of the hyena wolf piercing the silence of the desert as it loped through the night.

The pass broke and the desert widened. As the sun began its descent, the valley transformed into an uneven, golden-brown terrain pockmarked with cacti, aloe, and creosote bush. Mala checked her spyglass. No sign of animal life in any direction, though she knew bands of native Cahuilla people were nearby, hidden in the nooks and crannies of the desert. She did not think the peaceful tribe would accost her, but one never knew.

Yet another worry.

The temperature, as hot as mage-fire just a few short hours ago, had plunged. Mala shivered and took a fur-lined cloak out of her Pouch of Possession. The horse had slowed to a fast trot, exhausted. She stopped to water him, every passing second feeling like the edge of a blade sliding along her skin. She estimated she would reach the Crater of the Snow Moon just before nightfall. Once the moon rose, the dhampyr would find her, and she had to gain the shaman's help before then.

The landscape changed again, the wide-open vistas of the desert contracting into a region of beige soil and standing stones carved by erosion into mythic sentinels of another age. Mala did not consider herself a spiritual person, but the solemn presence of the stones and the blush of dying light left her in awe at the grandeur of creation. The distinctive flora of the region, trees with stunted, upward-facing branches that ended in tufts of spiky green needles, reminded her of the shaman who lived nearby, working his charms with arms raised to the heavens.

The body of the horse started to droop. His labored breathing had become worrisome. Unlike humans, horses did not know when to stop, and Mala knew her mount was approaching a danger zone. After consulting her map and her compass for the hundredth time, she exhaled in relief when she spotted the distinctive white peaks jutting upward like swords, marking the border of the Crater of the Snow Moon.

A barrier of jagged rock that ran for miles and averaged a hundred feet in height, the massif was thought by most travelers to be impenetrable, formed by a geological hiccup. That still didn't explain the bizarre whiteness of the rocks, and Mala thought the entire formation, including the ancient crater hidden from view on the other side, had been created by some long ago battle waged with magic.

She also knew the rock face, almost sheer and running all the way around the crater, was not impenetrable. On her first and only visit to consult the shaman, led by a Cahuilla guide in exchange for five sacks of Mayan chocolate, she had carefully marked the entrance on her map. As before, she rode alongside the barrier rocks until she spotted the distinctive three points, thrusting upward like a trident.

What mattered now was finding the shaman—and convincing him to help in time.

If he could at all.

Mala debated leaving the limping horse behind. Fearing the dhampyr would just slaughter it, she dismounted and led him around the lip of sandstone that obscured the narrow passage through the rock. The walls of the pass hid the declining sun from view, and Mala pressed forward, eager to escape the claustrophobic passage.

She emerged to find a giant depression surrounded by a wall of serrated rock. Except for an oasis of rainwater in the center, the crater looked similar to tales of the surface of the moon from spiritmancer legend, pockmarked and barren. The only difference was the brilliant white color of the sand, as if whatever force had bleached the rock had whitened the crater as well. During the day, she remembered the reflection of the sun on the sand being so blinding white that she could barely see.

Though desolate, the Crater of the Snow Moon was a very beautiful place.

"Hello!" Mala shouted, cupping her hands and listening to her own echo. "Shaman!"

Did the medicine man know what manner of creature pursued her? Was he choosing to stay hidden and leave Mala to her fate?

She led the horse to the pool of water in the center of the crater, scanning the rapidly darkening rock face.

Nothing. No one.

Though not born to magic, even she could sense the tellurian energies humming in the air. The Cahuilla revered the crater and thought the ancient lake that must have once resided there was the birthplace of all life on Urfe. Every generation, they sent their greatest shaman to live alone inside the sacred space, guiding the tribes and probing the secrets of the crater until he died and the next shaman took his place.

What if the tradition had been interrupted? What if this was a time of transition, or one of Lord Alistair's death squads had found the entrance and slaughtered the shaman?

The sun disappeared behind the rock wall, casting the land into shadow. The time of the dhampyr. Mala's breath came in frosty exhalations as she continued calling out for the spiritual leader, trying to devise another plan if he failed to appear.

Sensing a presence behind her, she whirled, fear pumping through her veins as she faced the pool of water shimmering in the moonlight. Expecting to find the arrogant face of Nagiro, she instead saw an old brown woman wearing a headdress made of dirty feathers. A sheepskin shawl wrapped her legs and torso but left her arms bare, exposing sagging triceps and lined skin that reminded Mala of a discarded coconut shell.

Mala's hand slid to her sash. This was not the shaman she had seen years ago. Had there been a changing of the guard, or had he assumed a new form?

"I need your help," Mala said. "I am—"

"Mala of Clan Kalev."

Mala started. She noticed the woman was standing atop the water with no support. "How do you know me? Have we met before?"

"Not in this body."

Mala nodded. "This, then, is your true form?"

"You misunderstand me. I am now the keeper of the energies. I have become one with the past keepers."

"I don't understand."

"Nor would I expect you to." The old woman's voice had a hollow ring, as if she was not quite there. A golden-brown mist had begun to form at her feet, the color of the desert, creeping slowly off the water. "It is against the laws of my people to come uninvited to this place."

Mala had never been one to ask permission, or forgiveness. "I don't seek to cause disrespect, but I need your help. Urgently. I've nowhere else to turn. I'm being followed by—"

"I know what you've brought here. The nature of your enemy."

"Then you understand why—"

"Silence!"

Mala realized the shaman had somehow expanded in size, a head taller than she had been. Mala blinked, wondering if the mist and the darkness and her exhaustion were causing her to hallucinate. She had been looking right at the woman.

"The appearance of the unclean thing has already desecrated our lands. You have broken our laws. You have no voice here."

Mala folded her arms, waiting for her to continue. The shaman, she knew, had appeared to her for a reason.

The old woman lifted her hands, and the mist and water rose with her, as if attached to her body. As the water fell away, she held her palms to the sky and waited. Moments later, the cawing of a raven pierced the night, and a pair of the large black birds approached, swooping in to perch atop her hands. The medicine woman whispered to them before sending them away with a flick of her wrist.

"You have two choices," she said. "Stay as the slave of my tribe for a year, working the wells and using your talents to hunt for game. That is the price of trespass. To leave the tribe before the year is finished is to bring death upon your head."

"And the second?"

The shaman swept a hand in front of her, dispersing water and mist, seeming to part the darkness itself. "Those who seek my wisdom must pay a price. Those who seek my aid, a greater one. I will treat you as a seeker, if you so desire."

The cold dry air stung Mala's throat when she breathed. The sickle of moon hung upside down above the rocks, its silver sheen a reflection of the icy temperature. "I don't think wisdom can help me, unless you can tell me how to escape the dhampyr. Or perhaps you could kill him for me?"

"I do not take life without reason, and the dhampyr has done me no harm."

A sudden thought hit Mala. "What if he follows me here? Won't he be trespassing, as well?"

"He will surely follow your scent through the entrance. You are the one who led him here. He would not have found me on his own. You bear this responsibility."

In the distance, a jarring howl caused the hair on Mala's arms to rise. The maddened bray of the hyena wolf.

Mala took a step towards the shaman, causing the water of the pool to rise defensively in the air. "How can you help? What is the price?" Mala waved a hand in disgust. "Tell me, then."

"The price is a memory."

Mala blinked. "What?"

"My people are disappearing. Fading into the mists of time, as people do. My power is one of the few things that sustain them. To do what I do, to be what I am, requires great cost. I give of myself and get nothing in return. I cannot increase of my own volition, so the only way to compensate, to give more of myself . . . is to take from someone else."

Mala shifted her stance. She did not understand what the old woman was talking about. "What is it you want from me?"

"I will take the memory of a loved one. Someone near and dear. The love can be familial, romantic, or friendly, but it must run deep. I will know once I begin if it is enough, and I warn you, do not choose lightly. I will take another if it fails. And the erasure of both will be complete."

Mala could tell by the old woman's face that she meant every word she had spoken. And Mala believed she had the power.

What would it mean, to lose a memory? Would she even notice it was gone?

Whether she experienced a sense of loss or not, something would be ripped from her, and she despised that. She hated to feel helpless, hated it more than anything else. Yet if she did not pay this price and fulfill this transaction, she feared she would no longer have a life to live.

"Your decision?" the shaman asked.

Another howl, closer than before.

Who should she choose? Her parents were not an option. Those memories were sacrosanct. She thought of Allira and Marguerite, her closest friends, and wondered if those ties were strong enough. She couldn't take the chance of losing a memory for no reason.

Two men entered her mind: Gunnar and Will Blackwood. Men for whom she bore complicated feelings. She already had to choose between them once, ending in the death of her longtime companion and lover. She had detested that choice, and hated the shaman for making her choose again. Perhaps one day, if she lived through this, Mala would return and find a way to force her to return the memory, if such a thing was possible.

Yes, one of the two men. That should suffice. She took a deep breath and tried to soak as many memories inside her as she could, trying to keep something hidden deep down, in places no shaman could reach. Maybe she could circumvent whatever terrible magic would strip her mind. "If I do this, what will I receive in return?"

"I shall imbue you with the power of the cougar. You will be able to flee the dhampyr, running day and night."

"How long will it last?"

"A week, perhaps."

"Your proposal is flight, in exchange for a memory? Nothing more?"

"You prefer to be a slave, then?"

Mala snarled and paced beside the pool. Running day and night at the pace of a cougar for a week—if the magic lasted that long—should get her to New Victoria. There she would have options. In a worst case scenario, she had enough funds stowed away to purchase a magical escape.

"What will you do when he comes?" Mala asked.

"That depends on him."

"If you don't help him, he might decide to kill you."

"I will not offer the dhampyr the same advantage as you, if that is your concern. I will offer him nothing at all."

Mala gave a curt nod. She had been thinking exactly that. "Then you will flee?"

"Do you not understand? I will not flee the crater. I cannot."

"Why?"

"Because, child, I *am* the crater."

Closing her eyes, Mala hugged her arms and said, "Will I keep my possessions?"

"Yes."

The adventuress sighed, opened her eyes, and gave a single, grim nod. "Then so be it."

Without warning, the shaman drew her hands together in a clap, startling Mala. The old woman grew in height again, rising to half again her original size. The mist came with her, and the water boiled, and the darkness coalesced in her hands. She began to sing in her native language, a powerful lament that echoed through the canyon, rising in volume until it filled Mala's head with a tornado of sound, impossibly loud, power thrumming through the words, causing her to feel weak and dizzy. She stumbled as tendrils of mist shot forth from the pool and enwrapped her, propping her up as they swirled faster and faster around her, stuffing her mouth and nose with the smell of moisture on stone, a silent erosion that lasted for millennia, a thousand millennia, the power of the ground and the sky and the world itself. Mala moaned, bowing under the weight of the mist as it seeped into her head, probing.

She screamed.

The singing continued, louder than before.

Mala fell to the ground and pressed her hands against her temples, trying to lessen the pressure. "Make it stop!" she screamed. "It's killing me!" She felt something rip, as if a hand had scooped something out of her skull, and she screamed again, and again, and again.

Then it was over. Mala bent double and dry-heaved, unsure exactly what had been done and unable to pinpoint where it hurt. She just knew something terrible had happened. Something irrevocable.

Footsteps crunched on the ground behind her, from the crevasse through which she had entered. With a shudder, she pushed to her feet and pointed a shaky finger at the shaman. "Fulfill your promise, woman."

The shaman swept her arms into the air, agitating the water until it roiled like a boiling kettle. This time she chanted instead of sung, corralling the mist and the darkness, though when the mist came this time it felt different, protective. Moments later, just as a dark form emerged from the entrance to the crater, Mala sensed a transformation. She looked down and saw that instead of arms, she had four legs and paws, and a sleek golden coat, and muscles that rippled along her skin. It was odd; she did not feel as if she had become a cougar, as the lycamancers could do. Rather, she felt as if she were *inside* one. As if whatever forces the shaman commanded had congealed into animal form, a token protector that would shield Mala from harm.

With a powerful push, she leapt into the air, clearing ten feet or more at a time as she bounded toward the nearest rock wall. As her claws found purchase in cracks a human or a wolf would never be able to use, carrying her quickly up and over the barrier, she heard a long scream in the background. She couldn't tell if it was male or female or animal, the dhampyr or the shaman. Unsure what type of power the shaman wielded, or how the old woman would fare against Nagiro, the Mala-cougar didn't wait to find out.

17

As Val struggled to rise off his back in the sewer muck, paralyzed by the blast of the stunsphere, the trio of sorceresses clothed in filthy patchwork dresses drifted steadily towards him and his companions. Linked arm-in-arm, the two women on the outside waved a hand as they prepared a spell. A regiment of black sash fighters with weapons raised rushed down the corridor behind them.

Val seemed to have taken the worst hit, and it wasn't just physical. The blast had addled his brain and he couldn't find the concentration to use his magic. Not only that, he was slipping further into the muck by the second and was in danger of suffocating.

Beside him, whirling in one direction and then the other, trying to decide what to do, Synne seemed unaffected by the blast, and must have hardened her skin in time. The movements of their serpentus guide, ranging twenty feet ahead looked torpid, and he was trying to shake off the effects. Val had the fleeting thought that Sinias might have some innate magic resistance.

"You must fight the effects!" Synne shouted at Val, as their enemies drew closer. "Or we are all doomed!"

"I can't even think straight!"

"Push through! Use your magic!" She whipped towards the serpentus. "Did you betray us, snake man?"

Sinias hissed as he raised his hooked staff. "Attack, you fool."

Though Val tried to overcome the shockwave with sheer force of will, he couldn't seem to do it. It took all of his energy to stay awake and keep his head out of the muck. As the battle raged around him, he fought the enervating effects of the stunsphere with every ounce of mental concentration he could muster.

With a worried glance at the sorceresses, Synne decided to engage the fighters, who had drawn closest and could easily cut him down. Without a word, the warrior-mage leapt into the fray, surging above the muck to kick the lead fighter in the chest so hard he flew backward and slammed into two other men. Before anyone else could react, Synne spun and backhanded another man and then delivered a back heel to the temple of a cutlass-wielding woman, dropping her unconscious.

The entire group of fighters hesitated, cowed by the fury of the majitsu, and then a cone of gray light struck Synne in the back, sending her sprawling. Val saw Sinias raise his staff and swipe at the floating trio of women with the spiked iron bauble. As one, they cackled and drifted backwards as another streak of grimy light struck Sinias in the chest. It caused him to grunt and stumble, but he pressed forward, almost catching one of the women in the leg with a reverse swipe, this time from the hooked end of the staff.

Definitely some magic resistance.

The snake man withdrew a stoppered yellow bottle from an inside pocket of his cloak, twisted off the top with his pincers, and flung it at the three sorceresses. The bottle released a cloud of noxious green smoke that expanded to obscure them from view.

Synne managed to stumble to her feet and block the first few blows that came at her. Still, she was surrounded, and one dagger thrust got through, nicking her in the side. A majitsu's shield was not all-powerful, Val knew. Not even close. They could stop blows from the weapons they could see, but could not protect themselves on all sides or from spells.

He had to help his companions. *Fight it, Val. Burn the effects away.* Screaming to raise his adrenaline, he managed to rise higher out of the muck, though it felt as if he were pushing through tar. He felt his magic stirring but could not seem to force it to the surface.

Synne somersaulted up and away from her attackers, landing on her heels halfway up a wall and then vaulting behind the entire group. She spun to attack with the graceful leaping movement of the majitsu, delivering a flying knee to the unfortunate fighter at the rear. The burly gypsy's head snapped back as blood sprayed from his nose. Synne became a whirling dervish of pain, punching and kicking and spinning, silver belt bobbing, delivering knockout blow after knockout blow. Only four fighters remained to stand against her when another cone of gray light smashed into her, this one thicker and uglier than before, crushing her against a wall not far from Val. As she slumped, he saw the light in her eyes flicker and then dim.

"Synne!" he roared, though he still couldn't get up. A quick glance revealed that Sinias was backing towards Val, retreating before an onslaught of magical gray arrows. One of the sorceresses broke away and tried to soar through the noxious cloud he had emitted, but a fit of coughing doubled her over and forced her back. Still, they could bombard him from afar with impunity.

Val forced his gaze inward and snarled, reaching for the wellspring of magic, feeling it slip away whenever he tried to corral it.

The remaining fighters rushed Synne. When she tried to move, another blast of magic slammed her back into the wall. This time she collapsed. Another hit like that, Val knew, and she might not get back up.

The sight of the gypsy fighters closing on his wounded friend enraged Val so much that a flood of adrenaline caused a surge of power to burst out of him, wild and uncontrollable, sending a shock through his nerve endings and burning away the effects of the stunsphere. It also blew a hole in the sewer at his feet. Too surprised to take flight, he managed to arrest his fall at the last moment, just before he hit the patch of solid ground fifty feet below him. In the corner of his eye, barely visible in the dim light, he saw Sinias and Synne in free-fall, accompanied by a pile of muck. Val scurried aside as Synne scooped up the serpentus at the last moment and landed hard on her feet. Majitsu had a way of falling softly from great heights, and though reeling from the blasts of gray magic, she was still upright, staggering as if drunk.

A pair of arrows *thunked* into the ground at Val's feet, followed by a green bolt of power. A flood of dirty light lit the darkness, illuminating the three sorceresses and the remaining fighters hovering at the edge of the hole Val had just created.

"Move!" he shouted, throwing himself away from the opening as another volley of arrows hit the ground. They had landed in a tunnel far beneath the original, a much narrower passage with rough rock walls.

After they scurried out of range, Sinias produced a silver glow orb the size of a golf ball, illuminating an intersection ahead. Val worked to fight the remaining effects of the stunsphere as he turned awkwardly back towards the hole. No one had come after them.

Synne staggered against a wall, holding her side. "Can you fight?"

Val gave a grim shake of his head. "Doubtful. I still feel fuzzy, and that blast took a lot out of me. You?"

She had to stifle a moan of pain. "Yes, though I fear I may be compromised." The admission seemed to pain her more than her wounds.

"Broken ribs?" he asked, eying her hand against her side.

"Aye."

"The black sssash is no longer caussse for concern," Sinias said. "They will not follow."

"Why not?" Val said. "They know we're injured."

"Becausssse you created a tunnel out of sssolid rock, yesss? And becausssse we have landed in the lower levelsss. They will fear the inhabitantsss here more than they asssspire to relieve usss of our posssesssssionsss."

Almost as soon as Sinias spoke the words, the sound of booted feet carried down the tunnel, and they heard voices conversing in the thick brogue of the black sash gypsies.

"Unusssual," Sinias said.

"I guess they're not that terrified," Val said.

Synne stifled a gasp as she stood up straight. "These are assassins, not opportunistic thieves. We must flee."

Val turned to follow Sinias into the intersection, hesitated for a moment, then turned to the left.

"Hurry. Before they sssee the light."

"Link arms," Val commanded. After they obeyed, taking a cue from the sorceresses, he whisked them down the curving passage with his magic, skimming above the ground much faster and quieter than they could have run. The miniature glow orb cast light in a ten-foot radius. With Sinias pointing out the route choices in silence, Val flew for long minutes, using up more precious energy to secure their escape. Carrying other people while flying was very draining, even if just skimming the ground.

The serpentus finally signaled for Val to rest, and he set the others down to take a closer look at their surroundings. The sinuous nature of the lower tunnels made it look as if some giant worm had burrowed them out of rock and dirt, and some later culture had come along and crusted its slime with a layer of rough-cut stones.

"Which way?" Synne asked, peering behind them.

Sinias swayed his neck on a diagonal. "We shall try to the left."

Val crossed his arms. "Try? Are you lost?"

"I wasss lossst the moment we fell into the floor."

"Then where have you been leading us?"

The serpentus turned his nose to the air, sniffing. "Fleeing our enemy, and following the ssscent of water. Zagath's men ussse the underground riverss and lakesss for transssport. There will be accesss pointsss nearby. To the upper level."

"I hope you're right," Val asked. "Have you ever been to this section before?"

Again the diagonal head roll, which Val knew signified denial or confusion. *Great*, he muttered to himself. They were lost with no food, couldn't retrace their steps for fear of running into the black sash raiding party, and if the rumors were to be believed, even more dangerous creatures inhabited the lower levels of Undertown.

The air had cooled and smelled of minerals. Sinias drew his cloak tighter as he started down the passage. Due to Synne's condition, Val insisted on bringing up the rear, and the majitsu struggled on gamely in front of him. He knew from experience how painful even a single fractured rib was, and he suspected she had multiple.

If he was stronger, he could have tried the Spirit Map spell that had saved him beneath Leonidus's dungeon, and which he had been practicing. He had managed to cast the spell inside Salomon's Crib, illuminating the layout in his mind, but had been unsuccessful with larger areas.

"Why do you think they followed us?" Val asked as they walked. The lingering paralysis from the stunsphere was finally dissipating.

"It isss ssstrange," Sinias agreed. He turned his shrewd yellow gaze on Val. "Perhapsss they ssseek you."

"Me?"

"A wizard alone and vulnerable. If captured or killed, another dagger in the ssside of the Congregation. Perhapsss there isss a mole in the Congregation."

Synne turned her head sharply at the comment.

"Only a few people know I'm down here," Val said. "All of whom I trust."

Except Lord Alistair, who has no reason to send me on a mission and then kill me.

"What about your people?" Val said suddenly. "The other serpentus in your tent?"

The forked tongue darted quickly out of thin lips, angered. "Sssagana would never betray me."

Never say never, Val thought, though he kept the sentiment to himself.

After they passed through the next intersection, the new tunnel doubled in size and had a three-foot wide trench running through the middle. The canal was half-filled with murky water, and strange sigils were carved into the exposed stones at the top of the channel.

He wondered if these were some type of ancient sewers, buried deep beneath the earth. If so, who had made them? Where did they start and where did they end? Or were they perhaps some sort of waterway for ancient vessels?

When asked, Sinias rolled his neck and declared he had never seen this portion of Undertown, or anything like these canals. As they debated whether to press forward or try doubling back, they heard footsteps echoing in the distance. Left with no choice, they continued down the new tunnel, emerging into a rounded chamber with rock walls inset with human bones. Another canal flowed through the cross-corridor. Oddly, all four branches of the canal ended—or began—at a waist-high circle of stone in the middle of the chamber. They cautiously approached the barrier, peered over it, and realized it was the lip of a large pit that dropped into blackness.

"Did you hear that?" Val asked.

"Yesss."

As Synne rested a hand on the lip of the basin, her other hand clenched at her side, Val heard it again: a faint susurration that grew in volume as they listened. The sound of something, perhaps a large body, swishing against stone.

Val turned to his left. "I think it's coming from that tunnel."

"Aye," Synne agreed.

The two of them peered into the darkness. "Should I flood it with light?" he asked.

Sinias hissed behind them. "You might not like what you sssee."

Val backed away from the passage. "What if we're just going deeper and deeper into someplace we don't want to be? We need to find a way to double back to the hole in the ceiling."

"Or perhaps we make a stand here, before we're cornered," Synne said. "I can manage the pain."

Val noticed the sweat on her brow and the clammy pallor of her skin. He didn't doubt her courage, but he knew she might not survive another blow from one of the gypsy sorceresses.

The weird swishing sound increased in volume. It was clear something was coming. Something large.

Footsteps echoed in the corridor behind them, followed by the faint sound of arguing voices.

"Perhapsss there isss a better way," Sinias said, with a gleam in his eye. "Perhapsss we could sssolve two problemsss at once."

Val caught on quickly. "I can shield us down one of the passages while it plays out. Best case scenario, they kill each other off. Or we step in and finish off the winner."

"What if whatever approaches is too powerful?" Synne asked. "For the black sash and for us?"

"Then I distract it while we run. I think it's worth a shot." Val eyed the knobby ends of the bones poking out of the walls, gleaming in the dim light of the glow orb. "We're running out of options, and I don't like the idea of going any further unless we have to."

Both the swishing sound and the footsteps grew in volume, as Val herded the others a hundred feet down the corridor. He motioned to Sinias to extinguish the glow orb, and they hunkered down in the darkness, pressing their backs against the wall, staying well away from the murky depths of the canal running through the center of the passage.

Val tensed as his eyes adjusted to the darkness, working to manage his fear of the unknown. He ran through his spells in his mind, thinking of how much energy he had left and what might work best in this scenario. As drained as he was, he didn't think Spirit Fire was a good idea. He might have enough strength left to call it forth, but only for a moment. Moon Ray took much less power but required a celestial light source.

As he continued to think, light flared into the intersection, revealing the shadowy figures of the remaining black sash gypsies. Five fighters and three sorceresses.

The swishing sound had ceased. Odd. Val flinched at the light, though he knew they were hidden in the darkness. That would change if one of the sorceresses decided to illuminate the tunnels one at a time.

Which is exactly what they did. The three women split apart, each of them drawing light from a torch and flaring it down the three corridors. Synne gripped his arm, but Val had prepared for this contingency. He created a wall of darkness in front of them, an anti-light spell that snuffed motes of light instead of enhancing them. The spell wasn't perfect but at this distance it should be enough to shield them.

His strategy worked. It felt odd staring at the wall of light a foot from his face, yet unable to see the others right beside him.

The sorceress standing at the beginning of the passage lingered for longer than Val liked, squinting as if trying to decide if something was wrong. Just as she took a step down the corridor, the swishing sound returned, much louder than before, and a huge, maggot-white head burst out of the well in the center of the intersection. The body was that of a wyrm, round and slimy, with black fangs and levered jaws more akin to a reptile. Before anyone could react, it lunged its sinuous body with the speed of a viper, and snatched one of the gypsy sorceresses in its mouth.

The thing kept spilling out of the well, filling the chamber with its bulk, crushing the black sash gypsies against the walls or forcing them to flee down the corridors. To Val's horror, the monster decided to pursue them down the corridor in which he and his companions were hiding. It was moving so fast there was no chance to avoid it. It was going to crush or eat them if he didn't do something. He thought he could outdistance it himself, by flying down the corridor, but that would leave Synne and Sinias at its mercy. Grimly, he prepared to blast it with Spirit Fire, though he knew the little power he had left would not stop a creature of that size.

As he gathered his magic, a mottled green torso rose out of the canal that straddled the middle of the passage. The newcomer had a wide scaly face, gills for cheeks, and nostrils even flatter than a serpentus.

A kethropi.

Val drew back as the wyrm flew down the corridor towards them. *It must be able to see through my spell. That or it can sense us in another way.*

"Into the water!" The same kethropi said, in a voice so gargled and accented Val could barely understand its English. But he understood all too well the fear and urgency reflected in the lidless yellow eyes.

Val had no idea how it planned to help or whether he and the others would be walking out of the lion's den and into the fire. Yet they had little choice. The kethropi was jabbing a webbed hand down at the water, over and over. With a final glance at the enormous wyrm, Val grabbed onto Sinias and Synne, took a deep breath, and plunged into the filthy canal. He squeezed his eyes shut and closed his mouth as the thick, viscous goop clogged his nose and clung to his skin.

Someone, he assumed the kethropi, took him by the hand and guided him lower. Five feet down, his hand was shoved against a metal bar of some sort. Val got the hint. He gripped the bar tight just before it surged forward, propelled as if shot from a bow.

18

After their journey across Praha, Will and his companions were hungry and exhausted. Skara Brae provided cheese wedges and potato dumplings, washed down with water and a shared flagon of granth, then led them to a secluded alcove furnished with reed mats and woolen blankets. There was even a wash room with a rudimentary toilet at the far end of the winding stone tunnel.

The Nilometer was so inaccessible and well-fortified that Will felt no need to post a guard. He fell quickly into a dreamless sleep, and woke the next morning when Yasmina gently prodded him awake. Dalen was snoring in a corner, and Mateo was just beginning to rouse.

As they gathered their rucksacks for the next stage of the journey, Will asked the group, "What do you think of the bargain I made with Skara?"

Yasmina fastened the clasp of her pewter cloak. "I don't think she means us harm. But I don't trust her, either."

"Aye," Mateo said. "You saved us from the brushfire, cousin, but we might be sticking our heads into the witch's oven."

Will took a drink of water and wished, as he did most mornings, for a double espresso from his favorite coffee shop in New Orleans. "I wish there was another way. Like I said before, one step at a time."

"I think the Nephili are a fairy tale," Dalen added, "but tales of the Old City of Praha have been around for ages. At least according to my Da. Aike, there's *something* on that bluff. Maybe it will help us find the Coffer thief—or maybe it will get us all killed."

Will knew that whatever happened on the next stage of the journey, the responsibility lay on his shoulders. He was the leader, and he had to own it. "Listen," he said, eying them one by one. "I don't mind if you back out now. All of you. I was the one who got us into this. I can follow Skara to this door on my own, and meet you at Tiny's when it's done."

"Krikey," Dalen said, "I thought you'd never ask!"

As the young mage shouldered his pack and walked towards the entrance to the alcove, Will's heart sank, though he couldn't blame Dalen for not wanting to join him on such a dangerous quest. Without a backward glance, the young illusionist walked right through the beaded curtain that shielded the alcove, leaving Will stunned by the sudden departure. He turned to see how Yasmina and Mateo would react, only to find all three of them—including Dalen—watching him with huge grins.

"What the—" Will spluttered. "I just saw you leave!"

Dalen broke into laughter as he put an arm around Will's shoulders. "I told you I was getting better."

"That was an *illusion*? I heard your voice, too!"

Dalen pulled Yasmina and Mateo into a circle with him and Will. "We may not be the most fearsome group of adventurers in the Realm, but lucka, we stick together."

"Aye," Mateo said solemnly, gripping Will's other shoulder.

When Will looked over at Yasmina, expecting a faraway wilder expression, he instead saw the genuine, infectious smile he remembered from years ago, when they had first met at Caleb's bar. Though she didn't speak, her steady gaze and private wink comforted Will more than any words she could have spoken.

Moved by the display, he pulled them into a huddle so tight their heads were touching. "Did I ever tell you guys I love you? Now let's go find what we came for."

A grime-covered young man who grinned far too much for Will's liking led them to the top of the Nilometer, where they found Skara Brae waiting in the cool fog of morning, again dressed in black leather and carrying her odd assortment of weapons. She had brought a companion: a handsome, well-built man with a trimmed brown beard and not a hair out of place. Will might have mistaken him for a dandy, except for the stern, unyielding gaze and the two scimitars sheathed across his back. The newcomer wore loose-fitting cotton breeches tucked into his boots, a hoop earring in his left ear, and a fur-lined cape thrown over a forest-green tunic.

After their guide slunk away, Skara introduced her companion as Bartu Sevenoak, and gave no further explanation. By the way she glared at him when he ran an appraising eye over Yasmina, Will could tell he was more to Skara than a hired hand.

When Will started to ask questions about their destination, Skara began walking towards town. "I have a simple rule in the morning: I discuss nothing of importance before my morning brew."

"I can relate to that."

"We'll stop at the Pagoda before we set off."

Without further explanation, she led them through the wild parklands surrounding the Nilometer and back to the busy docks. Near the center of the district, she cut to the right and took them four streets deep, then into a seedy little alley squeezed between brick warehouses. A hundred feet down, she ducked into a doorway with a sign that bore an image of a multi-tiered pagoda with a pair of dragons sleeping nose to tail at the entrance.

The name of the establishment was scrawled in a foreign alphabet that re-sembled Chinese characters. Unfortunately, Will's armband only translated spoken languages. "What's it say?"

Skara snorted. "No one knows. That's why we call it the Pagoda."

Bartu held the door as everyone filed into a low-ceilinged room dimly lit by hanging orb lamps with orange smoke drifting out, hazing the air with cit-rus-scented incense. A long wooden bar took up most of the room, packed with occupants from a variety of races hovering over steaming beverages. On the wall behind the bar, jars of tea leaves were stacked floor to ceiling, except for a glass case full of stoppered vials near the middle. Behind the counter, an Oriental man in a shimmering silk robe was busy extracting leaves from var-ious jars and mixing them with drops of liquid from the stoppered vials. He kept his long white hair tied above his head in a bun, and a manicured goatee flowed to his waist. Skara stopped to watch him work with a reverent stare.

A woman dressed in a kimono approached with an open palm, ushering them down a corridor to their left that wound through a nest of compact rooms filled with patrons and the omnipresent orange haze. While it might have been Will's imagination, the sweet smelling vapor seemed to relax him. When they reached an unoccupied alcove with a circular table big enough for the group, the hostess handed out menus and disappeared.

Will opened the menu, which was as thick as a phone book and had thousands of different concoctions on display.

"Lucka," Dalen said, as he perused the menu. "Dragon's Breath for travel to snowy climates? Leaping Grasshopper Mint for springtime courtship? Elixir of Owl for increased night vision? How are we supposed to choose?"

"It might be best if I ordered for the group," Skara said. "Something to pique the mind and provide stamina for the journey?"

Will and Mateo closed their menus at once, relieved. Yasmina kept flipping through the pages with interest, and Will remembered she was a tea aficionado back home.

"I'd like to try Alchemist's Morning Enlightenment," she said slowly. Skara rolled her eyes but honored the request when the hostess returned to take their order.

"These prices range from a single groat to incredible amounts," Yasmina said, still browsing the menu. "What sort of tea costs five hundred *platinum?*"

"Master Kuang is a genius," Skara said. "He carries every varietal found on Urfe, but he's also a *chayigong*, a brewer who infuses low-level magic into his tea. Duels in the docks have been won or lost according to who could afford the most expensive potions."

"So he's a tea brewing majitsu?" Will said.

"I suppose, of a sort. There are many types of *gongs*, each focusing on a different discipline."

"Cool."

"I thought mages were unwelcome in Praha," Mateo said.

"Exceptions are made," Skara said, giving Dalen a sidelong glance. "Especially for those who keep to themselves and provide a community benefit."

When the tea arrived, Will blew on the light brown beverage to cool it, then took an exploratory sip. It was packed with flavor, cinnamon and ginger and an herb he couldn't identify. Following Skara's lead, he found that hovering over the cup and inhaling the steam hastened the stimulatory effect.

After a spell of silent contemplation, feeling calmer and more alert, Will planted his elbows on the table. "What's the plan, Skara? I'd like to know what we're getting into."

The adventuress regarded him in silence as she took another sip. "I made some inquiries last night, while you slept."

"That was fast."

She exchanged a glance with her companion. "Those inquiries are why we're sitting at this table."

"Rumor is," Bartu said, in a quiet but commanding voice, "a certain legendary sword has returned to Urfe, wielded by a fair-haired warrior of gypsy blood."

A moment of tense silence encased the group. Will's hand tightened at his side, and he saw Mateo's good hand slip beneath the table. Yasmina had not moved but her eyes were alert, settling on Skara with a watchful gaze. Dalen had his face buried in his tea, but Will could tell by the clench of his jaw that he was paying attention.

Bartu noticed the change in atmosphere and gave a thin smile. "If we wished you harm, we would have never left the Nilometer."

"Unless this hypothetical sword does exist," Will said evenly, "and you need us to open the door for you before you try to take it."

"Why not use this sword ourselves?"

"I can think of a number of reasons. Maybe there's a guardian on the other side you need our help with, or a trap waiting for us. Maybe you don't wish to kill us at the Nilometer. Or maybe, and rightly so, you worry such a sword would not respond to your command."

"It is sentient, then?"

Will locked eyes with the warrior, returning his cold smile. *Let them stay in the dark about the mysteries of Zariduke.*

"Bah," Skara said, smacking a palm on the table. "Enough jostling by the Alpha males. What's yours is yours, Will Blackwood. Mercenary I may be, but I'm no thief or murderess."

"Assuming you would win that battle," Will said, taking another sip of tea. His blood was still hot from the exchange, and he wanted them both to know where he stood.

Skara's gaze rested on Dalen before flicking to Yasmina and then Mateo, as if assessing their strengths. "Maybe it would ease your minds to know that, even were I disreputable enough to break our bargain, I would think twice before crossing a companion of Mala's. I know her well enough to understand she does not lightly allow others to invoke her name. My point in bringing this up was to say I'm satisfied you've represented the truth, and I'm ready to proceed."

Will did not like them knowing about his sword. While Skara might fear Mala's wrath, his deadly muse was a world away. Yet they had little choice in the matter, if they wanted to find out who stole the Coffer. When Will glanced at his friends for support, Yasmina gave him a brief, barely perceptible tip of her head. Whether the wilder had some way of knowing if Skara was telling the truth, he didn't know. But it gave him some comfort.

"Let's move forward," he said, looking Skara in the eye.

After a curt nod, the adventuress took out a scroll from her canvas pack and unrolled it in the center of the table. The square of parchment with serrated edges contained a rough sketch of the city. "Because of my interest in cataloguing the creatures of Urfe, the legend of the Nephili has intrigued me for some time." She gently smoothed the surface of the map, as if lost in a memory. "This was my father's, and his father's before him. I come from one of the few families native to Praha."

"We've noticed a lack of children," Yasmina said.

"A number of small communities exist, in isolated pockets of the city far from the center. I cannot say," the corners of her lips turned upwards, "that my childhood was an easy one. In any event, long ago, in the year after my father was murdered, my grandfather bequeathed me the old journal of an explorer he had found, dated just before the turn of the last century. As you may know, the Volta river makes a sharp turn in the middle of Praha, cutting back on itself and almost enclosing the Old Town. A sheer, high bluff—which I suspect was formed long ago by some mage or power of the Nephili—rises up from the river to protect the Old Town, and is impossible to climb. A perpetual darkness encases the plateau, seething with strange magical energies that have thwarted all attempts to circumvent the Wailing Wall atop the bluff and reach the top through the air. The only known way to reach the Old City is via an ancient staircase cut into the bluff, and accessed through the Agora."

"What's your plan?" Will asked.

"I know it's possible because I've reached the bluff and heard the wailing of the Skinwalkers. I've never ventured further because the journal claims that certain death lies atop that bluff." She leaned forward, her eyes intense. "Unless, that is, one carries the Sephyr Wafer."

"How? Why?"

"The journal doesn't say. But the statistics of those who have gone before—and never returned—bear the truth of the tale. That was without the wafer, mind you. I admit my curiosity has almost propelled me forward before on many an occasion." She exchanged another glance with Bartu, one that hinted at a clandestine journey and shared danger.

"Where exactly is this storehouse you mentioned?" Will asked.

She pointed to a section of the city just within the boundaries of the map, along the northern course of the river. The closest points of interest were Pilgoth's Pillars and something called the Charred Monolith. "The temple is located in one of the most inaccessible parts of the city. Lucky for you, I've charted a path over the years."

"Lucky for you," Will said, "we have a way to open the door."

She chuckled as she rolled up the map, her eyes gleaming with anticipation. "I'll need to purchase an item for the journey, and hire a barge for the day. With any luck we'll reach the Old Town by nightfall."

"Is it smart to go at night?" Will asked.

"If we manage to procure the wafer, I'd rather not delay. Its strange properties might affect us in some way, or call out to those we'd rather not meet. Besides, does it matter at what hour we visit a place that knows not the light of day?"

Before leaving the Pagoda, Skara disappeared for a few minutes before returning with a box the size of a paperback book, wrapped in silky paper embossed with a dragon-themed design. Will assumed it was from the Pagoda. She placed the box in her backpack without a word.

Outside, Skara led them to another section of the docks, this one crowded and garbage-strewn and full of menacing characters that looked ready to slit their throats at a moment's notice. Halfway down a seedy alley lined with taverns brimming with patrons despite the early hour, Skara approached a low-slung warehouse with shouts emanating from inside. Bartu held open the rickety wooden door as Skara ushered everyone into a packed interior filled with unwashed men and women smelling of booze and tobacco. They were gathered around a commotion in the center. As Skara and Bartu pushed through the crowd, the patrons either scurried aside at once or took a long look at the party and thought better of standing their ground.

Will gawked when he saw why the crowd had gathered. In the center of the warehouse, a space was cleared around two combatants fighting inside a rectangular arena the size of a small living room, outlined by a two-foot high brick partition.

And the gladiators were giant spiders.

They were not as huge as the nightmares Will had seen in the Fifth Protectorate swamp or in the forest outside Leonidus's keep, but were large enough to cause him to shudder. One of the arachnids was midnight blue, and one was green with furry red streaks. Each had a body as thick as a cantaloupe and spindly legs that carried them swiftly back and forth, clacking and probing, looking for a chance to sink its fangs into its opponent.

Skara indicated for Will and the others to wait with Bartu, then disappeared into the crowd along the edge of the arena. Unable to look away, Will and the others watched in disturbed fascination as the green battle spider managed to flip its opponent onto its back, then bit into the soft abdomen. The blue spider spasmed and lay still, causing the crowd to roar in response. Coins exchanged hands in a flurry of activity.

During the commotion, Skara returned with a heavyset black woman dressed in a coarse woolen shirt and pantaloons with flared bottoms, her hair kept in short ringlets around her face that obscured her eyes. A swarm of tattoos covered her neck and the backs of her hands.

After they returned outside, Skara introduced the woman as Barge Master Meru.

"Good timing ye had," Meru said, in a lilted accent that Will could barely understand. She opened her palms and grinned, revealing two missing teeth in an otherwise perfect set. "De spiders picked me clean as that they always do you see."

Skara rolled her eyes. "Have ye *ever* won at the Kumo House?"

"Me smile every day is me winning, Skara-dee." Meru cackled and then unleashed a fast-spoken soliloquy incomprehensible to Will. *She's managed to thwart my magical armband*, he mused.

After a heated bout of negotiation, Skara and Meru settled on a fee for her services that seemed to include silver florins and a future line of credit at the Kumo House, as well as at the barge master's favorite tavern.

A light drizzle began as they walked a few blocks east to the river. Meru's boat was long and flat-bottomed, with a cluster of seats near the prow and a three-story pilothouse made of weathered gray wood that took up the bulk of the middle. Everything from animal skulls to fishing rods to kitchen pots hung from pegs attached to the outside of the pilothouse.

After shooing them into the cluster of seats near the prow, where a canvas tarp provided protection from the elements, Meru disappeared into the pilothouse. Soon a low purring arose, followed by the sound of water churning beneath the boat. Startled, Will and Yasmina exchanged a glance as they walked the perimeter.

"Skara," he called out, after seeing no sign of a mechanical engine, "does this boat have a motor?"

"A what?"

"How does it run?"

"Magic, I suppose."

"Are there any other boats that sound like this?"

After she answered in the negative, disinterested, Bartu scanned the horizon and said, "I've heard of mechanized boats that prowl the waters in the far northern seas. Never seen one myself, but I'd like to."

Startled by the possibility of crude technology, Will doubted that Meru had an engine beneath the boat, and suspected a former occupant had ensorcelled the boat to move on its own. He had no idea how this was done, or how long the spell would last, but the concept fascinated him. Or maybe the entire boat was a magical artifact crafted by some long-dead mage who had once navigated the waters of Urfe.

As the ungainly boat left the docks and chugged down the river, tunneling into the depths of the massive city, Yasmina moved to stand next to Will, joining him as he gazed at the far shore, bonded by unspoken memories of their home world. He knew the sound of the boat, whether magical or not, had affected her in the same way. Will ached at the thought of life back home, his friends and family and all the little pleasures he would never find on Urfe.

Such things he desperately missed, though if given the choice, he no longer knew which world he would choose.

At the moment it was irrelevant. What mattered was staying alive, finding the Coffer thief, and doing everything in his power to bring his brothers together again, alive and safe.

"I'll say this," Bartu continued, making conversation as he watched the river with trepidation. "Meru's more than she appears. No one knows the river better, and some say she's taken this rickety old vessel across the four oceans."

"What are you looking out for?" Will asked. "Are we in some danger?"

"Peril aplenty awaits those who ply the Volta. Pirates, river monsters, flying menaces from above, bandits who take aim at boats from ashore."

"Shouldn't we take more precautions?" Will asked, seeing no sign of weapons or defensive bulwarks on the boat. A long ripple in the water not ten feet away, a sign of some sinuous form beneath the water, caused him to lean away from the railing. "Especially since we're the only boat on the water."

A huge splash, coming near the ripple Will had seen, caused him to leap backwards. Noticing that Bartu and Skara didn't seem concerned, and were in fact regarding him with amusement, gave Will the confidence to peer over the side and watch as an oval mouth lined with fangs reached up to swallow the bloody contents of a bag floating atop the water. He looked up and saw Meru watching the scene from an open window atop the pilothouse. After the disturbance on the water ceased, she disappeared again.

"If she didn't gamble all her coin away," Bartu said, "Meru would be a rich woman. As long as I've known her, she's only been boarded once, and let's just say it did not go well for the trespassers. There's far more than junk inside that shack of a pilothouse she calls home."

While curious, Will's speculations on the barge master drifted away as he stood at the bow and watched Praha unfold before him. The cityscape was like a dark angel with wings spread wide, a vast sweep of plague-blackened towers and buildings. Every hundred yards or so they would pass beneath a curved bridge that arced high above the river, flanked by spires and carved with elaborate murals. The clouds were so pregnant with moisture it felt like twilight, though every now and then an orange light would flare in one of the buildings, the only sign of habitation since they had left the docks. Whenever a breeze sifted the clouds, Will would strain to catch a glimpse of countryside in the distance, but never saw beyond the endless horizon of diseased stone.

Whatever resources or cloaking devices Meru had at her disposal, no other river monsters appeared, nor did thieves or pirates accost them on the journey. An hour later, the boat drifted into a marina with a secure dock and boats slips at regular intervals. Once the vessel came to rest, Skara led the way onto the boardwalk. Meru never appeared, and Will assumed she was staying with the boat.

The boardwalk opened onto a grandiose plaza that ran for two hundred yards along the bank of the river, backed by a collection of domed palaces suspended high above the street with pillars, buttresses, and other architectural supports that formed an intricate pattern of their own. The decrepit state of the buildings failed to disguise their former grandeur.

The city was eerily quiet, the smell of old stone mingling with the fetid reek of the river. Skara and Bartu waved for everyone to follow, moving swiftly through the courtyard with weapons drawn and heads cocked for unfamiliar sounds. Once they passed beneath the linked undersides of the palaces, they saw that all the buildings in the district were suspended above ground level, though none as large or as grand as the ones facing the river. Delving deeper, they encountered a network of smaller and flimsier buildings at street level built among the curving support structures. It was as if two cities existed here, one on top of the other.

Skara trod a quarter mile down a wide boulevard and down two side streets before stopping to huddle everyone together. "The door to the storehouse is not far, but the city is a maze around here, with danger at every turn. Make sure we stay together. Never stray to investigate an unseen sound, not even for a moment."

"Don't worry about that," Dalen muttered.

Mateo had his urumi sword in hand. "What sort of danger?"

"Though the streets seem deserted, appearances are deceiving. There are denizens lurking that . . . are quite devious. Visitors are few and far between, forcing them to adopt clever tactics."

"By *visitors* you mean *prey*?" Will said. "Speak plainly, Skara. What's in here?"

She shushed him with a finger, and lowered her voice. "This was once the home of the menagerist's guild, before the mobs ran them off. Several of their ilk still remain."

"Lovely," Will muttered.

"I've been here a score of times to map the place, and only twice ran afoul of trouble. With any luck, we'll find the storehouse, retrieve what we came for, and be off before sunset."

Dalen shuddered within his cloak. "Lucka, let's make sure that happens."

"This way," Skara said. "Hurry, now."

Yasmina's face was grim when Will glanced over to see how she was faring. Her eyes betrayed his own thoughts: *what is there to do but carry on?*

As Skara had said, this part of the city was extremely convoluted. Streets and alleys intertwined in no apparent pattern, and often the road would rise without warning, turning into an aerial walkway or bridge that spanned a low building or empty canal. At times, Skara would squeeze everyone into an irregular gap between buildings, or drop down from a bridge onto a hidden connector.

Soon after they started down a long boulevard lined with tall stone buildings, a long hiss sounded from overhead, followed by a shrill cry. Instead of scanning the skies, Skara immediately ushered everyone through an arched entryway to their left.

"That was a rock wyvern," she said. "Everyone link arms and push into the darkness, then be still."

"Is it safe in here?" Will asked, feeling his way blindly ahead. He held Yasmina's hand on the right, and linked an arm through Dalen's on the left.

"Safer than out there."

"What about a light?"

"No lights. Further, now. Their sense of smell is extraordinary. Hopefully it was chasing something else, and will pass by."

After they stopped moving, they heard the distinctive cry several more

times, each louder than before. Will tensed as the flap of eldritch leathery
wings seemed to pass right outside the archway. Someone grunted to his left—
he thought it was Bartu—causing Skara to silence him with a harsh whisper.
Will wondered what had caused the composed warrior to move around.

"Mateo?" he whispered.

"I'm here."

"Just checking."

The cry of the great beast moved further and further away. Eventually Skara lit a match, exposing an anteroom with slender pillars and carvings of impressionistic landscapes on the walls. "What happened?" she asked, moving
towards Bartu with some concern.

"I tripped," he said.

"Tripped?" She looked around the empty room. "On what?"

"I thought I heard something over there," he said, pointing at a black hallway leading deeper into the interior. "I thought to position myself better in
case of attack, and must have stumbled."

Skara let it drop. After ushering everyone back onto the boulevard, she
scanned the sky for signs of danger, then hurried forward. More twists and
turns led to a dead-end corridor walled in by immense granite buildings.

"We've arrived," Skara said.

"Here?" Will asked. "This is the fabled storeroom?"

Skara grinned, took a step forward, and disappeared through the base of
the wall.

"Oh my," Dalen murmured, peering at the granite dead-end. "It's no illusion I recognize."

"Nephili magic is unlike any other," Bartu said, right before he stepped
through.

Will made his companions go before him, sucked in a breath, and followed.
The illusion felt oddly tangible, as if walking through a heavy mist. Or maybe
it was a portal instead of an illusion.

On the other side, everyone had gathered at the base of a black marble
staircase leading upwards into the gloom, enclosed within walls of the same
material.

"Remember that the Nephili lived in the higher reaches of the city," Skara said. "My grandfather's journal speculates that this staircase granted entrance to human workers to the Nephili storeroom for purposes unknown, with entry restricted by the door we're about to encounter."

With everyone close on her heels, the adventuress moved steadily up the claustrophobic passage, lighting the way with a lavender glow stone. The illumination soon revealed the top of the staircase at least two hundred feet above ground level, though not until they drew to within a few yards could Will make out the faint outline of a silver door with no handle, and the angular scrawl of runes etched top to bottom into the surface, so faint they had almost disappeared.

"That's the door?" Will said, in a low voice.

"Aye," she said. "If the journal speaks the truth, 'tis the chamber where the Nephili came to feed."

19

The river flowed lazily along, wide and blue and comforting, a waterborne magic carpet that could carry one anywhere, to the ends of the earth and beyond. Caleb wasn't sure how long his cheek had been pressed against the sun-kissed wood of the raft, or how long he had been gazing down at the hypnotic current. The weather was warm and languorous, a perfect summer afternoon. He could smell the forest along the bank and almost taste the breeze. Time felt irrelevant, the way it did when he was a child.

As if the world would go on forever.

"I don't know what you're talking about, you. That just makes me mad."

"Mad? Why would it make you mad? It's the dang truth. You should feel bad about it and apologize."

The voices did not startle Caleb. It was confusing, though. He didn't know who they were, but for some reason, he knew there were two other people on the raft with him. One of the voices belonged to an older man with a thick, uneducated drawl. The other speaker was a boy of around twelve. Both sounded Southern, from north Louisiana or Mississippi.

"I ain't apologizing for nuttin, cuz I didn't do it."

"You know you ate that butterscotch corn, Jim. You just forgot about it. Now c'mon and hand over that last piece."

"I ain't gonna do that, neither."

Caleb heard scuffling, and the raft started to tilt as the two scrambled for the disputed piece of candy. Wary of falling into the water, Caleb scooted towards the middle of the raft, where he saw a white boy with a dirt-smeared face and overalls sitting atop a burly black man.

"Oh, Huck," the older man moaned, as the boy twisted one of his arms, "don't make old Jim get up from here and lay a whooping on you."

"Looks to me like I'm doing the whooping," the boy crowed.

At the other end of the raft, Caleb saw a makeshift canvas tent, a couple of buckets, and a trio of fishing poles. As the two continued to struggle, a golf ball-size piece of caramel corn rolled towards the edge of the raft. Caleb walked over to pick it up, causing both of them to stop fighting.

"Hey," the boy said, holding out a hand. "Now just go ahead and hand that on over."

Caleb sat cross-legged on the raft. "Not until I get some answers."

The boy and the older man exchanged a look.

"Huh?" the boy said.

"Are you Huckleberry Finn?"

"Are you a white-tailed rabbit? Of course I am." He rolled off the older man, who kept moaning and complaining as he pushed to a sitting position.

"How long have I been here?" Caleb asked.

"What kind of a question is that?" The boy reached for a fishing pole, cast it out, and sat with his legs dangling in the water. "Who cares how long we've been here? We're here, ain't we? Isn't that right, Jim?"

"That right, Huck."

Huh, Caleb thought. Though his brain felt foggy, he seemed to remember that his favorite novel as a boy was *The Adventures of Huckleberry Finn*. And now here he was, drifting down the Mississippi with Huck and old Jim themselves. It was just as grand as he had imagined it would be.

The more he thought about it all, the past and the future and his own presence on the raft, the more *right* it felt. As if it had always been this way.

As if it always would be.

"Say, you," Huckleberry said, "why don't we split that candy up between us? Old Jim doesn't need it, anyhow."

"That doesn't sound very fair," Caleb said.

"That right, Huck. That ain't very fair."

"Why not?"

"Because," Jim blustered, waving his hands, "I'm the one had it first. At least gimme a piece. Split it three ways."

Over Huck's protests, Caleb split the caramel corn into three chunks and handed one to each of them. He bit into his own chunk and found it quite delicious.

"What's your name again?" Huckleberry asked.

Caleb thought for a moment, confused by the question. What *was* his name? Everything felt so warm and fuzzy. It came to him after a moment. "Caleb. Caleb . . . just Caleb, I guess."

"Here, then," Huck said, reaching for one of the poles. "Help me catch some dinner, Just Caleb."

A wriggling worm was already attached to the hook. Caleb held the rod in his hand, reveling in the familiar smoothness of the wood. What was better than floating free down the river on a lazy summer day and tossing a line into the water? He reached back, cast, and laid the rod in his lap with a contented sigh.

"Say Jim, tell us another story."

"Which one you want, Huck?"

"Hmm . . . how about the one where you made the world?"

"You already done heard that one."

Huckleberry jerked a thumb towards Caleb. "*He* hasn't."

"Oh. Well." Jim glanced at Caleb. "You want to hear it?"

Caleb shrugged. "Sure."

As he began to speak, Jim clasped his weathered hands behind his head and laid on his back, letting the sun warm his face. "Way back in the beginning," he said, in a voice of baritone honey, "when I was a little lonely one day, I made dem stars and dem galaxies, and then the ole Earth itself. It took me a few tries—"

Huckleberry rolled his eyes. "You mean a few *gazillion* tries."

"You always using dem big words, Huck. You want to hear this story or not?"

As they continued to argue, Caleb grew tired again, and set the rod down. He lay on his back near the edge of the raft as Jim resumed his story about making the world. He talked about the time before the stars arrived, and the time that came after they were gone. Somehow it all seemed to roll together. He talked about the meaning of life and how the animals communicate and where Atlantis used to be and other grand mysteries that Caleb listened to in fascination. At some point, his hip aching, Caleb turned to the side. He didn't want to stop listening but his eyes started to slip downward, into the hypnotic depths of the river.

"Don't look down there," Huckleberry warned. "We don't look in the water."

"Why not?" Caleb asked.

"Because you might not be able to look back. It won't be like this anymore."

"Like this?"

"You know, just the three of us, Jim's stories, the river, the fishing, the adventure. What else do you want?"

"Let the man make up his own mind, Huck. That's what it's there for, after all."

"*That's* brought us nothing but trouble," Huckleberry muttered.

"You always say that, and you always wrong."

"That's your *opinion*, Jim. You're not *perfect*, you know."

"Anyway," Jim said, "he should look if he wants to. Make up his own mind."

Huck threw his hands up. "Do what you want," he said to Caleb. "My advice is to make it quick and forget about it."

Now curious, Caleb leaned over and saw what he expected: a river of achingly blue water, too deep to see the bottom. Just as he started to turn away, he noticed his own reflection, and it caused him to pause.

And remember why he was there.

It all came back in a flash: Marguerite's death, the quest and the Tower of Elarion, the harem, the dungeon beneath Zedock's obelisk. He remembered, and he sat up, troubled by the stupor into which he had fallen.

"I told you," Huckleberry said, now chewing on a piece of licorice. "Here," he said, offering Caleb's rod to him again. "Help us catch some dinner."

Caleb took the rod, and his memories started to slip away as soon as he turned back from the water. He wanted to drift on that raft forever, bask in the glorious sunshine, listen to Jim spill forth the secrets of the universe. He sensed that he could do it, too. That this place was real, as real as anything else, and he could stay forever if he wanted. And he would be *happy*.

But it would mean losing everything else. His memories of Marguerite, Luca, and his brothers. That was a high price to pay for eternal bliss.

That, and Lord Alistair would never pay for what he had done.

He could barely hold onto that train of thought. He was already slipping into a dreamlike state again. When he looked over at Jim, he noticed the older man was now staring at him with a piercing gaze. His pupils were a well of sadness so dark and deep they eclipsed the hole in Caleb's soul. It gave him a moment of relief from the pain, and that made him furious. He never wanted to let go of that. Desperate for a way to escape this place, Caleb did the only thing he could think of to do. As Huckleberry protested beside him, trying to convince him to stay, Caleb leaned over and let himself fall off the edge of the raft, into his own reflection.

The water was freezing, much colder than he expected. The shock of it snapped him back to reality, and he sank far faster than he should have, as if gravity and water resistance didn't exist. He closed his eyes and kept on falling.

Without warning, Caleb found himself standing on hard ground. He opened his eyes and found himself in a Jurassic landscape of blasted rock, bubbling fumaroles, and muddy brown lakes on the edge of a forest with trees so tall it made him dizzy to look up at them. The air was fresh, though it smelled faintly of sulfur. Steam poured out of hot pots and geysers. The primeval feel of the place reminded him of *Rincon de la Vieja*, a national park in Costa Rica he had visited before he had settled into his thatched hut in Hermosa Beach.

A howler monkey roared from deep within the forest, setting Caleb's nerves on edge and causing him to spin around.

Which was when he saw Humpty Dumpty.

Who else could it be? The giant egg with arms and legs and a face, sitting on a freestanding, ten-foot section of stone wall, had been imprinted in Caleb's brain from a very early age.

Outside of a few Stephen King novels, Caleb hadn't done much reading in recent years. But he read a ton as a child, and Mark Twain and Lewis Carroll were two of his favorite authors. Given all that had occurred, he knew the tower was picking up on his memories somehow. He really hoped *It, Salem's Lot*, and *Pet Sematary* weren't next on the list.

"Humpty?" Caleb asked.

"Eh?" the egg said. It was peering intently at the primeval landscape with the rocks and fumaroles, and away from the old-growth forest.

"That's your name, isn't it? Humpty Dumpty?"

"Well if you already know, why are you asking?"

"Just checking. You don't happen to know where we are, do you? Is this a dream?"

"How should I know if this is your dream?" the egg said haughtily. "It surely isn't mine."

"Yeah. Okay. Listen, do you know how I can get out of here? I'm trying to climb to the top of a tower. Have you seen one anywhere close?"

"A rock tower? A flower tower? Say what you mean, and mean what you say!"

"A stone tower. Cylindrical and white, eight or so stories high."

"The tower is made of stories? How curious. How does that work, pray tell?"

"It's eight *levels* high," Caleb said in exasperation. A geyser hissed and bubbled to his left, followed by another ear-splitting roar from a howler monkey.

"Ah, why didn't you say so!"

"So you do know it?"

"I'm afraid not."

Caleb tried to remember everything about the book, but it had just been so long ago. How had Alice escaped? Wasn't there a queen involved?

A sudden crash shook the earth, followed by another. Some great beast roared in the distance, deeper within the Jurassic portion of the world, and Caleb cringed at the sound.

The beady eyes on the egg's face, which reminded Caleb of Mr. Potato Head, widened as far as they could. The shaking ground caused him to wobble atop the wall, to the point where Caleb rushed over to help steady him.

"Thank you," the egg said begrudgingly. "Most embarrassing, this precarious state."

"Is that a dinosaur?"

"A what?"

Caleb waved his hands as the thundering footsteps drew nearer, though nothing could be seen on the horizon. "A huge prehistoric lizard. Triceratops, tyrannosaurus rex, stegosaurus?"

"What strange words you know! I have no idea what you're talking about!"

"Okay, so what the hell is making all that noise, and is it going to eat us?"

"Why, it's a Jabberwock, that is. And *of course* it's going to eat us."

Caleb swallowed. Now *that* he remembered. He thought it was from a different book or poem, but who the hell cared. He backed against the wall. "What do we do?"

"How would I know? I'm just an egg."

A huge, misshapen form appeared in the distance, stomping out from behind a hill. The thing looked like a mishmash of a dinosaur, a catfish, and the mountain trolls that had attacked him on the journey to the tower. Sturdy hind legs and a thick tail supported a squat gray body covered in warts. Its membranous bat wings twitched as it walked, the two spindly arms ended in clawed fingers that opened and closed like a bear trap, and the Jabberwock's absurdly long neck supported a gilled face with whiskers and antenna poking out. At least fifteen feet tall, the monster ran upright, though at times the serpentine neck would raise and lower to sniff the ground or scope its surroundings.

"Don't you know anything helpful?" Caleb shouted, his stomach bottoming in fear.

"Like what?" the egg answered.

"Like how to get out of this world! Are there other people like me here?"

"There was a little girl once," Humpty said, twirling his thumbs nervously. "She even gave me some advice. Actually, she said a number of curious things, though she might have been addled. But one time, just before I fell for the seven thousand, six hundred and seventy-second time, instead of helping me up she looked at me with a very strange expression and said, "Humpty, sometimes death is the only escape.""

"That is not at all helpful," Caleb said, backing away as the Jabberwock caught a scent and started loping right towards them.

"Then might I suggest, as someone with full mobility and a less ponderous ratio of shell to flesh, that you run very swiftly for those tall trees?"

Caleb gave him a sharp glance. "Better," he said, and darted for the cover of the forest. The Jabberwock bounded after him, swift and terrible, causing a stampede of birds and smaller animals.

A cover of pine needles allowed Caleb to dash through the forest unhindered. Soon after he entered, he looked back and saw the Jabberwock passing right by the stone wall. Without missing a beat, the monster craned its long neck and gobbled up Humpty Dumpty in one bite.

That's just wrong, Caleb thought, although a wave of terror swallowed his indignation as he fled. The Jabberwock was gaining ground quickly, smashing through saplings in its path and knocking down larger trees with a swish of its mighty tail. Its deafening roar caused fear to pulse through Caleb.

A jagged cave mouth, tucked into a hillside, gave him a spark of hope. He drew closer and realized it was too small for the Jabberwock to fit through. But how deep was it?

Didn't matter. The chance for an escape gave him a burst of adrenaline, and he raced through the forest as the monster drew closer, the ground-rattling footsteps almost causing Caleb to trip.

A young fir grew near the mouth of the cave. Caleb whipped around it and darted inside, relieved beyond words to find the cave extended deep into the hillside. When he had gone beyond the reach of the Jabberwock, he turned in time to see the monster pull the tree out of the ground, toss it aside, and stick its long neck into the cave mouth.

Startled at how far its neck could reach, Caleb scampered deeper inside, until the poison-green catfish head jerked to a stop. The baleful red eyes stared at Caleb, and the whiskers surrounding the massive puckered maw twitched in the air like live wires.

Jesus Christ, he thought, as the thing strained against the rock, trying to force its way inside. This went on for several minutes until, frustrated by the effort, it snorted and laid its head on the floor of the cave, watching its prey.

With a shiver, Caleb turned to view his surroundings, surprised to find a teal light illuminating the cavern from somewhere in the distance. He walked towards the light and, after rounding a corner, found a small body of water surrounded by phosphorescent mushrooms at the back of the cave. After failing to find another exit, he lay on the cavern floor near the mushrooms, exhausted, trying to block out the breathing and snorting of the Jabberwock. Before long, his eyelids started to flutter. Nervous of falling asleep on that strange world, but not knowing what else to do, he let himself drift.

When Caleb stirred again, it took him a moment to remember where he was. His heart sank when he saw the glowing mushrooms and the cave pool. He was hoping to find escape through his dreams. Almost at once, he heard the heavy exhalations of the Jabberwock, though its breathing sounded more regular, interrupted by snorts that sounded more fitful than angry. He crept around the corner and found the monster's eyes closed.

Why wouldn't it just *leave*? Already weak in the knees from the thing's presence, Caleb backed away, thinking that if it couldn't see him when it woke up, it might go away.

Thirst scratched at Caleb's throat. He bent to sniff the water, and let it trickle through his fingers. It was very cold and seemed natural. *Oh well*, he thought. *If the point of this world is to kill me with dysentery, then so be it.*

The water slid cool and fresh down his throat. In fact, it was delicious. He drank his fill, feeling refreshed when he finished. After giving the cave another search for exits or hidden passages, he sat cross-legged near the pool and waited for the monster to leave.

Some time later, he heard scraping on stone, as if the great head was retreating through the cavern. The sounds of breathing ceased, and Caleb released a sigh of relief. He was starving and needed to search the forest for food. He made himself wait a little while longer, giving the beast time to wander away, before he poked his head out of the cave.

Night had fallen, though the temperature outside the cave was still balmy. Stars glittered in the sky. He wished he knew more about the constellations. Maybe he could at least confirm what world he was in.

Just as he started to search for a plant or a nut to eat, he heard a faint crashing through the trees. Dread filled his bones as the noise increased and a throaty roar silenced the crickets and rattled Caleb's eardrums. He scurried back into the cave just as the Jabberwock bounded into sight. As before, it ran to the cave and thrust its head deep inside. Caleb panted in the back of his hideout, horrified by the monster's swift return.

Why was it stalking him? Weren't there tastier things to eat on this world?

Eventually, the Jabberwock calmed down and fell asleep again. Frustrated and starving, Caleb spent another night in the cavern, waking to hunger pangs so acute he felt dizzy. He had no choice, he realized.

He had to eat those mushrooms.

With a deep breath, visions of horrid woodland faeries dancing in his head, he took a long drink of water and bent to sniff the shrooms. They smelled subtle and earthy. The problem was that blue-green phosphorescence they emitted. Were mushrooms supposed to glow? They just *looked* poisonous.

Running a hand through his hair, hoping his extensive past experience with fungi of the hallucinogenic variety had strengthened his immune system, he took a bite of a medium-size specimen and let it hit his stomach. It tasted nice. He waited a while and felt no ill effects.

After that, he ate ten of the things, washed them down with water, and felt whole again. After pacing the cavern to stretch his legs, he took a nap, until a loud snort from the Jabberwock caused him to jump. Enraged at the thing's persistence, he grabbed a rock from the cavern floor, rounded the bend, and threw it right at its face. It smacked the Jabberwock on the gill, causing its nostrils to flare and its eyes to burn with hatred. It made a renewed effort to push inside, causing loose stones to fall around the cave mouth.

Maybe not the best idea.

But Caleb was growing desperate. How long could he stay inside this cave before his food source ran out? Or he went insane from loneliness and boredom?

There was someplace he hadn't explored, he realized. Eager at the thought, he stripped down and plunged into the icy water, wondering if he could handle the cold. The pool was clear, and after a few long dives, he spotted the pebble-strewn bottom. He swam back and forth along the floor, shivering, his lungs close to bursting.

He surfaced and dove two more times before he saw them, lying on the bottom like a gruesome underwater cairn: a loose pile of human bones, stripped of flesh and scattered by the passage of time. After ensuring he had scoured the entire bottom of the pool, he toweled off with his clothes and ran in place to get warm.

So someone else had been here, he thought grimly.

And they hadn't made it back.

Had something killed his predecessor? Or had that person let himself slip into the cold waters, tired of eking out an existence in a cave on some abandoned world?

Two days passed, and then two more. Every day and night the same. As always, the Jabberwock would eventually retreat from the cave mouth, but every time Caleb ventured outside, it would return within minutes, either alerted by his smell or by some perverse machination of the tower.

Caleb began venturing further into the forest, sprinting in different directions until he heard the Jabberwock return. That practice ceased when he found nothing on his sojourns and almost got caught by the monster. He felt the wind from its iron jaws snapping shut inches behind him as he dove into the recesses of the cavern.

Caleb howled in frustration. He no longer feared death, but he couldn't die *here*, not like this. Not with so much to do back on Urfe.

Yet for the life of him, he couldn't think of a good option besides waiting the Jabberwock out.

The problems with that were twofold. One, he had the sense the monster would never leave, that it had marked Caleb as its prey and would see it through to the bitter end.

And two, the mushrooms were almost gone.

Three more days passed. The food situation was critical. Though he might have imagined it, Caleb began to sense a triumphant gleam in the Jabberwock's eye, as if it knew the end was near. Scratching at his beard, craving something to eat besides blue mushrooms, Caleb thought for the millionth time about everything that had occurred. The dream, the tower, the trials before this one. Nothing sparked a new idea.

Out of sheer desperation, he did something he had not yet done. He walked right up to the Jabberwock, inches from the tentacles around the ugly maw, and talked to it.

"Listen up, dirt bag. I need to get out of here."

A snort in response.

"You want to eat me, do you? If I give you a finger, will you go away? An arm?"

The eyes burned like lasers, following Caleb's every movement.

With a snarl, Caleb reared back and threw a heavy rock he had concealed in his hand right at the monster's snout. It struck hard, causing it to roar and open its puckered maw.

Exposing something Caleb had never noticed before.

Something which caused him to stare, dumbfounded, at the sight.

Inside the Jabberwock's mouth, seared like a scar atop its slimy red tongue, was the image of a tapered, ivory-colored spiral identical to the shape of the staircase in Elarion's Tower.

The monster unleashed a roar that threatened to shatter Caleb's eardrums. He stood his ground, thinking about what that symbol could mean, as well as his conversation with Humpty Dumpty so many days ago.

What strange words you know! I don't know what you're talking about!

Okay, so what the hell is making all that noise, and is it going to eat us?

Why, it's a Jabberwock, that is. And of course it's going to eat us.

What do we do?

How would I know? I'm just an egg.

Don't you know anything helpful? Like how to get out of this world?

There was a little girl once. She looked at me with a very strange expression and said, 'Humpty, sometimes death is the only escape.'

The Jabberwock continued to roar, opening its maw so wide Caleb thought he might be able to walk inside.

Sometimes death is the only escape.

With a start, Caleb thought he knew the answer—and it absolutely terrified him.

Was Humpty saying he was supposed to let the Jabberwock *eat* him?

Despite being a ludicrous suggestion, what if he was wrong? What if he stuck his head in that monstrous mouth and the creature ripped it right off his shoulders?

The beast kept roaring, as if to reinforce his conclusion. *Go on*, it seemed to mock him. *Give that great idea a shot.*

Old Caleb would have done anything to avoid that terrible pain. He would have waited until the last mushroom was gone, until his emaciated flesh hung from his bones, until his choice was to take the risk or perish. Even then, he probably wouldn't have had the courage. He would have slipped into the water and drowned, just like those other poor souls, rather than die of hunger or walk into the lion's den.

And even if he decided to go through with it, what if he was wrong? What if some other solution would present itself at the last moment, when he was on his deathbed?

On the other hand, what if this was *the* opportunity? Maybe the spiral symbol wasn't always on the beast's tongue, and this was a sign. What if it was now or never, bucko?

He took a deep breath, his head spinning. *Sometimes death is the only escape.*

That phrase didn't sound like something Alice would have said. Not from what he remembered of the book. It was incongruous, bizarre.

A message.

With a snarl, he stopped thinking it through and trusted his gut, which told him this was exactly the kind of twisted trial the builder of the tower would dream up. "Hey you!" he shouted. "Bend your ugly mug down!"

As Caleb stepped closer, one of the huge red eyes focused on him, and the maw swept downward to gobble him up. As soon as it opened wide, Caleb dove inside. The last thing he saw before those awful jaws closed was the dark tunnel of the Jabberwock's throat and, at the red throbbing end of it, an open wooden door.

-20-

The frenzied bark of the hyena wolf, evidence that Nagiro had survived the encounter with the shaman, persisted during Mala's nighttime flight from the Crater of the Snow Moon. Eventually the maddened shrieks and jibbers faded away, the dhampyr no match for the magic-enhanced speed and constitution of the spirit cougar.

The desert persisted in various forms as she ran through the mesas and sprawling highlands, through canyons and valleys, in and around rock formations that grew more and more fantastical. Mala felt the rippling of the feline muscles, the wind in her face, the heat from the noonday sun, and the chill of the desert night. She could see for miles ahead, leap streams as wide as a gladiator pit, hear the bats flapping past her ears at night, smell the paintbrush and the desert lilies and the musk of fleeing game.

A dhampyr could only shift at night, and her cougar form was preternaturally fast. Reaching New Victoria ahead of Nagiro was no longer a problem—as long as her avatar did not dissipate too early.

Yet the dhampyr was not her only worry. Bandits traveled the byways, and even more dangerous were the delver outposts at the reclusive entrances to the southern reaches of the Darklands, concealed behind boulders or inside rock piles. She kept alert for any sign of their presence.

Once the desert receded and the semiarid plains began, she worried about an encounter with the Congregation death squads. She saw three of them, a pair of tusker raiding parties and a larger regiment that included a mix of human mercenaries and Protectorate soldiers. The humans had a wizard with them, a woman whose arrogant chin and cold blue eyes made Mala's blood run cold. The Mala-cougar slunk into the nearest thicket and went miles out of her way to avoid them.

During the night, she smelled or heard many creatures she would not want to test her mettle against, especially in animal form and without access to her magical items. A few cats larger than she but which had no reason to approach. Packs of wolves she knew she could outrun. And later that night, when trapped on a ledge high above the valley floor, she had to risk a precipitous leap to clear a pygmy basilisk whose secretions would paralyze her.

Yet the most dangerous element to the journey were the intelligent beasts of the Ninth. She saw no sign of the solitary monsters that roamed the deserts, but once she reached the highlands of Caddoland, she had to be wary of rock fiends and burrow wyrms. Luckily, she saw neither, and managed to avoid the scorpion hybrids as well. Just when she thought she would escape the highlands unscathed, a pair of cockatrices cornered her in a gully. The cockatrice, a five-foot lizard with the head of a rooster, was a vicious beast that owed its bizarre existence to a menagerist. They were often used to guard the isolated compounds of wizards in the region.

Mala suffered a flurry of claw and bite wounds before she managed to kill one and escape the other, fleeing before more of their vile kind arrived. Though aching from her wounds, she dared not stop to lick them clean.

After leaving Caddoland, she veered southeast, soon reaching the lakes and forests that signaled the approach of the southeastern corner of the Ninth Protectorate. The spires of New Victoria lay but a few hundred miles away, a pittance to her feline avatar.

At first, she worried she would lose herself in spirit form, and worked hard to think of herself as a human being. Yet the primal thoughts of the cougar never seemed to intrude on her mind, and her thoughts turned to trying to regain her lost memory, whatever part of her the shaman had stolen. Yet there was nothing to remember, not even an itch she felt unable to scratch. She recalled making the bargain, and sensed she had lost someone, but did not know whom. Her memories of her family seemed intact.

But she would always know someone was missing.

Not long after she spied the Great River and followed its swift southern course, the spires of New Victoria appeared on the horizon, glowing like giant colored candles. The sight never failed to move her. For better or for worse, though not even a legal citizen, the city had become her home.

As she reached the outskirts, her form began to shift, and she stopped running as her spirit animal dissolved. There was no pain to the procedure, and soon Mala found herself crouched on the ground in the same clothes she had worn before the transformation, all of her possessions intact. She had not known hunger or thirst while imbued with the constitution of the spirit cougar, but now she was starving and exhausted.

With a firm set to her jaw, she walked the rest of the way into the city, determined to hire a coach and then collapse into a chair at her favorite pub.

When looking for work or taking the pulse of the city, Mala preferred the pubs and taverns with a more interactive clientele, such as the Gryphon's Beak or Folly's Wager or the Minotaur's Den. When she craved privacy and respite, creature comforts, and the best ale and warm pies in town, she went to The Velvet Temple.

The shrine at which the patrons worshipped was not one of religion, but hearth and hospitality. Located along the boundary between the Thieves Quarter and Live Oak Junction, an artists' district filled with quirky shops and residences interspersed among the thick foliage, The Velvet Temple charged double the price of other pubs, appealing to Uptown residents who wanted a taste of the edgier arts scene, or a quiet place for a tryst. Neighborhood types from Live Oaks frequented the pub as well, when they had the coin.

After scanning the room with her customary caution, working hard not to collapse before she reached a secluded nook by the fire, Mala slid into the green velvet-coated booth and, with a sigh of pleasure, relaxed for the first time in weeks.

She estimated she had gained two days on the dhampyr, and it would take him some time to locate her inside the city, especially if she desired to stay hidden. She didn't yet know her course of action, but she had decided one thing for certain on her long cross-country journey from the Barrier Coast.

She wouldn't use magical means to escape the city, and she wasn't staying on the run.

She was going to confront the wretched dhampyr.

Here and now. In the city.

This was *her* town.

If she had a chance to beat the dhampyr, it was in her own territory, with time to plan. Turning over Magelasher might buy her freedom, but that was one thing she was never going to do.

The soft illumination of the tabletop glow-orb warmed the room, a luxury in this part of the city. She ordered a plate of venison, candied yams, the vegetable medley, and a pitcher of the finest ale this side of the Great River. A minstrel strummed softly from a corner, accenting the susurration of lovers and old friends. The fire crackled, steaks sizzled, a gentle rain shower tapped against the windows and then made a polite exit.

When Mala's meal arrived, the aroma of charred game and cinnamon-topped yams almost made her swoon. She kicked off her boots and curled into the booth, sighing with pleasure. As she finished her meal and relished her ale in silence, deep in the abyss of her thoughts, her attention turned to the reason she had joined the gypsy caravan to avenge her parents in the first place.

Kjeld.

An involuntary shudder passed through her, which in turn caused her to clench her mug in anger. The very thought of the red-bearded giant was enough to cause her face to feel hot and her heart to thump against her chest. Frightened like a little schoolgirl. Her hand slid to Magelasher, stroked the leather-wrapped hilt.

Soon, warrior-mage, she whispered. *Soon.*

Yet even to have a chance to confront the First Don of Majitsu, she had to elude the dhampyr. With a deep breath, she drained her ale and paid the bill. She had a warm bed to fall into, and business to conduct in the morning.

After stepping onto a sidewalk lit by mauve glow orbs attached to silver lampposts, Mala glanced down the high street in both directions, looking past the shuttered shops and restaurants for a sign of anyone out this late who might pose a threat.

Except for a few arm-in-arm strollers, Live Oaks was empty. Another reason Mala frequented The Velvet Temple: it lay within walking distance of her home in New Victoria.

She followed the street until it crossed over a swampy canal into the Thieves

Quarter. The change was marked by the absence of glow orbs and a worn cobblestone street that replaced the red bricks of the Live Oaks district. To a pedestrian unaccustomed to the serpentine lanes and peaked roofs of the Thieves Quarter, the shadows would seem alive, every corner and darkened window a robbery waiting to happen.

Right after the footbridge crossed the canal, the shadows congealed, and she made a sharp left onto a cul de sac dotted with commercial warehouses shuttered for the night. Looking back to ensure no one had followed, she stepped between two tin-roofed buildings, hopped a stone wall that ran behind them, and found herself on a footpath that tunneled beneath a canopy of vine-laden oaks.

It was one of the secret places in the city. Few knew it even existed. The land bordering the two neighborhoods was public trust, one of the green spaces the city had allocated to clean the air and provide erosion barriers. Too swampy for parkland, and too overgrown for tourists or commuters, she had rarely seen anyone use the path.

A hundred feet in, she crossed back into Live Oaks, swept aside a curtain of Spanish moss, hopped another wall, and strolled into a quirky neighborhood of garden paths, swaths of trees and tropical vegetation, and bungalows hidden deep within the foliage. Home to artists and wealthy residents seeking privacy, it was a small but mazelike community secreted within the thick jungle canopy.

Several turns later, down a twisting lane overgrown with bougainvillea and then through a locked iron gate, Mala felt her step lighten as she beheld her stone bungalow for the first time in many moons.

After pacing the clearing around the house, she unlocked the door and searched the interior, ensuring no one had trespassed during her absence. She climbed to the second story, then through a trap door that led to the flat-topped roof. An enormous live oak loomed above the house, and she used a rope ladder hanging just above the roof to climb into the higher reaches. She had a series of steps and platforms built into the tree, an elaborate tree house that allowed her to spy on the neighborhood from above, or escape into the canopy in case of an attack. She checked to ensure everything was as she had left it, then returned to the house.

Mala yearned to crawl into bed, but first she approached a wooden door reinforced with iron bands. A padlock also protected the door, but the real defense was the magical ward built into the mechanical lock which, if the correct numbers were not selected, would release a lethal dose of mage-fire.

She entered the code and breathed a sigh of relief when the door opened to reveal the large closet housing her spare weapons and chests of coin and magical items.

Everything looked intact. Knowing Nagiro was loping along in the moonlight that very moment, she studied her collection. Most of the major arcana she had found over the years had been procured for her clients, and her past few adventures had dangerously depleted her supplies.

In the treasure room of the sorcerer king, along with Magelasher, she had managed to pick up the decagon of Kirna Tuluth, a ten-sided amulet commissioned by an ancient king of Persia for his wife. According to legend, the bearer of the amulet was supposed to keep a strand of his or her beloved's hair inside the talisman. The magic would connect the two souls. She wore it around her neck, though how it worked, Mala didn't know. She could always consult a magecrafter. Regardless, she didn't see how it could help her against the dhampyr. As she paced the room, she saw nothing at all that would give her a real chance of victory.

After replacing her stock of fire beads, she filled her purse with coin and decided to seek out an old acquaintance. Hardly a friend, for there are no friends among thieves, but someone who was at least not her enemy.

Someone who had access to powerful resources and would entertain her proposal of a business transaction.

Mala was wise enough to know she needed help, and she was going to her first home in the city, the storied Thieves Guild of New Victoria, to attempt to get it.

The next morning, after coffee and breakfast in a neighborhood café tucked inside a palm grove, Mala returned home to don a light blue traveling cloak over her leather pants, sleeved blouse, and jewelry. The cloak would help shield her identity and allow her to conceal an array of weapons and magic items.

After returning to the Thieves Quarter, she progressed deeper into the seedy neighborhood, passing a string of dive bars, flophouses, pawn shops, and random businesses that were barely-concealed fronts for money launderers. The potholed streets and decaying buildings, the shouts of the street vendors, the smell of cheap ale and manure and greasy kebabs: it all brought her back to the time when she had walked these streets on a daily basis, plying her craft and making deals and frequenting the taverns.

She hesitated to call it nostalgia. That period of her life had been too harsh for that. But it was something. A part of who she was.

Though haggard in appearance, the Thieves Quarter was not a slum, or nearly as impoverished as it looked. Most of the city's criminal elite lived in the district, in well-guarded compounds hidden within the maze of narrow streets. No beggars clogged the intersections, because they all begged outside the quarter. Off the main roads, there were gems to be found, good restaurants and rogue-oriented blacksmiths and specialty shops of all sorts. If one knew where to look and how to avoid being robbed, the Thieves Quarter offered some of the best, and certainly the most eclectic, shopping in the city.

Mala had no time for that. The clock was ticking.

Keeping a tight grip on her weapons, she strode through the quarter and entered the central plaza, a busy square with attractive gothic architecture hidden behind the grime. The plaza was home to a constant stream of shady denizens and no-nonsense professionals, clustered in pairs or small groups around the benches and fountains, sipping coffee or grog as they planned heists and conducted negotiations. No street performers called out for coin in this plaza, no tourists dared cross the patterned tiles.

On the far side, a spiked iron gate rose high above the crowd, guarding a crumbling brick mansion whose turrets and peaked towers took up almost an entire city block. The headquarters of the New Victoria Thieves Guild.

Except for wizards, who tolerated the organization because it provided useful services and helped regulate crime, no one who valued her life went through the front door of the Thieves Guild. After debating which secret entrance to choose, Mala ducked into an alley to the left of the mansion, following the muddy lane until it intersected with another, and then another. Slipping inside an old building that looked abandoned but which she knew was crawling with guards, Mala lowered her hood and entered.

Dusty, antique timepieces covered the wall, an old clock shop gone to seed. A fresh-faced lad drew his knife when he saw her. As he took a threatening step forward, an older rogue with an eye patch backhanded the weapon out of his grasp.

"What're ye thinkin', boy? Don't ye know who this is? If me old eyes don't deceive me, that's Mala of clan Kalev standing in front of me. She'll take yer knife and shove it backwards up yer arse before ye can blink."

"Brock," Mala said with a nod to the older man, as the younger thief retrieved his weapon. She knew Brock Bentgill to be a skilled and clever thief who had managed to stay out of prison for decades.

"Are ye a ghost, or back in the fold now?"

"Neither, I'm afraid. I need to speak with Dashi."

The old man's eyes slipped away. "If yer not on the ledger, I'm not sure I can—"

Mala snapped her fingers twice to cut him off. "Tell him I have a proposition for him. He'll see me. I'll wear a hood if he desires."

Brock clicked out of the side of his mouth. "Aye, lassie. That I can do. Get her a glass of ale if she wants," he said to the younger man, "and try not to get yerself killed."

The younger thief, whose name was Benji, threw Mala a nervous look. He didn't bother offering her ale, instead waiting in sullen silence for Brock to return. One of the grandfather clocks chimed the hour, startling Mala.

Minutes later, Brock returned with a trio of guards and curled a gnarled finger. "No need for a hood, he says. Yer still family."

Mala knew that was a lie, and that either they were taking her on a secure route she already knew by heart, she wasn't coming out alive, or they wanted to gauge her reaction for some reason. She followed behind as Brock led her through the rear of the clock shop and into a conjoining derelict building, then through a long stone tunnel set with wards. She knew the route well.

Once inside the guild, Mala collected stares from every cutpurse, assassin, and beggar they passed in the halls of the old mansion. In her day, she had been the youngest person to obtain guild master status in the history of the organization. Yet climbing the ranks so fast had left enemies in her wake. The cutthroat internal politics of the guild was one of many reasons she had left.

Brock led her through a series of hallways to a quiet wing marked by fading Oriental carpets, expensive tapestries, and a variety of daggers and lock picks displayed in glass cases on the walls. The air smelled of incense and leather, and had she not known better, Mala might have let her guard down. Though this area of the guild was reserved for meetings with visiting dignitaries and city officials, she knew the eyes and ears of the guild were behind every cabinet and tapestry. All manner of traps, from poison darts to remote magical detonators, lurked within the furnishings.

Brock rapped on a door with a raven's head knocker, then pushed it open. Inside, a lean and very tall man of mixed Asian descent, two decades older than Mala, afforded her a pleasant smile from a high-backed armchair.

"It's been some time," Dashi said. He pointed towards a matching armchair across from him. "Please, sit."

A vain man who colored his black hair, he was wearing his typical outfit: red silk shirt over brown leather pants, silver city boots, and an assortment of jewelry almost as extensive as Mala's. Dashi was an expert swordsman, and kept a rapier within easy reach on a table beside his armchair. His sword was called Soulskein, and was reputed to be sentient.

During Mala's time at the guild, Dashi had been a high-ranking council member who had recognized her potential and lobbied for her ascension to guild master. He had brought her along and taught her many valuable lessons, both in craft and in politics. After she left, he had risen to the rank of First Guild Lord, second only to the Guild Maven, Ilianna Nightwing. One of the most powerful non-wizards in the city, Ilianna ruled the guild with an iron fist, and had not been happy to see Mala go. There were too many insider secrets at stake. Only an oath by Mala, and Dashi's intervention on her behalf, had prevented a bloody confrontation.

Mala knew she risked a lot in coming back, perhaps even her life. But she felt she had no choice.

"You never write," she said, in a playful tone.

"And would you have returned my letters?"

"Of course. You'll always be my mentor, no?"

"One wonders who would mentor whom, these days. You have much experience in the field, Mala. If the rumors are to be believed, and some are quite unbelievable, you have traveled the breadth of Urfe since you left the guild."

"Yes, I have traveled far. Though in the ways of prose and politics, I fear I'll never be your equal."

Dashi tipped his head forward. "The years have softened your edges. Charm was never your weapon of choice."

"Nor is it now," she said coldly, lest Dashi or anyone else listening think for a single moment that any of her edges were less rough. "It was simply a statement of fact."

Dashi's hand fluttered, and out of nowhere he produced a tiny blade, an inch-long thumb dagger with a poison tip that he wove between his fingers almost too fast for her to follow. The Guild Lord had the nimblest fingers Mala had ever seen. "Have you come to rejoin us, Mala? For one so young, I can only imagine the limits of your potential."

Mala knew he wanted to ensure she would not become a rival, and also suspected his words were some sort of veiled political message to the unseen observers. Everyone knew Dashi had designs on the maven's power, and that he didn't want to wait another decade or two for her to step down.

"I'm afraid not. As I told Brock, I have a transaction to propose."

After a moment, the thumb blade disappeared. Dashi opened a palm. "I no longer entertain commercial proposals, but for you I'll make an exception." *This better be good*, his tone implied.

"Obliged," she murmured.

"Intrigued," he replied.

Mala drummed her fingers on the smooth fabric, choosing her words carefully. "Someone is seeking my head. An Alazashin. He will come here, to the city."

Dashi's eyebrows lifted. Mala had known that would get his attention. Though they feared and respected the infamous league of assassins, the New Victoria Thieves Guild was no friend of the order. Every time someone in the city used their services, they took business that would otherwise have belonged to the guild.

The Guild Lord smiled. "Who have you offended?"

"Does it matter?"

"Surely it has something to do with your past involvement with the Alazashin? Some long-held grudge or slight?" He leaned forward, his smile turning cruel. "Just how *did* you escape their grasp? It's been the talk of the guild for some time."

"That's a story I'm not prepared to tell. Nor should it matter. I came to conduct business, not to arouse sympathy."

"Why would you need my help against a single assassin, in New Victoria? Or have they sent a team?"

"Not a team," she said evenly. "They've sent Nagiro. One of the dhampyr twins."

Dashi's eyes widened. "That is . . . unfortunate. For you, that is."

"It's also an opportunity." Mala smirked. "For you, that is."

Dashi's eyes bored into hers.

"Imagine," she said, "the value of such a prisoner. Nagiro is one of the Zashiri. Some say he is next in line to the Grandfather, should the old man ever die."

"I thought the Alazashin do not bargain for hostages?"

"That rule applies only to the common body. To my knowledge, one of the Twelve has never been taken."

"So you don't know for sure."

"Nagiro knows the secrets of the mountain. I believe they will open their strongboxes—pour them in your lap—to see him returned."

Dashi cast a greedy look around the room, as if hoping no one else was listening—or at least no one unfriendly to him.

"We both know one of the Alazashin will never willingly give up secrets," she continued, "but we also both know that is not a problem for the guild."

He answered with a shrewd glint in his eye. "Your timing is quite interesting. I wonder if you're aware of the Congregation's recent interaction with the Alazashin?"

"I'm afraid not. I just returned from the Mayan Kingdom."

"Unearthing the Coffer of Devla, if I'm not mistaken."

Her eyes narrowed. "So you've heard."

"Possibly before you unearthed it." He steepled his dexterous fingers, pressing them against his mouth. "I also know it's been stolen."

"As I suspected. But by whom?"

"Both the Alazashin and the Congregation are trying to find out. The Congregation has sent a promising young mage by the name of Val Kenefick in pursuit. A spirit mage, no less."

The name caused her to start. *Val Kenefick.* How many spirit mages in New Victoria could share the same uncommon first name? Was it possible Will's brother had joined the Congregation under an assumed identity?

"And the Alazashin, well," the corners of Dashi's lips parted, "someone apparently desires to interrogate you."

"It won't help them, because I've no idea where it is. But no matter. What will it be, Dashi? Will you help me?"

"As I said, your timing is interesting. The Congregation and the Alazashin have broken the accord, and their assassins are no longer welcome in the Realm. Should we manage to capture Nagiro, we could barter for his return to the mountain *or* hand him over to the Congregation. In exchange for a slew of magical items, of course." His eyes sparked as his long fingers twitched in his lap. "What did you have in mind? A dhampyr is exceedingly dangerous, Mala. Even one who is *not* a world-class assassin."

"Please, Dashi, tell me something of which I'm unaware." She leaned forward and spoke in a conspiratorial tone. "But here is what I need."

21

Val hung on for his life as the metal bar whipped around a corner in the sewer canal, moving faster and faster and faster. They must have been traveling sixty miles an hour, and he could only hope Sinias and Synne were alive. He tried not to think about the filth that filled the canal. It was the most disgusting thing he had ever experienced. As the metal contraption kept speeding forward, he worried about having enough air to complete the journey, as well as the nature of their rescuer. Where were they being taken?

Just before he thought his lungs would burst, the iron railing slowed and then came to a stop. Val shot upward without waiting for someone to grab him. When he reached the surface, gasping and covered in muck, he was surprised to find himself in a huge underground cavern. The sewage had a far thinner consistency, allowing him to swim through the dark green water. The smell was still bad but not overpowering, compared to what he had just experienced.

Not far in front of him, the water merged into an underground beach made of turquoise-colored sand. The solid ground beyond the shore was an island of sorts, about as big as a football field and riddled with canals that fed into the rock walls of the cavern.

Glow orbs strung high on the walls cast a jaundiced light throughout the grotto, and a squat black structure dominated the center. Plenty of people were milling about, loading crates onto small vessels or congregating around canvas shelters. Everyone looked armed and capable.

Synne and Sinias emerged beside Val, followed by a pair of kethropi. Though Val knew Synne must be in severe pain, she gave no sign of it. The serpentus had a rigid set to his face, as if he had just returned from the front lines of a war. His pincers shook as he reached into a pouch, withdrew a vial, and took a deep inhalation. The journey had caused the golden lacquer on his pincers to flake away, exposing the dark green surface underneath. "Zagath," he rasped, as a score of armed men approached the edge of the water.

"You've been here?" Val asked.

"The trident," Sinias replied, as if full sentences were too much for him after the journey.

Confused at first, Val took a look around and noticed most of the men and women had a tattoo of a barbed trident on the sides of their necks, jabbing upward. There was a tall, wiry redhead leading the group, dressed in leather breeches and a sleeveless vest with knives strapped into the pockets. His wary eyes canvased Val and the others as he beckoned for them to wade ashore.

There wasn't much of a choice. As he emerged dripping from the water, Val inhaled his own stench and recoiled at the bits of unnamable substances clinging to his hair and clothes. A bout of nausea overcame him, and he leaned over to retch.

The approaching men laughed at the condition of Val and his companions. "Got a ride on the mercart, did ye?" one hooted.

"Don't know how much Zagath pays 'em for a ride through the sewer, but it ain't enough for me. Ye smell like a pile of corpses covered in pig vomit."

"Thanks," Val said dryly.

The redhead stepped forward. "Fancy a bath before ye meet the king?"

"As long as it's not in sewer water."

He grinned and led them along the side of the cavern to a place where two wooden blockades cordoned off a portion of the surrounding lake. The dammed water was not exactly crystal clear, but it looked clean enough. The man pointed at the channel leading through the rock wall on the far side. "That one leads to the Great River."

Val didn't bother asking questions. Nor did he bother with modesty. After stripping off his clothes, he set his staff down and dove into the cool water, rubbing the muck off his body and hair as if covered in fire ants. Synne followed suit, though she dove deeper and cleansed herself calmly beneath the water. Sinias elected to stay ashore, miserable and silent.

After Val and Synne emerged, one of the men threw them each a towel and a pair of cotton breeches and shirts. They slipped into the new clothes and retrieved their belongings out of the pockets of their old garments, leaving the soiled rags where they lay. "Burn them," Val muttered.

The redhead led them to the heart of the island, which bristled with armed denizens of both genders, as well as different races. During the walk, he saw canoes and other small watercraft slipping into and out of the canals strung along the perimeter.

"Do you know where we are?" he whispered to Sinias.

"I have never ssseen thisss."

They approached a squat and unimaginative structure built of interlocking, rough cut stones the color of powdered graphite. It was a somber contrast to the eerie beauty of the blue-green sand. The building straddled the convergence of a dozen canals, and it had a utilitarian feel, as if it had once served as an administrative center for some ancient race of cavern dwellers.

Their guide led them to a canoe moored alongside one of the canals. Val, Synne, and Sinius crowded inside with the redhead and three other men, all of whom bore the trident tattoo. One of the men untied the vessel, then guided it down the canal and into the structure. Val and one of the taller men had to duck their heads to clear the bottom of the entrance cut into the stone wall.

Inside was no different. Stark, dimly lit, crisscrossed by canals.

"Who built this place?" Val asked.

A bearded man missing half an ear spoke up. "Dunno, mate. Zagath found the place abandoned and took it for his own."

"What was that thing that attacked us?"

"Eh? Which one?"

"A giant white worm or something. It came up through a well."

"We call those *larvies*." A grin split the edges of his ruined mouth. "Want to know why?"

"Probably not."

"We call 'em larvies cuz we think they're just the larvae of something much bigger." The hardened smuggler shuddered. "Thank the Queen it can't get up here. Zagath thinks whoever built the canals used to feed on the larvies, but I dunno. Maybe it was the other way around."

"What's down there? Inside the well?"

The man shrugged. "Zagath sent some men down, once. No one ever came back."

Inside the structure, the canoe passed through a series of interconnecting canals. Every now and then, a kethropi could be seen swimming in the dark water, and one time a pair of females surfaced to deposit a waterproof sack on the floor.

Their canoe approached a stone wall, the top of which disappeared into the gloom above, and Val again had to duck as the canoe passed into a large chamber, the terminus of the canals. In the center, resembling the hub of a wheel with the canals as the spokes, was a circular basin of water with a throne floating atop it. Lounging atop the high-backed chair, half in the throne and half in the water, was a being whose head and torso belonged to a human male, yet whose lower half was scaly and mottled green, like a kethropi. Though the mermerus had human facial organs, he also had gills on the side of his neck that opened and closed as he breathed.

"Welcome to my palace," the mermerus said, with only a trace of the gargling voice distinctive to the kethropi. "I am Zagath."

After tying off the canoe to a wooden post, the red-haired man stepped out of the vessel and waved at them to follow. Val offered Synne a hand, knowing she was in pain, but she cut him off with a glare. Sinias took another deep sniff from his stoppered vial and followed them on shaky legs.

Val planted his staff on the stone floor and drew up tall. He was representing the Congregation and needed to act the part. "Thank you for saving us."

"It's not often that a Congregation mage comes to visit. In fact, if memory recalls, you're the first. Welcome, Valjean." He bowed in his chair towards Synne. "Lady of the Rigid Hand. You are welcome, too. And Sinias! Well met again. I assume you were selected to guide our illustrious visitors?"

"Yesss."

"As you can see, I've had to move my base of operations. I daresay it's an improvement. We can reach anywhere in the city from here, and even the gulf." Zagath turned the chair to address Val again, the dangerous smile returning. "I only found this place once the black sash forced us deeper inside. Unless one has wandered these tunnels for years, one would never find one's way home."

"There's no need for threats," Val said. "We came on business."

"Not a threat, mage. Just a statement of mutual understanding."

Val summoned a flicker of Spirit Fire to play across his fingertips. "Then I suppose we understand each other."

The mermerus arched his eyebrows at the display. "I've been aware of your presence since the moment you entered Undertown, but I confess the purpose of your visit eludes me."

"The Congregation desires your assistance with a simple question."

"Nothing to do with the Congregation is simple, and information is power."

A green-gilled head broke the surface of the water. Zagath paused to converse in the language of the fish men. After the kethropi slipped beneath the surface again, Val said, "The Congregation is seeking an artifact that has returned to Urfe."

"The Coffer of Devla."

Val spread his hands. "You have good sources."

"I *am* the source."

"Then that bodes well for our inquiry. We wish to know who stole it, and where they took it."

"Most understandable," Zagath said. "The Coffer is a grave threat to the Congregation."

Val knew what Zagath was doing: bargaining for the price by elevating the importance of the request. "Grave is an overstatement. We view it more as a nuisance."

"A simple nuisance has brought you all the way to Undertown?"

"They have hardly sent an elder mage."

"Yet they sent a spirit mage, no less. One who completed the Planewalk on his own, returned the Star Crown, and has the ear of Lord Alistair."

Val didn't respond, stunned that he knew those facts.

"No one in New Victoria," Zagath said, leaning forward on his watery throne, "has the eyes and ears that I have."

"Impressive," Val murmured. "Conducting an empire from such an isolated location."

Zagath leaned back in his chair. He seemed both pleased and troubled by the compliment. "Do you know why I live beneath the surface, mage?

Surrounded by filth and muck, doomed to a half-life of stench and darkness? I have an empire, yes. But it is not one that pleases me."

The mermerus spun his floating chair slowly in the water, as if collecting his thoughts. Val glanced at Synne and found her gaze roaming the chamber, wary.

"I am . . . unwelcome . . . in the Kethropi Kingdom. The oceans and seas are not safe for me. Oh, there are plenty of uncharted pockets in which I could dwell. But I am both human and kethropi. I desire society. The sunlit world of men and its pleasures." He smirked. "Certain companionship. Yet *these*," he swept a hand towards his legs, "limit me to a half-life. We mermerus, you see, cannot survive fully in the water, and on land, without moisture, my poor scaled limbs will suffocate. Thus I conduct my business from this waterlogged tomb." His green eyes blazed as he planted his hands on the side of his throne. "My men saved your lives in the tunnels. Even without an answer to your question, I consider you in my debt."

"So you know who took the Coffer?"

"I was approached by someone for the job. I don't know who stole it, but I know who ordered it done."

"And where it now rests?"

Zagath gave a single, brief nod.

"What is it that you want?" Val said.

"The one who ordered the Coffer stolen is a very dangerous adversary. A person it would be unwise to cross. A wizard. This, too, impacts the price of my knowledge. I am a reasonable man, and there is one thing I desire above all others. Yet it lies in the heart of the Kethropi Kingdom, and I am unable to reach it myself. But you, mage. You can get it for me."

"Go on," Val said.

"You will hear many things about me from the kethropi." He grinned again. "Most of them true. Not long before I was banished, I uncovered knowledge of a legendary trident—the inspiration for my organization—that allows its bearer to swim the oceans without air, and walk at will on land. An artifact made specifically for a mermerus. Yet the trident rests in an ancient temple sunk deep beneath the ocean. The kethropi care not for this artifact. They have no desire to walk on land, and should they have the need, they have their own mages and ensorcelled items."

"Why not get it yourself?" Val asked.

"I would be caught and imprisoned before I swam within a hundred fathoms. This, then, is my price for the knowledge you seek. The retrieval of the Trident of Terengotha."

Val glanced at his companions. Sinias was gripping his staff just below the spiked iron bauble, observing the exchange with an impassive air. He brought his vial to his face now and again, rolling his neck after he sniffed. Synne was standing between Val and Zagath's men, ensuring no one got too close.

Val knew this was his decision to make. "If I retrieve this item for you, how do I know you'll keep your word? As you said yourself, the possessor of the Coffer is a dangerous enemy to cross."

Zagath gave a harsh laugh. "More dangerous than breaking a promise to the Congregation?"

"No," Val said quietly. "Not more dangerous than that."

"As I thought. Bring it to me, mage. Bring me the Trident and we will conduct business."

"How do I find you again?"

"Step foot in Undertown, and I will know."

Lord Alistair leaned back in his chair and took a long sip of granth. "Interesting."

Six hours earlier, Val had returned from his journey to Undertown, blindfolded by Zagath's men as they led Val and the others to the surface. Sinias had already been paid, and he left them at the entrance to the Goblin Market, still shivering with cold, his reptilian eyes flat and menacing, proclaiming he hoped never to see either of them again.

After returning home for the longest shower of his life, Val treated Synne to dinner at his favorite pub, then reported to Lord Alistair in the study of his St. Charles manor.

"Interesting," Val repeated. "Yes, it was definitely that."

"Do you trust him?"

"In my career on Earth, I was a lawyer. I'm a pretty good judge of when someone is lying. I think Zagath wants this Trident—desperately. I also think he knows it would be foolish to cross the Congregation."

Lord Alistair crossed his legs. "The Trident of Terengotha does exist. Its creation is well documented. Whether it resides in this ruined temple is another matter."

"Should we bring Zagath here and force him to divulge the information?"

"Unfortunately, I fear he'll be wary of just that, and take precautions to avoid us. If we lose the opportunity, we might not get another. No, better to attempt the retrieval, and if that fails, pay him another visit."

Val read between the lines. *If I die or fail on my mission, the Congregation will send someone who can get the job done.*

"He gave me a nautical chart he acquired from a kethropi boundary surveyor who found the temple," Val said, holding out a vellum scroll.

Lord Alistair unrolled it and examined the map. "You understand this?"

"Zagath interpreted for me."

"What if someone else has reached it first?"

"I asked the same question. Zagath said it's very remote, and no one outside the kingdom knows about it. He said it took him years of searching to find the location."

"And why did he himself not retrieve it?"

"He was caught and imprisoned before his planned expedition."

"Does that not strike you as contrived?"

"It does."

"And?"

"I think Zagath isn't telling us the whole story. I think maybe he tried to go himself and couldn't get the Trident for some reason."

Lord Alistair pressed his lips together. "Perhaps a guardian or danger of some kind? How long would this journey take?"

"According to Zagath, the temple rests on a sunken landmass outside Kethropi City. I suppose we could fly there, or take a boat."

After another long sip, Alistair steepled his fingers against his lips as he considered the situation. "The Congregation is in possession of two items, Skincloths, that allow for underwater exploration. They were developed by a powerful aquamancer ages ago."

Val chuckled to himself. *We call it scuba gear.*

"The Skincloths allow the wearer to breathe and speak underwater, swim with ease, and walk on underwater surfaces as if on land."

Val nodded. "I'm game, if you think we have time. How long does it take to reach Kethropi City?"

Lord Alistair looked amused. "As long as it takes to reach the Sanctum."

"A portal?"

"Of course. If you choose this route, I'll allow a companion mage, though I'd prefer it not be someone from the Congregation. For the same reasons as before."

"I'll go," Adaira said, as she stepped into the room. Though the door had been cracked, Val had thought they were alone in the house.

"You forgot to knock," Lord Alistair said, with a frown at his daughter. "I thought you were away for the day."

"And Father," she said sweetly, taking a seat beside him in a richly upholstered chair, "you're forgetting something about the kethropi. They're very concerned with formality, and Val will need a representative who knows their customs. They're too important an ally to ruffle feathers."

Val wanted to tell Adaira not to put herself in danger, but he dared not intervene.

"You're right," Lord Alistair said calmly. "It would be prudent to send an emissary. It would be good training for you."

"Thank you," she said after a moment, surprised by the acquiescence. "It will be good to see Riga again."

"You are *not*, however, to accompany Val on his mission."

"What? But I can—"

"Silence!" he thundered. "I'll brook no discussion. You defied me once already, and I'll not return you to danger." He turned to Val. "I'll hold *you* responsible if she does not remain in Kethropi City during the journey. Yes?"

"Understood," Val replied. Adaira wouldn't like it, but what could he do?

"Do you have anyone else in mind?" he said to Val. "A majitsu won't have enough magic for a sustained journey with the Skincloth."

"Zagath mentioned runes on a door inside the temple. It might be helpful to have a bibliomancer along, and I happen to know a talented one."

Lord Alistair steepled his fingers. "A good point. If he agrees, Dida is an acceptable companion." He clapped once and stood. "Now, if you'll both excuse me, I have a speech to prepare."

Later that night, Val met Dida and Adaira on a cobblestone street outside the entrance to The Gryphon's Beak, a popular pub near the Guild District that catered to seasoned adventurers.

After they exchanged greetings, Val opened the heavy oak door, releasing an aroma of wood smoke and fat drippings from the open grill built into the rear wall. Patrons congregated around high tables spread throughout the room. It was a boisterous and edgy crowd, armed to the teeth.

Pennants, flags, and coats of arms from around the world hung above the bar in the center of the establishment. Val aimed for a table by the fireplace where a burly one-armed man sat alone, drinking a mug of foamy red ale. The tables around him were unoccupied, as if the other patrons were wary of sitting too near.

It was the same table at which Val and Dida had met the grizzled explorer the first time, and his scarred face broke into a scowl as the three of them approached. Val smiled to himself. Rucker was as unchanging as the tide.

As usual, the adventurer's long gray hair was caught in a ponytail, and he wore a battered leather breastplate with a sleeve attached. A shorter sleeve covered the stump of his other arm, and a pair of serrated hunting knives hung from his hip. There was no sign of his multicolored ring, but the silver battle-axe he had taken from Myrddin's Tomb dangled menacingly from his leather belt.

"I don't like the looks of this," Rucker drawled. "Can't an old man drink in peace?"

None of them had seen Rucker since their return from the alternate dimension on the other side of the spirit fog. Adaira approached Rucker from behind and wrapped her arms around his neck, causing the gnarled warrior's cheeks to flush bright red. He spluttered as she disengaged, looking as helpless as Val had ever seen him.

"I missed you," Adaira said.

Rucker grunted in response, then exchanged a forearm clasp with Val and Dida that almost resulted in the shattering of Val's ulna.

"Take a seat, then," he said, waving a hand at them. "Ye look like fools standing around without a beer."

A slim waitress came over to take their order, winking at Val when Adaira wasn't looking. After she returned with a round of ale, Val said to Rucker, "We need your help with something."

"I told you before, I don't get involved."

"Unless there's a sick relative who needs your help," Val said.

"Bah! Are you related to me? Didn't think so."

Adaira patted his hand. "We just need some advice. I promise."

"I trust a promise from the three of ye about as much as I trust a fox with me chickens."

"We're just waiting on Synne," Val said. "As soon as she arrives we'll—"

A commotion near the entrance interrupted him. Val turned to see a hulking man with a long red beard berating someone at the door, as if trying to bar them from entering. When the person tried to slip past him, Val saw a shaved head and lithe figure, and realized to his surprise it was Synne. His shock increased when he realized the identity of the bearded man: Kjeld Anarsson, First Don of Majitsu. Next to his enormous frame, Synne resembled a starving urchin.

The cavernous establishment was very crowded. Somehow, Val had missed Kjeld on his way inside. The man was obviously drunk, and he was shoving a finger in Synne's face.

Val rose to intervene, but Rucker grabbed him. "Boy, that's Kjeld Anarsson."

"I know who it is," Val said in annoyance. "And that's my majitsu he's bullying."

"Better bullied than lying on the floor with yer throat ripped out."

As Val shrugged him off and strode towards the door, he heard Kjeld roar, "The Don you dueled was my first cousin!"

"The girl who hung herself was my little sister," Synne replied, thrusting her chin forward and squaring her shoulders for a fight. "And it's your cousin's fault she's dead."

"Lying wench!" With a strangled cry, Kjeld took a swing at Synne, so fast Val could barely see it. Somehow, Synne reacted in time, and after she blocked the blow she went low for a leg sweep. As inebriated as Kjeld appeared to be, he sidestepped the maneuver, graceful as a ballerina, then caught Synne by the throat with one hand and lifted her straight in the air. Her eyes bulged at once. She managed a shortened combo kick to his midsection, but he didn't even react to the blows. Val realized the towering majitsu was about to squeeze the life out of her, right in front of everyone. Enraged, Val summoned Spirit Fire to his fingertips, though too many people surrounded the combatants for him to use the spell. He waded through the crowd, worried he wouldn't reach Synne in time.

"Don Anarsson!" Adaira shouted from behind him.

The command in her voice caused the crowd to quiet. Kjeld turned to face her, holding Synne like a rag doll. She was gasping for air and clutching at her throat.

"Release that woman at once!"

His eyes widening at the sight of the Chief Thaumaturge's daughter, Kjeld snarled and tossed Synne to the side, against a wall. As she crumpled to the floor, Val extinguished his magic and rushed over to her, but she pushed him away and stood by herself, wobbly on her feet. He knew she had a bandage beneath her robes to cover her broken ribs.

"Adaira," Kjeld said evenly, "this woman is responsible for the death of my cousin. Honor demands I settle that score."

"If I am not mistaken, your cousin fought a duel according to the regulations of the Code of Majitsu—and lost. According to those same regulations, there is no outstanding honor debt. Stand down, commander."

With a visible effort of will, Kjeld maintained his composure and performed a half bow. "My lady," he said tightly, and then strode towards the door. On his way out, Val saw him glare at Synne. An unspoken promise to finish the job.

A posse of Kjeld's supporters followed him out the door, and they disappeared into the night.

"That's not an enemy you wish to have," Rucker said, when they returned to the table. Dida looked disturbed by the violent encounter. While Synne said nothing, her normally steady hands were shaking as she sat, and an ugly purple bruise had blossomed on her neck.

"He was about to kill her," Val snapped at Rucker.

"He wouldn't have killed her. Not in here."

"It didn't look that way to me."

"I can take care of myself," Synne said.

Rucker snorted. "Sorry lassie, but not against that monster, you can't. He's too ambitious to risk his rank over an unauthorized murder. He was just blowing off steam. But don't get in the way of that one. I'm not even sure Spirit Fire would stop him. Some say he's as powerful as an elder mage, and no one disputes he's as nasty as a cornered wererat."

"Powerful men think they can get away with anything," Adaira said. "It's despicable. He's three times your size," she said to Synne, "and your superior as well."

The majitsu didn't respond, and Val could tell by her darkened brow that Adaira's words had only angered her more. Synne was as proud as anyone he had ever known, and the head of her beloved order had just embarrassed her in public, as well as questioned her honor.

Eventually the conversation turned to the trip to Kethropi City. Val filled Synne and Rucker in on the details, and asked if they knew anything helpful.

"I know nothing of such things," Synne said to Val, "except I wish you wouldn't go someplace I cannot accompany you."

Adaira leaned a little closer to Val, and he caught a stab of jealousy in her eyes.

"I appreciate the concern, Synne," he said. "Unfortunately, the Skincloth can only be used by a mage."

"I could accompany you through the portal. Stay with you until you leave for the temple."

"We'll be fine," Adaira said. "There's no danger in Kethropi City."

"As you wish," Synne murmured, with a respectful tip of her head.

"What about you?" Val said to Rucker, unrolling the nautical chart that Zagath had provided. "Do you know anything about this?"

The adventurer studied the vellum scroll. "I haven't heard of this trident, but the description of a ruined temple beneath the ocean, in that part of the world, smacks of the lost civilization of Kau-Voa."

"Ah," Dida said, lifting a finger in the air. "Yes, I hadn't thought of it before."

"The what?" Val asked.

Dida assumed a scholarly air. "Kau-Voa is rumored to be an ancient civilization that existed long ago, deep in prehistory. Perhaps during the Calaverian Age."

"That sounds like the myth of Atlantis."

"I'm unfamiliar with that legend."

"Don't worry about it."

Dida sniffed. "The kethropi are notoriously bad historians. I have no doubt that significant historical sites exist within the boundaries of their kingdom, unknown to the outside world. If this lost temple really is a remnant of the Kau-Voa, the chance to study it firsthand would be extraordinary!"

As Dida made notes in a journal, Val continued to probe, but neither the bibliomancer nor Rucker had anything else of value to add. Almost no humans had visited any part of the Kethropi Kingdom, since the water-breathing requirement made it a tad difficult.

Disappointed by the lack of knowledge, Val sat lost in his thoughts until the conversation turned to the recent state of war declared by the Congregation. Rucker slammed his mug on the table in disgust.

"Isn't the Realm territory enough for that father of yours?" Rucker said to Adaira.

"Threats have been made by the Mayan Kingdom," she said stiffly. "He cannot project weakness to our enemies."

"Weakness? The Congregation?" Rucker guffawed. "The Battle Mages are formidable, but they're hardly a threat to storm the walls of New Victoria." He wagged a finger. "My guess is this pretext of squashing the so-called *revolution* is a way to whet the public's appetite for war. He wants the Mayan Kingdom for himself, and the bigger prizes further south. It's bad business, pushing into a neighbor's homestead," he said, with a shake of his head. "Bad business."

"*Dean Groft* is bad business," Val said. "He's with the Revolution, and that should be enough to scare anyone."

"Aye. 'Tis true. But still—and no offense to all of ye—a government with no check on its power worries me even more."

"It's getting late," Val said, as he drained his mug. "We should rest before our journey."

Rucker folded his arms as they stood to leave. He looked at each of them in turn, but his eyes rested longest on Val. "Ye watch yourself now, lad," he said. "In Kethropi Kingdom, as well as right here in New Victoria."

22

"Did the Nephili have a religion?" Will asked suddenly, as he stared at the outline of the seamless door to the storehouse. He and the others were standing at the top of the enclosed obsidian stairway they had found by walking through a secret entrance in an abandoned section of the city.

"What an odd question," Skara said. "I've no idea. Why do you ask?"

"I don't really know. Maybe just looking for insight into their nature."

"I think they *were* the religion."

Mateo was standing next to Yasmina, holding the urumi blade in his hand. "If we can open the door, should we expect a guardian inside?"

"I've no doubt the storehouse was once protected by something I've no wish to face," Skara said. She had looped the corded glow stone around her neck, and was holding her cudgel in one hand, the bladed cane in her other. "The question is whether the guardian survived the plague and the passage of millennia."

"Say your prayers to fallen gods," Will said, locking his wrists as he held Zariduke at arm's length.

As soon as the ensorcelled blade struck the door, a dull green light outlined the surface of the portal. Instead of a clean swipe, or encountering the natural resistance of stone, Zariduke instead bit deeply into the substance of the door, as if cutting into a force field. Arms straining with the effort, he grunted and thrust harder, afraid the sword would get stuck if he lost momentum. Mateo offered to help but Will shook his head and put all of his strength behind the effort, shoving the blade forward millimeters at a time until it finally broke through and the door dissolved into motes of green light.

"I have no idea what kind of magic that was," Will said, panting from the effort, "but it wasn't normal."

In disbelief, Skara stepped carefully through the open space where the door used to be. "At last," she breathed. "The storehouse is open."

Bartu followed behind her, both scimitars in hand, as everyone entered a circular chamber the size of a small pond. Like much of the architecture in the city, the surface of the floor was made of smooth black stone with no visible seams. Spaced throughout the chamber were slender pillars of the same onyx hue, bending to connect the floor to the walls like the curve on a 3-D graph, or disappearing into the darkness above their heads to support an unseen ceiling. These pillars were of varying sizes; some as thin as a finger, some as thick as a light pole. Most incredible of all was the pool of thick gray energy seething in the center of the chamber. The storehouse gave Will the impression of being inside a giant, three-dimensional wheel with a hot tub of dirty water serving as the hub.

As he and the others carefully approached the basin, which resembled a viscous bank of thunderclouds caught in the center of the floor, he looked down and realized the dirty mass of energy was swirling torpidly in random patterns, as if confused.

"Over here!" Dalen called out. "Look at this!"

Everyone turned, astonished to find the illusionist in a corner of the room, waving his hand through a portion of the wall. After getting everyone's attention, he stepped all the way through and called back for them to follow.

Will entered last, passing through the illusion into a corridor that curved away into the darkness. On the left side of the passage was a succession of pronged silver stands as tall as Yasmina. They were empty except for the four closest to the illusory doorway. Cradled atop each of these stands was a single disc-shaped object glowing with the same greenish tint as the door to the storehouse.

"Sephyr Wafers," Skara said in a reverent voice, reaching up to grab one of the plate-size discs. "Just as the journal said."

"You sure you want to do that?" Will asked.

She ignored him and plucked one off its stand, cradling it in her hands. Everyone tensed as Skara turned it over. It bore no markings of any kind. "It doesn't weigh very much."

As she carefully placed the wafer in her backpack, Will wanted to scratch an itch that had formed from studying the design of the storehouse. He reached up to take one of the wafers and returned to the main chamber, followed by Mateo, who watched as Will knelt in front of the basin, careful not to touch the surface.

Will wasn't sure what he planned to do, perhaps just see if the wafer or the pool reacted to the proximity of the other. Yet when he held the green disc above the surface, it dissolved to dust in his hands. It happened too fast for him to react, other than to watch in shock as the cloud of powder disintegrated into the pool, followed by a crackling sound that caused sparks of colored energy to dance within the basin. The gray mass began to stir faster, and an emerald flame shot along a grid of previously invisible lines throughout the floor of the chamber. The flames leapt onto the connecting pillars in the room, flowing into them and causing them to glow. Neither Will nor Mateo was standing on one of the lines on the floor, though Mateo had been grasping one of the pillars with his metallic hand. He jerked away but seemed to suffer no damage.

A scream came from inside the secret chamber Dalen had found. Skara Brae stumbled into the main room holding her arm out in front of her. Her leather shirt was burnt through near her left triceps, the skin blistered and raw. She was holding a wafer wrapped partly in a cloth in her other hand. The others followed her out but appeared unharmed. Bartu had retrieved Skara's cudgel.

"What happened?" Will asked.

"I was leaning against the wall when I got a shock—Bartu! Your hand!"

Everyone turned to regard the warrior, who was staring down at his left hand, the fingers of which had been burnt to white bone underneath. His palm was a pulpy mass of bloody flesh that made Will wince.

"I'll get the healing salve," Skara said. "You didn't even cry out!"

As if just realizing he was in pain, Bartu howled and bent over his hand. The adrenaline of the situation must have caused a delayed reaction.

Will noticed the colored sparks in the basin glowing brighter at the same time he heard a hum from overhead, followed by a gathering of white light in the darkness directly above the basin. "Get back!" he cried, just before the light coalesced into a beam that shot downward, curving towards Will like a heat-seeking missile. Without thinking, he raised the sword in defense instead of his shield, which was still strapped to his back. Zariduke caught the beam and absorbed it, though the impact moved him back a step.

In the corner of his eye, he saw Skara move towards the exit, followed by another stab of light arcing towards the adventuress. Again, from his position directly underneath the source of the magical beam, Will was able to intercept the missile with his sword.

"I think I just activated the defense system," he called out, then noticed someone was missing. "Where's Yasmina!"

"Here," she said. "In another of the corner tunnels."

"Stay put," he said, trying desperately to figure out what to do. Why had he been so stupid? He had just wanted to see if he could help in some way, lift the terrible curse of the city.

The situation grew worse when he noticed that Zariduke had turned a few shades darker than its normal sheen. Will grew cold. The strange beam of light must have affected the sword in some way, perhaps even infected it with the disease plaguing the city.

The white ray had not struck again, making him think it was motion activated. He took a deep breath. He had gotten everyone into this, and had to get them to safety. "Skara, will you risk running for the exit? I think I can cover you."

"You *think*?"

"Do you have a better idea?"

The adventuress muttered something too low for him to hear, then called out, "On the count of three?"

"Run fast," he replied, then began to count. On three, he heard her rush across the floor behind him. As he suspected, her movement initiated two strikes of light from above. He managed to swipe them both, dissipating the energy, then studied his sword.

It had turned even darker.

"I'm out!" Skara yelled.

No no no. This can't be happening. Everything they were fighting for, the Revolution's hope against the Congregation, Will's ability to defend himself and his companions, hinged on the power of the sword his father had bequeathed him.

He risked turning his head. The movement incurred no response from the defense system. He saw the horrible wound on Bartu's hand and did not want to think about what a direct blow from one of those beams would do.

As far as he could tell, there was only one way out of this predicament. "Get out of the room," he called out in a flat voice. "All of you."

"What about you?" Dalen said quietly. Everyone must have noticed the damage to the sword. "Perhaps I could try an illusion."

"It's too risky. Better if I face it head on."

"Cousin, my hand did not react when the light struck. Perhaps I can use it in defense."

"And maybe the light beam is a thousand times stronger than what passed through the pillars."

"I still think—"

"Go!" Will roared. "All of you! On my count!"

Without waiting for a response, he craned his neck to face the shaft of darkness overhead, and counted to three. Behind him, everyone made a mad dash for the exit, and he blocked two more blasts. Yasmina called out to say they all were safe.

At least I've done my duty.

He stood rigid by the pool, terrified to move. Zariduke had turned a deep, ugly brown, and he knew in his heart that whatever strange disease had ravaged the city had infected the magic of his sword as well. He found he was not as concerned with his personal safety as he was with Zariduke. He knew all too well that the sword, and not he, was the hope of the Revolution, the guardian of his companions.

Which meant that the sword, and not Will, had to make it out of that chamber in one piece.

He turned slowly as he raised his shield, prepared to throw the sword through the portal.

"No!" a voice called out, clear and firm. Yasmina. "Don't do it, Will. Use the sword."

He hesitated, gripping the buckler tight. Though he hated to expose Zariduke to another beam, he sensed she was right: the shield would not withstand the magical blast, and using it would likely get him killed.

"I know what you're thinking," she said, "and it's not worth it."

"I'm a believer in causes, Yaz," he said. "In personal sacrifice for the good of all."

"I'm a believer in the sanctity of life. Which I believe is more valuable than *any* cause."

Skara and Bartu remained silent, but Dalen and Mateo chimed in, echoing Yasmina's concern, pleading with Will to use the sword to escape even if it destroyed the blade.

Will stared down at the compromised weapon. "Even if I use it, I might not make it through."

"Take the chance," Yasmina urged. "We know the sword can stop it. It's not Zariduke we need—it's you."

"That's not true and you know it."

"It *is* true. I need you. I need Will Blackwood, my friend for many years, the guy at the bar who always made me smile. Do you know who else would never forgive you? Do you think Val and Caleb care about that silly sword? Your brothers need you more than ever, Will." She took a moment to gain control of her emotions. "I'm afraid Caleb won't come back to us without you. He loves you and Val both, but he worships you. Respects your integrity. You're his lifeline, Will. His beloved baby brother. You always have been. And I know Val well enough to know he'll never recover."

Whether calculated or not, Yasmina had found an argument that spoke to him. And she was right. His brothers needed him, badly, with or without the sword.

After taking a few quick breaths for courage, knowing he might not make it out, he backed towards the exit as fast as he could, using Zariduke to fend off three more rays of light. The impact of the final blast sent him tumbling through the open portal, where his friends caught him before he fell down the stairs.

Everyone tensed, but no more beams followed. The defense mechanism must have been keyed to the central room in some way, which Will had suspected.

As they descended the marble stairs, his eyes lowered to his sword. Zariduke was still in one piece, but the legendary sword had turned the color of deepest night, from tip to hilt, and felt lighter than before, as if the magic that sustained it was gone. He felt numb as he waved it around.

"Cast a spell, Dalen," Will said harshly, as soon as they returned outside.

"What?"

"An illusion of any sort. Right here in front of me."

His friend complied, waving his hands to create an image of a hill troll looming over the party, smacking its lips in hunger. With everyone watching, Will gripped Zariduke and ran it through the heart of the illusion. He felt numb as Dalen's illusion flickered but held. The snip-snap of blue-white light from the sword was so faint it was barely visible.

Dalen swallowed and dispelled the illusion with a flick of his hand. No one spoke as Will grimly turned on his heel and headed back the way they had come, towards the river and the waiting barge.

Though an occasional shriek or deep-throated bellow accompanied their passage, imparting a vivid reminder of the menagerists who used to occupy this part of the city and perhaps still did, the party returned to Meru's vessel without incident. The barge master was waiting on the deck when they arrived, drinking from a battered gourd and chewing on a wad of something in the side of her mouth. After a curt greeting, she returned to the pilothouse and ignited the boat's power source.

Once safely on the river, Skara used her good hand to extract a tiny tube of healing salve from her pack, then applied the ointment to her and Bartu's wounds. The salve did not have the miraculous effect of stronger healing balms Will had seen, but it closed the wounds and eased the pain.

When Skara asked her companion about his hand, he probed his palm with his other hand, declared he was fine, and moved away. Her eyes followed him, though Will was too preoccupied with his sword to think much about it.

As the sun descended, casting the gloomy city into deeper shades of gray, the party discussed what had occurred in the storehouse. Was the bizarre pool of energy the source of the wafers, or did it only consume them? Would the city come back to life now? Outside the storehouse, they had seen no further sign of regeneration, but maybe it would take time. Why had a few of the wafers been left behind by their creators? Why not try to use them all?

Yasmina remarked that the shape of the room, an ellipsis with four passages in the corners that spiraled away from the center, resembled the shape of a galaxy. Had the Nephili arrived from beyond the stars? Or was the storehouse merely inspired by the heavens above, an ode to the beauty and mystery of the multiverse?

The others came to the conclusion that Will had drawn when the wafer had dissolved in the pool and ignited the room: somehow, the architecture of the city was magically connected, perhaps even alive in a way that none of them understood. This would explain how the plague had spread, and why it had stopped at the borders of Praha. This could also mean the builders of the city were connected to the city itself, sensitive to any damage incurred.

As curious as it all was, Will couldn't bring himself to care about the discussion. He had only wanted to bring a spark of hope to the doomed city, yet he had succeeded in single-handedly derailing their quest, and possibly the entire Revolution. How could he return with a broken sword? What would he tell Tamás and the council?

How would he help his brothers?

He thought of Mala, and her final words before they parted. She was right, of course. Being a hero was a fool's game, and he was Fool in Chief. Deep down, did he *want* to sacrifice his own life? Did he have no identity apart from his prowess in battle, or the praise and adulation of others?

Who was the better human being: Mala, who might be selfish but placed a high value on the sanctity of her own life, or Will, who stumbled blindly forward, risking life and limb for inchoate causes that bolstered his reputation?

Mala had true confidence. She knew exactly who she was and lived her life by that code.

Will had spent his life in search of meaning, doing everything in his power to please and help others—and now he had paid a terrible price for his choices.

The barge passed by the docks and kept going. Soon, the towers and spires atop the bluff of Old Town emerged in the distance, a great gaping darkness looming in the middle of the city. Will gave a little shudder at the thought of entering the Agora and scaling the Wailing Wall without the use of Zariduke.

As if reading his thoughts, Mateo wandered over to offer up a spare dagger he kept in his pack. Will tried to act grateful as he accepted, but felt only shame and humiliation. His cousin patted him on the back and reminded him that every weapon was simply an extension of the spirit of the fighter, even a weapon such as Zariduke.

Will flashed a bitter smile and returned to watching the river.

Dalen and Yasmina kept their distance, sensing Will needed to be alone. On occasion, when one of them caught his eye, he converted their sympathetic glances into pity, whether they meant it that way or not.

Bartu had spent the entire journey alone at the stern of the boat, muscular arms folded, watching the receding tunnel of stone with an impassive expression. As the bluff drew ever nearer, its sheer walls seeming to rise straight out of the river, Skara wandered over to stand beside Will. She placed her hands on the railing and leaned into the wind.

"I'm not your friend," she said, causing Will to bark a laugh.

"The feeling is mutual."

"But let me offer some advice. I'm a teacher to my acolytes, both in the martial ways of baritsu and in the discipline of the mind. And I can state with impartial clarity that if you do not regain your focus, you will die on this journey, and imperil our lives as well."

"My sword is broken, Skara. What if you didn't have your weapons?"

"Are you familiar with baritsu?"

"No."

"It's a derivation of the martial arts of the Orient, adapted to the needs of urban environments. Instead of fighting samurai on horseback or engaging in hand-to-hand combat in fields of war, baritsu utilizes the principles of everyday survival common to all slum dwellers. In short, we do anything and everything we can to stay alive, with any weapon available."

"That reminds me of my own teacher," Will said, still staring into the distance. His heart grew heavy at the thought of Mala. Not just her distance—physical and emotional—but how cruel her laughter would be when she heard of his reckless behavior.

"Which was whom?" Skara asked.

"The same person who sent us to you."

Skara's tone took on new respect. "Mala? I've never known her to take on a disciple."

"I was hardly a disciple. It was . . . a necessary circumstance."

"I know Mala well enough to know she does not suffer fools. Whatever the circumstance, she must have thought highly of your potential."

"We were paying her to guide us. She wanted to keep us alive. That's all."

After a long moment, Skara said, "I don't know her that well, but did Mala tell you how we met?"

"I've been wondering about that."

"It was many years ago. She might not appreciate me telling you, but she was looking for a particular weapon in Praha. One she never found, at least to my knowledge."

He thought about it for a moment. "Was it a cat o' nine tails?"

Skara pressed her lips and nodded. Will decided not to tell her that Mala had found the scourge at last.

"Slight as she is, Mala is the greatest opponent I've ever faced. We sparred briefly, in my arena in the Nilometer, and I was unable to touch her. It's not just her skill in battle, but her willingness to use anything and everything at her disposal to prevail, and her cleverness in so doing. Though her style is different, she embodies the principles of baritsu. Are you aware of the nature of the particular weapon she sought? The cat o' nine tails?"

"Not really."

"It was crafted specifically to kill majitsu."

"Okay."

After a moment, Skara said, "Mala fears those who wield magic, Will. She fears them with all of her being."

"That seems like a healthy point of view."

Skara pushed away from the railing and stared him in the eye. "Fear may keep you alive, but it will eat you from within, and color all of your actions. Fear will keep you from truly being awake. As capable as Mala is, she is ruled by her fears."

He got the point she was trying to make, but it only served to annoy him. "I suppose we all have our faults. What's yours, Skara?"

"Mine?" she said, with an unhealthy chuckle and a glance in Bartu's direction. "Mine is the opposite of fear."

"Bravery?"

"Obsession."

She moved away to stand closer to the prow, leaving Will to his thoughts as the vessel rounded a bend in the river. Soon after, they navigated another turn, completing the C curve. The boat slowed and headed for shore as they passed the edge of the bluff, bringing a new sight into view: a jumbled collection of pillars, stela, and temple-like structures spread over a small plain, abutting the rear face of the massif. From the perspective of the boat, Will saw how the top of the bluff formed a high, flat-topped hill with sheer rock walls that looked impregnable. Atop the bluff loomed the shadows of the blackened palaces and arches of Old Town, swathed in darkness and, far below, bordered on three sides by the river. On the fourth was the plain of ruined buildings they now saw before them.

They had reached the Agora.

23

For some reason, after plunging into the Jabberwock's throat and surviving, Caleb progressed faster through the challenges of the tower. Or at least he thought that was the case. Maybe he had gotten off track somewhere, and was working his way back to the beginning. Maybe the tower had no end and he was stuck in an infinite loop. He didn't know. He could only press grimly forward, using the memory of Marguerite and Luca as a beacon on the hill, pointing the way to some unknown destination.

After the Jurassic version of *Alice in Wonderland*, Caleb popped into a barren wasteland akin to the surface of the moon. The blasted, rocky ground had a bluish-silver sheen that was almost metallic in nature. The sky was black and deep and the stars gleamed brighter than any he had ever seen, as if all other celestial firmaments possessed a filmy gauze obscuring the view. He felt as if he could reach out and touch these stars, and he saw two enormous blue spheres hovering in the sky behind him, a pair of moons glowing with a sapphire light so luminescent he almost had to shield his eyes.

Okay, then. So I'm not in Kansas anymore.

Able to breathe just fine, he caught a faint odor of limestone and chalk dust. As far as he could see, nothing but craters and piles of loose rock littered the lonely surface of the planet. After a time, a humanoid creature made of rock wandered into view, half Caleb's height but twice as thick. It had the look of hardened clay. No eyes or nose or mouth, just two arms and two legs, a torso, and a faceless head. Caleb scurried behind a boulder as the strange being lumbered past without a sideways glance.

More of them came and went, never interacting, never doing anything, an ongoing random procession that felt mindless. He finally got the nerve to call out to one of them. When he did, it stopped moving as if frozen in place. Almost, he thought, as if awaiting a command.

So he gave him one. *Start walking.*

And it did.

After a while, Caleb intuited that this place was a representation of his current vision of the universe. A lifeless place without hope or joy. The only break in the monotony were the two perfect orbs of beauty dominating the night sky, appearing so close yet forever unattainable.

He didn't need a PhD in literature to figure out what they symbolized. *Know thyself.*

As easily as the nature of this place came to him, so did the manner in which he could leave. *Build*, he commanded the stone creatures wandering aimlessly across the surface. His voice barely rose above a whisper, yet it resonated with power, and every rock creature in sight obeyed his command. They worked in silence, tirelessly, gathering the rocks and boulders strewn about the landscape into a central pile, just as Caleb had imagined. They built and they built for their sad human god, lumps of clay in his hands, until they had constructed an image he held clear in his mind: a tower of rock about the same size and shape as the Tower of Elarion.

After the last stone was placed, they filed away one by one, leaving as quietly as they had arrived. Caleb watched the last one disappear into the oddly sharp horizon, and when he turned back, a wooden door had appeared at the base of the tower.

He knew the drill.

On the next pass, Caleb was flying like a spirit mage in outer space, somehow able to breathe, exploring the bounds of the universe. Marguerite was flying behind him, as was Yasmina. There was nothing weird about having the two women together. Yasmina was a friend to them both, just as Caleb would have wanted.

The most beautiful scenery imaginable flashed by: planets and moons and suns, glowing nebulae and exploding supernovae so beautiful it brought tears to his eyes. He felt he had the power to go anywhere, explore any world, fulfill every desire.

Yawn.

As soon as Caleb saw an enormous black hole on the horizon, its spiral arm of kaleidoscopic gases the same shape as the staircase inside the Tower of Elarion, he veered right towards the center, shrugging off the screams and protests of Yasmina and Marguerite. He dove into the heart of the black hole, deeper and deeper, until the light was sucked away and Caleb found himself back in Freetown, just about to open the Coffer of Devla, right before the murder of Luca and Marguerite. Except it wasn't him who was about to open the Coffer, but another version of himself. He stood just outside the pavilion, watching it happen again in real time.

Now we're talking. A scenario I can get into.

Everything from that godforsaken night was the same: the high winds heralding a storm, the crowd of people gathered near the central fountain, glow orbs hanging in the corners of the open-air pavilion where the Coffer rested on a brick platform.

The Other Caleb had just opened the Coffer and was holding up the cloak he had found inside. The same cloak that Real Caleb was wearing. Waves of heat lightning brightened the sky as Other Caleb examined the inside of the chest. Beside him, Marguerite held Luca by the hand, watching with a bemused expression. The boy looked gravely serious, as if he knew something of import was about to occur.

"The Templar!" someone cried. "The prophecy is fulfilled! A true cleric has returned to the land!"

The crowd grew excited. Will and Mala entered the pavilion.

"Caleb?" Will said. "What happened?"

A deafening clap of thunder interrupted Other Caleb's response. Lightning ripped through the canvas roof of the pavilion. It burst into flame as the screams of bystanders pierced the air.

"Lord Alistair sends greetings," the wizard said calmly, right before he called down a wave of lightning to sweep through the four guards, filling the air with the stench of charred flesh.

It was going to happen again. Whatever Caleb was supposed to do differently this time, he wouldn't have time to stop the deaths of Luca and Marguerite. The electromancer was about to walk towards Other Caleb, and Marguerite was about to step in front of him, dooming her and Luca.

In the background, outside the pavilion, Caleb roared in denial. No one could hear him above the high winds and the chaos. He could see Marguerite gripping Luca tightly by the hand, gathering herself to act. Caleb felt his throat constrict with panic. He had thought he could change the outcome, but instead he was forced to watch in helpless horror. *No. God, no. I can't go through this again.*

Some poor soul standing next to him was holding out a dagger, as if that would help against a wizard or a majitsu. Caleb knew what it meant. He ripped it out of the man's hand, turned, and let the dagger fly as Marguerite had taught him. He was nowhere near as proficient as she was, but this time his aim was true. He hadn't bothered to throw it at the attackers, because they would surely have magical defenses in place.

Instead he threw it right at himself.

It was the only way to stop the carnage. His aim was true, even better than he had hoped, and he caught Other Caleb right in the throat. His twin dropped and writhed on the ground as blood poured from the wound. Some final thing shriveled and died inside him as Caleb watched his own self gurgle his last few breaths, dead by his own hand. Marguerite and Luca bent over him, screaming their denial, as Caleb rushed into the pavilion to pull them out of harm's way.

He never made it that far. The electromancer called down a lightning bolt with a familiar spiral shape, sent it slamming into Caleb, and the world went black.

When Caleb could see again, he found himself standing inside a tower with walls of pure ivory and an exquisite tile floor. The whisper of moonlight failed to penetrate the upper reaches of the tower. An array of weapons and heraldic shields hung on the walls. There were no doors or windows he could see.

If there were no windows, where was the light coming from? Perhaps a window atop the tower was open, yet he saw no stars.

From the general size and shape of the place, he got the sense he was back inside the Tower of Elarion. Had he traveled to the past? Was this a former incarnation?

A voice startled Caleb. "When time and space and self are abolished, what remains?"

"Who is that?" Caleb called out. "Who's there?"

No answer. The voice had sounded hollow, disembodied, gender neutral.

All at once, the moonlight inside the tower began to swirl and take shape as if congealing into a physical substance. It picked up speed, starting at the edges of the room and moving inward, with Caleb as the focal point. Moans emanated from within the strange cloud, as if from ghosts or lost souls trapped within. Caleb had the sudden terrifying thought that these were past victims of the tower.

The voice returned. "Are you the locust or the dream? The dream or the locust? Which is inside the other? Know thyself, traveler."

"I wish I did," Caleb said.

The churn of clotted moonlight took on a specific shape, an all too familiar spiral, and Caleb felt goose bumps rising on his arms. He stood very still in the center, afraid to let it touch him. It was all around him now, drawing closer. The voices grew louder and more desperate, wailing, eager. They wanted his warm blood and living essence, he could feel it. Wanted it as bad as he wanted to avenge Marguerite.

No, he thought with a snarl. Not that bad.

"Is there reality apart from self?" the voice intoned. "Or am I you as well as I?"

The spiral arm of moonlight swirled faster and faster, then began to pour into the tiled floor at a specific spot. As Caleb stepped back, he realized the floor was also in the shape of a giant spiral, taking up the whole room, and that the moonlight was pouring right into the center of the helix. The silvery light collected and then rose, forming a human shape with no face, a corporeal ghost that shuddered into being and drifted towards Caleb. He dove to avoid its grasp, and felt a stir of air so cold he knew the thing would freeze his bones if it touched him.

"What is reality?" the voice droned. "Is it the same for all beings?"

"Marguerite and Luca are reality," Caleb said. "Death is reality."

For a moment, the blink of an eye, the tower disappeared and all Caleb could see in the utter darkness was a mace hovering a foot above him, as if suspended inside an abyss. The mace had a black wooden handle and a dia-mond-shaped head formed of a crystalline substance. Before he could reach for it, the mace disappeared, and the ivory-walled tower returned. The ghost thing brushed against Caleb's arm. He screamed at the searing pain and stum-bled backwards, out of reach. His left forearm had blackened where the thing had touched him, as if stricken with frostbite. It went numb at once, and Caleb couldn't lift it.

The ghost was drifting towards him again. As Caleb dashed away in horror, seeking an escape, he thought of Marguerite and Luca with all his might, try-ing to get the mace to reappear. Nothing seemed to work. He grew frustrated as the ghost drew nearer, seeming to predict his movements in advance.

If it had not been the thought of his loved ones, then what had caused the mace to materialize?

"To expand thyself is to open the gates of the universe."

"Shut up!" Caleb screamed.

He grabbed a sword off the wall and jabbed it at the spectral assailant. It passed right through. The thing opened its mouth in a soundless scream, as if releasing the throatless voices trapped inside, then flew faster at Caleb. He rolled beneath it and sprinted away. Desperate, he began circling the room, yanking weapons and shields off the wall, trying to hurt it with daggers, axes, and halberds, hoping to find a magical weapon of some sort.

All were useless.

As he fled, Caleb tried to parse the words of the disembodied voice, but they made no sense. Despite the fact that the ghost warrior wouldn't let him concentrate, Caleb had never been much for philosophy. Clearly the maker of this twisted tower had some sort of agenda. For a while, during the journey, he thought he had it figured out—deny your desires, kill the self, blah blah blah—but this was something different. He had no idea what to do.

Still, he had to try something. If that thing grabbed him even once, Caleb had the feeling he would never escape its embrace. As he thought about ev-erything that had happened, the different challenges of the tower, the room disappeared and the mace reappeared, again for an instant, before the room returned.

"What's the trick?" he muttered.

"The riddle of existence is a mirror within a mirror, with no beginning or end, wrapping inward upon itself."

"Tell me something I don't know," Caleb said, reaching for the final weapon within reach: a two-handed broadsword with a bejeweled hilt that looked promising. As the ghost made another pass, Caleb jabbed straight into its chest, jumping to the side at the last moment, willing it to work.

No effect whatsoever. He tossed the sword aside in disgust.

"You know what I believe?" Caleb shouted. "I believe in the hand in front of my face." He stared at his hand as he ran and, to his great shock, the mace reappeared in the center of the room. Caleb was running along one of the walls. He dashed towards the center, but the mace disappeared before he could reach it.

Then he got it. He knew the nature of this final test, and he knew that it was his greatest weakness.

Know thyself. To reach the mace, all he had to do was believe.

Something he had never been able to do.

Okay, okay. I can do this. As he used up the last of his reserves dodging the deadly touch of the apparition, he shouted, "I get it! I really do! There's something out there running the show, and maybe you're it!"

Yet his words had no effect. Again he tried to think of his fallen loved ones, because if he believed in anything, it was in them. When that produced no results, he thought of his brothers and his parents. Still nothing.

Am I supposed to believe in myself? He wondered. Is that the point? Am I the only reality? Or is there no reality?

Know thyself.

All that nonsense philosophy was a distraction, he realized. Or at least not necessary to the solution. The inscription on the tower had told him what he had to do. He just had to figure out who he was, what he really believed in.

Nothing, he whispered. *I believe in nothing. That's the truth.*

The mace flickered into existence.

I believed in something, and I lost it. Someone took it away. So I guess I believe in suffering, and revenge, and that's about it.

This time, the mace stayed corporeal for an entire three seconds, but he wasn't close enough to reach it.

Caleb was almost spent. As the ghost flew at him again, he tried to feint to the left, but it cut him off. When Caleb dove to avoid it, the being's fingers raked him across the back. Caleb screamed from the pain, stumbled, and fell.

"None of this is real," he shouted, scrambling away on his back. "Goddamnit, none of this is real! None of it matters! This room isn't real. This tile floor, these ivory walls, this fake tower, your stupid disembodied voice! Give me the mace, you bastard! The mace is my suffering. My loss. My tool of revenge. My soul. My reality. So *give it to me!*"

As he screamed the last line at the top of his lungs, the room pulsed and then vanished, and the mace reappeared in midair, wrapped in darkness where it had always been.

Yet the ghost was there, too.

Caleb was still on his back, lying on a rough stone floor. The ghost was a foot away. As it reached down for him, fingers outstretched, Caleb rolled to the side as fast as he could, then jumped to his feet. He started for the mace, but knew he wasn't going to make it. The ghost was about to cut him off. Caleb's left arm hung limp at his side, dragging him down, and pain seared through his back with every step.

The mace was ten feet away, dangling in the darkness like a piece of exotic fruit. Using every ounce of energy he had left, summoning an image of Luca's smiling face, he burst towards the mace and launched into the air, grasping for it. The ghost met him halfway and flowed into him, causing the most intense pain Caleb had ever experienced, liquid fire shooting through his nerves. He screamed as his momentum carried him within reach of the weapon, and somehow he gathered the energy to wrap his fingers around the handle. The mace released from whatever force had suspended it, and Caleb clutched it as he crashed to the floor, losing his wind. Gasping like a fish out of water, blinking in and out of consciousness from the pain, he turned just in time to see the ghost reaching for him again. He knew he wouldn't survive another pass. As the spectral being's fingers reached for Caleb's face, inches away, he jabbed upward with the mace, connecting just before it touched him.

With a flash of light, both the ghost and the floor disappeared, leaving Caleb floating in darkness.

24

Mala shivered in the cool night air as she stood alone atop the burial mound, the wisps of moonlit fog indistinguishable from the fingers of Spanish moss hanging like shrouds off the oaks and willows.

The burial mound rose a hundred feet out of the swampland, its flat earthen top wider than the central plaza of the Thieves Quarter. It was both sacred ground and energy vortex, with magical currents so strange the Congregation had stopped trying to catalogue it and attributed it to a quirk of nature.

Earlier in the day, Dashi had listened to her plan, agreed to help, and even loaned her a powerful item: a wrist bracelet that would bind the dhampyr, or any other lycanthrope, to human form. Once entrapped, his men would attack the dhampyr en masse and paralyze him with a powerful poison.

Getting the bracelet on Nagiro's wrist, however, was Mala's job. Dashi refused to risk his guild members in such a dangerous endeavor, and until the bracelet was applied, the dhampyr could simply change form and flee, then alert the Alazashin of their treachery.

Or he might simply kill them all. Mala didn't know how many people Dashi had brought along, but he could only bring people he could trust with such a politically risky mission. A handful at most.

Not enough to best Nagiro.

She took a deep breath, inhaling the perfume of gardenia and decaying vegetation. The spires of the Wizard District loomed between the trees on the distant horizon.

The sun had just set. She expected the dhampyr to arrive soon, though Nagiro would expect a trick, and know she had exposed herself in such an isolated location for a reason. The questions were how long the Grandfather had given him to complete the mission, whether Nagiro chose to employ the darkness and mist to his advantage, and whether he knew Dashi's men were nearby.

A village lay half a mile to the west. After dinner, Mala had splurged on a flying carriage to take her to the settlement while daylight remained, reducing the risk of a surprise attack. Just before sunset, she had left the village and hiked quickly atop the mound, where she awaited the cover of darkness.

The moon had fattened to a juicy silver orb. The hum of insects dulled her mind, and to keep herself sharp during the wait, Mala recounted what she knew about dhampyrs.

The one foolproof way to spot one of the half-human, half-vampire hybrids was the wicked little spurs on their left wrists. Some said the dhampyr lacked a shadow, but Mala knew this to be a myth. She had seen Nagiro and Ferala in daylight on many occasions, casting a silhouette like anyone else. Other sources claimed the dhampyr lacked bones, abhorred the smell of carrion, and lived a very short life.

All legends.

Just as she began to catalogue what she knew were true characteristics of the species, a shimmering in the air caused her to leap away, roll, and come up with her short sword and sash in hand. The shimmering continued until a man with wild dark hair, a flat face, and eyes as cold as the grave materialized out of the mist in front of her.

He lowered the hood of his form-fitting white garment in disgust.

"What strange magic of yours is this, disrupting my Mirror Cloak?"

Mala knew the burial mound made compasses spin, spells go awry, and glow orbs malfunction. "No magic of mine," she mocked, giving him nothing.

"No matter. Nothing, not even Magelasher, will save you tonight." Nagiro stalked towards her, drawing a platinum-colored sword that caused her to back away. "You know this, Mala. So why stand against me? Especially here, at night? You're not one to think of the safety of innocents."

She loathed the offhand arrogance in his voice. "What choice do I have? Hide in plain sight and wait for the reaping? No. I will choose my battleground." She started spinning her sash, deciding to change her earlier strategy. She would tell him why she was here and lull him into complacency. "The burial mound is an energy vortex."

"I gathered," he said drily.

"Without the Mirror Cloak, the odds are more even."

The dhampyr showed his teeth. "Are they?" Without warning, he closed the ground between them almost as fast as a majitsu, slicing downward with his blade. It was all she could manage to bring her own sword up in defense and spin away. "Impressive you are," he said, continuing to stalk her with that infuriating grin. "For a mortal."

They exchanged a series of sword thrusts that left the underside of Mala's arm bleeding, centimeters from an artery. She managed to disengage by swinging the sash at his head and forcing him back.

"An energy vortex?" he said. "There must be more to your plan. I searched the trees and know you came alone. What trick is up your sleeve, treacherous one?"

"The Grandfather would never order my death. Why risk his wrath?"

"I wouldn't be so sure. The Grandfather is old, and more fickle with his edicts. But this is not about you, Mala. I came for the weapon. Leave it in my hands, and I'll decide whether to slay you as well."

She spat. "You'll twitch on the end of a blade one day, fiend."

"Perhaps," he said, amused, "but it won't be yours. What dark hold do you have over the Grandfather, Mala? I've always wondered."

"True love," she said, "as sweet and pure as a mountain stream."

The music of Nagiro's laugh masked the darkness of his heart. "I do miss your wit. You would have made a fine concubine, once I ascend to the Throne of Daggers. But then you're already accustomed to that role, aren't you?"

She pressed the attack, causing the assassin to skip back as he continued to laugh. "A sore topic, Mala? We all know you bewitched the old man. It was the only way. But you're a killer, just like the rest of us. Why leave the mountain?"

"I'm a killer, true. But I choose who I kill and why. You're nothing but a slave to the whims of a diseased old man."

The dhampyr leaped at her with a vengeance, catching her with a foot to the stomach that doubled her over. As his sword came down for the killing blow, she reached into her pouch and threw a handful of fire beads in his face, causing him to rear back.

She scrambled to her feet as the mist swirled around them, as if urging them on. Despite Nagiro's superior speed and strength, she managed to keep him at bay with her array of sword, sash, dagger, and fire beads, infuriating the dhampyr.

"You'll never outlast me," he said. "You already tire."

She didn't waste her breath denying it.

"Where is Magelasher? You'll tell me before you die, I promise you that."

Mala hadn't brought the cat o' nine tails, in case Dashi betrayed her and she needed a bargaining chip for her life. As powerful as the weapon was, it wouldn't afford her the same advantage against Nagiro as it would against an opponent with magical defenses.

As she stepped back to throw a dagger, Nagiro's form blurred, shifting into a hyena wolf with silver and brown fur. The huge beast snapped its jaws and leapt at her, causing her to execute a series of acrobatic maneuvers to avoid its claws, almost tumbling off the sloped edge of the mound. That was dangerous. She had to stay atop the earthen burial site to keep him from using the Mirror Cloak. When she finished a series of back handsprings and spun to meet the hyena wolf, the dhampyr had shifted back to human form, face twisted in fury, his sword sweeping towards her chest. She lifted her own blade just in time, but Nagiro raked his wrist spur across the side of her throat, narrowly missing her jugular and causing her to stumble. He shifted again, and Mala found herself flat on her back with the paws of a hyena wolf pinning her torso to the ground.

Blood seeped into her mouth as she twisted and struggled to no avail. The creature was far too strong. She gagged at the stench of its fetid breath, her chest crushed beneath its weight. With a blur, the dhampyr shifted to human form again, and Nagiro pressed the side of his blade against her throat. He sat astride her, pinning her arms to the ground with his knees.

"Let us try again," he said. "Where is Magelasher?"

She spat in his face.

"Witch!" he roared. After wiping off the spittle, he put the tip of his blade against her left eye. "Shall we start here?"

She tried to think of something, anything, that might help her escape. The golden bracelet, as slender as a wire, was concealed beneath her sleeve. It may as well have been in the Mayan Kingdom, because she couldn't move her hands. Yet if she didn't slip the collar onto Nagiro, she knew Dashi wouldn't help her.

"Why come after Magelasher?" she said, trying to buy time. "Instead of the Coffer of Devla?"

"Not to worry, love." He leaned over to let his long hair fall in her face as he patted her check. "Ferala seeks the Coffer, and she knows where it is. She'll kill your blond companion and his friends, then bring the Coffer to the mountain. I assure you of that."

Mala felt herself go cold. *She'll kill your blond companion.*

If Ferala was tracking Will, the dhampyr would find him and kill him. Of this she had no doubt. Neither Will, nor anyone else with him, was ready to face the likes of Ferala. Nagiro's twin was even more ferocious and deadly than he was.

The revelation gave her a burst of adrenaline, and Nagiro saw it in her eyes. "I've struck a nerve, eh? Is the blond one a lover?"

"Nagiro?" she said, shuffling her feet as close to her buttocks as she could, and tensing her torso.

"Yes?"

"Catch."

She spat again, this time aiming for his eye. Like a slap, spitting was a maneuver that served to unbalance more than harm. As the spittle flew towards Nagiro's face, causing him to flinch, Mala thrust upward with her heels with all her might, unbalancing the powerful dhampyr just a fraction, for the briefest of moments. It wasn't enough for her to regain her feet, but she was able to slip an arm out and fling her hand at his face, again aiming for his eyes.

Instead of batting her hand away, he bit down on it with the precision of a striking snake, sinking inch-long fangs into her forearm. Mala screamed at the pain but fought through. The eye strike, too, had been a distraction. Her bodyweight had shifted enough to allow her other hand an inch of space, and she managed to reach into her pocket and extract the wrist collar. Contorting her slender wrist with the dexterity of a master thief, she freed her hand even further, reached up, and slapped the golden band around Nagiro's wrist.

There was a flare of orange light. Nagiro jerked his arm away with a scream, as if the collar had seared him. Mala scrambled away in the confusion, her arm aching. Thank the Queen that dhampyrs were sterile and their bite could not make others of their kind.

"What is this?" he said with a snarl, holding his arm in pain. He tried and failed to yank the slender wire off his wrist. "You think this will save you, witch? I'll take you to the mountain and flay you alive!"

"Having trouble with the bracelet?" she mocked.

His face contorted, and he concentrated as if trying to shift form. When nothing happened, he stared at the wrist collar in horror, screamed his rage to the night, and rushed forward. Mala had backed all the way to the edge of the mound. When the dhampyr was halfway to her position, the ground burst apart, trapdoors of dirt-encrusted wood hinging open. Dashi and ten of his followers jumped out of their hiding spots to surround Nagiro, cutting him off from Mala.

The dhampyr howled in fury and replaced the hood of his cloak, causing his form to blur. As before, he didn't quite disappear, instead leaving a silver shimmer in the air. The thieves raised their azantite-tipped arrows that Mala suggested they bring. Rumor held that piercing a dhampyr's skin with enough azantite would kill it, though she was unsure of the truth of that legend, or how much azantite was required.

Before anyone got a shot off, Nagiro pounced on the nearest thief, who had dropped his bow to reach for his sword. Nagiro tore his throat out with his wrist spur. Spinning as fast as a tornado, he whipped his sword into another, gutting a woman with the platinum blade. As he spun again, Mala heard the *thunk* of a quartet of arrows piercing his cloak, and Nagiro staggered. Azantite was sharper and stronger than any metal, and another round of arrows dropped him to his knees.

With the dhampyr distracted, Dashi slipped behind him and threw a net that rendered the creature immobile, caught in purplish strands that hardened to the strength of steel.

"Impressive your kind is," the Guild Lord said, holding Soulskein aloft in precaution as he stepped towards the trapped dhampyr. "But there are what, a few dozen of you on Urfe?" He pointed the tip of Soulskein at Nagiro's throat. "Majority rules, I'm afraid."

"You'll start a war with the Alazashin," Nagiro hissed.

Dashi shrugged. "Lord Alistair already has. And I'm betting on him."

*　　　*　　　*

For the second time in two nights, Mala collapsed into her chair at The Velvet Temple. After rendering the dhampyr unconscious with tranquilizer darts, Dashi and his minions had carried him back to the Thieves Guild in a private carriage. She knew they would keep him locked in a secure cell, guard him with all of their resources, and decide how best to exploit him.

Mala idly wondered how far the Grandfather would go to ensure the return of his favored assassin, or whether he would leave Nagiro to his fate. She also wondered, now that Dashi had the Mirror Cloak, when he would make his bid to usurp Ilianna.

Once the food arrived, rabbit stew served with rosemary biscuits, Mala turned her attention to the decision at hand: whether or not to fulfill her lifelong quest of confronting Kjeld, or instead try to save Will Blackwood's life.

Mala didn't know why the knowledge that Nagiro's twin was after Will had given her such a burst of adrenaline. She did not think it was because she loved the impetuous warrior. She had to admit she had feelings for him, but she had never known love of *that* sort. If so, she thought she would have felt it somewhere by now, deep down inside, and known for sure.

Was it because Will was a companion in arms?

A good man?

The best hope for her people?

Since when did any of that matter? Truth be told, she didn't think any of it did.

So why couldn't she let this go? All of a sudden, she realized what it was, and it made her beer taste rank.

Fear must be the source of her sudden urge to help Will. Another excuse not to face the majitsu who had haunted her nightmares for her entire adult life.

Yes, she was sure of it. She felt for Will, and did not want to see him come to harm, but her own cowardice in confronting Kjeld was the real reason she couldn't get the young warrior's predicament out of her mind.

Still, even after she had admitted this sad fact to herself, why couldn't she seem to stop thinking about him?

And if not Will, whose memory had the shaman taken from her?

*   *   *

The next day at noon, Mala stood in front of a two-story stone residence on Magazine Street. A handsome but typical dwelling in this part of town. She had spent the morning making discrete inquiries about the home of Val Kenefick, the spirit mage she suspected was the alias of Valjean Blackwood, Will's older brother.

Her inquiries led her to a carriage driver named Gus, who had given her the address. Not after Mala had offered him good coin—for some reason, the man was fiercely loyal to Val—but only after she had told him that his brother's life was in danger.

Gus could drop her at the residence, he had said, and nothing more. He didn't have a key, and what she did after that was her business.

Mala had never met a lock she couldn't pick. Eying the simple wooden door with an expert eye, she expected a deadbolt, or an iron bar that would have to be slipped off. If it proved difficult, she could always pry a window or take to the rooftop.

Oddly, the door opened without resistance. She crept inside, knowing Val was away on a mission for the Congregation, unsure if anyone else was around. It made her nervous to sneak into the home of a wizard. The Val Blackwood she had known had been unable to access his powers, but apparently things had changed.

And how in the world had he managed to join the Congregation so quickly? As a spirit mage, no less?

She detected no physical traps, and any magical ones would have snared her already. She stopped to eye a strangely hypnotic tapestry on the wall that depicted two wizards facing each other across a rock bridge spanning a bottomless chasm. The artistry was exquisite, and she wondered at its origin.

There were signs of recent use in the kitchen. Before she descended to the cellar or climbed to the rooftop, she found what she was looking for in one of the bedrooms: a pillow with a few short strands of blond hair.

Neither Val nor Caleb had blond hair. Unless someone else had slept in the house, there was a good chance the lock belonged to Will.

Still muttering to herself that she should be looking for a way to challenge Kjeld, Mala took the decagon of Kirna Tuluth out of a pouch. The beautiful amulet was embedded with tiny pieces of amethyst that formed a ten-pointed star. Earlier that morning, she had consulted a lore master about its usage. She turned the face of the amulet clockwise until it clicked. When it popped open, she laid the strand of hair inside and closed it, then slipped the silver chain around her neck and held the amulet in her palm, staring at it.

She owed this man from another world nothing. Yes, they had once saved each other's lives, but those debts had been paid. Yes, his lips tasted nice and his strong arms felt good around her waist, but she could find a dozen men that very night who made her feel the same.

So why couldn't she leave him to his fate?

She depressed the lever on the back of the decagon and spun the face, unsure if anything would happen. At once she felt the amulet merge into her hand, as if sinking through flesh. The sensation was not painful but caused her to step back in shock. The room started to fade, and just before the blackness enveloped her, she thought again about what a coward she was for running away from the monster who had murdered her parents.

25

The portal to Kethropi City was located beneath the Sanctum. Lord Alistair himself saw Val and the others off, along with Professor Azara and a retinue of majitsu guards. Dida had never seen a bilocation portal before and was highly impressed with the experience, inquiring how it compared to an elder bibliomancer's method of long-distance travel, the deployment of mathematical interdimensional constructs infused with magic. No one in the room had any idea what he was talking about.

As Val, Adaira, and Dida faced the archway of liquid silver, Professor Azara explained that a high-level spirit mage could use the portal not just to bridge locations in an ephemeral state, but to transport items or people as well. Since this feat was far too advanced for Val, she brought the three of them through the portal, then stepped back through.

They arrived in a well-appointed chamber in a portion of Kethropi City located on the surface of the ocean, a tiny floating island built out of coral and reserved for visiting dignitaries. Val wondered how they kept it afloat and anchored it.

Beautiful mixed-media artwork made from repurposed ocean objects, shells and dried sea creatures and various species of coral, adorned the pebbly walls. They were met by a small contingent of kethropi led by Riga, who Val had learned was niece to the reigning king, and ninth in line for the throne. As soon as they arrived, Riga moved forward to greet them, using the rolling gait of the kethropi. Riga wore a floor-length sleeveless dress that shimmered in shades of green, made of dried seaweed enhanced with silk, interwoven with tiny pearls. Blue-green scales covered the exposed portions of her body, her face was gilled at the cheeks, and she had nostrils so flat they were barely perceptible.

The other representatives had scales of varying shades of blue and green.

Val assumed that Riga, along with her retinue, had been imbued with the same magic that had allowed her to attend the Academy. That or the entire chamber was ensorcelled.

Lidless eyes the color of dull amber flickered with warmth as Riga raised the back of her hand in a limp-wristed gesture of greeting. "Well met, Val and Adaira. And Dida! I thought you would have returned to your kingdom by now."

Adaira executed a flawless kethropi hand movement of her own, and then greeted Riga by her long official title—in the gargled language of the fish-people. Murmurs of surprise and approval rose from the kethropi contingent.

There were no tables in the chamber, but a servant brought a tray of tea and water. The other kethropi remained standing as the visitors caught up with their old classmate. Adaira expertly straddled the warmth of the reunion with the professional niceties of a diplomatic mission. She knew all the right things to say and when to say them, leaving Val impressed by her ambassadorial skills.

From Val's briefing, he knew the kethropi were a reclusive race. Not just because of the obvious difficulties in communication, but also due to a culture of insularity born from apprehension of the outside world. Though the kethropi had plenty of mages and a formidable army—unmatched on the oceans—they never involved themselves in surface conflicts. They also disapproved, for the most part, of contact with the surface races outside of trade or diplomatic purposes. An invitation to visit their kingdom was an extremely rare prize, usually extended to aquamancers from friendly nations.

Which was why, in exchange for helping the Congregation find the Trident of Terengotha, Lord Alistair had agreed to give the kethropi Zagath's location in Undertown. Val had learned that Zagath, after he was banished, made a habit of selling kethropi secrets to foreign governments.

Neither Val nor Adaira was comfortable with the double-cross, but it was out of their hands. Too much was at stake to allow a criminal to stand in the way of recovering the Coffer of Devla.

As they sipped seaweed tea, a surprisingly refreshing beverage, Val and the others learned a bit more about their mission, including the history of the trident. They were told that interracial marriage and procreation were forbidden among the kethropi, and all mermerus were born sterile. Riga did not say it, but Val got the sense they were heavily discriminated against within kethropi society.

Three centuries before, a mermerus named Terengotha surprised the kethropi by exhibiting magical ability, the only known wizard of his kind. Desirous of a life above the surface, he had crafted his trident in secret over many decades, fulfilling a lifelong ambition. Before he could escape with it—unauthorized surface visits were forbidden at the time—his lover betrayed him to the authorities. Terengotha was imprisoned and the Trident ordered destroyed. To everyone's surprise, no one, not even the most powerful kethropi mages, could shatter the weapon. Fearing it would be too much of a temptation to other mermerus, the queen ordered the Trident sent to a deep and lightless part of the ocean, dropped into an ancient temple that was legendary among the kethropi.

"You see," Riga said, her wide mouth contorting into a grimace, "Zagath is a liar. One of the reasons the Temple of Dagarithaloggathva—shall we call it Dagavi?—was chosen to hold the Trident is because it lies at a depth too deep for the gills of a mermerus."

"I didn't realize they were limited," Adaira said.

"Oh, yes. Even a hundred fathoms is unobtainable to them."

"But couldn't a kethropi retrieve it?"

"Kethropi have no desire for such an item," she said contemptuously. "Still, realizing that an unscrupulous sort might be swayed to retrieve it for a fee, the location was chosen to dissuade kethropi as well. The temple belongs to the ruins of a lost civilization that now lies deep beneath the ocean, far from our cities."

Beside him, Val could see Dida's curved nose twitch with excitement.

"Intriguing," Adaira said.

"Perhaps, perhaps not. The civilization was rudimentary, as you will see from the crude temple design. Civilizations have risen and fallen on Urfe for years untold, perhaps hundreds or even thousands of millennia, and we are not a people who dwell on archaeological concerns. Yet we are not, unfortunately, a people without superstition. The area of the ocean in which these ruins are found is a small one, and one which our people believe is inhabited by ghosts."

"Ghosts?" Adaira echoed.

"Just like surface dwellers, we too have our fears of the dark. Many centuries ago, expeditions were mounted to the area in which this temple rests. None returned, giving rise to the legend that the ghosts of this lost civilization lure visitors to their doom. Nonsense, of course. Yet something happened on the expeditions, and the only sanctioned visit in the past few centuries was to dispose of the Trident."

"Zagath mentioned runes of some sort," Val said. "On a door."

Riga emitted a string of squishy syllables Val suspected was a curse. "More evidence of his lies. Zagath could not possibly know anything about the temple beyond what the legends say, and there are certainly no reports of any runes. I suppose the Trident could still be there, though perhaps some sea creature has dragged it away. I know not. If you must go, please be careful in these waters. In fact, I'll be sending a regiment of kethropi to guide you."

Val said, "That isn't necessary—"

"Thank you," Adaira said, smoothly cutting him off. "The Congregation very much appreciates the thoughtful gesture."

Riga crossed her arms and gave a sinuous half-bow.

Hours later, Val squatted on the floor of his bedchamber, peering down at the ocean through the glass floor. They had just finished a dinner of the freshest, most delicious sashimi he had ever had in his life, accompanied by a spectacular seaweed salad and a bottle of imported rice-wine from the Nippon Islands. Riga had dined with them, and the conversation had lingered long after they finished. He and Dida were scheduled to depart for the ruins at first light.

Schools of minnows and tropical fish darted to and fro beneath the glass. A short way down, backlit by an aquamarine light that illuminated the ocean to a depth of a hundred feet, he could see the glow of Kethropi City, a watery glimpse of slender towers and underwater bridges and geometric collections of transparent spheres that had the appearance of bubbles captured in midstream. It was all interwoven among a vertical, kaleidoscopic coral reef which Val guessed a kethropi wizard had adapted to suit the city. He wished he could visit more of it, and that his brothers were with him to appreciate the experience.

The sheer bizarreness of his surroundings made Val miss home desperately, and especially his brothers. It was one thing to journey to an entirely new world and appreciate its wonder and beauty—and another thing to do it alone.

Someone knocked on the frond-shaped door of the bedroom.

"Come in."

Adaira stepped inside, latching the odd door behind her. With her hair unbound and her silver nightgown clinging to her lithe form, she was a shimmer of loveliness as she strode across the glass floor.

All of a sudden, Val found that his loneliness had dissipated to a faint, aching whisper.

"Be careful tomorrow," she said.

"I was planning on it."

"No unnecessary risks. I mean it. The Congregation will survive without the Coffer."

Val forced a reassuring smile. Unless the Trident was nowhere to be found, he had no intention of coming back without it. Too much was riding on the success of the mission: curtailing the Revolution, his standing within the Congregation, the safety of his brothers. Even his future with the woman standing in front of him, whose lightly scented perfume of sea salt and rose petals was making him light-headed. Lord Alistair wasn't about to hand over his daughter to a failure.

She draped her arms across his shoulder. "Listen to Dida. He's less prone to take unnecessary risks."

"Until he's presented with an opportunity for scholarly research," Val said wryly.

"True."

He noticed a shadow behind her gaze. "What's wrong?"

"Nothing."

"It's not Synne, is it?"

"What? No, of course not. I may not like the fact you're going to be in constant proximity to another woman, but I understand the mage-majitsu relationship. In fact, I wish she were here to protect you."

He smirked. "Is that so?"

Adaira slid closer, brushing against him and slipping her hands into his hair. Her voice turned throaty. "Perhaps not this very instant."

"A majitsu's duty only goes so far."

She gave him a playful smack on the cheek. "Were you this impertinent with all your past women?"

"Only the ones I like."

"I see. So you *do* favor me?"

"Maybe a little."

"I happen to have noticed," she said, flicking her tongue across his lips, "that we are no longer in New Victoria, under the watchful eye of my father's guards."

"Not even on the same continent."

"Or on a continent at all."

He scooped her in his arms and carried her to the bed. Below them, a pair of zebra fish darted into a maze of coral that resembled miniature fluted trees.

"You're sure there's nothing bothering you?" he asked.

She put a finger to his lips and smiled, trying to hide the worry in her eyes. "Just make sure to come back to me."

He cupped her face in his hands. "I will. I promise."

"You're very good at telling people what they want to hear."

"I'm even better at following through."

"Let's see about that," she whispered, and the rest of their conversation took place without words.

The next morning, Val and Dida were both disappointed to learn they would not be descending to view more of the city. Instead, just after dawn, a cadre of six kethropi warriors carrying long barbed spears met them on a coral platform attached to the floating residence. All of the kethropi except one, a bulky female with bright blue scales, were bobbing in the water and holding onto a ladder attached to the platform. Riga and Adaira were there as well, to see everyone off.

Before the sun had risen, Val and Dida had donned the magical, paper-thin

Skincloths. The flesh-colored mesh material even covered their faces, though Val found that he could still talk, see, and breathe.

Riga introduced the female leader of the fighters as Kiva. Val assumed she, too, had an enchantment in place allowing her to speak and breathe. After goodbyes were said, Kiva cupped her hands to her mouth and emitted an ululating cry resonant with the distinctive gargling sound of the kethropi. Minutes later, a pod of dolphins arrived, and the kethropi warriors fitted eight of them with saddles made of seaweed rope and whale bone. Another dolphin carried their supplies, including Val's staff.

The kethropi knew where to go. After climbing onto their frisky dolphin mount—it took Dida eight attempts—and letting the kethropi strap them in, Val kicked above the water to wave goodbye to Adaira. Her confident parting smile gave him strength as the dolphin plunged into the icy depths.

The Skincloth allowed Val to breathe and see just as easily beneath the waves. With the taste of Adaira's lips and smooth skin still swarming his senses, he clutched the saddle as the cetacean sped through choppy waters.

It was not an easy ride. The dolphins were prone to diving without warning and swimming underwater for a time. For most of the ride, the landscape was the unchanging blue of deep-water ocean, swells and gulls and wind when they surfaced, strips of kelp and seaweed clinging to Val's face and hair. According to a map of the world's oceans Riga had shown them, he gathered they were aiming for the western part of the Atlantic, due east from the tip of Florida. He wasn't positive, but back home he thought it would put them smack in the middle of the Bermuda Triangle.

This did not inspire confidence. Was there a correlation between the strange occurrences in this region back home, a lost civilization, and the kethropi's fear of ghosts?

Gripping the reins and constantly holding his breath when they plunged was very taxing. Every hour or so, the dolphins let them dismount on an island or an atoll, or even just bobbed in the water, long enough to let Val and Dida recover. When they stopped for the night on a deserted beach covered in palms, Val and Dida collapsed on the sand and, after a meal of fresh fish and coconut, slept right through to morning.

By early evening the next day, as the sun began to sink into the pink-and-green horizon, they arrived at their destination.

It looked no different from the unchanging watery horizon that extended in every direction as far as the eye could see. With a limp flick of her wrist, Kiva halted the dolphins and proclaimed they had arrived. Grateful beyond words the outbound journey was over, Val unhooked himself and fell back into the water, buoyed by the waves. After a meal of dried seaweed and chunks of raw tuna, Kiva gave a signal, and two of the kethropi took hold of the whale skin bag holding the weapons and supplies.

She took out a blue glow stone and handed it to Val. "Make sure not to stray."

"Don't worry."

Val found the descent into the lightless ocean a terrifying experience. Though beautiful—the variety of aquatic life forms took his breath away—they were free diving thousands of meters beneath the surface, solely dependent on the Skincloth for survival. What if the magic gave out? What if it had a depth limit? What if he ripped it on a piece of coral?

Not just that, but the deeper they went, the more menacing the sea life became. A black-finned shark passed above them that must have been forty feet long, a goliath who didn't even register their presence. Schools of electric eels, puffer fish, and spiny lionfish drifted past. A few hundred feet down, a family of seahorses as big as buffalo darted towards them, forcing the kethropi to brandish their spears. Val reared in shock when a fish with enormous jaws, its dagger-like teeth glowing with bioluminescence, passed right beneath him. Yet the two creatures that caused the most alarm were a spotted blue octopus and a jellyfish with a pink body and multicolored tentacles spread around it like streamers. Kiva gave both these creatures a wide berth, rerouting their descent to avoid them.

Dida was not the best swimmer, but he managed. Val estimated they were a thousand feet down when they first glimpsed the seabed, a mass of gray rock pitted with watery depressions that resembled the pockmarked surface of the moon.

Just after the bottom came into view, Kiva pointed behind Val and Dida. They swiveled and saw, in the distance behind them, a low, oval-shaped building resting on the ocean floor. A short tower jutted upward from the far side of the oval. The entire structure appeared built of the same dull granite as the sea floor.

Even stranger, they noticed as they swam closer that a set of steps extended from the flat roof of the oval building, rising straight up the side of the twenty-foot tower. He and Dida floated above it to examine it. The tower sides were made of thick stone, and the aperture was just wide enough for a person to step through. Val leaned over the edge and used the glow stone to peer inside. More steps led down, and he could just make out the stone surface of the bottom.

As Kiva swam over, the other kethropi hovered off to the side, giving the structure apprehensive looks.

"The temple?" Val asked, surprised he could speak this far below the surface.

Kiva's return nod looked unnatural, as if she were using the movement for his benefit. Whatever spell had allowed her to walk on land and use English, it had either worn off or did not work beneath the surface. She was forced to communicate with Val and Dida with hand gestures and other body language.

"We can converse down here?" Dida said. "What a marvelous invention these Skincloths are."

The bibliomancer led the way as they circled the perimeter of the structure. Except for the top of the tower, there were no windows or openings of any kind. The design was rudimentary and solid.

"Riga was right," Dida said, disappointed. "There's no sign of any runes."

"Which makes me wonder about the Trident," Val said.

When they returned to the top of the tower, Kiva pointed down into the opening, then opened her palm as if releasing something.

Val got the hint. "The Trident was dropped inside?"

She nodded again.

"No one's actually been down there?"

This time she shook a finger.

"That would have been nice information to know," he muttered. "Dida, any idea what this place is?"

The bibliomancer rubbed his pointed chin as he bobbed in the water. "I've never seen anything like it. The design of the main structure is quite primitive, and the oval shape is odd. What is the purpose of the tower? Why the steps?"

"Does anything about the legend of Kau-Voa match what you're seeing?"

"I do not believe so," he said slowly. "The presence of the granite sea-bed, however, suggests it was once dry land. We might be looking at the remains of a wholly undiscovered civilization." He gave Kiva a sheepish glance. "Or at least undiscovered on the surface."

When Val breathed it felt normal, though bubbles formed outside his mouth. He hovered for a moment with his hand on the lip of the tower, thinking as he watched the bubbles drift away and dissolve. Never had he experienced a silence so vast and profound. The ocean heaved with life and mystery, and for a moment he was in awe at the wonder and terror of it all, of how life itself had started in these solemn depths.

"I guess we're going down there," he said finally.

Kiva waved her men over, and they reluctantly swam towards them, barbed spears at the ready. After conversing in their garbled language, Kiva selected one of them to go first. The kethropi she chose drew away, and Val held out a palm.

"This is my expedition. I should be the leader."

Kiva tried to protest, but Val extended the glow stone and swam head first down the tower. Having no idea what lay below them, he reached for his magic and kept it ready. He assumed his spells would work this far beneath the surface, but he had no idea. Why hadn't he discussed that with Riga?

The steps inside the chimney descended to fifteen feet above the granite floor. As Val floated into the chamber, he righted himself and saw that the structure was just as plain on the inside, made of unadorned stone walls. Five passages exited the room through rectangular openings in the rock.

The room was empty. No sign of the Trident.

Dida, Kiva, and the rest of the kethropi followed him down. The lidless eyes of the kethropi darted around the water. Val didn't blame them. The whole place was strange. Why was there an intact structure at the bottom of the ocean? Why no proper entrances?

The five passageways were very slender, no wider than the tower chute. Val approached the entrance to each with his glow light. Except for the corridor in the middle, located opposite the bottom of the tower, each of the passages curved away in a sinuous pattern, twisting like a snake. The central passage proceeded straight into the heart of the temple.

"May I?" Dida asked, pointing at the glow stone. Val handed it over. The bibliomancer took an exploratory step into the central corridor, and then a few more. "Oh my," he said.

Val followed him in. "What? I don't see anything."

"Look into the distance. And then at your feet."

Val did as he asked, then lifted his eyebrows in surprise. "It's going down."

"Correct."

After taking a glance at the sloping tunnel, the kethropi warriors muttered amongst themselves and backed into the main chamber. Kiva made a series of hand gestures that Val interpreted as *hurry up human, my men are nervous and won't stay down here forever.*

He took the glow stone back from Dida and walked slowly down the curving passage on the far left, wishing they had someone experienced with traps. Yet no dangers arose as the watery stone corridor twisted deeper into the structure, dead-ending after a hundred feet or so at a circular chamber the size of a home swimming pool. Along the perimeter of the chamber, a set of stone steps led down a few feet and then disappeared, as if a circular basin had once existed in the center. Val walked down to shine the light into the water, but it was too dark to see.

Had someone dug a basin at the bottom of the ocean? Or had this once been dry land?

The kethropi stayed at the top of the steps. No one, Val included, wanted to dive down the hole that punched through the ocean floor to see what was inside.

As he continued to shine the light around the room, they noticed the faint remnants of prehistoric rock carvings etched into the granite wall. Though too faded too make out specific images, the carvings had a fluidity that surprised Val. Not that he was an expert in prehistoric art.

"Fascinating," Dida said, gently pressing his thumb against a wavy bit of line. "This was etched with a sharp object. From what I can tell, these are quite rudimentary carvings, indicative of a very old society. Yet they are utterly distinct in design. I have never witnessed anything like it."

"They're so . . . graceful."

"Yes. Yes. It's as if they started writing in cursive before they learned to print. Utterly fascinating."

Val had to almost drag Dida out of the room, he was so intrigued by the find. They continued to explore and found an identical scene at the end of each of the side passages: circular steps leading down to a central basin, rock walls with faded prehistoric art. With no option left, they cautiously proceeded down the straight central corridor. The slope was very gradual and, by the time they reached the enormous ivory archway at the end of the corridor, they had walked a hundred yards past the length of the outside portion of the temple.

Even more bizarre than the existence of the oval archway was the alien scrawl of runes etched into the ivory surface. Runes crafted in a spidery, free-flowing pattern similar in design to—yet far more advanced than—their prehistoric counterparts in the chambers above.

The archway was easily ten feet high, with a similar diameter across its widest point. Kiva floated in the water just behind them, and the rest of the kethropi hung back, spears at the ready.

"Do you recognize these?" Val asked Dida, who was staring in fascination at the runes.

Val's friend clasped his hands behind his back as he studied the ancient script. "They're unlike any I've ever seen," he said finally. "Unless I'm mistaken, it is most certainly a language. An advanced one. Even at a glance I can see evidence of grammatical markers, phonemes and morphemes. Yet the differences are profound . . . almost as if it developed out of context with any other known language."

"You can tell all that already?"

The bibliomancer blinked. "I could be wrong."

Val tapped the archway. "How long can ivory survive underwater?"

"This isn't ivory. It's albalium."

"What?"

"An extremely rare stone found deep beneath the surface, related to tilectium. So deep only a few samples are known to exist."

"What do you think that means? Who built this?"

"I don't know," Dida said slowly. "But there are obvious similarities between the runes on this archway and the crude carvings in the chambers above. Certain stylistic markers. I get the impression the prehistoric civilization that built the rock temple was trying to . . . *copy* . . . these runes."

"These Skincloths won't last forever," Val said, feeling a little shiver pass through him as he started through the archway. "Let's get on with it."

26

"Ye know me can't stay on de river at de night," Meru said, as Will and the others disembarked onto a blackened stone wharf at the edge of the Agora. The long shadows of dusk had fallen across the water, bruising the surface.

"Understood," Skara said. "We'll meet you here in the morning."

If we make it out alive, Will thought darkly. He was afraid to use Zariduke, feeling as if the blade might shatter and be forever lost. With no way to combat the abilities of the Nephili or other magical creatures they might encounter, he did not relish the thought of spending the night in the Agora, the Old Town, or anywhere else on the forsaken plateau that rose hundreds of feet above their heads.

As the barge disappeared into the twilight, Skara set down her pack and took out the silk-wrapped box she had brought from the Pagoda. She cut the ribbon on the lid and opened it, revealing six miniature teapots with corked spouts. "Don't waste a drop," she said, as she handed them out. "These did not come cheap."

Yasmina looked doubtful as she held her teapot in her hands. "And these are?"

"According to the journal, the guardians atop the Wailing Wall—the Skinwalkers—are meant to deter all living creatures from entering Old Town. They operate by smell, however, and Master Kuang has developed a potion that will render the scent of a human being undetectable."

"For how long?" Mateo asked.

"He estimates eight hours."

"Why do we apply it now, and not at the base of the bluff?"

"First, because I've no idea how acute a Skinwalker's sense of smell may be. Secondly, because the Agora is infested with a particular species of vampire bat that can smell human blood, as well as echolocate their prey."

"Thank you for providing us with two thoroughly disturbing scenarios to anticipate," Will said. "Skinwalkers? Have you ever seen one before?"

"I've spent the night in the Agora, on more than one occasion. I've seen strange lights coming from the Old Town that no one else has seen. I *know* there's something there. I've also stood at the bottom of the Wailing Wall and heard the cry of the Skinwalkers, who are said to wail for their lost lives for eternity. But no. I have never seen one myself. The journal speaks of faceless creatures who cannot be harmed by normal weapons, but the entry is brief. Even the old explorer who left the journal never made it past the Wailing Wall." She held up the teapot. "I aim to use it to walk where no one else has tread, at least for long centuries."

Ever since they had disembarked, a covetous light had entered Skara Brae's eyes. Whatever happened from here on out, whatever she thought she knew or didn't know, Will knew she was going the distance.

"Why do you trust this journal so much?" he asked. "What if it's wrong about the Skinwalkers?"

Skara ran a finger along the blade of her hatchet, as if debating whether to answer. "Because the explorer who wrote it," she said at last, in a soft voice, "was my great-grandfather. He came to Praha from Moravia long ago, searching for the fabled treasures of the Nephili. My father stayed for the same reason, though he drank himself to death in frustration. I plan to change the family destiny."

"We should go," Bartu said, with an intense glaze to his eyes. "The sun sets."

Skara turned to face him, but he had already started towards the Agora.

"Bartu!"

He turned, expressionless.

"Are you feeling all right?"

"Of course. Why?"

"Because you seem to have forgotten the way," she said, giving him a long look before starting down a weed-covered walkway that wound through a maze of obelisks and rotundas.

"I must have," he said, with a grin. "Too many knocks on the head."

Will had no idea what was going on with Bartu, but all he could do at this point was keep an eye on him. As they headed into the heart of the Agora, Will was reminded of Roman ruins he had seen in photos, though on a far grander scale, and all of it blackened by the plague fire that had ravaged the city. The silent remains of pillars, stela, temples, and other monoliths overshadowed them as they traversed vast stone plazas or crept through narrow passages that Skara had scouted on previous visits. Rodents and feral dogs slunk through empty buildings and scampered over mountains of rubble. A smell of rot and decay lingering in the air made Will question the source of the odor, as there was no sign of habitation.

The base of the massif rose ever closer. As the darkness continued to mature, cloaking the Agora with a Stygian pall that kept the party in a tight line, faces grim as they picked their way through the ruins, a rustling arose in the distance. The sound reminded Will of crickets, except more high-pitched and interspersed with vibrating chirps.

"Bats," Yasmina said.

Skara swore. "I wished to make the climb before dark. It's not far now."

The wilder cocked her head. "They're still some distance away, and if they stay their course, will pass to our left."

"I hope you're right, wilder."

"Why don't we just wait for morning?" Dalen asked, nervously eying the sky. "Send someone back for more tea?"

"My grandfather speculated the wafers would disintegrate if carried too far from their source. It's best to try straightaway for the wall. Hurry, now."

They soon emerged into a large courtyard that stretched to the edge of the massif. Pillared rotundas, concentric archways leading to smaller plazas, and a host of long buildings that looked administrative surrounded the plaza. Though impressive, none of the buildings had the same grand, otherworldly feel as the rest of Praha. Had there been a human population that served the Nephili and called the Agora home? If so, why had the plague affected it?

When the party tried to skirt the edge of the courtyard, following Skara's lead, a high pile of rubble between two buildings blocked the way.

"That wasn't here before," she said.

"How long ago was your last visit?" Mateo asked.

"A few months. Something piled these rocks together."

Mateo turned over one of the stones. The ground underneath was dry and free of insects. "I don't like the idea of climbing over this barrier in the darkness, without knowing what awaits."

They all agreed, though no one liked the look of the hidden interiors of the buildings surrounding the courtyard. Skara decided to save time and risk exposure by pressing through the center of the plaza. They abandoned the single file line and bunched together, creating a ring with Dalen in the center.

Halfway across, with the base of the massif tantalizingly close, Will heard the slap of boots on stone, and whipped around to see a group of people dressed in rags pouring out of the buildings. At first he thought they might be ghouls of some sort, but as Skara ignited a glow stick and Dalen expanded the light to encompass the plaza, Will realized the forms sprinting towards them were human, though some of the filthiest he had ever seen. They brandished knives and clubs and swords which they held like thugs instead of trained warriors, and desperation was etched into their faces. They also had numbers on their side. At least a few dozen were rushing towards them, with more pouring out of the buildings.

Will and the others fanned out, surrounding Dalen and creating space to move without breaking the circle. Will was unused to the weight of Skara's cudgel. Zariduke could have cut through these untrained ruffians like a scythe through tall grass.

Sensing they could overwhelm the small party, the ragtag group of thieves and beggars rushed forward. Skara threw a pair of daggers that stuck in the throats of the first two. Though weakened by the absence of natural light—creating illusions in dim lighting required advanced techniques—Dalen managed to sow confusion with muted bursts of color, as well as shadows that took shape and leapt at the assailants.

Yasmina and Mateo kept the first wave at bay with their lengthier weapons, Yasmina's long staff cracking skulls and kneecaps, Mateo's urumi sword snapping like a whip as it bit deep into the flesh of any who came near. A quick glance to the side told Will that Skara and Bartu were holding their own as well. The tall warrior had lost one of his scimitars in the storehouse, but he swept his remaining one back and forth with expert ease, cutting the throat of one attacker, then blocking the weak thrust of another and spinning to slice him across the back.

As the screams of victims shattered the night silence, Skara went to work with even more efficiency. After throwing her knives to deadly effect, she swung her hatchet by its chain and let it fly into the face of the nearest assailant. She jerked it back and felled another, and whenever an attacker pressed too close, she jabbed with the bladed cane.

Yet the ragtag group kept coming, driven by greed and hunger, knowing precious few targets ventured out to the wasteland of the Agora. Will's turn came when two of the assailants charged him, one wielding a rusty spear and the other holding a club above his head.

Lesson the first: always be aware.

Without time to think, he moved swiftly to his left, cutting off the holder of the club from the burly man with the spear. Will blocked the club with his shield, but didn't see a good opening to swing the cudgel. Instead he dropped the bulky weapon and whipped his dagger out in one smooth motion, stepping inside to thrust into the man's gut. He ripped through muscle and pushed the man away in time to blade his body to the side to deflect the spear thrust of his other opponent. He snapped a kick to the man's groin, causing him to double over, then followed up with a fierce blow to the head with his shield, knocking him senseless.

Someone jumped on Will's back. He roared in fury and spun, then bent and threw the person over his shoulder without using his hands, as Mala had taught him. The woman who had jumped him lay gasping for breath as Will heard footsteps to his left. He moved fast enough to avoid the sword thrust, but the woman on the ground grabbed his ankle and jerked, causing him to stumble and lose his grip on the handle in the middle of his shield. Someone else tackled him from behind and managed to knock his knife away. Weaponless, Will found himself fighting for his life on the ground, with no idea how his friends were faring. He could only concentrate on staying alive.

The woman screeched and dove across the ground, trying to claw out Will's eyes. He met her with a head butt to her nose, knocking her back. Someone was still on his back, trying to pin his arms for the swordsman taking aim in front of him. The man on his back was quite strong, and he rolled once, leaving Will belly-up and exposed to the sword. Will worked desperately to free himself as the swordsman moved into position, but Will couldn't free his arms. The man had him caught in a bear hug and was enormously strong.

Lesson the third: cheat.

Though Will's arms were trapped, he managed to reach behind his back with one hand, found the man's groin, and squeezed with all his might. The grip lessened as the man gasped in pain. Will jerked his head back, impacting soft facial tissue with his skull, and the man's arms fell away just in time for Will to roll off him and avoid the downward thrust of a sword.

He leapt to his feet without using his hands. *Lesson the second: strike first, and with intent.* Before his opponent could recover, Will grabbed the hilt of the sword with both hands, covering the man's wrist. As his opponent tried to pull the sword back, Will summoned the power in his muscular forearms, stepped to his left, and made a bowing motion as he bent the man's wrist towards the ground.

The man made the mistake of trying to hold on to his sword. Unable to resist the force of Will's maneuver, trapped by his own grip, the brittle wrist bones snapped like dry twigs, and Will jerked the sword away as the man screamed.

Two more people rushed towards him, one with a dagger and one with an old hatchet, but he squared his feet and prepared to engage with his captured sword.

It didn't take long. Will batted away the hatchet thrust, slicing an arm on the backswing before using the superior reach of his sword to stab the man with the dagger before he had a chance to engage. Will turned to finish off the man with the hatchet, but found him running away.

A quick glance told him no one else was coming for him. All of his companions were still standing, and a mass of thieves were dead or writhing on the ground, the rest dashing for the safety of the buildings surrounding the plaza.

I survived, he thought, as he retrieved his shield.

I survived without Zariduke.

"To the stairs!" Skara said. "There could be more on the way."

Though everyone had nicks and wounds, no one cried out as they raced for the side of the courtyard abutting the bluff. Skara jumped onto the raised base of a rotunda and off the other side, then sprinted to the bottom of a set of stairs cut into the cliff. It would be an arduous climb but he knew they could manage.

That was, until the vampire bats arrived.

A third of the way up the staircase, the rustle and chirp of the bat swarm returned, increasing in intensity. As they drew closer, he heard a new sound, the scratching of nails back and forth on leather, amplified to the millionth degree. When he glanced behind him, the darkness seemed to have congealed, somehow deeper than the night—and was moving towards them. Within moments the outline of furry bodies took shape, thousands of them, beating their wings in a furious rhythm as they flew towards the exposed party.

"Lucka, I thought they couldn't smell us!" Dalen called out.

"The blood from the battle must have drawn them," Skara said. "They'll eat us alive up here!"

For the first time since he had met her, Will heard desperation in the voice of the hardened adventuress. He understood. They couldn't fight something like that.

A voice rang out above him, clear and commanding. "Hold still!"

Yasmina's voice.

"Wilder, what are you—"

"Silence! No one move a muscle."

Will craned his neck and saw that Yasmina had turned to stand with her heels planted on the steps in a precarious position, arms raised to the sky with fingers spread, as if making her presence as large as possible.

The flap of leathery wings was deafening, driving a stake of fear into Will's heart. As the swarm drew closer, less than a hundred feet away, chittering and shrieking, Yasmina made a call of her own, a shrill and piercing cry that reminded Will of an eagle. She prolonged the cry as the bats flew into them, landing on the rock face and perching on the bodies of the party members. One landed on Will's head and dug its claws into his skull to hang on.

"Don't move!" Yasmina shouted again. "No matter what!"

The stink of the flying mammals, ammonia and urine and musky glands, made Will want to gag. He winced at the pain of the claws and it was all he could do to hold still and not scramble to escape, though he knew it meant certain death.

A number of the bats took turns flying right at Yasmina, turning away millimeters before smacking her in the face. She continued the shrieking cry and upturned her hands above her head, enticing two of the furry beasts to land in her palms. They walked back and forth in circles as they chirped and showed their fangs. After a time they flew away, and then one by one, the rest of the colony peeled off the cliff and took flight, gathering again in a swarm before darting into the night.

Will let his weight sink against the cliff wall, feeling shaky from the brush with death. Blood dripped onto his face from the claw wounds on his head, and from Yasmina's wounds above him. Though painful, he did not think they were serious. He called out to the others and everyone seemed shaken but fine to continue.

"Thank you, wilder," Skara said, in a strained voice. "You saved us all."

"They're hungry," Yasmina replied quietly. "Not malevolent."

"Would that have stopped them from drinking our blood?"

"Let's just hope their decision holds."

"What did you do?" Will asked.

"It would be hard to explain."

"I sort of figured."

The party resumed climbing. Less than a hundred feet remained. Just as Will began to feel hopeful, a new sound pierced the air, a keening moan even louder than the din of the bats. It was a vaguely human cry, though filled with a pathos so terrible it seemed to scrape along the inside of Will's skull. He could hardly stand the noise, and thrust his hand over his ears.

"The wailing begins," Skara said. "Stay strong. Don't let it affect you."

How could we not? Will whispered to himself. *Will this night never end?*

"Are those the skinwalkers?" Mateo asked.

"Aye," Skara said.

"So we approach the Wailing Wall?"

"Gypsy, this cliff *is* the Wailing Wall."

More voices joined the first, creating an awful chorus that caused waves of gooseflesh to tumble across Will's skin like a chill wind, raising his hairs and setting his teeth on edge.

"Should we turn back?" Mateo said. "Have they not seen us?"

"They see nothing. Their sense of smell alone guides them."

"And the blood drawn by the claws of the bats? Will that not overpower the potions we drank?"

"Let us pray Master Kuang is the genius I think he is. Now *climb*."

When they reached the top, every muscle aching from the climb, Will joined the others as they faced an awful sight. Standing at the edge of the cliff, spaced ten feet apart as far as he could see in the moonlight, was a line of tall humanoids as white as grubs. At first he thought they were wearing pale suits of some sort, but as they drew nearer, he could see the blue veins threaded throughout their bodies, the bunching of muscle beneath their skin. They were hairless and featureless, with no sexual or facial organs except for the bulge of a nose pushing against taut skin. When Will stared closer, he saw their nostrils opening and closing as if breathing. The skinwalkers were looking straight ahead, their gazes fixed at the edge of the cliff. As he watched them, Will was filled with the certainty that these things, these *abominations*, had once been normal human beings who were forced to stand sentry for eternity over Old Town.

And he also sensed they longed, more than anything else in the world, to return to their former state.

Behind the line of skinwalkers stood the palatial ruins of Old Town, giant smudges of chalk pressing against the darkness. Skara waved everyone on, stepping carefully forward as if afraid to make a sound. Will could scarcely believe the Skinwalkers would not notice when they passed, yet one by one, they slipped between the nearest pair of wailing figures, their still forms filling Will with a terrible sadness. Just after he was through, he heard the sounds of a struggle behind him, followed by a man's bellow. He whipped around to see one of the pale beings holding Bartu by the arm, and two more converging. More and more seemed to notice, causing them to rush towards Bartu, the wailing increasing in frenzy as if maddened by the catch.

"Bartu!" Skara screamed.

Bartu had been guarding the rear of the party, and everyone else was safely through the line. The creatures surrounding the debonair warrior were ripping him apart with their bare hands. Bartu screamed, but it wasn't the scream of a terrified man. Instead it sounded enraged, inhuman.

The Skinwalkers moved incredibly fast, more like animals than men, and before Will or any of the others could react, they had surrounded Bartu so completely he could no longer be seen. Skara rushed towards her fallen lover, weapons in hand, ready to plow into the entire pack. Will caught her by the waist and yanked her back. The distraught adventuress tried to shake him off, but Will kept his grip.

"Let me go!" she cried, raising her cudgel.

"Look, Skara! Look at him now!"

Yasmina gasped, Mateo swore softly under his breath, and Dalen took a step backwards in shock. Skara finally looked up and saw what the rest of them had noticed: a pulsating pillar of flesh where Bartu should have been, changing shape and color as it rose out of the circle of Skinwalkers. At first Will thought the monsters had caused the phenomenon. But as Skara stopped moving to stare at the awful spectacle, she lowered her cudgel and whispered, in a horrified voice, "Doppelganger."

The creature changed form into a variety of shapes as the Skinwalkers tore into it: first a sticklike insect a foot taller than a man, then a werewolf bristling with fur and claws, and then into another Skinwalker that seemed to blend perfectly with the others. Yet somehow they knew the difference, and continued to tear into the creature. Finally it turned into Bartu once more, sobbing, pleading in the fighter's voice for Skara to save him. Will had loosened his grip, and she moved towards the thing as if seeking a final moment with her companion.

Will caught up to her and wrapped his arms around her. The Bartu-thing had disappeared again, enveloped by Skinwalkers. Will cringed at the sound of flesh ripping apart, but the circle was so tight that, thankfully, he and the others were spared the sight of the carnage. Skara collapsed into his arms, leaden with grief.

"Skara," he said gently. "It wasn't him. We have to go."

"I knew something was different. I knew it wasn't him. I knew it. Back in that dark room . . .we heard him groan . . . the doppelganger must have taken him." She spat. "The filthy *bastard*. I'll hunt its kind to my dying breath."

"Will!" Yasmina said sharply.

He looked up and saw, to his horror, that one of the Skinwalkers had broken from the pack and started walking in his direction, sniffing the air like a bloodhound.

"We have to go," he said to Skara. "*Now.*"

She complied, but it was too late. Somehow the rest of the pack had picked up the scent and moved to encircle the party. When Will and the others tried to walk quickly away from the edge of the cliff, and then run, the wailing Skin-walkers loped to surround them.

"Any ideas, Yaz?" Will asked in desperation, but she had nothing to say. Like the rest of them, the wilder was backing away from the enclosing circle. There was nowhere to run.

"Why aren't they attacking?" Will asked in a low voice.

"I think I know," Skara said, as she reached into her pack and withdrew the wafer, careful to use a rag instead of touching it.

"Let me," Mateo said, holding out the palm of his metal hand. After a moment's hesitation, she passed him the green disc, and he held it high above his head.

The skinwalkers lifted their snouts and drew nearer, sniffing the air as Will and the others pressed closer together. The creatures drew to within five feet of Mateo then stopped moving. They stood in place for a long moment before some of them moved away and returned to their posts. Nine remained behind to form a line beside the party. These nine fell silent and began walking in unison towards the ruins of Old Town.

"Aike, what are they doing?" Dalen said.

Mateo was still holding the wafer above his head, afraid to lower it and upset the skinwalkers. Will looked from the wafer to the pale humanoids and back again. "I think they want us to follow them."

27

When Caleb could see again, he was back where he had started the odyssey, inside the Tower of Elarion. Only this time, he was standing on an iron platform atop the spiral staircase, looking down at the floor far below. All of his pain had disappeared. He checked his arm and felt his back; the frostbite marks were gone.

At least one tangible reality had endured: he still held the mace in his hands. It was about three feet in length, from the bottom of the black wooden handle to the tip of the crystalline, diamond-shaped head. Though heavy, it felt balanced as he swung it back and forth, and the craftsmanship was exquisite. He knew he could learn to use it.

There was no railing to keep him from plunging off the precipitous platform, and the vertigo was making him dizzy. As he started to climb back down, a voice in his head startled him.

Reach up.

Caleb whipped his head around but saw no one.

Reach up, it repeated.

It was not the same disembodied voice from the room with the ghost. This was the voice of an old man, and it possessed a gentle, even melancholy, timbre.

Caleb looked up and saw nothing but the rough, tapered stone ceiling of the cylindrical tower. With a shrug, he reached up a hand—

And found himself standing outside, his feet planted on a white stone surface, bleached and pitted from the elements. He squinted from the sudden brightness of the sun, and a cool breeze caressed his skin. To his left, far below, a midnight blue ocean heaved against a rocky shore. A line of golden-brown hills stood on his right.

The scenery was all very familiar, and he knew he was standing atop the Tower of Elarion.

"Er, behind you," the voice said. "I seem to have faced you in the wrong direction. Not quite as impressive that way."

Startled, Caleb turned to find a spindly old man with wispy gray hair, a sloping forehead, and gnarly eyebrows. He was dressed in a white dress shirt, dark wool slacks, and a tweed jacket, all of which had seen better days. He looked to Caleb like a semi-retired, adjunct professor at a community college on Earth.

"You're the owner of this joint?" Caleb asked.

"I'm afraid not. Elarion died long ago. He was a good friend of mine, though. Or let us say he was an *interesting* friend. Actually, he was just interesting."

"Then who are you?"

"Ah, yes. I forget we've never met. The third brother. Or second, to be exact, if we're discussing birth order. You really do favor the clans, you know."

Caleb took a long look at the old man's knowing silver eyes glittering with intelligence. He remembered a story Will had told them when they first arrived on Urfe. "You're Salomon, aren't you?"

The old man bowed.

"According to my brother, you're either a crackpot or a two-thousand year old wizard of immense power."

Salomon looked wounded. "That awful birthday is at least a decade or two away. And immense is a relative term, my boy. Let's call me . . . seasoned. No, that sounds like a steak. How about weathered? No, that's even worse. Capable? Tenure material?"

"Do you control the tower now?"

Salomon spread his hands. "This thing? I had nothing to do with it. I merely decided to meet you here and have a little chat after your ordeal."

"About what?"

"I'm curious as to what happened inside. Every experience is unique, you see, and I'm interested in yours. Congratulations, by the way. You've accomplished a very rare feat."

"You mean you don't already know what happened?"

"Why does everyone think I'm omnipotent? Higher technology to a less advanced civilization . . ." he muttered, trailing off. "I know many things about the tower—one of Urfe's most fascinating landmarks, by the way—but nothing of the individual journeys. The exclusive eternity of the mind and all that."

"I don't understand."

"To be honest, I don't either. Elarion was a genius. He coined the term quantum magic. Urfe's equivalent of Sigmund Freud, Einstein, and Tesla all rolled into one."

"Um, how do you know about those people?"

"I've taken quite a liking to your home world. I lived there for some time, you know. Prague, Vienna, Berlin, New York, Knoxville. A fascinating place in so many ways."

Caleb waved a hand in dismissal. He just wanted to get down to business. "Did you heal me?"

"Your wounds were not the sort to survive a metaphysical journey."

"You mean they were all in my head?"

"Yes, and no. They were very real within their particular milieu. A death in the tower is a death on Urfe. So, too, is the decision final if you choose to remain within one of the scenarios."

"But how can that be real?"

"I believe the answer to that question, my boy, is rather the point."

"What do you think about it?"

"What do I think?" Salomon said, surprised. "Hmm. Well, I suppose that denying the self or the multiverse is a rather pointless task, in the end. Time and death may be illusions, but is the very illusion not real to itself? The world, unfortunately, is real; I unfortunately, am Salomon."

Caleb thought about it for a moment, then slowly nodded. "I can dig that."

"It's rather profound, no? Except Borges said it, not I. Wordsmithing was never my gift."

"You said that every experience is unique. So I'm not the only person who has made it out of the tower?"

"Who told you that?"

"The Brewer."

"Hmpf. No, there have been others, over the centuries. Not many. The vast majority of travelers perish or choose to remain inside, in another reality. Or the same reality, in another mind or multiverse. I'm unsure how to parse it."

"If lots of people die, then why are there no bones in the tower?"

Salomon frowned. "Good question. Maybe no one's survived for a thousand years? Maybe the body follows the mind? Maybe animals wander in and take them? I've no idea. Now, suppose we discuss your experience—"

"Why has no one ever taken the mace before?"

"You see, that's part of the reason I came. That was Elarion's personal weapon. It disappeared with his death, and I've heard of no one seeing the mace on their visit to the tower."

"When was the last time you interviewed a survivor?"

Salomon squinted as he thought. "Twelve hundred years ago?"

Caleb put a hand to his temple. "Maybe you just forgot? Sometimes I can't remember what I had for breakfast."

"No, no, I wouldn't have forgotten something like that. I'm quite sure."

"Does the mace have any powers?"

"I don't know that, either."

"Can't you, you know—" Caleb wriggled a hand—"figure it out?"

Salomon's eyes slipped downward. "Ah, no. I'm afraid not."

Caleb's eyes narrowed. "You can't or you won't?"

The archmage fell quiet for a moment. "I'm truly sorry for your loss."

His words caused Caleb to stand rigid, clutching the mace as if it were a buoy thrown to someone drowning at sea. "This is all your fault," he said, taking a step forward as his face darkened. "If you hadn't sent us here in the first place, they wouldn't have died."

"It's possible they might have died even sooner," Salomon said gently.

"OR NOT AT ALL!" Caleb roared. "Get the hell away from me, old man! Get me off this tower!"

"I will," the wizard said. "You have my word. Just as soon as I hear about your journey." A mug of beer appeared in his hand. "Here, maybe this will help you—"

Caleb smacked the mug away, and it shattered on the ground. He stepped on the broken glass and snarled. "Why are you so interested in my family?"

Salomon clasped his hands behind his back and formed a meek, lopsided smile. "I'm afraid I can't speak to that. I'm truly sorry."

"Then I'm afraid I can't tell you what happened inside the Tower."

Salomon grimaced and wrung his hands. "Fair enough, I suppose. Fair enough. What if I were to propose a trade?"

Caleb's voice was low and venomous. "What sort of trade?"

"In exchange for your story, I agree to transfer you not just off this tower, but to a location of your choosing."

Caleb thought about the implications for a moment. His first impulse was to go straight to Lord Alistair and attempt to kill him. *No*, he decided. *That would be foolish without the Coffer, or without any idea what the mace does. I'll only get one chance at Lord Alistair, if that, and I have to be ready.*

Or at least more ready than I am now.

He thought some more. "You can't bring them back?"

Salomon's eyes were faraway. "I'm afraid no one can do that."

Caleb swallowed his disappointment. "Can you heal my mother?"

"The injuries of the mind are beyond the power of even the most accomplished cuerpomancers, which I most certainly am not. Transfer to a new location is all I have to offer, as that is a minimal . . . intervention."

Caleb crossed his arms. "Fine."

Salomon rubbed his hands together. "Wonderful."

"Take me back to Bruce first. He'll want to know I'm all right. I'll tell you both what happened at the same time."

As soon as the words were spoken, Caleb found himself standing near a fire pit by the entrance to the tower, with Salomon right beside him. To their left, the Brewer was sitting cross-legged on the ground beside their packs, strumming a homemade stringed instrument that resembled a lyre. When he saw them materialize, his eyes grew very wide, and he leaped to his feet and began belting out a deep-throated song about returning home from a journey.

It took the rest of the day for Caleb to relate his experiences inside the tower, and Salomon listened intently to every word, interrupting only to clarify a description or to ask a follow-up question. According to the Brewer, Caleb had spent three full days inside the tower. The Brewer had tried to check on him, but the door wouldn't open, and he could find no other way inside.

Caleb refused to elaborate on any of the reasons for his various decisions, which disappointed the archmage. The Brewer sat open-mouthed throughout the tale, refilling Caleb's flask of water whenever his throat grew dry, and roasting a pair of quail over the fire once the sun began to set.

After Caleb finished talking, the wizard looked towards the sea as if digesting the information. "Thank you," he said softly. "Where is it you wish to go?"

Caleb inclined his head towards his older friend. "I want to take him with me."

"Take me where?" the Brewer said. "What are you talking about?"

"That will be fine," Salomon said.

"Hey—what's fine?"

When Caleb said where he wanted to go, one of the archmage's crooked eyebrows curled higher, and the Brewer held out a hand. "Now wait—"

"Do you want to go or not?" Caleb said.

"I . . . yes, I'll go if you want."

"Do it," Caleb said to Salomon. "Now."

After the Brewer rushed to gather his pack, Salomon reached into a pocket of his tweed coat, opened a small vial, and tossed a powdery emerald substance onto Caleb and the Brewer. As soon as it touched them, they started to dissolve, and Salomon shook the powder over their dappled white mare and Caleb's larger mount. Moments later, there was nothing left but Salomon himself and the flicker of the campfire.

Deep in thought, the archmage stepped closer to warm his hands by the embers. The least interesting brother in the beginning had turned out to be the most promising case study of all. For as great as Salomon's power was, he still had absolutely no idea what the Coffer of Devla actually was, who or what had made it, and how Caleb had managed to use it. As far as Salomon knew, Devla had not made himself known to the Roma people for centuries untold—if he ever had in the first place. Salomon did not profess to know very much, but he knew that time was an ageless thing and that countless suns and moons had risen on countless worlds and universes. As Elarion had sought to explore with the tower, the nature of all reality was an enigma so great that Salomon shuddered at its weight, and he foreclosed no possibilities.

"Most curious," he said to himself as he began studying the signature of Caleb's spirit residue. "I really thought he would ask to join one of his brothers."

28

After Val and Dida passed through the oval archway in the temple on the lightless bottom of the ocean, using a glow stone to examine the bizarre runes writhing across the ivory-white surface, Kiva had to issue a series of harsh commands to get her troops to pass through. On the other side, the tunnel was the same size and shape as the entrance portal, and crafted from the same white stone. The smoothness of the walls imparted the feeling of walking through a giant egg.

Everyone bunched together as they traversed the final length of tunnel, soon emerging into an enormous chamber crafted entirely of albalium. Val's mouth dropped when he saw that the walls were covered in sophisticated drawings and runes similar to those on the archway—except these runes were glowing, as if coated in bioluminescent paint. To his unpracticed eye, the chaotic scrawl of the runes looked almost digitized in nature, as if some mad, ancient, multi-handed genius had gone berserk on Photoshop.

This cavern, too, was oval-shaped, as was the basin that comprised most of the room, the size of a Ferris wheel lying on its side. As in the rooms above, a set of steps encircled the basin, leading to the darker water below. Even without the runes, the precision of the chamber walls spoke of intelligent design.

"So much albalium," Dida murmured. "This is an extraordinary find. Unprecedented. And these runes . . . they look so fresh."

Around the perimeter, the walls and ceiling had caved in at four spots equidistant from one another. The destruction gave the impression there had once been a cave-in, blocking the exit passages. As Dida began to wander giddily about the room, studying the spidery runes, Kiva and her warriors fanned out near the archway and stood rigidly awaiting orders.

Disappointed to have seen no sign of the Trident, Val studied the imagery interspersed among the runes, elaborate drawings of scenes so bizarre they left him breathless with the thrill of discovery, as well as unnerved. He saw a boiling ocean surrounded by flaming volcanoes and sheets of fire that fell like rain. Weird jungles with blue soil and mushrooms instead of trees, some as tall as skyscrapers. Clear cavern streams filled with sponge-like creatures that resembled human brains.

Along the wall opposite the entrance, Val found a set of images that caused a chill to sweep down his spine. The scenes portrayed a group of short, pale-skinned humanoids standing on steps in a rock-walled chamber. The steps led down to a basin, where the humanoids were using long-handled brushes to wash the bulbous head of a creature half-submerged in water.

"Dida, get over here."

The bibliomancer gasped when he rushed over. "The rooms from above! Before they filled with water!"

In other parts of the chamber, interspersed among the runes, were similar scenes: pale humanoids cleansing the heads of these creatures, bowing before them, offering them sacrifices. In one disturbing image, a man hung from a pair of iron rings set into the wall, next to a figure wearing ritual beads and the decapitated head of a seal. The shaman was pulling the victim's entrails out of a wound in his side and feeding them into an oval maw surrounded by needle-like teeth. It was unclear what creature the mouth belonged to, but Val noticed with a start that the walls of the room in that image were albalium.

"Great stones," Dida whispered. "They're worshipping the beasts."

"Our geomancers speculate," Dida said thoughtfully, wagging a finger in the air, "that at least one, and perhaps many, vast bodies of water exist within the core of Urfe. Perhaps the ocean floor on which this temple rests was once the surface. Perhaps these basins once tapped into an ancient underground aquifer, reservoir, or even a sea far below the surface."

"Something else comes to mind," Val said. "Think about the design of the temple. The sole entrance via the tower. The narrow passages. The progression from the upper to the lower levels."

"It all has a ritualistic feel," the bibliomancer murmured.

"As if they're terrified of those beings in the images—thus the rock walls and narrow passages, keeping them inside—yet also worship them. And the runes and walls in this room—I don't think primitive humans did this."

"Agreed."

"What if those things were part of an advanced civilization? What if they gave these humans tools and language and who knows what else? What if they were their *gods*?"

"This place could be tens of thousands of years old," Dida said in awe. "It would explain why there's no trace of anything except the rock."

Val swept an arm around the rune-covered walls. "And whoever—or *whatever*—did this."

They kept moving. Near one of the cave-ins opposite the archway, Dida grew excited as he pointed out what appeared to be the hilt of a weapon sticking out of the rubble. Val got Kiva's attention, then swam over for a closer look. When he peered into the debris, he could tell the hilt belonged to a sapphire blue, five-pronged trident as long as his staff.

A prolonged gurgle came from behind Val. He spun to find Kiva staring at the weapon.

"Is this it?" Val asked. "The Trident of Terengotha?"

"Indeed."

Val felt a wave of relief. He had begun to suspect the Trident had been lost or stolen away. After Dida checked for wards, Kiva pulled the Trident out of the rubble. Though elated by the completion of the quest, a troubled thought entered Val's mind.

If the kethropi expedition had once dropped the Trident through the tower opening, how had it gotten all the way down there?

It was almost as if the Trident, lying conspicuously among the rubble, had been *placed* there.

Kiva waved for her warriors to head for the exit, and started swimming across the chamber with the artifact. With a shrug, Val called out to Dida, knowing it would be hard to pull him away from the runes. As the bibliomancer turned to respond, a creature rose out of the basin, startling everyone and leaving Val weak in the knees, gaping in disbelief.

A nest of tentacles appeared first, grasping onto the top of the steps with suckered appendages. The tentacles straddled the basin from all sides as it continued to emerge, rising to a height well over ten feet. The tentacles converged into a thick and rubbery torso of grayish hue that reminded Val of seal blubber, atop which sat a bulbous head with two eyes and a maw filled with teeth as long and as sharp as daggers. Once the thing stood upright, using the steps to support its tentacles, the milky pupils swept the room, large and liquid, shining with intelligence. A pair of tentacles ending in pincers extended out from each side of the torso, pinching the water like a crab in front of the strange being.

Before anyone could react, the creature used one of its tentacles to sweep up a kethropi and hold him high off the floor. It gazed on the kethropi warrior with a contemptuous air as another tentacle snaked over to tighten around his neck, decapitating him with a jerk.

Stunned by the violent display, the rest of the kethropi regrouped to attack the creature as green blood fanned into the water. Thrusting spears bounced off the thing's rubbery flesh as it lurched out of the basin, using its nest of tentacles to carry it swiftly back and forth around the chamber, scuttling like a crab.

One of the kethropi rushed for the exit. A tentacle lashed out like a whip, almost severing the kethropi's arm. The being's pincers snatched another kethropi and drew him close to its maw, attaching to his face as he screamed and kicked his legs. Moments later, the creature tossed the mangled corpse into the water.

All of this had taken place in seconds, yet three kethropi were dead. Val had seen enough. He extended his hands and Spirit Fire erupted through the water, causing Val to wonder if it was a good idea to release energy like that through a conductor. The black lightning sparked more than usual as it slammed into the torso of the creature, causing it to scuttle backwards with an ear-splitting shriek. A gaping wound appeared in the center of its chest, muddying the water, but the powerful magic did not disintegrate the thing.

Its movements took it within reach of another kethropi. As the fish man darted forward, prepared to thrust a spear through the creature's eyes, the beast suddenly stopped moving, growing as still as a placid lake. The kethropi's spear lowered, and he hovered in the water as if confused, ensorcelled in some manner. With a shocking burst of speed and power, the creature scuttled closer and hugged the kethropi to its chest, coiling its four arm tentacles around the warrior's body. After a wet crunch of bone, the creature let go, and the kethropi sank lifeless to the floor.

Dida was busy inscribing the outline of a glowing wall in the center of the room, cutting the creature off from the remaining members of the party. Val knew the spell; the runic magic was strong enough to stop a stone giant.

Yet the tentacled thing moved right through it, slowing just a fraction.

Val felt fear coil tightly around him.

Calm and collected, the creature wrapped a nest of tentacles around the limbs of the nearest kethropi warrior. As the fish-man tried to free himself, the monster jerked straight out with its tentacles, quartering him.

Only Kiva was left, and she looked terrified, unsure what to do.

"Stop!" Val yelled, trying a different tactic. "Why are you attacking us?"

To his surprise, the thing stopped moving and turned to face him. As they locked eyes, Val felt an overwhelming sense of awe at the vastness of the intelligence reflected in those silvery orbs.

A voice resounded in Val's head, deep and sonorous.

You are human but can speak with your mind.

"I didn't know that," Val said, using his voice. "What do you want with us? Why do you kill us?"

Your ancestors betrayed us. We had an agreement.

"Those weren't my ancestors. I'm sorry for whatever it was they did."

You tended to us, and we gave you things. Was it not enough?

The longer they talked, the more Val found himself immensely curious about the origins of this amazing being, overwhelmed by its presence.

We taught you how to burn and how to speak. You served us for millennia.

His arms hanging loose at his side, his magic forgotten, he asked, "How old is your race?"

As old as the stars that struck the oceans.

"Where did you come from?"

From the beginning.

Val felt the urge to lie prostrate in worship. Yet dimly, in the back of his mind, he heard someone calling his name. He turned and saw Dida and Kiva suspended in midair, enwrapped in tentacles that now seemed beautiful and powerful to him.

Look at me.

Val obeyed.

Will you tend to us, human? We will find you a mate and start anew.

The mention of a mate sparked a memory in Val's mind of someone fair and golden, with turquoise eyes that mesmerized him just as much as this tentacled being's stare.

Allow you to produce children and serve us as before.

What greater calling could there be, Val thought, *than to spend my life in service to these great beings with Adaira by my side?* As her image sharpened, a series of numbers flashed in the air in front of Val's eyes, a pattern that snapped his mind awake.

"Don't look at its eyes," Dida called out. "It's hypnotizing you!"

Ignore him.

Val teetered on his feet, his attention attracted to the flashing numbers, but also drawn to the mesmeric voice in his head.

Serve us.

Dida screamed as the tentacles started to tighten his body, and that piercing human cry brought Val all the way back.

Dida. My friend. This thing is killing my friend.

Val roared and blasted the creature with Spirit Fire, this time aiming for its eye. It gave an inhuman screech as the eye melted, and released Dida and Kiva. Val almost emptied his store of magic, burning a hole right through the creature's head. Its shriek reverberated through the water and caused Val to clamp his hands over his ears. Yet still it didn't fall. *How is it still alive?*

Kiva raised the Trident, then changed her mind and joined Dida and Val in a mad rush for the exit. Val looked back and saw the creature heave, press one of its tentacles to its eye, and rush after them.

As they fled past the basin, another creature rose out of the water, smaller than the first and with beige spots on its head. It swept an imperious gaze around the room and saw its wounded companion scuttling across the chamber.

Dida was frantically inscribing runes in midair with his hands as they raced for the archway. Both creatures followed them into the oval tunnel. Val's terror made him want to vomit, but he pressed forward, turning only to release a weakened bolt of Spirit Fire the lead creature barely noticed.

They were almost to the archway. Val prayed the things could not fit through. Yet the creatures had gained so much ground that even if Val and the others made it out, a tentacle was going to catch one of them by the legs and drag them back inside. Dida was bringing up the rear with his ponderous strokes, and Val feared he wouldn't make it. Just as they cleared the portal, Val turned to help his friend, raising his staff. The beige creature was less than ten feet away. A tentacle shot towards the white archway to ensnare Dida. As Val moved to intercept it with the staff, the tentacle stopped in midair at the entrance to the archway, and a bolt of electricity arced back through the water, causing the creature to seize up. A sheet of purple light filled the egg-shaped opening, and Val recognized another of Dida's barrier glyphs, this one stronger and more focused in the smaller space of the archway.

As Val and the others fled down the narrow tunnel, back into the temple and out of reach of their pursuers, the eldritch beings released a cry with an entirely different timbre than before, keening moans of rage and eternal despair.

Terrified the creatures would pursue them, Kiva led them up through the ocean without delay. She didn't seem to understand Val's worry about the bends, the deadly decompression sickness caused by surfacing too quickly, but the Skincloths must have protected him and Dida, because they arrived unharmed. Val felt immeasurable relief at the familiar sight of the moon and stars, of the fresh cool air on his cheeks.

The dolphins arrived soon, nuzzling Kiva as if relieved. Distraught by the decimation of her team, shaken to her core by the encounter on the ocean bottom, the kethropi leader grimly led them back to the underwater city, stopping to rest for a mere two hours on the return journey. Val was so exhausted when they arrived that he embraced Adaira and fell straight into bed.

The next morning, Adaira had the unenviable task of managing the diplomatic fallout from the disastrous mission. She decided to stay another day to help smooth things over, but Lord Alistair ordered Val and Dida to return immediately to New Victoria. After Val said his goodbyes to Adaira and promised to meet her soon, Alistair opened a portal and took him and Dida through.

Later that same evening, Val found himself back inside the rock-walled head-quarters of Undertown, facing Zagath again on his floating throne. Val held his staff upright in one hand and the Trident of Terengotha in another. He was alone this time—or so it appeared.

As promised, once Val had stepped foot in the entrance to Undertown by the Goblin Market, a heavily armed contingent of Zagath's men had arrived to meet him. After insisting on a blindfold, they had led him on a long walk through the sewer, and then a ride on a canoe. No black sash accosted them along the way, as Val knew they wouldn't.

Zagath's eyes latched onto the Trident as soon as he saw Val. Outside of the water, the sapphire artifact did not gleam so brightly.

"You've brought it," Zagath said.

"You sound surprised."

"I am . . . impressed."

"Because we overcame the horrific guardians you conveniently forgot to mention?"

"I don't know—"

"Don't lie to me," Val warned. "You couldn't have known about the runes unless you were inside the temple. You saw those things, too."

"Bah! You succeeded, did you not? I knew a powerful mage would be the only way to defeat them."

"I didn't defeat them. A few of us barely made it out, and the rest were killed."

"Collateral damage is always unfortunate."

As his magic boiled inside him, Val worked to control his utter distaste of Zagath. This was a business transaction, nothing more, and he had to see it through. "I'm curious: how did you descend so low, and how did you get away?"

"I had my own version of a Skincloth, and was the only one smart enough not to go through the archway." Zagath shuddered. "What are those creatures, anyway?"

"I have no idea. I just hope I never see one again."

The crime lord rose on his throne, exposing the scales on the lower half of his body. "Give it to me."

"Give me the name of the Coffer thief."

"First the Trident."

Zagath's shrewd eyes slipped to the side, and Val heard the bristling of weapons. Val knew it was bad business for Zagath to give up the name of a fellow criminal, and he feared a double cross.

After a long moment, in which Zagath was no doubt judging Val's strength and contemplating the wisdom of attacking a representative of the Congregation, he said, "I've no wish to quarrel, mage. You've earned your fee."

As soon as Zagath told Val the name of the buyer who had approached him about stealing the Coffer—someone named Takros of Crete, a name Val had never heard before—he extended the Trident. Yet when Zagath reached for the weapon, Val said, "If you're lying, I'll return for you."

Zagath's smile was like the stab of an icicle. "Return where, mage? You have no idea where you are."

Val's return smile was just as cold. He tossed the Trident to Zagath, then reached inside his cloak to extract a silver bauble the size of a golf ball. Val threw it on the ground. Instead of shattering, it expanded to form a portal that opened onto a room inside the Sanctum. The shadowy forms of the gathered mages, including the unmistakable silhouette of Lord Alistair, could be seen in the background.

"They've been waiting to hear from you," Val said.

Zagath's eyes bulged when he saw who was on the other side of the portal. After a long pause, he bowed deeply and said, "The name I've given you is true. You have my word."

"Excellent. Oh, and one last thing," Val said. "To reward the kethropi for their assistance, I agreed to give them your location."

Zagath gave a strangled cry as he rose on his throne.

"You brought this on yourself by putting my team's life in danger. Five kethropi didn't make it back. Still, we're not in the business of double-crossing

partners on a deal—which is why I'm giving you a half hour start before I reveal this exact location to the kethropi raiding party waiting in the river. I'd
leave now, if I were you. I suspect it won't take them long to locate the connecting tunnels."

"You've destroyed my livelihood! Everything I have!"

"The Congregation knows you've been allowing the black sash access to
Undertown in exchange for a fee. You're lucky they agreed to let you live. Look
at it this way, Zagath. Now that you have the Trident, you can set up operations in any city, wherever you wish." Val's lips parted in a thin smile before he
stepped into the portal. "It just won't be in New Victoria."

29

With their hands on their weapons and their eyes in constant motion, Will and his companions followed behind the Skinwalkers on a steady march atop the bluff through the abandoned streets of Old Town. As pale and silent as death, the terrifying beings seemed to know exactly where they were going, never pausing to gain their bearings.

A luminous moon should have cast more light on their surroundings, but whatever spell or unnatural darkness cloaked the ancient city prevented Will from getting a good look at his surroundings. It was as if Old Town was not real on some level, a murky impressionist painting hovering somewhere between reality and imagination. Yet sometimes, out of the corner of his eye, the looming shadows would congeal enough to reveal a collection of architecture similar to the rest of Praha, and even more grand: hovering palaces and elaborate arched bridges spanning towers and obelisks and pyramids, viaducts that led to columns and ziggurats and cupolas, everything interconnected with a symmetry that spoke of vision and genius beyond Will's comprehension. Perhaps, he thought, mortal eyes were not meant to gaze directly upon the wonders of Old Town, and he could only truly see the city when he wasn't looking.

Or perhaps it was simply cursed.

Fearing the wrath of the Skinwalkers, no one dared use a glow stone. In cautious whispers, they debated whether they should keep following their guides or try to escape, and they came to the conclusion that, even if they knew where to go, the Skinwalkers would hunt them down and kill them. *No mortal weapon can harm them*, the journal had said.

Will didn't know whether that proscription included Zariduke, but the question was irrelevant. The plague-blackened sword strapped to his back now felt like the hump of a cripple, an ill-fated burden that was his alone to bear.

Judging from the size of the bluff on the map, Old Town could not be more than a couple of miles across. After navigating the broad stone streets for less than half an hour, the pale creatures stopped in the center of a wondrous sight that had more solidity than the rest of the buildings: an amphitheater soaring high above their heads.

The ground-level ring of high-backed thrones fit for giants spanned fifty feet in diameter, while the next row up, more than twenty feet above their heads, was double the size. The higher reaches of the amphitheater were lost in the darkness above. The structure resembled a cone of enormous size balanced on its tip, and Will had no idea what supported it.

The Skinwalkers spread out to encircle the party. When the creatures started walking forward, tightening the circle, Will wondered if they had herded them through the city to perform some type of ritual sacrifice.

Once the party was gathered close together, the pale beings stopped moving. Will glanced down and noticed the blackened marble at his feet was a shade lighter. As his fear and confusion reached a fever pitch, the ground beneath them started to shift. It took a moment to understand what was happening, but when the ground looked as if it were rising, he realized the entire section of marble on which he and his friends were standing had started to descend.

Dalen's eyes bulged with fear, and Mateo started to jump to higher ground. Yasmina laid a hand on his arm. "I wouldn't," she said, eying the Skinwalkers.

Like Mateo, Will's instincts screamed at him to leap up while he still could, but the presence of the pale guardians and his curiosity at what lay below kept him—and everyone else—from taking action.

The slow moving platform did not have sides or railing. Descending into utter blackness was disconcerting, but a flicker of colored light soon appeared beneath them. The light grew steadily in size, clarifying into a circle of polychromatic color that seethed and flowed below them, a perpetual churn with no pattern as far as Will could tell.

"Does your journal have anything to say about this?" Will said through grim lips.

"This is uncharted territory," Skara said. Though weary and grief-stricken, there was an undercurrent of wonder in her voice.

"Whatever those lights represent," Dalen said, "it's no illusion."

"Is it magical in some other way?" Mateo asked.

"Not that I can tell. Lucka, I've no idea *what* it is."

"Yaz?" Will asked. "Can you see anything?"

"Only that the bottom is near. And I can sense a . . . presence."

"A malevolent one?" Skara asked.

"It's unclear. A life form unlike any I've encountered."

"The Nephili," Skara whispered.

It became clear they were sinking into a chamber of some sort, and in its center was a pool of roiling energy similar to the one in the storehouse, about the size of a large hot tub. Only the energy in this basin was brightly colored instead of dull, as vigorous as the other was torpid. A polychromatic Rorschach blot in constant flux.

Skara stepped to the very edge of the platform and peered down. "What on Urfe is that?"

"My guess?" Will said. "It's a healthy one of those *other* things."

"Krikey," Dalen said.

Mateo returned the wafer to Skara's backpack and was staring wide-eyed at the floor, gripping his urumi blade.

It seemed as if the platform was heading straight into the basin of energy, causing Will to prepare to leap away, but then he realized it was positioned to land just alongside it. Yet instead of striking against the floor, which looked crafted of pure silver, the platform dissolved under their feet as they landed, depositing them gently and causing everyone to gasp in wonder.

Skara raised her weapons. "What magic is this?"

Now that they were standing right beside the basin, they could see tiny bubbles of color covering the surface, constantly forming and evaporating, along with wavelike swells that simmered and churned beneath the surface. The prismatic light was so bright it took Will's eyes a minute to adjust to the rest of the room. Yet he gawked when his vision cleared. The walls of the spherical chamber, which spanned at least two hundred feet in diameter, were crafted of the same pure silver as the floor and divided by onyx partitions into shelves about three feet in height. Tall and slender objects with spines crafted from a single piece of precious stone filled the shelves. There was a section filled with ruby-bound volumes, another from moonstone, another from emerald, and so on.

"Is this a *library*?" Will said.

"Look!" Dalen said. "Inside the basin!"

Will whipped around to find the colors inside the strange pool gathering into the shape of a city so beautiful it took his breath away. Not just any city, but a city he recognized from the height of the buildings and the unique, interlocking nature of the architecture.

The city was Praha, as he imagined it must once have looked, beautiful beyond imagining.

"A most exquisite vista, is it not?"

Will spun again. The voice, as dry and raspy as a whisper in the desert sun, had come from his left. At first he saw nothing, but then he noticed, down a darkened passage set between two shelves, the outline of a shadow-encased form reclining on an ebony throne. The being was very tall and angular, its fingers as long and delicate as a blade of grass. Enormous almond-shaped eyes with silver pupils regarded them in solemn repose, and knife-edged cheekbones slashed down its face to create gaping holes in the fleshless face. Will could not tell if the being was made of bone and shadow, or was cloaking itself with magic.

Skara released a strangled cry. "Nephili! You exist!"

"As do you, hominid, unless my eyes deceive me."

"After all these years of searching. Decades, centuries. My family . . ."

Her voice trailed off, overcome by emotion.

"Come no closer," the Nephili warned, after Skara took a few steps forward. Will and the others moved to stand beside the adventuress, close enough to see that the Nephili was ensconced at the entrance to a deep alcove. Behind the throne he could see more of the silver shelves, filled not with tomes but with gemstone-covered ampules, chests, urns, and other containers.

"How are you alive?" Skara asked. "Who are you? Are there any others?"

"I am the first and last of my kind. My true name, if spoken to hominid ears, would rattle your delicate bones and release your mind from the tenuous tether of its soul."

"Not much for modesty," Will muttered.

"What is modesty to one such as I?" the Nephili replied. Apparently it had sharp hearing. "What is left to me except the insanity of truth?"

Despite the being's haughty rhetoric, it had yet to stir from its throne, and Will got the sense it was barely alive, too weak to move and clinging to consciousness by the thinnest of threads.

"We came to make a bargain," Will said. "We have something you might want."

"You do indeed. But it is not the *tjulkych*."

Interesting, Will thought, that his armband failed to translate the word. Maybe it was on the blink. "The what?"

"That which the angry one carries on her back."

The Nephili was looking right at Skara Brae. Slowly, keeping her hand on her cudgel and maintaining eye contact the entire time, the adventuress took the Sephyr Wafer out of her pack and held it high. "No?" she said, in a challenging tone. "This is of no desire to you?"

Its laugh was the crunch of dead leaves in a cemetery. "Desire? What do hominids know of desire? Of promise and disappointment, rebirth and damnation, of the infinite melody of that theme? That which I *desire* disappeared from this world a thousand and more moons ago. There is only release left for me, escape from the prison of corporeality."

"Then why did the Skinwalkers lead us here, if not to carry the wafer?"

"They were programmed long ago. Far before the affliction that doomed my kind. My life force keeps the guardians alive, and that is all."

Programmed, Will thought. *Interesting terminology.*

"Then I don't understand," Skara said. "What is it that you want?"

As if leaning into the gale force wind of a hurricane, the Nephili bent forward so slowly it pained Will to watch. It used its elegant fingers to probe the shadows coagulated on its chest, withdrawing a plague-stained, three-pronged dagger with a wavy hilt. With the torpid curl of a wrist, it dropped the dagger beside the throne. "I want you," he said, as if the effort had expended half of its life force, "to end my existence."

After a moment of stunned silence, saddened by the thing's awful state, Will blurted out, "We've brought you a wafer. Will it not help?"

A snarl twisted its aquiline features. "A single *tjulkych*? Do you think we did not try to reverse the affliction? The handful we left at the *kvulnych* were a fool's prayer for a miracle that will never come. All races fade to oblivion, and our time has come."

"What about this pool?" Will waved a hand towards the basin of chaotic energy at their side.

"When I die, so will the wellspring. It is weakened beyond repair. Before we crafted this funereal chamber, the wellspring reached above the surface, to the very top of the amphitheater, a fountain of life to us all. A single wafer would only prolong my cursed existence. What is the value of an eternity in exile, helpless inside this prison, the last of my kind? The affliction is too strong, and I've not the strength to take my own life. Take the blade and dip it into the pool. Restore its power."

Skara moved to take the knife, but Will beat her to it, grabbing the dagger and backing away as the Nephili watched over them. He doubted whether this enfeebled being could help them, but he asked anyway. "Not long ago, a thief opened a portal in Praha and stole something very valuable. The Coffer of Devla. We need to know who stole it, and where it is now."

At the mention of the Coffer of Devla, the Nephili seemed to draw back upon itself, sinking deeper into the chair. Almost as if it were frightened.

Or maybe it was Will's imagination.

"Can you help us?" Mateo asked, moving to stand beside his cousin.

"If the thief did indeed depart from our city, then yes, I can aid you. But you must promise to do as I ask in exchange."

"Oh, we agree," Skara said softly, her hand slipping towards her bladed cane. She did not look happy that Will had grabbed the dagger, and he knew she would fight him for it if she had to.

"And how do we leave?" Will asked.

"Unless I am restored, returning to the surface is impossible." As Will's heart sank, the being's left hand upturned in its lap, the shadow fingers stiffly unfurling. "Yet there is another way. A portal left by a hominid who sought me long ago, brought here by the guardians."

Will didn't need to ask how that turned out. "A portal to where?"

"Wherever you wish to travel."

"Where is it?"

"In the chamber behind me."

"Then why haven't you left?" Will asked. "Can't you escape the plague by going someplace else?"

"Do you not yet understand the nature of this place?" it said, as if talking to a child. "We came as a seed and of one body we remain. To use a hominid analogy, the city is our flesh, our flesh the city. The wellspring, the *tjulkych*, the *kvulnych*, it is all one. I could no more leave than you could step out of your own skin. A hominid portal is a worthless device to us."

Will felt sorry for the wretched state of the Nephili, but he was also growing tired of its condescending attitude. "Then find our thief, send us out of here, and we'll give you what you want."

"How do you propose to do such a thing from afar?"

"How long will the portal last?"

"Long enough to do as I ask before you leave."

"I'll stay," Skara said.

Will moved to face her and saw an unhealthy gleam in her eye. It felt as if she were looking right through him, but then her eyes latched on to the knife, and she took a step forward. Mateo noticed and stepped between her and Will.

"Don't try it," Will said to Skara in a low voice. "I'll give you the knife, but don't try to use it before we open the portal. We'll be stuck down here forever."

Her eyes flashed. "Do you think I wish to kill him in this wretched state? I want him *restored*."

Her comment took him aback. "You're both mad," Will muttered, then raised his voice to the Nephili, though he had the feeling it had heard the exchange. "We agree to your terms."

The being was staring at Skara, and when it spoke, its voice dripped with contempt. "This one will approach me to retrieve the portal. You will lower the dagger into the wellspring to restore it as I search for your answer. We shall proceed from there."

Will turned to his companions and encountered no dissent. Skara had already started walking towards the Nephili with her weapons drawn, giving the throne a wide berth. She stopped as she passed the Nephili, and Will heard the being whispering something to her, presumably instructions. After a moment,

Skara threw back her head, howled with forced laughter, and continued into the treasure chamber behind the throne.

"Tell me of this thief you seek," the Nephili said to Will.

Will and Mateo gave him every detail they could remember from that horrible night in Freetown when the electromancer had slain Caleb's family. When the tale was finished, the Nephili told them to approach the basin. Will took a spare cloth out of his pack and used it to hold the three-pronged dagger as he knelt in front of the geyser-like pool of bubbling color. Faint pops and crackles emanated from within, yet he felt no heat, detected no odor.

His companions and dear friends, Yasmina and Mateo and Dalen, stood behind him. As Will lowered the blade, the colored energy took shape as before, forming an image of Praha that began to transform as soon as it materialized. *It's moving it with its mind*, Will realized.

At first he thought the scene was dissolving, and wondered if the Nephili had lost the strength to continue, but then he realized it was changing too fast to follow, as if a movie reel of the city was playing at warp speed.

My God, he's not just moving it. He's sifting through time.

With a deep breath, Will did as he was asked and dipped the blade into the pool. As soon as the blade made contact with the seething energy, he felt a slight resistance, akin to pushing through a soft gel. He lowered it all the way to the hilt before drawing it out. Right before his eyes, the tip of the blackened metal turned to silver, so bright it glowed. The phenomenon continued down the blade until the entire dagger gleamed like new. Even the hilt was affected, changing to solid diamond as Will watched in awe.

"Lucka," Dalen whispered behind him.

The speed of change inside the pool had slowed considerably, now revealing the image of a splinter-size man with a ferrety face, holding a platinum bag as he stood alone on a street in the dystopian cityscape of Praha. Will watched him smash a crystal sphere on the ground, opening a portal that the man stepped inside.

"This is whom you seek?" the Nephili asked.

"That's him!"

The image resumed shifting, again too fast to follow. Eventually the surface returned to normal, and the Nephili said, "It is finished. Fulfill your promise, hominid. Bring the restored dagger to me."

Mateo laid a hand on Will's shoulder, his voice urgent. "The sword, cousin. Try the sword."

Will knew at once what he meant. In fact, selfishly, he had thought of little else since the Nephili had first mentioned the restorative power of the basin. Slowly reaching back, Will dropped the sword he had picked up in the Agora and slid Zariduke out of its scabbard, barely daring to breathe as he gripped the weapon in his free hand and lowered it towards the basin.

What if it only worked on Nephili weapons?

What if the magic of Zariduke blocked the process in some way?

What if it disintegrated inside the strange energy?

Catching his breath in anticipation, he dipped the blade into the basin and, after a long moment, withdrew it. His disappointment, when he saw no sign of restoration, physically pained him.

"I'm sorry," Yasmina said, as Mateo squeezed his shoulder.

After a long moment in which the weight of the world seemed to rest on his back, Will turned away, only to notice that a tiny gleam of silver had appeared at the tip of the legendary blade. Stunned, he clutched the hilt tighter as he turned to thrust the blade into the basin again, but then saw that he didn't need to: the plague-damaged sword was transforming before their eyes, the touch of silver continuing to envelop the blade, slowly but surely returning it to its natural state.

Mateo and Dalen whooped in joy, Yasmina hugged Will from behind, and he stood there feeling both elated and numb, shocked by the sudden reversal. Dalen cast a simple illusion, an image of a tree, and Will swept the blade through it.

The tree disappeared in a snip of blue-white light.

Will blew out a long breath and gripped the weapon in both hands, a jumble of emotions pouring through him as Skara returned from behind the throne bearing a jade-colored glass prism.

"It's full of Nephili artifacts," she said in a stunned voice. "Unlike anything I've ever seen. It's a priceless collection. Miraculous."

"Hand me the gateway stone," the Nephili said.

"Who's the thief?" Will asked. "Who sent him?"

"I do not speak in hominid names. But all will be revealed."

"What caused the plague?" he said suddenly, feeling as if he had to know.

"All species decline," the Nephili said, after a moment. "Even ours. Entropy and corruption are the cycle of nature."

Will could tell there was more to the story, far more, but that the Nephili didn't have the time or the inclination to tell him.

"Save your pity, hominids. I doubt your own pathetic kind will see the end of the millennium."

"You think so little of us," Skara mocked. "Yet we've outlasted you. You're the last of your kind, a fading shadow."

The Nephili seemed to straighten in his chair, his voice soaked with scorn. "Outlasted? You who have barely seen the passage of an *ilych* dare to reproach *us*? We who have seen the glaciers come and go, many times over? We who have watched your kind evolve with the animals in the steaming jungles and boiling plains? We who exist in a manner beyond your comprehension, we who built the *vynilych*, we who wrote new laws of nature? Now give me the dagger and the gateway stone, little hominids. Do not break your bargain, or I will eat your souls instead."

"Give it to him, Skara," Will said. "Now."

Looking as meek as a lamb, she approached to hand the emerald prism to the Nephili, who slowly upturned his palm to receive it, as if receiving an offer from a lowly subject. But then Skara held the wafer out to him as well.

"Skara!" Will shouted. "What are you doing?"

The meekness in her posture disappeared. "Do you think I want to slay a shriveled shadow such as this? I desire a trophy for my hall, not a desiccated cadaver."

The being rasped another laugh that sent a chill arcing down Will's spine. He hurried over to brush Skara aside and extend the three-pronged dagger to the Nephili. "Open the portal, and I'll give you the knife. Skara, if you have any sense at all, you'll stop this madness and come with us."

"So many gifts," the Nephili mocked. His long fingers closed on the prism as his gaze shifted to Skara. "I'm afraid I need a taste of the *tjulkych* to open the portal. I haven't the power."

"You're lying," Will said. "You didn't mention that before."

"I do not lie, hominid. You did not ask."

"Don't do it, Skara," Will warned.

But the adventuress had already snapped off a sliver of the emerald disk, which broke apart like a piece of hardened clay, the inside as bright as the surface. Skara tossed the piece to the Nephili, and it landed on his chest. He stared down at it as if too weak to take it, but then the sliver of wafer levitated into the air and flew into its mouth.

Within moments, the being eased out of its chair and stood before them on wobbly legs. A pair of angular wings, hidden behind his back when he was seated, unfolded as he rose. Still hunching, the Nephili turned away from them as its form started to solidify, filling out before their eyes. When it turned around and drew to its full height, exposing a naked but sexless form, its wings had turned as white as fresh milk, its flesh tinged with a deep golden hue that seemed more like molten metal than mortal flesh. The radiant being drew to its full height, standing more than nine feet tall, so beautiful Will felt dazed as he gazed upon the glory of it.

He felt a nail dig into his elbow, hitting the pressure point and causing him to wince. "Don't look at it," Yasmina said in a harsh whisper. "Look anywhere besides its face."

Though it took an act of immense will, Will shuddered and did as he was told, jerking his gaze to the side. *What have we unleashed?*

With a barely perceptible flick of its wrist, the Nephili sent the prism of solid emerald flying twenty feet away, in the direction of the basin. It shattered to expand into a translucent portal, beyond which could be seen a parched brown hillside spilling into a body of water the color of a glacial spring.

The Nephili closed its long fingers around the hilt of the knife, the movement so precise and beautiful that Will was spellbound. He felt as if he could watch it perform such simple actions forever and ever.

Yasmina squeezed him harder. *Snap out of it, Will.*

Yet the Nephili broke its own spell as it tipped back its head and roared like a pride of lions, a sound so booming and terrible and fraught with power that Will rocked back on his heels. "Flee while you can, hominids, for my bargain with you ceases once the portal closes."

Will clutched Zariduke as he turned to his friends. "Go!"

Yasmina had to yank Dalen and Mateo away by the collar, but then one by one, the three of them slipped through the portal and disappeared. Will avoided looking at the Nephili as he turned to Skara, her cudgel and bladed cane poised for action. "Come with us, Skara."

"I have unfinished business." Rather than appearing awed by the Nephili's presence, she looked as focused and aware as he had ever seen her.

"You'll be stuck here forever, even if you do survive."

"There are other gateways inside that chamber. I know it in my bones. That and far more."

"So you would slay me first, hominid?" the Nephili said in amusement, looking down on her as a cat eyes a mouse creeping towards its hole.

"This is suicide," Will urged. "Get out of here."

"There is more to Skara Brae than meets the eye," she said. "I've been waiting my entire life for this moment. If I die, then so be it."

Will looked back and saw the portal start to shimmer. "Last chance."

With a single flap of its wings, the Nephili skimmed lightly atop the floor, drawing closer to Skara as it flexed its limbs, awakening from its long period of dormancy. "Perhaps I shall conduct a final concert before I take my own life."

As Will watched in dread fascination, Skara broke off another piece of the wafer and shoved it into her mouth. Her body went rigid as the Nephili roared in laughter. It twirled the diamond hilt of the dagger through its elegant fingers, and Will could feel the power emanating from the creature. He wondered how Zariduke would fare if he were forced to fight it.

As Skara's eyes bulged and her skin became imbued with a golden tinge, she stumbled drunkenly around the room, as if trying to regain control of her actions. "The p-p-power," she stuttered, right before she started to jerk and dance like a marionette, her weapons clanging to the floor.

"Very good," the Nephili said. "An entertainment most splendid."

Will turned back to the portal. It was starting to close. He couldn't leave Skara like that, and in desperation, he rushed towards her, thinking to pick her up and carry her through the gateway himself.

"I told you to leaveeeee!" the Nephili roared, opening its mouth and releasing a blast of energy that pushed Will away at the same time he felt a force tugging at him from behind, as if the basin were a giant magnet. Unable to stop himself, he tumbled backwards across the floor and through the shimmering oval of the portal.

30

Will shielded his eyes with a hand, the sudden bright sunlight and endless blue sky a shock to his system after the lightless expanse of Old Town Praha and the gloomy lair of the Nephili.

The portal had deposited them on a golden sweep of beach that spilled into a sea the color of crushed blueberries. Behind them was a range of parched brown hills speckled with shrubby vegetation. There were no buildings or people in sight, no animals roaming the hillsides. "Does anyone have any idea where we are?"

"I see no sign of a thief or the Coffer," Mateo said, bending down to touch the sand and ensure that it was real. "I fear the Nephili has tricked us."

Yasmina planted her owl staff on the ground, the light breeze ruffling her hair. "If we were back home, I'd say we landed on a Greek island."

"Huh," Will said. "Can you see anything in the distance, Yaz?"

"As far as I can tell, we're alone here."

As the others continued to absorb their surroundings, Will verified that all of his possessions were intact, including his paladin's shield and armband and, most of all, Zariduke. A rush of emotion overcame him as he held the sword in his hands, its magic restored to full power.

Will turned to find Dalen staring at the line of hills behind them with an uneasy expression. "Are you okay?"

The young mage looked as if he had seen a ghost.

"My, my," a familiar mocking voice called out, before Will could ask Dalen what was wrong. "I've never seen such a ragtag band of adventurers."

Will's jaw slowly dropped as a lithe figure emerged from a rocky outcropping at the base of the nearest hill, less than a hundred feet from their position.

"I must confess, Will the Builder, that I'm as confused as you look."

"Mala?" he said, incredulous.

Her smirk expanded as she approached, clad in black leather pants tucked into calf-high boots, a lace-up crimson top, her weighted blue sash, and the usual dazzling display of pouches, weapons, and jewelry. "I assure you I am not the Queen of Albion."

"But how did you get here? Where are we?"

"I was going to ask you the same questions."

The adventuress swept her eyes across the group, acknowledging the others with a curt greeting as she fingered an amulet around her neck. "If I'm not mistaken, we're on a Minoan isle, though I've no idea which one. I arrived minutes ago, through a device that . . . allows the bearer to travel to the location of another."

"A portal?" Mateo asked.

"Of sorts. I fear . . ." Fingering the sash at her waist, she turned to regard the hills in the distance. "How did you arrive?"

Will exchanged a glance with the others. For a moment, he thought the Nephili might have sent them to his home world, but Mala's presence seemed to confirm they were still on Urfe. "It's kind of a long story. We're supposed to be tracking the Coffer thief."

"You came through a portal? From Praha?"

"That's right."

"And no one else came with you?"

"That would be rather impossible."

"Why?"

"As you said, it's a long story."

Mala pursed her lips as she swept the horizon again. "Then I suppose it's time for an exchange of tales. The danger might not be as imminent as I thought, but until I know what in Queen's Blood is going on and where we are, we should all be on high guard."

"I might be able to help," Dalen said, in a strangely subdued voice.

All eyes turned to the illusionist. His face had paled, and his eyes kept roving side to side. "What do you know?" Will asked. Where are we?"

"I think I've been here before," he replied, as if in a trance. "Long ago."

Yasmina laid a hand gently on the illusionist's shoulder. "Dalen? Are we in danger?"

"Quite possibly. I . . . can explain."

"Let's continue this conversation in a more secluded location." Mala said. "I noticed shelter when I arrived. Come."

Without waiting for a reply, the adventuress turned and led them back to the outcropping, into a little cove shielded from view by an overhang at the bottom of the hill. Mala sat lotus-style facing the sea as the others dropped their packs and spread out in a loose circle on the sand. Will opened a flask of water and took a long pull, then laid Zariduke in his lap as he listened to Dalen's story.

"I told you I'm from Hellas, a city in Macedonia," the illusionist said to no one in particular, staring off at the sea. And you've all heard me speak about my Da. But the truth is that I'm Minoan, not Macedonian—and I haven't seen my Da for a very long time."

"Why lie to us?" Will asked.

"Because the Minoans," Mala said, "are shunned throughout the region, outside of their own islands."

"It's true we're an insular people," Dalen said, "and have a reputation for witchcraft and dark sorcery."

Will started to laugh, since Dalen was about as edgy and darkly sorcerous as a Disney character, but the illusionist's face was more troubled and somber than he had ever seen it, and Will's laughter faltered. He realized how very little he knew of Dalen's true past.

"Lucka, we're also very clannish. Often our youth are sent to live as servants with older, more prosperous relatives. For those who possess magic, if we're lucky, we become apprentices." He took a deep breath and released it. "I have an uncle named Takros. He's a Kalaktos conjurer."

"By the Queen," Mala said. "I know of these wizards, and of Takros in particular. He's a well-known collector with a fearsome reputation."

"Have you worked for him?" Will asked.

"Contrary to public opinion, there are some assignments even I decline to take."

"It's true," Dalen said, staring stone-faced at the sea. "My uncle is a very bad person."

Will frowned. "What exactly is a Kalaktos conjurer?"

"An illusionist like myself," Dalen said, "only with far more power. Enough to enter the ancient brotherhood of Kalaktos. When I turned ten, Takros visited my family and demanded I live with him and become his apprentice. As weak as I was, I was the only one of my cousins with true power. Still, when the time came, I would never have survived the trials of the brotherhood. I haven't the strength."

"Don't sell yourself short," Will said. "You've improved so much. So this is why you left home?"

Dalen lip's parted in a soft smile. "Krikey, no. I was too young at the time to realize any of this. Yet my parents knew what sort of man Takros is, and that he would try to corrupt me, even if I survived the trials. They also knew he wouldn't take *no* for an answer. When my parents tried to put him off by claiming I was sick, he sent a message to the entire village, an elaborate phoenix illusion that delivered his demand for my services and dissolved once the sun set. I was enraptured, and the rest of the village demanded that I go with Takros, fearing his wrath. I was too young to know any better . . ." Dalen reached down and scooped up a handful of sand, then let it trickle through his fingers.

When he didn't go on, Will said gently, "What happened?"

"My parents smuggled me to Macedonia on a fishing boat. They paid someone to take me on board against my will. I was kicking and screaming the whole way. We lived near the harbor and, just after the ship left, I saw Takros swoop down from the sky in a flowing white cape . . ."

Dalen stared down at his feet. Yasmina put a hand on his shoulder again.

"He was riding a flying bull with wings, a *fornostos*. I thought it the most magnificent sight I'd ever seen and couldn't believe how unfair it was that I couldn't go with him. I hated my parents for sending me away and tried to fight my way off the ship. I did the one thing they told me never to do: I used my magic and cast a weak illusion, trying to scare the captain. It had the opposite effect: he understood the situation at once and his role in the affair, and it terrified him. To this day, I'm surprised he didn't head back to shore and turn me over to my uncle. Instead he hustled me below deck—right after I saw my family's home burst into flames."

Yasmina clapped a hand over her mouth, Mateo looked away, and Will felt sickened by the tale. He noticed that Mala's face had gone rigid, and the emotion in her eyes surprised him.

"My parents didn't die in the fire, but they might as well have. With their home destroyed and no savings, they were forced to live on the street. They died before I could see them again, and I never got to . . . I never told them I was sorry. The family I was sent to live with in Macedonia—distant relatives of my mother—wanted nothing to do with me. They called me a filthy Minoan and turned me away."

"When you were ten?" Will said, incredulous.

Dalen clasped his hands around his knees. "I survived. Aike. We don't need to discuss the details. When I was twenty, I had scraped together enough coin to purchase passage—working passage, mind you—on a ship to New Albion. I wanted a new start, someplace no one would recognize my heritage. I found such a place in New Victoria, but a tusker raiding party found me just as fast."

Will looked at his friend with new eyes and mad respect for surviving the ordeal of his childhood.

"You thought you'd been here before," Mala said. "What did you mean?"

"We visited my uncle once, when I was very young. It's one of my earliest memories. He lived in a lonely manor on a hill just like the one behind us. Lucka, that was so long ago . . . but I remember the color of the beach and the sea so well, the shape of the island, those three peaks in the distance . . . I'd swear this is the same island."

"Then where's the house?"

Dalen shrugged. "This all happened a long time ago. With all the plunder he's collected, he probably has a palace in Knossos by now. Krikey, the way you're all looking at me . . . forget it. The past is the past."

"Could this be an alternate dimension?" Mala asked.

Dalen shrugged, and Will could tell by the look on his face that, despite his brave words, the return to his homeland had shaken him badly. After a long silence, Will turned to Mala. "What do you know about Takros? Do you think he could have the Coffer?"

"It's quite possible. He's known to be a voracious collector with an abundance of coin. Yes, I wouldn't be surprised."

"If the Coffer is somewhere close . . . do we have a chance against him?"

"By *we*," she said, with a cold smile, "I assume you mean your little band of heroes, since I've no intention of confronting a Kalaktos conjurer anywhere, especially in his own abode. As to whether you can defeat him . . . I suppose that depends on whether you can get close enough to use that ensorcelled blade of yours." Mala's voice turned mocking. "A task fit for a hero."

"Even with the sword," Dalen said, "I don't see how you'll get close to Takros. He's one of the most powerful illusionists on Urfe. He'll make you see things . . ."

"We'll deal with that when the time comes," Will said grimly.

Some time later, as the sun began to sink into the sea, the horizon a forge of molten light, Will and the others stood atop the highest hill on the island and surveyed the beautiful but desolate vista. The island was quite small, perhaps a kilometer across, and the deep blue water extended as far as they could see. Except for birds and insects, they had still seen no sign of habitation or wildlife.

"Did the Nephili make a mistake?" he wondered. "Send us a few thousand years back in time?"

"I don't know," Mateo said, "but we should shelter before dark."

"Aye," Mala said, twirling the weighted ends of her sash as she scanned the hills in the distance.

"Perhaps a return to the cove?"

"Why not stay here?" she replied. "Judging from the sky and the terrain, there's little chance of rain, and I'd prefer to keep to higher ground."

No one disagreed, and the party selected a spot shielded by boulders at the edge of the hilltop. They created a loose circle with their packs and dug into their rations before bed. It was not cold enough to risk a fire. As they ate, darkness crept down the stippled hilltops in the distance before merging into the ocean and swallowing the island whole.

After dinner, Will and his companions recounted their adventures in Praha to Mala. She listened with interest, especially as they described the Old City and the encounter with the Nephili, and her eyes sparked when she heard about the treasures of the storeroom. "Skara and her obsessions," she said when they were finished, shaking her head. "You're certain she didn't make it out?"

"It didn't look good," Will said.

"'Tis a pity." Mala took a long swig of grog, leaned against a boulder, and swept a hand across the group. "That was quite a story, and you all look exhausted. Rest. I'll keep first watch."

After everyone but Mala was asleep, Will yawned and pushed to his feet, unable to stop his mind from spinning in a hundred directions. The clear night and absence of light pollution made it seem as if he could reach up and touch the stars.

"Trouble falling asleep, Will the Builder?"

He sat cross-legged on the ground next to her. When he felt her watching him, he turned to lock gazes with her extraordinary violet eyes. Her copper skin seemed to glow in the moonlight, and her wavy hair was unbound and loose on her shoulders. "Why are you here, Mala? You never told us."

After hesitating, she told him of the dhampyr twins and Ferala's quest to find the Coffer, and how the amulet had allowed her to reach Will.

"So there's a vampire super assassin after the Coffer?"

"You stand little chance against her, Will. She's the most efficient killer I've ever met."

"And you came here to protect me."

"To warn you."

He laced his fingers behind his head and leaned against a rock, touched by her decision. The sound of katydids in the low shrubs was mesmeric, and the air smelled of lavender. "And now?"

"I don't see how Ferala could have followed you here. You've bought yourself some time, but if you do manage to recover the Coffer . . . be warned."

"Thank you," he said simply. "For coming."

She looked as if she were going to retort, then gave a curt nod and returned to staring into the darkness. He reached out, cupped her chin in his hand, and gently turned her head. "I wasn't sure I'd ever see you again."

She didn't respond, nor did she turn away.

"What happens tomorrow?" he said.

"Whatever the dawn brings."

"You know what I mean."

"And you know who I am, and where I stand."

She still had not pulled away, but the look in her eyes did not match the tone of her words. He said, "You know who I am, too. But I also know we both feel something."

"One kiss does not a wedding make."

He chuckled. "You're not the marrying type."

"Ah, Will the Builder, light dawns at last."

He moved his hand to the back of her neck and drew her closer, breathing in her scent. "You know what I think, Mala?"

"Pray tell," she said, their faces inches apart.

"I think we're done talking."

When he moved to kiss her, her lips parted to meet his, but at the last moment she placed a finger on his mouth. "Lesson the Tenth," she whispered, so close the warmth of her breath sent tingles shooting through him. "Never betray the watch."

Her loose hair was tickling his neck and arms, and the taste of her finger against his lips was like nectar. He wanted to take her in his arms and press their mouths together, and he sensed she wanted the same thing.

But she was right. He couldn't jeopardize the lives of the party, and felt foolish for putting either of them in that position. With an effort of willpower that caused a shudder to roll through him, he pulled away, and they both returned to observing the hillside.

"There's something I should tell you," she said after a spell. "About your brother."

Will jerked his head around. "Caleb?"

"The other."

"Val?" He leaned forward, intense, the passion ebbing. "What about him?"

"When I was in New Victoria, I encountered a carriage driver named Gus—"

"I remember him. He took us on a ride around the city when we first arrived."

"According to Gus, he is now your brother's personal driver."

Will blinked. "I don't understand."

"He claims Val is a member of the Congregation. A spirit mage, no less."

Telling Will the universe was made of Cool Ranch Doritos could not have surprised him more. "Val? The Congregation? There has to be some mistake."

"I agree it sounds implausible, and I've no idea of the veracity of the information. I thought I should pass it on."

"Did he say anything else? What else you do you know?"

"Nothing, except I visited a residence on Magazine Street where the driver claimed your brother has been staying."

"Salomon's Pad . . ." Will put a hand to his forehead, feeling dizzy.

"I wasn't in a position to ask more. Especially if Val has truly joined the Congregation."

"That can't be . . . that just can't be true."

Will jumped to his feet and paced back and forth beside the camp, trying to grasp what Mala had told him. How had Val escaped from wizard prison— or was that vision some kind of illusion? It had felt so real, and that was Val's voice.

Could there be any truth to Gus's story? If so, then it meant Val had acquired much greater control over his magic. Yet it still seemed impossible. More likely, Val had tricked the carriage driver into believing he was a Congregation mage for some reason, or else he had convinced the Congregation to release him in exchange for some service Val was providing. Yes, these were scenarios Will could envision. His brother was incredibly smart and resourceful. Yet what kind of Devil's bargain had he negotiated for his freedom? The longer Will thought about it, the more confused he grew.

No, he decided at last, just before he dropped off to sleep when his vigil ended, what she told him couldn't possibly be true.

The next thing Will knew, someone was gently shaking him awake. He blinked and opened his eyes to find Dalen peering at him in the darkness.

"Krikey, Will, wake up. You have to take a look at this."

Will sat up and reached for his sword. "What?"

"Just come. Better if you see for yourself."

"How far are we going? What about the others?"

"Not far."

The moon hung low in the sky. Dalen was the last watch of the night. Will followed him a short ways to the southern edge of the hilltop, overlooking the side of the island where the Nephili portal had deposited them.

Will peered into the darkness as waves lapped faintly ashore in the distance. "Am I missing something?"

"Stare at the hill we sheltered under when we arrived."

"What do you mean?"

"Just do it. I'm going to bend the moonlight."

Will rubbed sleep from his eyes. "You're going to what?"

"Krikey, just watch."

As Dalen concentrated on the shadow of the hilltop barely visible in the distance, Will followed suit, uncertain what Dalen was trying to tell him. At first nothing happened, but then a shimmer took place in Will's line of vision, as if the darkness was taking shape. The distortion grew in size until it formed the rough outline of a large structure atop the hillside. Will watched as the image coalesced into the wispy, silvery, inchoate image of a spired fortress built right onto the hilltop, a fairytale castle made of dreams and moonlight. The castle came in and out of focus, flared bright for a moment, and then disappeared when Dalen waved a hand.

"Is that a new illusion?" Will asked with a yawn. "That's really impressive, but couldn't you have shown me in the morning? Or did you need the moonlight—"

"Lucka, Will, that was no illusion!" Dalen was staring at the spot where the structure had appeared. "That's a real keep under a permanent cloaking spell. A *wizard's* keep. The work of a master."

Will's jaw slowly dropped as he stared through the night at the seemingly barren hillside. "You're telling me that thing has been there the whole time—that it's sitting there *right now*?"

"That's why the portal brought us here. It was right above us the entire time."

"But who . . ." Will let the question slip off his lips, because the troubled look on his friend's face told him everything he needed to know.

"He's on the island with us," Dalen said quietly. "My uncle."

"Listen, I'm sorry I got you into this. I had no idea."

"How could you? Queen's blood, don't be a *krakator*. It's no one's fault but his."

After they stared into the distance for a while, Will said, "I have to get inside that keep, Dalen. But I understand if you can't come with me."

The illusionist's hands twitched at his side. "I don't know what I can possibly do to stop him, but you'll need me there more than ever."

Will gripped his friend by the arm, moved by his bravery. "So what do we do? How do we get inside if we can't even see it?"

"I'm unsure, but I'll need to get closer to investigate. I don't fly very well, but I can manage well enough to take a look around."

"Now?"

"Illusomancers work with light and shadow, the sun or the moon or an artificial light source. There might be a moment at sunrise or sunset, a transition, when it's easiest to glimpse the keep, but those will be the times it's best guarded. I suggest going now, before dawn." He flashed a weak smile. "Maybe he'll be asleep."

Will rubbed his chin as he considered the situation. "Okay. I don't mind if you fly above the keep to take a look, but we're going down there with you. I don't want you that close by yourself."

They woke the others and explained the situation as Dalen manipulated the light to allow the rest of them to see the keep. Everyone agreed it was best to go straightaway and find an entrance. As they broke camp and set off down the hill, Will was surprised to find Mala joining the group. "I thought you had no intention of confronting a Kalaktos conjurer in his own abode?"

"I don't."

"Then why are you coming?"

"You seem to have forgotten we're trapped on a barren island in the middle of the sea. I've no way home, my rations are dangerously low, and I don't fancy camping alone on a sorcerer's island. My choices, unfortunate as they are, seem to be starving to death on a hillside or searching this keep for a portal or some other way to reach the mainland."

"Or maybe you just can't bear to see me in danger."

She patted his cheek, smirking. "As I said, I've no intention of facing Takros, but I'll do what I must to leave this prison."

He could see in her eyes there was more to the story, and he smirked right back at her, having learned much in the ways of Mala. No matter what happened, he doubted there was a white picket fence in their future—and that was okay. He was no longer a white picket fence kind of guy.

It took them less than an hour to descend the hillside and traipse across the island to the beach where they had first arrived. The incline above them was quite steep, and having seen how the keep was built into the rocky slope, its walls rising steeply around the edges, he doubted they would be walking in through the front door. This was a wizard's keep, built for magical access and egress.

"Be careful," Will said to Dalen, as the illusionist rose into the air to probe the perimeter. "Come back if there's any sign of trouble."

"Don't worry," Dalen muttered, and disappeared into the night.

"I can see it now," Yasmina said, as she stared up at the darkened hillside. "The absence of life, the interference in the natural world, the pattern of birds and insects."

"You can see all that in the dark?" Will said.

"It's a remarkable illusion. I can hardly believe it was right in front of us." She turned to him. "I won't let it happen again."

"Hopefully we'll never *need* that particular talent."

"I worry about Dalen," Mateo said, moving to stand beside Will. "How he might react to the presence of his uncle."

"I think he's stronger than any of us realize," Will said quietly. "And I'm not talking about his magic."

"Aye. But family ties are an unpredictable thing."

Tell me about it.

Mala crossed her arms, peering up at the illusion. "My monocles of true seeing would have rendered this process much easier."

"What happened to them?" Will asked.

"I sold them."

"Who sells a pair of monocles of true seeing? Sheesh."

"Those who bribe customs officials not to imprison them for an illegal transport of goods and coin."

By the time Dalen returned, the sun had still not risen above the water, though the sky had started to lighten. "We should hurry," he said. "It took me some time to find the top of the wall, and I smacked into it a few times—I can hardly pierce the illusion while flying—but once I gained the ramparts I was able to see the keep from a better vantage point. It's a simple design except for the minarets and I think he must have studied the Bavarians and added elements from Minoan tradition—"

"*Dalen,*" Will interrupted. "Is there an entrance we can use?"

"I found a courtyard with a large door that appears promising. Though I've no idea whether it's locked."

"Can you take us to it?"

"I'll have to make two trips. I'm not strong enough to fly everyone."

"Okay, then." He exhaled a long breath. "Let's hope your uncle's a late sleeper."

Dalen flew Will and Yasmina up first. They linked arms with Dalen in the middle and rose slowly in the air, circling the hill on a diagonal before climbing the sky on a vertical escalator. At first Will thought Dalen was taking it easy for them, but then he saw the exertion on his friend's face and realized that only recently, during his time in Freetown, had Dalen perfected the art of flying.

The sensation was amazing and Will wondered if Val had experienced it. Once they cleared the top of the hill, Dalen asked them to put out their hands and feel for the wall as he began slowly moving inward.

"Here," Will whispered, once he felt the invisible surface. He and Yasmina let their fingers trail against the wall as Dalen climbed higher. When it leveled out he set everyone down, then warped the moonlight to illuminate the keep.

The top of a six-foot wide stone parapet emerged beneath their feet. The view from up close was magnificent; a forest of misty spires and ramparts with a watery consistency that made Will feel as if he were on the inside of a dream. Below them, Dalen pointed out a courtyard surrounded by sheer walls rising a hundred feet on each side. There were no visible entry points other than the outline of an arched doorway leading into the keep.

"It's the only entrance I could find," Dalen said.

Will looked down. Though it appeared as if he were standing on a cloud, giving the disconcerting impression that he might fall through at any moment, the surface felt solid enough. "You're sure this is a real castle?" he asked Dalen.

"Lucka, you're not falling to your death, are you?"

"It's just weird."

"It will get even stranger when I leave to get the others and you're standing in the middle of the sky. Would you rather wait here or down in the court-yard?"

"Here," Yasmina said, holding her staff as she peered into the ephemeral enclosure beneath them. "I can't say why, but I think it's better if we all go down together."

"I'll trust your Spidey-sense," Will said.

"Don't touch your sword to the illusion," Dalen warned. "It might alert my uncle, if he's not already watching."

"Okay. Try to hurry."

The illusionist nodded and took flight again. Once he did, the ghostly out-line of the castle disappeared, leaving Will and Yasmina with the uneasy sensa-tion of standing in midair a hundred feet above the hilltop, swathed in dark-ness. Yasmina linked an arm through Will's as they waited, peering around for signs of a disturbance. When Dalen returned with the others, he set them all down as the wall coalesced beneath their feet.

"Ready?" Dalen asked, after giving Mateo and Mala a moment to digest the sight of the courtyard, the wraithlike spires and ramparts hovering all around.

"Fascinating," Mala said.

Mateo bent to touch his metal hand to the surface of the wall. He rapped it lightly and stood. "It feels real enough."

Dalen had everyone link arms again, and tried lifting the entire group into the air to test the weight. "I can manage," he said through clenched teeth. "Barely."

Will unsheathed Zariduke and held the sword in both hands. "Take us down."

After a laborious descent, the surface of the courtyard coalesced beneath their feet, a smooth obsidian surface that spread to encompass the entire floor and walls of the enclosure. The dark surface was so glassy it reflected the waning light of the moon like a mirror. Will noticed there were no visible breaks or seams on the architecture and knew he was looking at the work of an artis-amancer. "Dalen, did you illuminate this?"

The illusionist swallowed. "No."

"You think it was your uncle?"

"Possibly. Or a spell triggered by our presence."

Only the door, a solid block of wood with a carved bull's head in the center, had a different surface from the polished black stone of the courtyard. A large iron ring set into the bull's nose served as the handle.

Mala and Dalen inspected the entrance and declared there were no traps or illusions they could find. The smell of brine drifted off the sea, and the sky crept closer to dawn.

"I guess we know what to do," Will said, as he strode towards the door. Behind him, everyone clutched their weapons tight, poised for action. Moving as quietly as he could, Will reached for the iron ring and pulled.

31

The door to the keep didn't budge when Will pulled on the iron ring. He tugged harder and got the same result.

"It seems real enough," Mateo said, stepping up and trying with his chain-mail glove, still to no avail. "So why won't it open?"

"Everyone," Yasmina said, with a catch in her voice, "needs to turn around."

Will spun to find the moonlight coagulating into six pillars in the center of the courtyard. As the party watched, unsure what to do, the pillars solidified and then transformed into humanoid shapes that quickly became recognizable.

The faces, bodies, and even the weapons of the spectral gray forms were mirror images of Will and his friends.

"Dalen?" Will said. "What is this?"

"I don't know," the young mage said. "I . . . this is far beyond me."

The six simulacrums raised their weapons and stalked towards the party, each seeking out its counterpart. Will tried to back away but found he had no choice but to face off against himself, unless he wanted to lower his weapon and see if his pseudo self would harm him.

A risk he wasn't about to take.

His opponent stabbed at Will's heart with a sword of hardened moonlight, a weapon the exact size and length of Zariduke. Will lowered his shield to block it, relieved the shield held, and then raked the edge of his blade against the side of the creature. He was disappointed when the thing failed to dissolve. *It's something more than magic.*

His twin utilized the same feints, strikes, and fighting style as Will himself. After a furious bout of sparring, neither was able to gain the upper hand. At one point, they crossed blades, nicking each other on the arm. The light touch caused a searing pain to shoot from Will's shoulder to his wrist, as if the blade had shot fire through a vein. "Their weapons are real!" he shouted. "And they hurt like hell!"

His opponent did not react to the touch of Zariduke, nor did it seem to tire. How was he supposed to beat a better version of himself?

A glance at his companions told him they were in a similar predicament. Mala was exchanging a dizzying series of blows with her opponent, an operatic ballet of skill and violence. Just as with Will, neither was able to penetrate the other's defenses, nor did Mala's fire beads have any effect when she tossed them into her twin's eyes.

Yasmina tripped and fell as she battled her opponent, barely reaching her feet in time to block a blow from her doppelganger's staff. Mateo's urumi sword cracked over and over on the obsidian floor as he fought like a cornered wolverine to gain an advantage. Will had never seen a fight with two urumi blades before and, if he wasn't fighting for his life, would have been fascinated by the snapping blades.

Dalen was locked in hand to hand combat with his opponent, trying to wrestle him to the ground, when a thought occurred to Will. "Dalen! Try flying us out of here!"

In a burst of strength, the mage pushed away from his opponent and levitated to gain separation. To Will's horror, the replica creature rose with him, drifting as easily as a moonbeam on the currents of air. It grabbed Dalen and pulled him down, causing the mage to land hard and twist his knee. Dalen shrieked and backed away as the thing pounced on him. Will roared and dashed to his side, driving Zariduke hard into the fake Dalen's back. Zariduke cleaved through it as if carving a piece of clay, and the moonlight golem dissolved into gray motes of light at Will's feet.

I just hadn't hit them hard enough.

He turned just in time to ward off a blow from his twin. After sparring for a moment, he worked his way across the courtyard until he could turn and slice downward across the back of Yasmina's pseudo-self. The thing evaded the blow at the last moment, and Will found himself in a new fight.

As Will faced off, Yasmina struck her twin with her staff to no effect, as if she had struck a block of wood. Out of the corner of his eye, Will saw his own twin approaching from the side. "Cut him off, Yaz! Use your reach!"

She stepped between the two Wills, jabbing with her longer weapon. Yet he knew what he would do in that situation, how quickly his twin would pierce her defenses and run her through. He had moments to save her—so he had to beat the other Yasmina even faster.

The moonlight staff swept downward. Will blocked the blow with his shield, spun inside, and jabbed upward. He caught the thing just under the chin, wincing as his blade drove straight through the head of the false Yasmina. It, too, disintegrated, though Will heard a scream as he whirled to his left.

Yasmina was crumpled on the ground, shrinking to avoid a blow as the other Will loomed over her. Its sword was facing downward and about to descend.

Will would never reach them in time. As Yasmina raised her hands to ward off the blow, a meaningless gesture, Will threw his sword like a spear as Mala had taught him to throw a dagger long ago, on the trek to Leonidus's castle. The weight was different and the throw would not have won any javelin competitions, but the distance was not far, and his aim was true. Zariduke pierced his twin in the back just before it stabbed Yasmina. A shower of dispersing grey light rained down on her as Will ran to retrieve his sword. He whirled to find Mala and her opponent dashing and tumbling across the courtyard, and Mateo backing his opponent against a wall. They traded lashes until Mateo executed a sudden maneuver that resulted in an entanglement of the whip-like blades. Will's cousin dropped his weapon and lunged with the speed of a boxer, jabbing with his left and throwing a straight right with his chainmail glove. His twin threw up an elbow to block the blow, but the ensorcelled glove blew right through it and smashed into its face. Mateo kept coming, trapping his twin against the wall and pummeling it over and over with the chainmail glove until it dissolved. Will's eyebrows rose as Mateo's final blow passed through the motes of light and shattered a portion of the obsidian wall behind him.

One to go, but it's the hardest of all.

As Will and Mateo rushed to help Mala, her twin used its sash and short sword with ruthless efficiency to keep all three fighters at bay. It spun in a circle, unflagging as it pressed the attack as efficiently as Mala herself, patiently awaiting a crack in its opponents' defenses. Every time Will or Mateo would try to slip closer, her twin would lash out with a blade or a well-timed kick while managing to fend off the attacks of the real Mala, whose exhaustion evened the fight.

The fake Mala whipped two daggers out of its gray boot and threw them at Will. He barely got his shield up in time. After catching Mateo with a back heel that sent him sprawling across the slick surface of the courtyard, the final twin flipped to the side in an aerial cartwheel and pressed a furious attack that resulted in a long cut on Mala's left forearm.

Mala, he wanted to scream, *why do you have to be such a badass!*

They just needed an opening for Will's sword or Mateo's gloved fist, but they couldn't seem to get it. The moonlit simulacrum was too good. Mala had encountered the one opponent she couldn't defeat in battle: herself.

"Will."

The soft, wounded cry had come from behind him. Yasmina's voice. He turned to find her limping to her feet, holding her left side as blood leaked through her fingers. She was pointing at the center of the courtyard, where four more pillars of moonlight were congealing, slowly taking shape once again.

Oh my God. The ones we've killed are reforming.

"It's a deathtrap!" he shouted. "We have to get out of here!"

Mala risked a glance to the side. "Find an exit, Will! I'll hold her off!"

With a renewed burst of energy, Mala redoubled the attack on her twin, keeping it occupied in the seconds before the other doppelgangers formed. Mateo stayed with her and managed to lash her twin with the urumi blade, though the weapon had no effect.

During the fight, ever since his twin had disintegrated, Dalen had stood in front of the door and tried to find a way inside. By the frustration on his face, Will guessed he had run out of options.

Think, Will.

The surface of this courtyard, the floor and high walls, are obviously meant to reflect light of some kind. Is that how the magic works? It reflects moonlight and sunlight to form simulacrums from the presence of intruders? Shut up, Will. It doesn't matter how it works. What do I know about Illusomancy? Nothing. But illusions . . . illusions rely on subterfuge, at least back on Earth. Sleight of hand.

Deception. Maybe there's some genius mathematical concept behind all this, a point of convergence of the mirrors that I don't have time to decipher.

Or maybe there's a simple trick.

"Dalen!" he shouted across the courtyard, as the pillars grew more corporeal. "Does an illusion require an observer?"

"What?"

"Do I have to look at it to be fooled?"

"Yes, for the most part."

"Close your eyes and walk through the door."

Dalen started to respond, then raised his eyebrows as he understood the import of Will's suggestion. He turned and led with his hands, walking straight towards the wooden door.

And ran smack into it.

"Hurry, cousin!" Mateo cried.

Will glanced to his left. The moonlit warriors were almost complete.

Dalen started speaking very fast. "There's a school of practice in Kalaktos... a yin and yang sort of philosophy that balances spirit and body . . . my uncle studied the drosoulites for some time and concluded the refraction curve acted in inverse proportion to the magical—"

"Dalen, what are you talking about!"

"Walk through the wall on the other side, Will. Directly opposite the door."

"What?"

"You were on to something. Close your eyes and walk right through it."

Left with no choice, Will swallowed his objections and did as Dalen asked, racing to the obsidian wall opposite the door and shoving against it. It was solid stone, its glassy surface reflecting the battle taking place behind it. Will closed his eyes, prayed to all the gods in the multiverse, didn't bother raising his hands, and took a step of blind faith.

There was no resistance. He took another step forward, and then another, and then opened his eyes and gawked at what he saw. He quickly closed them and backed away. When he opened them again he was back in the courtyard, watching the mirror images of his friends spring to life. "This way!" he roared. "Everyone to me!"

He gave instructions as they rushed over, and everyone but Mala managed to slip through the illusory wall. The adventuress had almost backed her way to the wall, but couldn't get free of her twin long enough to slip through. All of the other mirror images except Will's own had dissipated, bolstering the theory that the presence of the mirror images was a response to their own. But his twin was about to close the gap and converge on Mala.

"Step backwards towards the wall," he shouted. "You're almost there."

"Where? I don't have eyes in the back of my head!"

She was going to need his help. He could step up to defend her, but there was no guarantee he could hold her twin at bay, and his own twin was closing fast. "You have to trust me, Mala. Do exactly as I say."

She replied with a nod as she beat back another sword thrust. He gave her instructions to follow—three steps to the left and two steps back—until she was standing right in front of him. Either she trusted him fully or they were both about to die.

"Close your eyes," he said, right before he took her in his arms, shut his eyes, and fell backwards through the wall.

"You can let go now," Mala said, as she and Will opened their eyes on a shiny silver floor that reminded Will of aluminum, except the surface felt like stone.

After disentangling from her embrace, Will glanced at Yasmina, who looked pale and ready to collapse from the wound she had received. Yet even she was craning her neck to absorb the sight of the vast hall spread before them, stretching for at least two hundred feet and soaring to a ceiling high overhead. The walls and ceiling were made of the same material as the floor, giving the impression that the surface of the entire gallery was a giant reflective shell.

The contents of the grand hall were just as impressive. Mind-bending blown glass statues of varying shapes and colors dotted the room, impressionistic pieces that brought to mind the works of Dale Chihuly plastered all over museums on Earth, except these were larger and far more intricate, comprised of otherworldly patterns and swirls that exuded a hypnotic effect. Similar chandeliers hung from the ceiling, though the soft violet light illuminating the room derived from a different, unknown source. Also interspersed throughout the gallery, and arranged along the walls, were translucent crystal pillars bearing a single item on the inside, as if hoarding a secret egg: horns, rings, shields, weapons, decanters, staves, potions, scrolls, cloaks. The jagged tops and edges of the slender crystals, each of varying heights but some taller than Will, looked natural, as if plucked straight from a mine.

Normally he would have longed to explore the contents of the gallery, but at the moment he only had eyes for a single piece resting on a tall, three-pronged golden stand in the center of the room.

"The Coffer," Mateo said, staring in reverence at the legendary artifact.

"This is a museum," Mala said softly.

"Greetings," said a voice with an accent similar to Dalen's, resounding throughout the vast hall. "Especially to my nephew. An impressive performance, deducing the location of the entrance. I look forward to beginning your apprenticeship. We have many years to recapture."

Dalen lowered his eyes, and Will saw his friend's hands trembling at his side.

"You destroyed my family," Dalen said.

"My brother transgressed against the laws of our people. He knew the consequences."

"They were protecting their son!"

Will put a hand on Dalen's shoulder and stepped forward. "You have something that belongs to us. We're taking the Coffer back to Freetown."

"One is curious how you circumvented my offshore wards and arrived on my island. I assume a portal of some type, yet I detected no magical signature. In any event, your claim of ownership is an interesting one. Did you not steal the Coffer from the tomb of the sorcerer king?"

"It belongs to my people," Mateo said. "To the followers of Devla."

"Ah, I see. The prerogative of divine right. I assume you have the proper papers, stretching back to the origin of the multiverse?"

Will spoke to Mala in a low voice. "Give me your Pouch of Possession."

"I don't think—"

"Do it," he said, and somewhat to his surprise, she lifted a small velvet bag off her corded leather belt and handed it to him. When they had found the Coffer, he had seen the same pouch magically expand to fit the Coffer inside.

"See that it's returned," she said.

Will re-strapped his shield to his back, as it would do little good against a sorcerer, unless those runes had a power he had yet to unlock. He raised Zariduke in his right hand and gripped the pouch in the other, then started walking towards the Coffer. Before he drew within ten feet, a bottomless pit opened in front of him. Will reeled, stumbling backwards at the edge of the precipice. A sinuous gold dragon roared out of the pit and leaped at him, shimmering with power, and Will raised his sword in defense. He swung at the dragon's head but the sword passed right through it, causing it to disappear with a snip of light.

Laughter rang throughout the hall. "You see what I wish you to see," Takros said.

With a grimace, Will closed his eyes and started forward again, this time more slowly. "Not if my eyes aren't open."

"Is that really the wisest course of action?"

"Will!" Yasmina screamed. "Watch out!"

Will opened his eyes as someone jerked him backwards, just before a dagger-like shard of glass struck the floor at his feet. Instead of shattering, the shard came to an abrupt stop, poised on its tip on the reflective surface, then flew upward to merge with the chandelier directly overhead. Mala had pulled him back, yet as she helped him regain his footing, a searing light emanated from the floor, blinding him.

"Did you think my powers were limited to pure illusion?" Takros said. "Did Dalen not prepare you to face the might of a Kalaktos conjurer?"

It took a few moments for Will to see again, and when he did, spots of color still danced at the edges of his vision.

"As impudent as you are, I'm uninterested in needless confrontation. I'm a collector, as you know, and not an unreasonable man. I am willing to strike a bargain."

Will exchanged a glance with the others, not trusting the situation. "Your terms?"

"Are non-negotiable. Your sword and my nephew for the Coffer. A fair trade, I believe. One priceless relic for another, and the return of my rightful property."

After a moment, Dalen stepped closer to Will and whispered, "I'll go. And do my best to get the sword when I can."

Will put a palm on Dalen's chest and gently pushed him towards the others. "You're not going anywhere."

"We can't fight him, Will. Especially not here."

Will ignored his friend and tilted his head towards the ceiling. "Neither of those is on offer, Takros. Ever. Why don't you show yourself? Maybe we can come to an agreement in person."

"As a rule, I prefer not to stand too close to a sword with the power to penetrate magical defenses. Even a weapon as powerful as this does not cause me concern in my own keep, but I've lived a long time, and am a prudent man."

"Don't you mean cowardly?" Will said. "Along with vindictive and murderous?" Mala grabbed his arm but he shook her off. "You took Dalen's childhood from him. Burned the home of your own *family*."

"Silence!" Takros roared. "You know nothing of our traditions."

"I know any tradition that requires blind servitude and lets you get away with murder is a tradition that needs to be abolished."

The violet light in the room started to pulse, throbbing as if alive, and streaks of silver light bounced between the floor and walls.

"Why anger him?" Mala whispered, but it was not Will's sense of justice alone that fueled his words. Takros wasn't going to give up the Coffer. If they were to have any chance of victory, he had to distract him and make it personal. He drew everyone to him and gave the Pouch of Possession back to Mala, whispering, "Go for the Coffer on the count of three. Dalen, disguise her as best you can."

Mala frowned but took the pouch. "What are you doing?"

"He's a collector like the sorcerer king. I'm going to hit him where it hurts. One, two, *three*!"

Will stepped forward and held his sword in the air. "I'm coming for the Coffer, Takros! Give me a fair deal or I'll take it myself!" Out of the corner of his eye, he saw Mala standing behind Mateo and Yasmina. As Dalen's hands twitched, Mala blurred and then disappeared. Mateo and Yasmina raised their weapons to protect Dalen as Will strode to the nearest crystal pillar and cut downward with his blade, aiming for the emerald goblet imprisoned inside.

Before Zariduke struck home, an unseen force lifted him into the air and held him high above the floor. The light in the room pulsed again, revealing Mala slinking towards the Coffer, the illusion dispelled.

"Fools!" Takros said, as shards from a chandelier above Mala dropped like falling knives. She leaped to the side, barely avoiding being skewered.

Will wanted to sever the magical force suspending him in midair, but to do so would mean plunging thirty feet to the floor.

"The Coffer for the sword and the boy," Takros said. "I won't ask again."

"Save your breath," Will said. He swept Zariduke in a wide circle, counting on Dalen to arrest his fall as the sword severed the ties of magic. He plummeted towards the floor, felt his descent slow, and landed hard on one knee. After pushing to his feet, he lunged with Zariduke to shatter one of the crystal cases.

"Enough! My offer is revoked, and all your lives forfeit!" Takros roared.

The violet light flickered in and out like a strobe light. Shadow forms streaked across the room, swirling around the party. Will whirled one way and then the next, trying to discern the nature of the threat, when he heard a crack above his head. He looked up to find that an entire chandelier had shattered, dozens of the dagger-like shards streaking towards him as if guided by an unseen hand. He had no time to reach for his shield or even drop to the ground and protect his vitals. As the shadow beings converged and the daggers arced into him, he realized he had grown overconfident. He could not win this battle, not even with Zariduke.

I've failed my friends, he thought as the blades pierced him. *And I'll pay the ultimate price.*

As he cringed, he realized the shards had stopped driving into him, only pricking the outer layer of his skin. Will stood very still, thinking Takros had decided to halt the attack. The shadow beings looked frozen as well, trails of smoke suspended in the air around the party.

"Don't *ever*," an achingly familiar voice called out from behind him, "threaten the life of my brother."

The magical daggers surrounding Will fell lifeless to the floor as the light in the room flared and the walls exploded, showering the vast hall with shards of silver. Streaks of rippling black lightning came next, twin arcs of destruction that disintegrated the chandeliers and the shadow creatures and five of the crystal pillars. As Will turned in awe towards the source of the devastation, he saw his oldest brother standing in a fine wool cloak and high-collared shirt near where they had entered the hall, his hands slowly lowering. Beside him was a lithe woman with a shaved head and a thin black robe cinched at the waist with a silver belt.

A majitsu?

"Val!" Will cried.

His brother held out a hand to quiet him. "Takros! My name is Val Kenefick, and I come on behalf of the Congregation of Wizards of New Albion."

"So it's true?" Will whispered.

A large bag at Val's side lifted off the ground and flew forward, landing near the center of the hall, rattling as if filled with coins. He glanced around the ruined hall with a haughty expression. "I've come to take the Coffer, and bring you coin in exchange."

There was a long silence inside the gallery. Barely able to process what was happening, Will looked back and forth between his brother and the shattered walls, which had exposed the courtyard as well as a nest of marble-walled rooms and corridors.

"The boy stays," Takros said at last, still hidden.

Val glanced at Will, who shook his head.

"I'm afraid not," Val replied.

The voice rose in anger. "You dare to enter my home and make demands? I'm unfamiliar with you, mage, but even if you speak the truth and represent the Congregation, the Sanctum is a very long way away."

Val sneered. "Do you think our power is limited to the walls of the Wizard District? And do you not recognize the nature of the magic I wield? I'm a *spiritmancer*." He tossed a circular silver disc, too large to be a coin of the Realm, toward the center of the room. "I represent the imperial might and interests of the Queen and the Protectorate, but if you doubt me further, then behold the seal of Lord Alistair himself. He commissioned this visit, and will come himself should I fail to return with the Coffer."

The disc levitated and flew into the far recesses of the hall, where it disappeared. An even longer silence ensued.

"A bag of coin is far from sufficient payment for a relic such as the Coffer," Takros said finally. "It's worth far more."

"You'll find the contents of the bag greater than you expect," Val said. "And I didn't come to negotiate."

The bag of coins also lifted off the floor and disappeared. After a moment, Takros said, "Very well. I wish no quarrel with the Congregation. Take the Coffer and be gone from my island. I'll consider the exchange a favor."

"The only *favor* that has occurred," Val said, "is that I've spared your life."

With that, the Coffer of Devla raised off its golden stand and floated over to hover beside Val. Will felt himself lifted off his feet, along with the rest of his companions, and the entire group, including the Coffer, took flight into the courtyard and up the high walls of the keep, soaring high overhead before descending to the beach near where they had entered.

Dawn had risen and a ginger sun lit the horizon. Stunned by the sudden turn of events, Will looked back to find no sign of the spired keep atop the hill, as if it had all been a dream.

Yet there was nothing illusory about his brother's presence on the remote Minoan isle, standing in front of Will and clasping him warmly by the shoulder, his eyes full of love and relief. Val looked the same as ever, his trim dark hair and patrician features, the intelligent green eyes that missed nothing. Only one thing had changed: as with comparison photos of United States presidents Will had seen—taken before and after their terms—his older brother looked as if he had aged a decade in the months they had been apart. Touches of silver now streaked his temples, his face was more lined, and his stare felt heavier than before, as if the weight of a great secret bore down on him.

Val's voice was husky. "I thought I'd never see you again."

"Me, too."

Dalen cleared his throat, and Will turned towards his companions. Yasmina, who had met Val before, was staring at him with a steady but cautious gaze. He seemed to relieve her worries by walking over to embrace her, after which Will introduced him to Dalen and Mateo. Dalen seemed in awe of Val and thanked him profusely for not handing him over to his uncle.

"Our *cousin*?" Val said to Mateo.

Mateo flashed a huge grin. "Well met, Valjean. Your two siblings have caused quite a stir in Freetown."

"I'm sure they have," Val said faintly.

Off to Will's right, he found Mala standing with a hand on Magelasher as she eyed the majitsu who never strayed far from Val's side. The mage-warrior was keeping an eye on everyone, though especially Mala, somehow sensing the adventuress was the greatest threat.

Val nodded at Mala. "It's good to see you again. Thank you for protecting Will."

"I'm not sure who is protecting who these days. Though you seem to have surpassed us all in that regard. Your intervention was quite timely."

Val glanced at the keep. "I spent half my power in that display, and I'm not sure who would have won had Takros chosen to engage. He's a very powerful mage, and I'm unfamiliar with the skillset of an illusionist. I hear it's a deadly art in the right hands."

Dalen paled at the admission, and Will shook his head in disbelief. "I've said it before, and I'll say it again: I'd *never* bet against my oldest brother in a negotiation. How'd you find us, anyway?"

"It's a long story, but once I learned that Takros stole the Coffer, Synne and I took a portal to a nearby city, just out of sight to the west. We flew the rest of the way. Once we landed, I picked up the spirit signature of Dalen's magic and followed it through the illusion in the courtyard."

The young mage looked sheepish. "I should learn to disguise that."

"It's a good thing you didn't. Will, I need to talk to you alone for a minute."

"Sure. Should we set camp first?"

"Walk with me."

After hesitating, Will followed his brother, leaving the others milling about in confusion. Val even made Synne stay behind while he and Will walked to the edge of the shore, the sun warming their cheeks as gulls circled in the clear sky overhead. For the first time in months, Will felt as if things might be okay. Now that Val was back, surely they could work together to bring Caleb to his senses.

"You don't look as surprised to see me as I am to see you," Will said.

"I was shocked, believe me." He smiled. "When have you ever shown less emotion than I have?"

"True."

"I knew you were after the Coffer, so it wasn't a *complete* surprise."

"How did you know?"

"Don't worry about that right now. Listen, Will, there are some things I need to tell you, and we don't have much time."

"We don't? Why not?"

"Because Lord Alistair will open a portal soon, and he's going to expect the Coffer."

Will was too stunned to speak.

"I know it's a lot to digest—"

Will put a hand up to cut him off. "Did I hear that right? *Lord Alistair?* Here?"

"He'll arrive any moment."

"Val—you can't give him the Coffer!"

"That's an even longer story. I'll tell you everything, but first I need to tell you a few things. While we still have time."

Will grew very still. "You're really working with the Congregation? It's not a trick?"

Val hesitated. "It's not a trick, but . . . it's complicated. You haven't seen what I've seen."

"Apparently not."

"I'm doing it to help you and Caleb," he said, lowering his voice as if Synne might overhear. "Among other reasons. There's someone I wish you could meet, a woman, and I've had some experiences that have caused me to question the Revolution. In fact, I don't think it's a good thing anymore. And it's definitely not something you should be involved in. But all that's irrelevant now."

Will put a hand to his temple. "A woman? Who? You don't think the Revolution—haven't you been in prison? I don't understand any of this."

"Nor should you. The Congregation freed me in exchange for helping them with a mission. I went to a place, an alternate Urfe, and I've seen what happens when the common . . ." He took a deep breath and looked away, as conflicted as

Will had ever seen him. For a moment, Val looked as if he was about to make a confession, then thought better of it and stayed quiet.

"What is it?" Will put a hand on his brother's arm. "Tell me."

Val looked him in the eye. "I'm sending you home."

"You mean to Freetown? I don't think that's a good idea, unless you mean with the Coffer—"

"Not Freetown, Will. *Home*. Earth. New Orleans."

Will froze. "What are you talking about? I'm not going anywhere. I've got friends, duties, the sword and the Coffer . . . and I haven't even told you about Caleb. You have to listen to me. He's gone insane with grief . . . we have to help him."

Val looked worried at the mention of their middle brother. "Where is he? I have to find him quickly, before things get any more out of control."

"I don't know where he is. He ran off on some quest, mumbling about a dream and having to fight Lord Alistair. You have to understand what happened to him—"

Will cut off as the air beside them shimmered. A tall man with a high forehead and regal bearing materialized, stepping out of the portal as his gray cloak with silver trimming fluttered behind him. He carried an azantite scepter, and bejeweled rings adorned every finger. Will knew at once who he was.

The opaque portal remained in place, a displacement of the air that bent the light in an oval behind Lord Alistair. His eyes moved to regard Synne hovering by the Coffer, and a satisfied smile graced his lips. "I see my faith in you was not misplaced."

Val gave a slight bow. Mateo and Dalen were staring white-faced at the Chief Thaumaturge, Yasmina looked as collected as ever, and, strangely, Mala was nowhere in sight. Will glanced up and down the beach, and over at the parched hillside, but it was as if she had disappeared. Dalen looked too distracted to have cast an illusion. Had she seen Lord Alistair and decided to escape?

Yet if she had a way off the island, why not use it before they entered the keep?

"Shall we proceed?" Lord Alistair asked.

Val glanced at Will. "We're ready."

"Ready for what?" Will said.

"Send him home, please."

"No!" Will cried, certain that Lord Alistair had the power to do exactly what Val had asked. Will reached back to grab his sword, yet before he could grip the weapon he found himself caught in an iron grip. Though he had not heard her move, Synne was holding him from behind, pinning his arms at his side. Will bucked to free himself while Mateo and the others watched in shock, not daring to intervene.

Val removed Zariduke from its sheath and handed it to Lord Alistair.

Will gasped in disbelief. "No!"

"I'm sorry. This sword has caused us so much trouble. Dad should never have left it for you. But it's all over now. You're going home, and no one's coming after you."

"You're not listening. The sword and the Coffer are the only hope we have! How can you trust him? He probably killed our father!"

"No," Val said, shaking his head. "We believe another mage did that. It's one of the reasons I have to stay here."

"So Groft didn't have the sword after all, but wanted us to believe he did," Lord Alistair mused. "A clever ruse."

"Why would anyone do that?" Will said. "That doesn't make sense!"

"To make the Revolution appear stronger than it really is," Val said. "I've made my decision, Will. I'll send Caleb as soon as I can."

Lord Alistair unfurled a hand, and another portal opened beside Will, one that displayed a street scene full of people in modern dress, motorized cars, electric lights, and the familiar sights and sounds of Magazine Street. *Home.*

"Don't!" Will cried. "I can't go back yet!"

Val lowered his eyes. "I'm sorry. It's the only way I'll know you're safe."

"Dammit, Val! You're not my protector anymore!" Will felt frantic as he looked at his brother and then Lord Alistair, and saw the inevitability of his fate in their eyes. "What about my friends?" he said, looking at Yasmina and the others. "Their safety is *my* responsibility."

Val turned to Lord Alistair, and the Chief Thaumaturge considered the question. "As long as they renounce their participation in the Revolution, then I have no quarrel with them."

"Thank you," Val said. "Yasmina, would you like to go home?"

"I am home," she said simply.

Surprised by her answer, Val seemed to take in her appearance for the first time, the pewter cloak and owl staff, then pressed his lips together and nodded.

Even if Lord Alistair was telling the truth—which Will doubted—he knew by the set to Mateo's jaw that he would never renounce his people. "He won't let them go, Val. He'll stick them in the Fens."

"He will if they keep their part of the bargain. It's their choice."

Will knew his brother was not in charge, and had no say in the matter. After Synne released Will, Lord Alistair flicked his wrist, causing Will to drift closer to the portal. In the background he saw Mardi Gras beads strewn on the traffic lights and oak trees, heard the clamor of tourists on the street. He tried to make a grab for the sword but couldn't free himself from the grip of Lord Alistair's magic. In fact, he couldn't move a finger.

"Val," he pleaded a final time, as the gateway drew nearer. "Please listen. Don't do this. I have to stay here and help Caleb, and these people need us. *Our* people."

"Goodbye for now, Will," Val said softly. "I love you."

As Will drifted into the portal, screaming at Val to listen, the beach and the brown hills and everyone around him disappeared, leaving Will hurtling through space and time, one world gone in an instant and another revealed.

Except Will did not land on Magazine Street in New Orleans, back on Earth as he expected. Instead the image of his home city disintegrated around him, as if it were a one-dimensional facade that had conveyed a false impression of depth, and behind the crumbling motes of light he saw damp, rough stone walls streaked with grime. His breath fogged the cold air as his surroundings clarified to reveal a ten-foot wide cell with a door of grated iron and a tiny hole in the corner. He rushed to the door, failed to budge it, and gripped the bars of the dungeon cell as the terrible reality of the situation set in.

-32-

In the amphitheater of the Nilometer, surrounded by tiers of empty alabaster rows soaring overhead and a score of dead bodies on the floor, Ferala grabbed the last remaining fighter by the throat and held her in the air. All around them, the macabre, lifelike remains of an array of exotic creatures bobbed from slender wires strung across the amphitheater.

The dhampyr's slender fingers tightened around the throat of the mercenary. With her other hand, Ferala held the tip of her dagger an inch from the poor woman's eyeball. "Where is Skara Brae?"

The woman couldn't stop her hands from trembling. Despite living in one of the most dangerous cities on Urfe, and having faced countless monsters and cutthroats, the cold fingers and piercing crimson eyes of the dhampyr assassin frightened her more than anything she had ever faced. "I don't know! The last I heard she'd gone off to the Old City again, her and Bartu."

"You understand," Ferala said, "that a single cut of my blade is fatal? You've seen my handiwork all around, yes?"

"I have," the woman whispered. A contingent of Skara's disciples had chosen not to flee the wrath of the dhampyr. One by one, they had all fallen. She was the last.

"Then you understand the consequence of lying to me? I assure you I will know if you're withholding information."

"I swear it! Skara left and we haven't seen her for days!"

"And the others? The bearer of the sword and his companions?"

"They left together with Skara and Bartu on a barge upriver."

"Who was the barge master?"

"Meru. Her name is Meru. You'll find her at the docks every morning, or at the Kumo House spending coin."

After a few more questions, satisfied the woman knew nothing else of interest, Ferala traced a thin line across her throat with the dagger, causing her paroxysms of pain as she collapsed to the floor. Within moments, the powerful toxin ensorcelled into the blade worked its dark magic, and the last of those who had remained to challenge the dhampyr was dead.

Frustrated by the lack of progress, wondering why Skara and the others had failed to return, Ferala started to change into her bat avatar when she received another telepathic message from the Grandfather, the third in as many days.

Ferala!

As she had the other times, Ferala ignored her superior's call.

You know the laws. If you do not return to the mountain at once, I will be forced to replace you.

Ferala continued the transformation, hovering in place by flapping her membranous wings. No, she would not be returning to the mountain. Nagiro was the only living soul she loved, and the Grandfather had refused to barter for her twin brother. Knowing an assassin would be sent to quiet Nagiro, Ferala would have to find Zariduke, trade it to the Alazashin for her brother, and in the process inflict as much suffering as a human soul could bear on those responsible.

Just before she soared up and out of the Nilometer, Ferala took a final glance at the preserved menagerie in the amphitheater. To free her brother, she would travel to the ends of Urfe if she must, and when she had finished with her mission, perhaps she, too, would build a shrine like this one, a mocking tribute to the humans who had dared commit this deed.

Or at least what was left of them.

-33-

Tamás led the survivors of Freetown and the contingent of Roma warriors protecting them, two thousand blades strong, on the march through the valley in the driving rain. They had evacuated hours before the sky filled with smoke on the horizon behind them, and reports of the final attack by the Congregation's tilectium airships trickled in. Freetown, city of hope and refuge, symbol of the Revolution, capital of the Roma clans and other oath avoiders, was no more.

The wizards had razed it to the ground.

The green, sprawling valley extended for miles in all directions, bordered to the east by a range of white-capped mountains. A hundred yards ahead, on the bank of a gushing stream, the Prophet was camped with several thousand Devlans, some of them trained fighters but most ascetic devotees pitifully short on battle experience. Still, Tamás needed every hand he could get, and hoped to join forces with the Prophet before the long journey to the Great River.

Tamás gave the signal to his commanders to halt. Accompanied only by Caleb and the Brewer, he rode ahead into the camp of the Devlans. For reasons unknown, after Caleb had left on his mysterious journey, the Prophet and his followers had departed Freetown in the middle of the night. Tamás had not heard the Devlans mentioned again until Caleb reappeared in Freetown, stepping through a portal with the Brewer in the middle of the Red Wagon Tavern. Holding a mace with a diamond-shaped head, Caleb had looked around the inn and demanded to see the Prophet at once.

Reports had arrived that another attack by the Congregation was imminent. Tamás had already convened the council to discuss the evacuation. A scout had reported that the Prophet had gone east, into the valley, and Tamás knew the Prophet might be more willing to listen if Caleb was with them. With or without the Coffer, it was time to begin the long march east to New Victoria, hoping for a miracle along the way.

Caleb had barely said a word since his arrival. Now, as the middle Blackwood brother rode side by side with the Brewer, the only person in whom he confided, the rain slid off Caleb's black cloak without dampening the surface, as if unaffected by the weather. It was the same cloak Caleb had taken from the Coffer, and Tamás wondered at its nature. Caleb's new mace hung by his side, and the edges of his leather vambraces were visible as he gripped the reins of his powerful steed.

Tamás was surprised when the Prophet himself rode out to meet them, accompanied by a woman with skin as dark as ebony, a young mage with wild brown hair, and a muscular man with a shaved head and tattooed forearms, wearing very strange clothes and staring at Caleb with a shocked expression. To make matters even more bizarre, an enormous harpy eagle took flight from a nearby cottonwood, cawing before soaring away into the rain-streaked sky. Tamás hoped it was not a spy for the wizards.

He focused on the Prophet. "Greetings."

Beside him, Caleb nodded at both the woman and the man with the shaved head, who had the bearing of a seasoned warrior. "Lance. Allira."

Though the woman did not reply, her eyes glowed with warmth, and Tamás sensed an empathetic soul. He wondered who she was.

"Caleb?" Lance croaked. "How did you get here? Where are Will and Val?"

"We can exchange proper greetings later," Tamás interrupted. "As you might be aware, Freetown has been destroyed. Death squads roam the Ninth, the airships could appear at any time, and according to reports from New Victoria, the Protectorate army has gathered outside the city. We have to assume the Congregation has decided to secure the Ninth and eradicate all non-citizens in the process. If we do not take action . . ."

He trailed off, as everyone present understood the situation. Unless they swore fealty to the Congregation and renounced their heritage and beliefs, it was genocide or the Fens. And Tamás sensed that for the Roma clans, even if they acquiesced, there was no turning back. The black-sash gypsies had pushed

Lord Alistair too far, and he would never accept a vow of fealty even if the Roma Council opted to give him one—which they never would.

Yet even if every able-bodied free holder in the Ninth joined the fight, their numbers would be pitifully small compared to the Protectorate Army, and a mote in the eye of the wizards. To stand a chance, they needed a groundswell of support from the commoners in New Albion, or the intervention of a foreign power, or the return of the Coffer and the resurrection of a legion of true clerics and a hundred thousand paladins.

They needed, in short, a miracle.

"My followers are prepared to offer our unconditional support in the struggle," the Prophet said.

Tamás blinked at the rapid offer. Good. At least the Prophet grasped the dire nature of the situation.

"We have only one demand," the Prophet continued, "and it is non-negotiable."

"Yes?" Tamás said.

The Prophet turned his horse to face Caleb. "The Devlans will only follow the Templar into battle."

Stunned, Tamás found himself at a loss for words, quickly trying to think of a way to massage the situation. Despite opening the Coffer, the middle Blackwood brother was neither warrior nor leader, and had shown no desire to participate in the conflict. Yet before Tamás could offer a solution, Caleb urged his mount forward. A sudden silence befell the soldiers in both camps, and Tamás and the other delegates seemed to recede into the background as Caleb's eyes burned into those of the Prophet, neither man seeming to notice the rain slashing their faces or the wind whipping into their cloaks.

When Caleb finally drew tall in his saddle and spoke, his voice was as hard as a block of azantite, and his words shocked Tamás even more than had the demand of the Prophet.

"I'm ready to lead you," Caleb said.

TO BE CONTINUED IN
WIZARD WAR
The Thrilling Conclusion to THE BLACKWOOD SAGA

Please visit www.laytongreen.com to stay up to date on
The Blackwood Saga and Layton Green's other work.

Acknowledgments

Yet again I owe an enormous thanks to my amazing editors Rusty Dalferes, Michael Rowley, John Strout, and Maria Morris for their continuing help on this series. Sammy Yuen delivered another knockout cover, and uber-detailed proofreader/formatter Jaye Manus is the best-kept secret in the book world. My handful of advance readers are also integral to the process—thank you so very much. Finally, a special shout to my nephew Luke Gifford for sharing his excitement about the series and reminding me of the thrill of discovery.

LAYTON GREEN is a bestselling author who writes across multiple genres, including fantasy, mystery, thriller, horror, and suspense. He is the author of The Blackwood Saga, the Dominic Grey series, and other works of fiction. His novels have been nominated for multiple awards (including a two-time finalist for an International Thriller Writers award), optioned for film, and have reached #1 on numerous genre lists in the United States, the United Kingdom, and Germany.

Word of mouth is crucial to the success of any author. If you enjoyed the book, please consider leaving an honest review on Amazon, Goodreads, or another book site, even if it's only a line or two.

Finally, if you are new to the world of Layton Green, please visit him on Author Central, Goodreads, Facebook, and at www.laytongreen. com for additional information on the author, his works, and more.

Made in the USA
Coppell, TX
12 October 2020

39681334R00215